THE QUEEN OF BLOOD AND FURY

C.M. QUINN

e-book ISBN: 978-0-6453153-2-5

To Brooke, one of the strongest women I've ever had the greatest honor of knowing. Your passion, kindness and ferocity inspire me every day. This one is for you.

CONTENT WARNING

This book contains themes of war, death, and grief. There is an escalation of some themes noted in book 1, and this book is intended for audience 18+. Please read at your own discretion. Below is a list of triggers:

- Blood
- Death
- Loss of a child (stillborn)
- Explicit sexual themes
- Some coarse language
- Mentions of slavery & genocide
- Torture
- Off-scene experimentation of prisoners

PART I

BLOOD

CHAPTER 1

"Another round of demons crawled from the pit today, mostly soldier-class demons. The King is pleased to see more join his army, though he left before the last demons dragged themselves out. A shame. The last one was a girl. I liked the look of her. A fire burned in her eyes."

—Excerpt from Commander Titania's diary

The crowds in the courtyard below screamed, scattering like ants.

Nimue watched as Lorca landed, wings flaring wide, a low snarl rumbling from his chest. He lifted his head, straightening up as he tucked his wings in.

You can land now, he sent.

She swooped down, landing with a stumbling trot. Her attempt at mirroring Lorca's ease in his dragon form spiked a low note of envy in her gut. The old demonic nature was rapidly pushing to the surface, devouring the traces of humanity within her. It was a far cry from when she lived as Wren the climber, scaling the cliffs without a care in the world. Now, a new future loomed before her. One haunted with an ugly past and more demons than she ever cared to reveal.

Graceful, Lorca crooned, and her trail of dark thoughts shattered into a thousand tiny shards.

Her gaze snapped over, anger giving to humor as a teasing note hummed down their bond. *Careful.*

Whispers filled the courtyard. The crowd watched her with wary, skittish eyes, reminiscent of the deer in the ancient woods that surrounded her old home, Fenware.

Beside her, Lorca's body flashed white for a second as he shrank into his human form. A couple of soldiers stepped forward, hands resting on their blades. An action she knew well. She dropped her head low, growing softly, as he approached the front door.

"Where's Helena?" Lorca asked.

The few armed men who guarded the front door glanced between each other before the door opened and Helena strode out, clad in an armored dress. Those cool, porcelain features curled into a ghost of a smile.

The knowledge that her capture and her sister's rescue had been part of another's agenda burned like poison in her mouth. She didn't like being played for a fool, even less now she had all her memories intact.

"Hello, Lorca—a bit much for your arrival, don't you think?" Helena mused as if Nimue wasn't looking at her like she wanted to set her on fire.

"You played us," Lorca accused.

Ignoring him, Helena eyed Nimue with a quizzical expression on her face. "Perhaps you'd like to change to your human form before my guards have heart attacks?"

A low growl escaped Nimue's lips as she called on the shift. The change came easily enough as her bones broke, reforming seamlessly into the smaller shape of a young woman. As the surrounding light dimmed, she strode forward. "Where's my sister?"

Helena turned to one of her men, gesturing for him to go inside. As the door groaned shut, there was a beat of silence. Even the whispers faded away, though all eyes lingered on Nimue, and the soldiers appeared ready to attack at any moment. Nimue's heart thundered. She knew Lorca likely sensed the biting agitation that hissed like an angry snake within her.

"Your sister is fine. I kept my word." Helena paused, casting a short look over the crowd before returning to her. "Shall we continue the conversation inside?"

Nimue felt Lorca's gaze on her, waiting for her to choose.

She let out a quiet breath and squared her shoulders. "I will see my sister first, and after that, we'll talk."

"Don't you trust me?" Helena countered.

"No."

Uncertainty flickered across the older woman's face. She must've known her betrayal would be discovered. Had she thought Nimue would forgive her?

Before Helena could reply, the front door flew open, and Ellie leaped out, clad in a high collared dress. She looked nothing like the timid girl Nimue had dragged from the brothel. Joy lit her face as she rushed past Helena, barreling into Nimue and wrapping her slender arms tightly around her.

"Wren!" Ellie cried, burying her head into Nimue's neck.

The sound of her old name cut her like a knife.

"I told you I would come for you."

Even as Nimue hugged her sister, something felt different. She and Ellie were now as far from blood as any two souls could be for in reality, she had been born from a dragon's egg her adoptive father had stolen from Lorca's court. Once more, she was as she was before her murder; a demon masquerading as a spirit, acting as if an ocean of blood did not sully her hands or that kingdoms had been decimated by her wrath.

Ellie pulled back, wiping her red eyes. "Helena said you'd come back."

Ignoring the sting of her failure to save the people of her village, Nimue looked at Helena. The anger at being used still burned.

"Did she now?"

The woman merely turned to the door and set off inside. "I think it's time we have a discussion."

Helena's office was choked with tension.

Nimue paced restlessly in the small room, her footfalls softly muted over the polished wood floor. The rush from the last day's battle was fading rapidly from her body. Only scraps of energy kept her standing.

She threw impatient glances at the door Helena had vanished through a few moments earlier. Her parting comment had been that she was off to fetch someone, though she'd refused to say who it was.

Lorca leaned against the wall, his arms folded across his chest, staring into space. A deep frown furrowed his brow. With him in the room, she didn't feel so alone. As Wren, she hadn't minded being alone, but now newly awakened as Nimue, something inside her had changed. An old ache for human company had returned, and she needed his steadying presence.

She'd wanted her sister there too, if only as assurance that Ellie was safe. But the girl had appeared so worn out that she hadn't argued when Ellie headed off to her room. She didn't want to think about the hell Ellie endured in the Pleasure District, not now when her temper was scarcely contained.

"I don't like this," Lorca grumbled.

She paused in the middle of the room. The rescue of her sister from the brothel and the unexpected change of plan when Helena murdered the madam had been part of a grand scheme she'd been unaware of. As Wren, she hadn't wanted to question too much back then. That blind, foolish trust and desperation had almost cost her dearly.

The door swung open and Helena swept in, followed by another woman.

Lorca's breath hitched as her own blood chilled.

The black-haired woman, with strikingly familiar features, stopped in the middle of the room, smiling at Nimue. The face in front of her was all too familiar. One plucked from the past and thrust before her.

Pain sliced through Nimue's heart, tugging at an old wound, and she struggled to find the words.

Lorca moved first. "You look like..."

"Litania," Nimue finished, her voice a hoarse whisper.

The pieces clicked into place. The bells ringing out across the city, the soldiers in Helena's courtyard, and this woman standing before them. A woman who bore a dead reckoning to the one who had murdered her and fled the mountains, forging a bloodline of her own centuries before.

The woman's brow furrowed. "Litania was an ancestor on my mother's side. I've never seen a portrait of her. I'm not sure one even exists." Her golden gaze flickered to Lorca. "She was a prominent sorceress in the Dragonir court, deeply beloved and very talented. Did you know her well?"

A look of pain flashed across Lorca's face.

Nimue itched to jump to his defense. She knew how much he had loved Litania, that her betrayal haunted him, even now. All that she had been to him, a real person of flesh and blood, reduced to this story told to children.

The familiarity in her voice was unnerving. Almost as if...Nimue stepped forward. "Who *are* you?"

"I'd hoped you'd recognize me, but I guess the new face makes that tricky," the girl mused.

"Sorcha?"

The deepened smile confirmed it. "Actually, that's not my name. My real name is Princess Sybilla Evior, of the House of Evior, heir to the throne of Danomir."

The room fell silent. Lorca's gaze darkened. She didn't have to hear his thoughts to know his mind, sensing that wild clash of emotion that raged within. His nostrils flared and his jaw clamped shut as he spun around and stormed out of the room, slamming the door behind him. Nimue flinched at the hard sound.

She drew in a deep breath, exhaling slowly, but it could barely contain the rage bubbling up inside of her.

Sybilla blinked innocently. "Did I say something wrong?"

Nimue shook her head. "It's not what you said. It's the resemblance you have to your ancestor, Litania." She paused, unsure of her words for a moment. "Litania was the reason the Dragonirs fell and why Lorca lost his entire world."

And why I lost my life and had to hide in the dragon's egg.

Sybilla straightened up and leaned against Helena's desk. "I'm sorry. I've grown up hearing stories about the fall of the Dragonirs, but none of them ever suggested Litania was responsible. Had I known..."

Nimue studied Sybilla and glimpsed unease in the girl's eyes. Long ago, she had prided herself in being able to read people—but Sybilla's games had left her feeling uncertain. Was she seeing the innocent air the Princess wanted the world to see? Or was this something genuine?

At that moment, she missed being Wren whose youthful naivety had always seen the best in people. Now, she didn't know what to think.

"Am I correct in assuming you were behind Helena's secondary plan?"

"Yes," answered Sybilla.

When she pulled her gaze from the wall, she sucked in a deep breath to steady herself.

"Did you ever have any intention of helping me find my people? Or was that all a lie?"

Sybilla stared back. "I didn't lie about that. I *can* help you. Your people are at the temple construction. That's the truth, but the Empress's infamous Gray Army is standing between you and saving them. You'll need my help to get your people out. Or are you confident you can do it without me?"

CHAPTER 2

"I have taken the fiery soldier demon Nimue under my care, much to my King's confusion. He sees her as weak and slow. While this is true, for now, I see what he does not—the girl watches and learns. I will forge her into a weapon that will bring kings to their knees."

—Excerpt from Commander Titania's diary

The thick fog was driving Flynn mad.

As the ship limped through the glassy sea, the sails propelled by the lightest of winds rattling through the rigging; the crew watched on. Men stood by, ready for the command of their captain. The man in question was at the wheel, casting a cool, assessing look over the water.

What he was looking for, Flynn didn't know.

He leaned against the railing. Something was wrong, but he couldn't put his finger on it. Mira huddled beside him, wrapped up in a black cloak, her blue eyes peering out from beneath the hood.

"This weather is slowing us down. The captain thinks it'll be another day at this speed," she said.

Flynn's grip tightened on the railing. "You heard what the men are saying?"

Mira glanced at him, one brow lifted. "You believe in sea monsters?"

"They seem like a superstitious bunch, but something feels off about this fog," he replied.

"It's just *weather.* You were never this jumpy on the cliffs." Her pale hands slid up and pushed the hood off her head. "Is this to do with your, well, your—"

"Maybe?" He sighed, rubbing the back of his neck. "Did we make the right choice?"

"Choice was in short supply. Besides, this mission is for you to learn about your magic. I'm just...." She paused, her gaze shuttering. "I don't like feeling useless, but right now all we can do is wait."

They stood there, silent in their thoughts. The fog billowed around them, the only sound coming from the gentle waves lapping at the sides of their vessel.

A scream sliced through the air.

Flynn spun around, thrusting himself between Mira and the cries. Human-like shapes vaulted over the railing, landing on the deck with muted thumps. Swathed in tattered dresses and draped in ribbons of seaweed, with long hair cascading over their shoulders, they stalked forward like creatures forged from nightmares. Paper-thin green skin stretched taut over bony faces, their lips pulled back into predatory grins, revealing rows of jagged teeth.

A sailor tried to run. The sudden movement shattered the slow advance and the creatures exploded forward. One of them dashed across the deck, barreling straight for Flynn and Mira.

"Stay behind me!" he yelled, launching himself at the creature.

Flynn yanked out the small dagger on his hip. The creature leaped back with a snarl; eyes narrowed at the blade. It focused on him and edged nearer. Flynn moved back, keeping Mira behind him.

That blackened gaze landed on Mira as it lunged forward. Its hand shot up and claws tore across Flynn's chest, the sting erupting across his skin, blood welling through his shirt. He slashed furiously at the creature desperate to drive it away, dodging every blow he could.

But it was fast and caught him on the arm and chest several times. Blood dripped in his wake as he pushed on. His foot kicked against something almost causing him to fall. He staggered and looked down.

An arm.

The creature rushed, slamming him to the ground. The dagger was ripped from his hand, and sent clattering across the deck. Straddling him, his hands pinned to the deck, the creature's sharpened nails bit into his wrists. Blood trickled through its grip.

It leaned in, snarling. "*Demon spawn...*"

Ice flooded his veins as he fought, trying to thrash the beast off. But the creature was stronger. Flynn was a child once more, trying to get a bully off him, helpless against their overwhelming strength. Panic surged in his throat, threatening to consume him.

I can't die here. Not like this.

The creature's head shot down, fangs exposed.

It stopped. A look of shock flashed across its face.

Flynn looked up at the blade piercing its throat, black blood trickling down the tip and onto his cheek.

He was frozen for a moment; then, the screams of the men and sounds of fighting ripped him back to reality. Cursing, he slammed his fists into the creature's chest and rolled it off him. He turned to the figure standing nearby.

Mira.

"You okay?" she asked.

He opened his mouth to respond when another creature launched at her from behind. Before it could reach her, a shadowy wave slammed into it, sending it flying across the deck. Flynn scrambled to his feet and dashed to his dagger, picking it up before darting back to Mira.

A man stood near the railing, his black cloak billowing around him. Obsidian eyes stared at Flynn, then snapped back to the creatures who were now frozen on the deck, leaving the surviving men to cower away.

Their dead eyes watched as the stranger raised his hands, ribbons of black energy swirling around his fingers.

Demon... The word lanced through Flynn like a clap of thunder.

The man slammed his hands together, sending a shockwave of energy exploding outwards. As it collided with the creatures, their bodies turned to dust on impact. A few darted behind the masts attempting to dodge the attack. Once the wave faded, they scattered and leaped over the side, hitting the water with a splash.

All that was left of their attack were the bloodied remains of slain sailors littering the deck.

The creatures vanished from Flynn's mind as the man dropped onto the deck and strode toward him and Mira. He stared at them with a curious glint in those fathomless depths.

"So, you're Atlas's son? Amara was right. Claudius was dumb enough to send you across the sea without protection."

Flynn opened his mouth to speak, but Mira beat him to the question, stepping forward.

"Who the hell are you?"

His gaze slid to hers, and a smile tugged at his mouth that didn't quite reach his eyes. "I am Castille, Commander of the Arzadan Archers, and loyal servant to the Demon Queen, Nimue." He turned to Flynn and gave a slight bow. As he rose, the smile tumbled away. "And I am here to protect you, something my dear idiot of a friend should've done himself."

CHAPTER 3

"We are put to work in the King's army. Training begins before dawn and finishes long after the sun has set. You are too tired to do anything but sleep when you finally reach your bed. This is our life now, they tell us. Live, train, then die for the King."

—Excerpt from Nimue's diary, soldier-class demon

The garden below was crammed with tents, wagons laden with goods, and soldiers busy readying weapons, tools, and supplies. For a moment, Nimue felt as though she were a queen back in the demon realm, watching the preparations for war. A tight knot squeezed low in her gut. No matter how much she tried to deny it, war was in her blood.

She mulled over Sybilla's words. Much had changed during her centuries of slumber in the dragon egg in Lorca's kingdom, and she scarcely recognized the world anymore. From what she'd gleaned during her brief studies of the kingdom and its history before her sister's rescue, there was little to allay her concerns.

The Gray Army, which served as the Empress's elite force stood between her and the survivors from her village. This army had brought the fae to their knees scarcely a year after her rise to the throne. Emerging from the mists, seemingly out of nowhere, it had descended with such fury that the capital, Toranelle, fell within a matter of days.

In her old form, with the other demons, she *might* have had enough power to defeat them. But this current body was too weak, and as she stood there gazing from the window, she felt like nothing more than an echo of her former self.

Drawing back from the railing, she returned inside. The room given to Lorca and herself was spacious and dominated by a large four-poster bed. She'd almost asked about different rooms, but then refrained. Rooms were in short supply because of the increased personnel around, and she wasn't some shy miss to be uncomfortable about sharing a bed.

Her gaze dipped to her hands, calloused from years climbing the cliffs. These weren't the blood-stained ones that had brought armies to their knees and burned empires to the ground. She scarcely recognized herself anymore.

Her eyes shut. Reaching down, she called on the power buried deep within. In her mind, her hand stretched out to the churning mass of darkness.

It hissed, retreating out of reach.

She tried twice more, but its refusal was a deafening roar. Frowning, she turned her focus to the glowing core of her soul. A thin red thread coiled around the sphere, flickering faintly. Her connection to her throne in the demon realm remained.

Retreating, she opened her eyes as the door cracked open. Lorca slipped inside. His green eyes met hers, unreadable for a moment. He made no move to her, as if he were waiting for her to do something, say *something.*

For the first time, she looked at him through new eyes. She felt awkward in a way that she hadn't in years. Uncertainty gripped her. He knew her name, but he believed her to be a spirit, a guardian of his people. He saw only the titles and roles she permitted the rest of the world to see.

Would he run like so many had when he glimpsed the monster within?

"Wren...Nimue. Can we talk?"

Nimue nodded. She owed him an explanation after all they had been through. He'd stayed by her side and almost died for her.

"If you're not Wren or the Spirit of the Mountain, who are you?"

"I *am* Wren from Fenware, and I *was* the Spirit who protected your people." She sighed, her shoulders sagging. "But I am also...more. I am a demon."

Something unreadable flickered in his eyes. For a moment, he said nothing and her heart froze. Was he disgusted that he'd given his heart to a monster?

"I didn't want to deceive you. Please believe me. I only got my memories back when I was tortured in the city. I understand if this is too much for you." She turned, unable to see the hurt in his eyes.

"Nimue..." The naked desperation in his voice tore at her. "I don't care. You're still the girl I fell in love with...and you should know my sister suspected the Spirit of the Mountain was in reality a demon."

She pivoted sharply. Her heart slammed viciously against her ribs, as if at any moment, it would cleave itself from her chest.

"What?"

A fond smile touched his lips. "Despite all the rules our mother gave us to leave you be back then, my sister ignored them. She would not tell me the specifics of *what* she saw but that it was enough to make her doubt you were truly a spirit."

"And the pair of you never uttered a word to your mother or anyone?"

"You kept us safe."

All she could do was stare into those warm, gentle eyes, that bore none of the terrible things she imagined.

She wasn't sure who moved first, but the next moment his hands were sliding around her waist, his lips finding hers. Desperation welled. Her hands clutched at his chest, yanking him close. They drank each other in, hungry for comfort, for something familiar—something grounding as the world outside went mad.

Her hands found the bottom of his shirt and tugging it free her fingers slid along his molten skin. He shuddered beneath her touch, devouring her with his kiss, his own hands sliding down, cupping her bottom. His desire pressed against her stomach, heat coiling tightly at her core.

Breathless, she pulled back. She caressed his cheek, tracing the shape of his jaw. Words escaped her but, for the moment, the madness churning within her stilled. A tiny thread of tension loosened in her gut.

His eyes shut as he leaned into her hand. "Sorry for storming off."

A bitter laugh nearly tumbled from her lips. That he had anything to be sorry for was absurd. Out of the two of them, she had far more to atone for. She kissed him again, then drew back and pressed her forehead to his as she slid her arms around his waist. The rich, earthy notes of his scent filled her lungs, reminding her of the mountains. Of *home.*

"I was tempted to follow you," she whispered, the corner of her mouth twitching.

A ghost of a smile pulled at his mouth. She ached to wipe away the quiet grief in his eyes.

"We could take your sister and go."

Her hand fell away, and she stepped back. "I wish we could."

"But?" In a single word, there was the weight of a thousand questions in it, and she felt the pressure heavy on her shoulders.

"The Gray Army," she said softly, glancing at the window. Her reflection stared back, all too mortal and weak. "I'm not what I once was. I—" She cut herself off. A knot of tension throbbed at the base of her skull. "I want nothing more than to fly to the temple and save my people. Demons below! I *wish* I could. But according to Sybilla, they stand between us and my people."

Lorca appeared beside her, and she felt him brush a hair behind her ear. "Do you believe her?"

"Honestly? I am unwilling to gamble on trusting her. Figuring out if my people are there is the priority."

His arms wrapped around her, drawing her into his chest. The steady drum of his heart throbbed against her. Instinctively, she leaned in, savoring his earthy scent.

"We will bring them home," he assured her.

She drew back. "Even if that means staying in the same city as Sybilla?"

"You are concerned about how I reacted before."

"I'm worried *for* you. It can't be easy to see your sister's face again, even if it isn't truly her."

A war of emotions passed over his face. The thread of their bond quivered as if he were fighting to contain the full force of his grief. Instinctively, she touched his cheek once more.

"Don't hide from me," she murmured.

His burning gaze locked on her face and his grief came crashing through, nearly forcing her to her knees. Seeing Litania's face again had ripped open old wounds that had been buried for hundreds of years.

Lorca shuddered beneath her touch. "I try to tell myself that I could not have prevented what happened...but that nagging voice haunts me. What if I had stopped her?"

"Even if that meant killing her?" He flinched beneath her touch. She gently kissed his lips and continued. "You could not know that it would be Litania who would lead to the destruction of your kingdom."

"If I had not been swayed by my heart and only listened to my sister. She knew Litania was not to be trusted. I should—"

"Then we would have never met and my village might never have existed. Who can say what this world would be if you'd struck her down? All we can do is move forward, one step at a time, even as our hearts ache for everything we've lost."

He crushed his lips to hers, leaving her breathless as she returned the kiss. To her dismay, he pulled away, pressing their foreheads together. His hot breath fanned her lips, leaving her aching to taste him again, to strip him bare and claim him.

A knock rattled the door.

The sound jerked her back to reality. She reluctantly withdrew from his embrace and opened the door.

Ellie greeted her. "You're awake." Seeing Lorca, she stepped back. "You're busy—"

"I'm not," Nimue cut in, standing aside for her sister to enter. "Please, there's someone I'd like you to meet."

Lorca stood as her sister came cautiously into the room, staring wide-eyed as he rose to his full height. He bowed deeply. "Please, call me Lorca. It is an honor to meet you."

"You're a Dragonir, aren't you?" Ellie said; she turned to Nimue, her eyes wide. "And does that mean you...?"

A knife twisted in Nimue's gut, guilt sour in her mouth. Neither Ellie nor Lorca knew what she truly was. The deception had never felt bitter before, like a poisoned chalice.

She forced a smile. “I have a lot to tell you.”

Lorca moved closer to the door. “I’ll give you some time. You have a lot to catch up on.”

Panic filled her. She opened her mouth to argue, but he smiled softly, a weariness peering through the mask he wore. A dull pain throbbed through their connection. She knew he needed to go.

“Rest. I’ll find you later,” she said.

Stepping forward, he kissed her. Firm, with a promise that passed silently between them. His gaze burned. “I’ll hold you to that.”

Then he was gone, the door clicking shut behind him. A beat of silence followed. Ellie stared at her sister, waiting. Shadows danced in those young cerulean eyes, unreadable to Nimue. She hunted for the words, to explain all that had happened.

So, she did what she did best from the moment she was ripped from the demon realm two thousand years ago.

She lied.

CHAPTER 4

The training is long and hard. It begins before dusk and stretches well into the night. They think to break us, to kill off the weak. I will not be so easily beaten.
—Excerpt from Nimue's diary, soldier-class demon

Sleep was a luxury Sybilla didn't have.

She stared down at the mountain of letters that had accumulated on her desk. No sooner had she sat down and began to sift through the reports when there was a knock at the door. Before she could even call out, Helena swept in, looking frustratingly polished and calm, as if she'd gotten a full night of sleep.

A faint floral note perfumed the air.

Frowning, Sybilla leaned back in her chair. "Well, don't you look rested?"

Helena smiled as she sat down. "That would be the benefit of lotions and a hot cup of tea."

"Must be a hell of a tea. I think I'll need it to get through these reports. Dare I ask if this is all of it?"

One could only hope.

"I suspect more will come in. We've begun gathering food supplies, weapons, and materials to make more, as well as organizing the men. It's going to take time to get everything done."

"We need to consolidate everything as fast as we can. It won't be long until Alexandria sends an army to reclaim this city. Is there any more resistance?" Sybilla asked, hoping that the day might not leave her with a pounding headache.

Helena peered out the window, silent for a moment. "Are you sure she won't send the Gray Army?"

There was a quiet air of concern in her voice, and her stony mask cracked to reveal a glimmer of uncertainty.

"I told you I foresaw the army from Midlan march on us. Alexandria won't move her Gray Army. Whatever she's protecting at the temple she's constructing is worth more than this city."

Her statement should have offered a measure of comfort, but the truth was, no matter how hard she tried to force a vision, she could not glimpse what was within those temple walls. Since taking the city, that gift had grown silent.

But so long as the Gray Army remained where it was the nobles were satisfied with her answers. No one wanted them marching on their city to become the next Toranelle, reduced to ash and ruins. A sentiment she shared.

Helena leaned back in her chair, resting one hand idly on the armrest. "There is the matter of your personal guard. I've gathered those I believe are suitable for the task, men you can trust. The captain is outside, if you would like to meet him? See if he appeases you."

It had been something she knew was coming, but the idea of being so closely shadowed was a foreign one. All her life, as Sorcha the traveler, she'd been left to her own devices, even in her scheming. Now, she needed to adjust to her new status as the lost heir to the throne.

"Very well. Bring him in."

One brow lifted faintly before Helena bowed, exiting the office for a moment. There was a murmur of conversation, then the door creaked open again. A young man strode in, perhaps five or six years older than herself, and at least a head shorter. He stopped in front of her desk, bowing deeply. Coppery curls tumbled over his forehead, framing a piercing set of green eyes.

She rose from her chair and walked over to inspect him. He turned, keeping his body facing her, his gaze never wavering. Not for a single breath. They stood close, a war of silence raging between them. It gave her time to examine him; the cut of his stance, the way his eyes regarded her with veiled interest. The sword at his hip was simple but well-made and his clothes had a hint of wear in them. A thin scar ran below his right eye.

"Permission to speak, your Highness?" She inclined her head in response, and he went on, "My name is Oren. I know you have no reason to trust me. So, while I swear upon my life, and that of my men, that no harm will come to you, I look forward to *earning* that trust. From this breath until my last, I am your shadow."

A trickle of ice slithered into the pit of her soul.

After living much of her life in obscurity, she knew it would take time to get used to the bowing and lowered gazes. Those who dared to speak to her did so with an air of caution.

By the time she navigated through the chaotic halls, bustling with soldiers and people readying the city, she was nearly ready to run back to her room. At least there it was quiet, and she felt more like herself.

Whoever *that* was anymore.

Oren and two of his men shadowed her. She'd tried to talk to them, but it had been like drawing blood from a stone. An endeavor she soon gave up on.

She pushed through the heavy doors into the ballroom, pausing at the sight of beds filling the entire space. Mercifully, only a few were occupied. Their losses and injuries in taking the city had been minimal. She burned the sight of the empty room into her mind. It would strengthen her later, remind her that calmer times were possible.

As she made her way down the long line of beds, she lingered with the injured, speaking softly, learning their stories. Each one she committed to her memory. Their faces too. A reminder of what she was fighting for.

When she came to the last few, a healer approached. A young woman, perhaps Sybilla's age, with sharp features hinting at some fae lineage and long black hair. A warm smile lit her face.

"Thank you for coming to visit them. It means a lot," the healer said.

"These are my people. It's the least I can do," she replied, casting her gaze over the room. Truthfully, it wasn't enough. She'd known there was to be a human price for her mission, but it was another thing to see it happen before her eyes.

Sybilla turned to meet with the remaining injured men when the ballroom door swung open. Helena strode in, her face flushed, shadowed by soldiers.

"Trouble in the city. There's been a demon attack, twenty men dead and twice that injured. They're being brought here now."

Well, so much for hoping there would be more time before things fell apart, thought Sybilla ruefully as she strode out of the room, falling in beside Helena.

"Is the area secure?"

Helena hesitated. "Yes, for now."

"Good. Gather the men and wake Wren in her room. Lorca is sleeping out in the garden. Grab him, too. Then we'll head out. I wish to get a handle on this before my aunt has an army at our gates."

CHAPTER 5

"The drums of war tolled across the camp at dawn, drawing us from our tents. The promise of battle filled the young demons. We envisioned our swords slick with blood and a field of dead at our feet. Today, we would become death incarnate."
—Excerpt from Nimue's diary, soldier-class demon

There's been a demon attack in the Merchant Quarter.

Helena's grim announcement and request for aid echoed in Nimue's mind as she dashed down the hallway. Men and women looked up, wide-eyed, as she darted past, leaping down the stairs two at a time. Out through the main doors, the front courtyard was a hive of activity. The heavy morning air, damp with moisture and sharp on the lips, washed over her.

Lorca had already shifted, stretching out his glossy wings in the glinting sunlight.

Closing her eyes, she called on her dragon form. Warmth erupted in her soul, bursting outwards along her limbs. A bright light flashed through her eyelids, dimming as the brief stab of pain ebbed away. Her eyes opened, taking in her higher vantage point and the stares that were on her.

Only Lorca looked at her with pride.

She unfurled her wings, tipping her head to the sky as a deep roar burst out, cracking like thunder as it ricocheted through the city. As it tapered off, she lowered her gaze and tucked her wings in.

Sybilla strode over, clad in leathers, a sword strapped to her back. Her eyes glowed brightly, magic crackling in her wake. "The men will meet us there. Can you or Lorca carry me?"

She can ride like her men, grumbled Lorca through the bond.

Sybilla's men stared at Nimue, no doubt having heard the request. She dropped reluctantly to her belly. When her revenge came for Sybilla's manipulations, it would be solely of her choosing. Now wasn't the time.

She eyed the girl as Sybilla climbed on, settling around her shoulders, hunkering low. "Ready."

Nodding, she unfurled her wings and leaped into the sky. Surging upward above the buildings, the wind caught her wings and steadied her ascent. When she was high enough, she glanced back, watching as Lorca flew to her. He was half her size, but was fast and fell in beside her with ease, gliding effortlessly.

The warm sea breeze sharpened to a chill as they ascended. Below them, the sprawling gray expanse of the city stretched out eerily quiet. There was a stillness that hadn't been there before, as though the city was holding its breath. Waiting, standing on the precipice of change.

An act of war had been declared by Sybilla.

Now it was time for the Empress's reply.

"Down there, by the docks!" Sybilla shouted.

Plumes of smoke coiled high into the sky from a market square, just a few streets back from the docks. Nimue angled down, shifting her wings slightly to catch the downward draft. Lorca shot past with wings tucked. Just as he hit the rooftops, he slowed sharply and landed in the middle of the square.

People screamed, darting out of the way.

A space opened for her.

She swooped down. Heart racing, she snapped her wings at the last moment, and hit the ground, landing with a hard trot. Biting pain shot up her legs as she nearly tripped, barely catching herself before she crashed into the stone. Her heart thundered in her chest.

Laughter bubbled through the bond as Lorca strode over, wings in. *Remind me to teach you how to land.*

She flashed her teeth. *I land with flair.*

Apologies. It was exciting to watch you nearly crash...with flair, he teased.

Nimue went to respond, but Sybilla gently touched her neck. "Uh, don't suppose you could lower down a bit?"

Half tempted to tell her to jump, Nimue dropped to her belly. Once Sybilla was clear, Nimue called on her human form. White light flashed, dimming rapidly as her body reformed. Lorca followed suit, striding to her side as he smoothed down his shirt.

His collar was opened, exposing bare skin. Nimue's fingers itched to trace every inch and to tear away the remaining fabric.

He stopped in front of her, his gaze darkening. "You look at me like that, and I will take you here, right now."

All the wicked ideas he had flashed through their bond, filling her mind.

Heat crept up her cheeks as she managed a quick wink. "Promises, promises, Lorca."

His eyes widened.

Leaving him to stare at her, she made her way over to Sybilla.

On the ground, Nimue could take in the market square. Shuttered stalls lined one side. On the other, a row of bodies was laid out, many torn to ribbons. Beyond them were injured men, sitting on crates or standing.

A few had bandaged limbs, the scent of their blood lingering in the air. Half a dozen lay on sheets on the ground. Healers moved among them, tending to the injured and carrying baskets of supplies.

Sybilla was talking with a group of men close by. As Nimue and Lorca drew closer, she turned and gestured to them. "This is Lorca, the Dragonir, and Wren, a dragon. They've come to aid us. Lorca, Wren, these are some of the men leading the charge in this fight."

Nimue tried to pay attention to the names as they were rattled off. She got out a few courteous greetings, but found her gaze drawn back to the carnage. Demon energy lingered in the air, calling to the darkness within her.

Sybilla's voice drew her back to the conversation. "Have the wounded moved back to the mansion. There are rooms and healers waiting. The sooner the better. It won't be long before we'll need every man."

The looming threat of a siege hung over them all.

And now, a demon threat was emerging. She had to figure out what was going on. Since her arrival in the realm two thousand years ago, and excluding her time in the egg, there had never been a coordinated attack before.

Nimue turned to Sybilla. "Lorca and I will inspect the market square and see if we can pick up any demon scent. We might be able to figure out where they came from."

Sybilla nodded. "Let me know if you find anything. I also would like to speak to both of you tonight when you're back at the mansion. There is more we need to discuss."

Lorca stiffened, but Nimue squeezed his hand warningly before he could say anything.

I don't like this, he sent.

She nodded to Sybilla, then led Lorca away from the group. Once they were out of earshot, she studied the sprawling square, pretending to be searching.

"I don't like this either, but it's just the two of us—" She cut herself off, thinking of Titania and Claudius. No. One had sworn from war, the other she'd rather burn alive. Shaking off the thought, she picked her words carefully. "We must play this game while we gather the information we need and figure out a way to rescue my people."

Lorca nodded when a scream pierced the square...and within seconds, more followed. Ice flooded down her back, plunging deep into her soul, right to the heart of the monster within. It howled back.

The demons had returned.

CHAPTER 6

"The King was not present at the battle today, so when the demon wolves went feral, we had no one to control them. They devoured a dozen of us when one came at me. I cannot explain what happened. It is a blur, even now. All I know is that I felt my hand come up and a single word burst from my lips. "Stop!" And then the beasts did as I commanded, yielding to me."

—Excerpt from Nimue's diary, soldier-class demon

Nimue took one look at the size of the space, of the men around them and the wooden buildings, and cursed. Lorca had shifted as soon as the first dozen demons rushed into the square, and was already stretching out his wings. A red glow welled up in his throat.

Lorca, no! Watch your fire!

His head snapped back. *You're not shifting?*

Nimue snapped her fingers, ribbons of black rippling up her arms. *I don't know if I can control the demons in dragon form.*

It was a lie, of course. She doubted her power would respond even in human form, but the odds were better than as a dragon.

Screams ricocheted across the square, dragging his focus away as a demon leaped up for his throat. Nimue lifted her hand and fire roared from her fingers. The blast slammed into the beast, exploding it on impact.

As the wisps of smoke cleared from where the creature had been moments before, a knife twisted deep in her gut. Cold recognition sparked at the fringes of her memories and shame seeped in like poison.

For it was a beast she knew only too well since she had forged them from her own bloodied hands.

A demon wolf left the fray and came to a stop in front of her. Its eyes, like glowing coals, burned through her. She sensed its interest, that demonic power brushing against her mind, hunting for a way in. But she was no soldier-class demon anymore, nor a mortal unsure of the world.

Her hand lifted, and once more, she called on the darkness, praying that it would answer.

Shadows flared around her hand. A bolt lanced through her head, and pain splintered down her spine. The throbbing sharpened, but she forced more magic out, commanding it to wrap around her arm. Nausea clenched her gut, but she held on, refusing to let the power seep away.

The demon leaped forward.

A single blast shot forward from her fingertips, shattering the creature into fragments. Acrid smoke rushed over her and the world lurched, sending her staggering. Bile burned her throat, the sour taste pooling in her mouth. She swallowed and looked across the market square where dozens of demons spilled in, rushing at the men scrambling to defend themselves. Lorca was tearing through the attackers, but more came.

If she couldn't figure out how to stop the demons, even changing to her dragon form wouldn't help. She couldn't risk using fire and accidentally setting light to the city, certainly not surrounded by so much damn wood.

The demons prowled closer.

Her head pounded in her chest as she lifted her hands once more, summoning the power to her mouth. She knew what she had to do. All she could do was pray her body didn't give out.

But as her lips opened, an eerie stillness caught the demons, and they shrank back with a hiss. Only one remained before her, with ears pressed flat against its head. The beast's eyes stared at her with a burning gaze. An ancient power, bound to the core of her soul, stirred and pushed upward. It sparked through her limbs like bursts of lightning splintering across her skin.

Waves of agony crashed through her, blinding white lights flashed across her vision.

A raging storm swelled in her skull, trying to break its way out. A new presence brushed her mind. It was cold, like the caress of death she knew so intimately, and had felt keenly once before, right at the moment Litania had driven the sword into her chest.

The demons advanced, their lips pulled back to low snarls that rumbled across the clearing. The screams of men and clashing metal rang loud around her, but she couldn't focus.

Every inch of her being was latched onto the magic, hauling it to a single point within. The command to stop the beasts rose to her lips when a voice slid into her mind.

Hello, old friend.

Shadows rushed up to consume her vision. She dropped to her knees, and an eruption of agony ripped through her core.

Within her, a dam broke, and an inhuman roar tore from her lips.

The abyss swallowed her whole, and she felt no more.

CHAPTER 7

"Whispers abound in the court about Nimue. Her power has garnered the King's interest. Have we finally found the one we need to rip that demon from his throne?"
—Excerpt from Lord Claudius Dellabore's diary

When Sybilla returned to the mansion, she found Helena waiting for her, a dark cloak set about her shoulders. Helena pushed back her hood and her shuttered expression darkened Sybilla's mood.

Whatever had happened wasn't good.

"What's wrong?" Sybilla asked.

Helena glanced back across the courtyard, silent as if she expected someone to listen in. "We found something you should see." There was a long pause before she spoke again. "It's not pretty. Spirits, it's fucking awful."

It was the first time she'd heard Helena swore. Her gut clenched. From the pale expression, tight mouth, and how her nails bit into her upper arm, it wasn't good.

She reached out, gently touching Helena's upper arm. "Show me."

To her surprise, they rode only a few streets before they came to an old temple. It was one of the dozens scattered across the city, remnants of a time when Alexandria permitted open worship of the spirits.

Soldiers stood guard out the front, indifferent to the rain that had intensified. Pools of shimmering silver scattered across the cobblestone road, rippling with every fat droplet that struck the stone. As she slid down from her horse, she passed the reins to a soldier who strode forward to meet her. Another man approached, his leathery face pinched with years of hardship, and eyes that cut like twin daggers. He paused, bowed deeply, and rose with a grim expression.

"I must warn you, your Highness, it's quite a sight in there," one said stiffly.

"Sir...?"

"Elmir, your Highness. Has Lady Adara briefed you on what is inside?"

Helena appeared at her side, her brow furrowed. Her cheeks looked chalky in the gloomy gray light, rendering her little more than a walking corpse.

"I did not think words would prepare adequately for the...horror inside."

"I see," Elmir murmured, lifting his piercing gaze back to Sybilla. "Well, your Highness, there have long been rumors of 'experiments' upon slaves, demons, even fae. Every so often, a body might be discovered discarded, but that was all... We had no more proof of it...until today. One of the noble families was caught red-handed trying to dispose of...their 'stock.' They led us here."

Her blood froze in her veins, the words lost on her lips. All she managed was a steely nod for him to lead her inside. She could barely trust herself to speak as she glided in behind him. Oren took up position on her right, and she met his gaze, but he hardly appeared surprised by the news. Had he known?

Questions tumbled away as she crossed the threshold. A faint coppery smell hit her first, thickening as they descended through another door and down a steep staircase. The walls pressed in tight on either side, forcing them into a single line. A row of lanterns spaced at regular intervals lit the way into the level below.

With every step, the stench soured. The bloody air tangled with shit and piss, and something that she knew all too well—rotting flesh. Her heart raced, fluttering like a nervous bird as she moved from the last step, and her mouth filled with ash. The sprawling room stretched further than she expected. One side was flanked by open cells, with trails of blood smeared along the floor. As if a body had been dragged inside.

From there, the sight only got worse. In a larger cell, tables were assembled in several rows, each with a corpse pinned down, cut open, and the skin peeled back. A few held demons, their blackened, matted fur stripped away in sections, exposing the dark red flesh beneath.

And at the rear of the room, the corpses of several men hung from their wrists. Peering closer, she noticed strange symbols carved into their skin, covering them from head to toe.

"What the fuck happened here?" she whispered hoarsely, pressing the back of her hand to her mouth.

Helena glided over to where two healers stood by a nearby bench. A dozen books were strewn across, cluttered with little vials and leather pouches. "Your Highness, this might offer some insight."

Oren slid in close, one hand falling to the small of her back. If anyone noticed the gesture, she didn't know—or care. He steadied her, and she offered him a jerky nod of thanks. He moved back, his hand falling away, as she reached Helena.

Both healers bowed at her, and the oldest one, a woman with wrinkled brown skin, held out a leather pouch. Sybilla accepted it and pulled back the leather tie, peering inside. It was empty, but she glimpsed the telltale reddish hue on the inside. She knew that powder anywhere.

"Hellis powder?" she wondered aloud, handing the pouch back. "Why would they use that down here?"

The red power was sourced from a remote mountain village, Fenware—or had been until the village's recent demise and enslavement of its people. She hadn't known its origins until Wren crossed her path. It was then she understood its rarity, and the more she read about it, realized its potency. A tiny pinch was enough to boost someone's magic for a brief time. And for those without magic, it healed and offered immunity to diseases. Supposedly, it even prolonged life.

The healer set the pouch aside. "It would appear many of the records were destroyed when the city was taken. What little we've found suggests they were testing it on those here. To what end, we're unsure."

Sybilla retreated, wandering to the closest table with a wolf. Its head had been removed and sat aside, the skull opened up. "And the demons? Were they given powder too?"

The woman shuffled after her. "We cannot be sure. There isn't anything in the diary."

Questions abounded with no answer, leaving her heart wrapped in ice. The myriad of the dead, their identities stripped away, left her sick to her stomach. She'd seen villages burned, suspected rebels hung, but this? The level of brutality? There was no care for human life. The people here were nameless, faceless things to experiment on and nothing more.

She swallowed the lump lodging in her throat and drifted over to the bodies hanging at the rear of the room. These bodies hadn't been cut open like the rest, and there was an air of deliberate intention with the marks. Every line seemed precise.

"And these?" she asked.

"This is most puzzling." The healer stood beside her, hands clasped behind her back. "Do you recognize them?"

"Should I?"

The pause made her frown. She studied the marks again with renewed interest. *Had* she seen them before? The whirling marks were strange, but tugged at no memory. Her mouth hardened into a thin line. She didn't like being in the dark, and this left her with a knife twisting in her gut.

"This city is over two hundred years old, and one of the oldest in Danomir. It has many underground tunnels and structures, some of which we know little about. There are even old wells and statues etched with strange markings. We didn't know what to make of them...and what is strangest of all," the woman said, pausing as she carefully reached up to spin one of the bodies around. In the center of the corpse's back was carved a large whorl lined with a strange line of symbols that Sybilla had never seen before. The woman spoke again. "These markings matched the ones we've found across the city. It makes one wonder just how long these experiments have been taking place."

She turned slowly, taking the room in once more, and feeling a shiver of ancient magic slide slowly over her skin. The hairs lifted along her arms. What had they been looking for when they used the Hellis powder?

It wasn't a cheap ingredient, which meant old money was likely behind this. She shivered.

What was all this for?

She barely made it to the next street before she dismounted, rushing over to the side of a building where she threw up. Shuddering groans racked her body as she heaved, whimpering until her stomach was empty and tears burned her eyes. The images of the bodies, torn apart and flayed open, seared in her mind.

Soft footfalls inched toward her. A hand gently peeled back her hair from her face until she finished. She wiped her mouth, straightening up. Oren stepped back, his gaze softening. The other mounted guards faced away, leaving the two of them to stare at each other.

For the first time, she noticed little details about him. The freckle beneath his right eye and the slightly crooked bend of his nose. The shadow of a beard along his jaw, and the tiny scar beneath his chin. He wasn't handsome in the classical sense, not like Claudius. But there was a sturdiness about him, and a look in his eyes that made her nerves settle.

She remembered his expression when they'd gone to the temple. "You weren't shocked by that."

His gaze shuttered. "I'd heard rumors, same as the healers. A few years ago, when I first started working with Helena, we investigated the stories. We found nothing, however, and after a while, there were no more leads. We should've looked harder."

"Oren—"

"Those people might not have been dead had we pushed harder," he ground out.

She gently touched his arm. "We cannot change the past. All we can do is make sure those responsible pay."

"And will you?" he challenged.

The doubt in his voice stung, but what proof had she given him she was different from her aunt? She stepped back, straightening her spine. "You will see. I will find those responsible. Mark my words, I will punish everyone who had a hand in that horror."

CHAPTER 8

"Claudius returned from the mountains, without Nimue by his side. When I asked about Nimue and their quest, he simply replied, 'she is staying in the mountains.' I reminded him that the fae call it their home, but he said nothing to this. I will never forget the haunted look in his eyes, like his soul had been ripped from his chest."

—Excerpt from Titania's diary

Titania sprinted down the hallway of Claudius's mansion, hurling herself around a corner and up the stairs, two steps at a time. A tentative hope had been sparked in her chest, tears threatening. She rounded the corner and plowed through the open door into his wing, and didn't stop running until she hit his bedroom. Without knocking, she threw the door open and burst through.

Moonlight lit his sprawling bedroom, touching the ornate furniture and his very vacant bed. The door to his bathing chamber was open. She started toward it when he strode through the doorway, tucking his shirt into his breeches. His dark gaze found hers.

"You felt it?" he asked as he moved to his dresser, grabbing a coat draped over the back of a chair.

"I thought she was dead," she whispered.

There was no mistaking what she'd felt. The eruption of magic down the bond she'd believed was lifeless. Even after eight hundred years, she recognized the roar of her queen's power.

"It would seem otherwise." There was a note of grief in his voice; the words scraped raw. He slipped the coat on. "Will you come with me?"

She stilled. "Claudius. Perhaps I should go alone..."

"You felt the pain. Something is wrong with her," he said quietly. "Regardless of our past, I have to go. I can't lose her again."

She didn't remind him that even an injured Nimue might try to kill him, anyway. Perhaps a part of him hoped for that. But even though half of Titania wanted Nimue to exact her revenge, the other half paused. Irrespective of their feelings for each other, the six of them had been ripped from the demon realm two thousand years ago.

Titania closed the distance, setting a hand on his shoulder. "You won't, but when we find her, let me speak to her first. It'll be safer that way."

He opened his mouth to say something, then shut it and nodded. Titania imagined the truth hanging over his neck like a blade, ready to deliver the killing blow. What Nimue would do when she saw him was anyone's guess.

They split their efforts in the hunt for their long-lost queen.

Titania stuck to the shadows, the domain of her powers, while Claudius darted over the rooftops, propelled by the wind he effortlessly controlled. The gusting breeze rattled through shutters and howled among the buildings as she sprinted through the alleyways and streets. No footfalls echoed in her wake, nor heavy breaths. The darkness ferried her along, yielding to her command as she swept seamlessly from one shadow to the next.

With the city under a strict curfew, the streets were silent. Doors were locked and windows shuttered. Only the patrols with their lanterns disturbed the night. Their soft voices echoed down the streets as Titania slipped past them unseen.

Every so often she slowed, lingering by their groups, listening to their hushed conversations. Most revealed little of interest until she heard snatches of a demon attack. She slowed, pressing into the long shadow thrown across the street by a warehouse. Concealed by magic, she watched as the men paused, taking a moment to drink from their waterskins. A faint sheen of sweat gathered on their faces from the humid night.

"You should've seen what that girl could do," one said.

The smallest of the group, his face half-hidden by shadows, shook his head. "Doesn't sit right in the gut, you know?" he muttered.

The original speaker snorted. "Your gut knows shit."

"Piss off, I'm right about this. Just you see."

The group finished drinking and set off. Titania watched their retreating forms, half tempted to follow them but her focus returned to the faint hum of Nimue's magic that drew her deeper into the Merchant Quarter. She glanced up to the rooftops where Claudius paused, peering over the edge. His jewel-blue eyes found hers and he nodded, then rose and darted off back down the trail.

It's not a damn race, she thought as she set off again, driving her feet onto the ground.

She steadied into her run. The hum grew louder in her ear, like a steady heartbeat. Her chest tightened as her magic called back, answering the command of a demon queen.

The feeling sharpened suddenly as she burst into a market square. Claudius dropped from a rooftop, landing silently beside her. He glanced at her, then back at the square. Tension tightened his shoulders as he moved forward.

"She was here," he said.

Titania felt it too, the aftermath of a fight, and the echo of Nimue's power.

But something else lingered. It was so faint she nearly missed it, yet she swore she had felt it before. That thread of ancient magic. But where? She racked the depths of her long memory, scouring for the truth. No answers appeared, and she floundered in confusion.

She trailed forward, unfurling her magic in a probe so that it spread out across the square. The remaining tendrils of magic that hung invisibly in the air drew to her, feeding in flickering images of the fight.

A black dragon carving its way through demons. Men, screaming. A girl wrapped in shadowy ribbons, her arms outstretched, as she advanced on a demon. Her face sharpened in Titania's mind.

She gasped, blinking the images away, and turned to Claudius. "I know who it is!"

Sybilla's mansion was a hive of activity even late at night. Torches lit the front courtyard, revealing the laden wagons and the flurry of soldiers that strode about. The front doors gaped open, and a steady stream of people filtered in and out. The scent of weapon oil and coppery notes of blood tainted the air. Injured men had been probably been delivered recently from the attack at the square.

Concealed by shadows on the rooftop across the street, Titania examined her way in. They could easily walk in, but the reason for their visit would raise questions. It was easier for her to slip in unseen for the moment, confirm it was Nimue, and then decided their next move from there.

She rose, squaring her shoulders. "I'll go in first."

"Titania—"

"It's better if I'm the first of us she sees."

The one she's less likely to kill on sight, at least.

She turned to him, taking in his tightened jaw and down-turned mouth, his eyes set with a stubborn edge. Lifting her brow, she gave him a single, lingering look, and his resolve cracked.

Scowling, he turned away. "Very well."

Titania reached out, gently touching his arm. "It's been eight hundred years. She may be willing to see you again. Just trust me, okay?"

Nodding reluctantly, he sat down on the roof. "Don't be long."

Nodding, she pulled away and waved her hand, bleeding into the shadows. The world dissolved into darkness around her, then burst into color as she materialized behind a wagon in Sybilla's square.

Turning her gaze to the front door, she stepped into another shadow, reappearing in the main foyer. Hidden, she eyed the other doors and the grand staircase. Titania hurried up the stairs, following the pull, drifting from shadow to shadow as she went along. Reaching the hallway, she passed busy men and women, their faces pinched. None noticed as she ghosted by and continued along until the feeling tugged sharply in her chest.

She paused at a shut door, pressing her palm against the wood. In a blink, she passed through and emerged into a palatial room. Her gaze was drawn to the four-poster bed and the sleeping girl. The furs pulled up around her so that only her head peeked out. A man slumbered in a chair beside it, hunched over, holding a slender hand.

Titania drifted forward, careful to maintain her concealment, lest she awaken the man. Beside the bed, she paused. The girl looked like the one who had once saved Titania. But there was no mistaking the magic that hummed from her loud and clear.

This was Nimue.

Realizing she must've possessed a new body in order to survive, Titania gently brushed her friend's forehead and entered Nimue's mind.

The room fell away as she appeared on a small clifftop clearing. A dark storm churned overhead, dark clouds split with cracks of lightning. The air was warm and humid against her skin, tasting faintly of salt and the city's fetid scents.

The real world is bleeding through, she thought, turning her gaze to the cliff's edge.

And there was her friend, standing over a blooming red flower. The gray glow from the storm framed Nimue's old form, brushing over the simple white dress and the thorny crown.

Nimue turned, surprise flashing on her face.

"Titania?"

CHAPTER 9

"I have been summoned to court by the King. Word has reached him of my unusual *talents. From the brooding expression of my guard, Titania, I am under the distinct impression this is not a good thing. But choice is not a luxury I have ever had. For now, I answer the call, like a dutiful soldier, and ignore the hunger of defying the summons."*

—Excerpt from Nimue's diary

The island emerged from the mist, the towering height of its lush green peaks a far cry from the snowy ones Flynn knew so well. Jagged cliffs of crisp white stone loomed on either side of a wide bay, striking against the dense foliage of the mountain. Set back from the shore, a bustling town reached high up the steep hillside. The rabbit-warren streets bustled with people resembling ants from where he stood on the deck. The island teemed with life, and people were unchained. Flynn suddenly ached for all he had lost.

Beside him, Mira stood silently, her arms folded across her chest. She hadn't said a word the whole day, though she remained on the deck, rather than hidden in the room. Flynn didn't miss the way she watched Castille, as if she didn't trust him.

He didn't either.

The man's smile never quite reached his eyes. The captain hadn't fought Castille's insistence to stay. There was a quiet familiarity with their relationship. As Flynn glanced back across the deck, he spied the pair by the wheel. Castille was chatting away, animatedly describing something with his hands while the captain chuckled.

Even the crew smiled at him and muttered teasing jibes.

It wasn't the reaction Flynn had expected, but his options were limited. The man had saved their lives, though he suspected it was for reasons beyond his knowledge at the moment.

"Quite a view, isn't it?" Mira murmured, drawing his gaze back to their approaching destination.

The quartermaster bellowed orders behind them. The men scrambled across the deck and up the mast. Flynn listened to the frenetic chaos as he watched the harbor grow closer. Several men awaited them on the dock, standing by as the lines were thrown across and the ship was secured. Men scrambled about the deck, orders shouted at a frenetic pace. The gangway was next across.

Once it was hauled over and lashed down, a few men hurried about and began ferrying crates off. Flynn kept close to Mira until Castille strode over, his hands clasped behind his back.

"There aren't any horses, so we'll be walking," he said. "Now, before we go, there is something I must prepare you for. You both know *what* I am, but these folks do not. Whatever you see, you cannot reveal your knowledge. That is all I ask. Do that and I will consider the life debt repaid."

"Life debt?" Mira echoed.

"I saved your lives, of course." His gaze flickered to Flynn. "The first lesson of our kind is this; honor every debt, even under pain of death."

Our kind...

Castille spun and strode to the gangway, leaving them to follow. Flynn felt Mira's gaze on him as they disembarked. No doubt she hadn't missed Castille's words either. The timely reminder that he wasn't like her, that he was something new and unknown. He wanted to assure her he was the same, but as he set foot on that pier, looking up at the town, a sense of power shivered down his spine. This island wasn't his home...and yet, something about it called out.

It lured him forward, one step after another, closer to something strangely familiar.

They walked through a village where silence followed, and gazes lingered. Flynn tried not to stare, but it was hard. He'd only ever seen a few half-blooded fae in the city, or those with faint fae features. Yet there was no mistaking the pointed ears, high cheekbones, and glowing golden eyes.

They looked first at Castille, their heads bowing as he passed.

Among them, he moved differently. His head up, eyes ahead, an air about him that hadn't been present before. Then the eyes of the crowds moved to Flynn and Mira, narrowing. Whispers stirred faintly, too quiet to decipher. By the time they reached the edge of town, he caught a louder snatch of conversation and realized it wasn't in a language he knew.

It was the first time he'd heard a language other than the common tongue taught from birth. The sensation of feeling like an outsider sharpened in his gut as they trekked up a winding road that led into the forest.

The humid air thickened. Sweat gathered on his brow and trickled down his face. His legs burned from the ascent, the first bit of real exercise he'd done since their capture. By the time the village was lost in the foliage and the call of birds sung out across the canopies, his breath was heavy. He pushed on, as did Mira, though she'd shed her cloak at some point and draped it across her arm.

Mira had asked about their bags as they left the pier. Castille merely remarked they'd be brought up later and that was the end of that conversation. She tried twice more, but he ignored her. Flynn offered her a smile, but she didn't return it. Her frown deepened.

"Ah, we're close now! Can you feel it?" Castille inquired.

"Feel *what?*" asked Mira through harsh breaths.

Flynn opened his mouth when the wind stirred through the trees, whipping up flurries of leaves and dust, carrying with it the tolling of bells. It pulled at his chest as if a string connected him to the sound and was pulling him forward. Mira called his name, but he couldn't stop himself as he set off again.

He didn't check to see if they followed him. Something had taken hold of him, guiding him along the narrow track. The tolling rang louder. As it faded off between each ring, he caught the sound of laughter and chatter, all in that same language he didn't know. But he didn't feel the same awkwardness he had with the villagers; no, this felt different.

The trees thinned away and he paused at the tree line. His jaw dropped. A large clearing was peppered with wooden huts that sat at the sides of a large road. It ran to a sheer cliff of white stone with an enormous temple carved into it. Towering polished pillars held up the entrance, three on either side of huge golden doors. On each was a different figure, some clad in flowing robes, others dressed like soldiers. One bore a golden thorny crown and a flowing black dress.

Flynn's gaze fell on the far right two.

One bore a dead reckoning to Castille, wicked grin and all, in a warrior's garb of polish armor, his hand resting on the pommel of a silver sword. Flynn's gaze lingered for a moment before it moved to the one next to him.

He didn't know who it was, not at first. The high cheekbones, sloping nose, and wide mouth set in a grim expression were not immediately familiar. Then he looked at the eyes, like polished black stone, that stared back with the same expression he'd seen before.

Atlas. His *father*.

Castille stopped beside him, letting out a low whistle as he slung his arm over Flynn's shoulders. "Time to learn about your history, kid, and see what you're made of."

CHAPTER 10

"The girl intrigues the King. She smiles and plays the role of a dutiful soldier. I do not miss, however, the way she studies everyone when they don't look at her. I caught her looking at me once and she offered a conspiratorial wink, then smiled as she slunk away into the shadows."

—Excerpt from Commander Titania's diary

The truth tumbled from Nimue's lips like an avalanche. The past three hundred years refused to stop as they spilled out; her death, the time slumbering in the dragon's egg in Lorca's kingdom, and the eighteen years living as Wren. When she finished, Titania wrapped her arms around her, rubbing small circles on her back. It took Nimue back to her youth when she was simply a headstrong soldier who needed a teacher. The girl who didn't know how to handle her emotions when everything spiraled out of control.

Only when Titania pulled away, offering a comforting smile, did she speak. "So, that man beside your bed?"

"Lorca," said Nimue, a smile pulling at her mouth before she could stop it.

Titania nudged her gently, grinning from ear to ear. "Oh, demons below, that *smile!*"

"Bugger off!" Nimue snapped, though, against her control, the smile remained.

Not like that, she was about to say, which was a lie. She'd already fallen over that edge and said those damning words. The one thing she'd never been able to say to Claudius. Her eyes widened. Oh Gods, if Titania was there, then that meant... She shrank away, her walls slamming back up, guarding her heart.

Titania seemed to sense her panic. "He's not in the room."

"But he's close?"

Titania took a moment to answer, her voice scarcely above a whisper. "Outside the mansion. He won't come unless you permit him."

She turned away, feeling the old wound reopen and grief wriggle up to her heart, squeezing it. An old memory took shape, the scent of new life... and then death filling her lungs. Tears threatened. Cursing, she drove the memory back down, clenching her hands into tight fists. She'd spent so damned long trying to move on, to *breathe.* How was it fair that he could just waltz back in and try to play the hero? She hated him for what he once meant to her and hated him for what he did.

"I don't want him anywhere near me. He can *rot* for all I care."

"Nimue—"

She wrenched herself away, throwing her hand up. Lightning erupted across the sky, the deafening bang quivering through the earth. "NO! I didn't spend so much damn time piecing myself back together for him to ruin it because he grew a conscience!"

Titania said nothing.

The wind howled between them, whipping Nimue's hair across her face. She stared back, defiant, ready to hear a plea for Claudius's redemption. That man only had *one* way he'd ever be welcome in her court and he'd not even tried that in eight hundred years. So why did she have to make any attempt at forgiveness?

She refused to forget...because that meant forgetting her daughter.

And she'd be damned if she let him take that from her.

Titania held up her hands in peace. "Then that's what will happen. I won't let him near you, but I'm going to have to come in the daytime to see you. Your body is a mess and Gods, you're weak. Weaker than I've ever felt."

Nimue flinched. She didn't want to accept the feeling her power had been scraped out of her, and that she felt weaker now than she had in death. Something was wrong with her magic, tearing her apart from within.

She shivered as a cold wind surged against her again, biting into her bones. Her soul ached, worn down, stripped bare of magic. She stepped closer to Titania, worry crowding her thoughts as she thought of Lorca.

"Lorca knows I am a demon and accepts me."

Titania tilted her head. "But does he know you're Nimue, Demon Queen of Azradan?"

"One damn secret at a time. If you heal me, Claudius and yourself could be exposed as demons. Are you sure?"

Titania snorted. "We shall be fine. Claudius can spin a lie better than most. It was how he served as your advisor for so long, remember? As for me, I consider myself rather clever. Back when we were all pretending to be spirits, I was beloved by many."

Nimue smiled. "You had what, six temples dedicated to you?"

"Five, actually. Atlas had six. Which reminds me, did you know he had children?"

"What?" The word slammed into her gut, ripping the air out. "That's impossible. We can't have children!"

Titania frowned. "We can if we're mortal, apparently. He was in your village and raised two daughters, though we found out that only one of the girls was his. He had a son, too. A boy called Flynn."

Nimue staggered back, the blood draining from her face. *Flynn?* He was a half-blood demon? Her stomach twisted. Gods, she was going to be sick. A way of nausea surged up her throat. The need for answers made her hand drop as she looked searchingly at Titania.

"What were the names of the daughters?" she asked softly.

"Ellie and Wren, I think?"

Her legs buckled as she dropped to her knees. Titania shouted her name, rushing over, but Nimue barely heard her. Ellie's beautiful face, her wonderfully *mortal,* gentle sister. Part demon. Like Nimue.

"Ellie...but how? I didn't sense any demon magic in her," Nimue whispered.

Titania sat back on her haunches. "Flynn's magic was bound. That's why we sent him to Atlas's old temple on the fae islands. Probably the same for her, I imagine?"

Bound magic. Atlas had likely been the one to spirit her out of Lorca's palace. The man was a master thief. There was no place he couldn't break into, magic wards or not. That had been why she put so much effort years ago to get him into her court. His ability to establish wards and bindings was also legendary.

No wonder her magic was bound so tightly.

But why had he done it? Why all the secrecy?

"He's still with the rest of my people, isn't he?"

"Refused to leave them. Made us take the boy instead and a sick girl. What was her name again? Mara?"

"Mira?"

"That's it. You know her?"

Nimue nodded, her mind still tangled with the news, as she replied numbly, "She was one of my climbers, same with Flynn." She fell silent again, pressing her palm to her face, and closing her eyes. Exhaling slowly, her hand fell away. "I can't believe I never knew. I mean, I have my memories back. I should've known about Atlas at least."

"To be fair, I didn't recognize him at first. He's not the man we knew," said Titania, an edge to her voice.

Nimue sighed deeply. "None of us are the same anymore."

She sighed and pressed her palms into the earth when a wave of nausea slammed into her, sending her staggering forward. Titania jumped up, catching her, calling out. The world lurched, blurring. The cold whisper of death called out; a bony hand stretched out from the shadows. The tempting promise of oblivion sang its deadly siren tune.

"I-I don't think I'm okay," she whispered hoarsely as she felt herself slip closer and closer to the hand.

Lorca's face flashed into her mind, his warm smile and gentle eyes. Her soul split as a single thought whispered through as she tumbled into the dark.

I wish I could've seen him again.

CHAPTER II

"Training is long and brutal. We spend hours with swords, daggers, and staff. Then I am required to study tactics, history, the forging of weapons, and politics. I can barely stand by the time I collapse into bed at night. We have repeated this for months now. I am being trained for something."

—Excerpt from Nimue's diary

Titania staggered back from the bed. A hand shot out, slamming into her throat. In an instant, she was shoved up against the wall. The man by Nimue's bed had her pinned, fury in his emerald eyes. Lorca, wasn't it?

"Who are you?" he snarled.

So much for the plan, she thought.

"Titania. I'm Nimue's friend."

"Why should I trust you?"

She held up her hands. "Because she's dying, and I won't lose her again."

Not again. Not like this.

He stared at her, his jaw twitching, a war of emotions raging in his eyes. A ragged breath tore from his lips as he stepped back, releasing her. Magic rolled off him, prickling against hers.

Rubbing her neck, she hurried over to Nimue, turning her focus to her friend. Worry tightened in her gut. Only the faintest hum of life flickered and it was growing weaker. With a deep breath, she sat down, gently taking Nimue's hands.

"Claudius Delmont is waiting outside—bring him to me," she instructed.

He froze, his anger giving way to confusion. "What?"

"He's like me, like Nimue. I may need an extra boost of energy and he's the only one who can help," she explained. "Now *go!*" Nimue doesn't have much time. I can hold her for the moment, but that won't last!"

His gaze flew to Nimue, grief stark in those jeweled eyes. In one look, Titania knew the feelings weren't one-sided. Nodding, he turned to leave but leveled one last warning her way. "Hurt her and I will tear you apart."

Then he was gone, the door slamming shut behind him.

Titania returned her attention to Nimue and opened her magic, pouring it down her hand and into the deathly pale girl on the bed. The thread binding the general to her queen, frayed by time and whatever was ailing Nimue, began to glow. Titania followed it, pouring all she had, descending into the darkness of Nimue's soul.

A storm raged around her. Howling winds and blackening clouds twisted and cracked with thunder. An icy wind slammed into her, sending a thousand daggers slicing at her skin, sinking deep. Shuddering breaths spilled from her lips, the cold air swirling against her cheeks.

Down she went, the thunder booming and lightning crackling across the sky. The storm grew stronger, the wind harder against her, trying to drive her back up. It wanted her out, to protect what little was left of Nimue's crumbling essence. A swath of emotions swept into her mind; desperation, grief, *fury*.

Splashes of memories darted past her, vanishing into the darkness as she pushed further down. Snatches of conversations reached her ears.

"You don't know the curse you have inherited. You stupid little fool!"

Titania knew the voice. It was the King who Nimue had slain to claim the throne.

Deeper she plunged, another voice crashing into her.

"Please, don't leave me! Don't go! I need you!" Nimue's hoarse screams choked with grief which followed the desperate plea.

Nimue's voice continued to tumble through the void, wrapping around Titania until she heard nothing else.

"Please, my baby, don't leave me! Come back!"

"This was your God's damned scheme? I will destroy you for this! I will rip apart everything you have loved and turn your kingdom to ashes."

A crash of thunder shattered the voices and Titania tumbled through a portal, silence slamming down around her. The world stilled into chilling darkness, the cold air still biting. She struck solid rock, pain erupting through her body, as if she'd just walked from the worst battle of her life—battered and bruised and bleeding. Wincing, she drove her palms into the ground and pushed up. Her legs wobbled, threatening to give out at any moment.

A portal open was above her, with a thin ribbon stretching down to her—a connection back to the waking world. She could just make out the storm still raging through the opening, but the sounds were far away. Frowning, she lowered her gaze and looked around.

"T-Titania?"

She spun. A few feet away, little more than a specter flickering in and out, was Nimue. Titania hurried over, heart pounding. Losing Nimue again wasn't an option. She couldn't endure that again.

"Who said you can die on us again?"

"I'm dying?" Nimue asked, her brow furrowing. Confusion deepened her frown as she blinked, glancing around. "Where am I?"

"You tell me. We were speaking when you suddenly collapsed. You're dying, which is why I'm here. Trying to find you, well, your soul given that seems to be the part currently splintering apart," she said, inching closer. "But there's something you should know. I sent Lorca to find Claudius."

Nimue flinched, hissing, her eyes black as death. "You did *what?*"

"You're dying. In this body, your connection to your throne is so weak you can't replenish it on your own. I need to give you a boost, but I can't do that alone. If I do, we both die. I don't know about you, but I like living. Lorca, I'm sure would feel the same. About you, I mean. I don't think he'd cry if I died."

A war of emotions raged on Nimue's face, her jaw twitching. "Fine, but once we're done, I want Claudius gone. I never want to see his face again."

It had been eight hundred years since Nimue and Claudius had fallen apart, and Titania had never been able to get a straight answer as to what happened. She wanted to ask, but it wasn't the time.

"Of course. Now, are you planning on just lying down and dying? Or are you going to fight? Not for yourself, but for your people and Lorca?"

That broke the last remnant of reluctance. Nimue nodded. Whatever her feelings for Claudius, her drive for the villagers and Lorca were greater.

More than she ever cared for her own kind, sneered an inner voice.

Shoving the voice away, Titania took Nimue's hands, when a warmth brushed her shoulder. A figure materialized beside her. Nimue's eyes widened, the blood flooding her face. The shock sharpened into cold anger as she looked at Titania while doing everything possible not to look at Claudius standing beside her.

Titania glanced at Claudius. "Ready?"

He nodded, his shadowed gaze never moving from Nimue. "Yes."

CHAPTER 12

"I understand now the role I am being groomed for. Little do they know what desires I have."

—Excerpt from Nimue's diary, soldier-class demon

A hooded figure awaited Sybilla in her office. Oren's hand dropped to his sword, but she grabbed it, shaking her head. His brow dipped, a question poised. She flicked her chin for him to leave, giving him a warning stare until he retreated. The door shut softly, though the footfalls indicated he remained just outside. The corner of her mouth twitched as she turned.

"I didn't think you'd come," she said as she shuffled over to one of the armchairs, and lowered herself down with a groan. The day had left her muscles stiff, her bones aching. A headache was already starting behind her eye.

A gentle laugh rumbled from the stranger as they pushed back the hood. Golden eyes stared back, glimmering with power. The sharp-featured, white-haired woman remained where she stood. Poised and with predatory grace, she reminded Sybilla of Aziah. Both were fae-born from the southern islands of the Mithra Archipelago. Both were spies and killers. Yet the one who stood before her didn't have the same sadness in her eyes, nor the loneliness that followed Aziah like a second shadow.

Sylvie Ryn had been forged by a different pain.

"We nearly didn't, but the Empress has become rather efficient in rooting out traitors. Our home was burned," the spy murmured, turning to the cold fireplace. "It seems her little inquisition into supposed traitors has gone beyond her attack of northern villages. Some of the remote areas near Grisk were hit, though reports claim it was bandits. Lies, the lot of it."

We? The air fled Sybilla, silencing her for a moment. "You're all here?"

At once, a tiny flame of hope kindled to life.

"We had nowhere else to go. Is that an issue?" Warning infused every word.

"Of course not. Dorian's knowledge in ancient languages might just save our necks here," Sybilla replied. Her eyes widened. "Does that mean she's here too? The girl?"

"She is."

Again, a silence followed, leaving to Sybilla if she revealed too much of her interest. After all, there was no one quite like Sylvie's adopted daughter. Not anymore, at least.

"Can I meet her?" The question was out before she could drag it back in.

Sylvie's mouth opened as if to argue, then closed. This was a mother who fiercely guarded her daughter, who Sybilla had only glimpsed once—an encounter she would never forget.

"I would prefer to keep her out of this, but it's safer if she remains with us. All that I ask is that you keep quiet about *what* she is and her abilities. That is the price of my aid." Sylvie moved away from the fire and sat in the other armchair. When Sybilla gave a nod of assurance, the spy continued, "I suppose we should discuss the recent matter of the experiments using Hellis powder."

The following day, as the rain continued its assault, Sybilla was taking a tour with General Galen along the wall when Aziah appeared. The assassin emerged from the shadow of the tower. The soldiers flinched and gave her a wide berth. Their mutterings trailed past Sybilla as she ordered Oren and his men to hang back, since a private matter needed to be discussed with her assassin. He gave her a reluctant nod, though his twitching jaw told her about his thoughts on that idea.

They proceeded into the tower, taking refuge in an empty meeting room. Gray light spilled in through a small window, creating a few small shadows in the corners. Aziah drifted toward one, as if by instinct, then turned and pushed her hood down. The cold promise of death never vanished from those ancient eyes. How many souls had been snuffed out, with those fathomless pits being the last thing they saw?

"Have you found your mate?" Sybilla asked.

Aziah's mouth tightened. "No, but that isn't why you summoned me. How may I serve you?"

"I need you to find out some more information about the temple that's being constructed beyond the capital. The surviving villagers from Fenware were taken there, and I want to determine their status."

Aziah's brow lifted. "They're probably dead."

"Perhaps, but unless I want my two strongest allies, Wren and Lorca, running off on some harebrained quest to determine *that* for themselves, I need proof. Can you do it?"

Aziah snorted. "I'm a little insulted that you have to ask. Consider it done, but will you be okay in this city?"

She thought about pointing out Oren's presence, but refrained. He was human. The threats Aziah referred to wouldn't be deterred by that.

"I'll survive. Find out what happened to the people of Fenware, then you can resume your search for Gabriel. I'll have my little birds seek for any trace of him." Sybilla closed the distance and reached out, squeezing her friend's shoulder. "It's the least I can do. Now, go."

Aziah's hand slid up to Sybilla's cheek, and the assassin and heir to the throne pressed their foreheads together.

"Don't get yourself killed, little one."

CHAPTER 13

"The nobles at court are like vipers, their every word drips with venom. Their arrogance betrays them, though. I watch them in the shadows, listen when they think I am absent, and learn. Secrets are the true power and that is how I will be Queen."
—Excerpt from Nimue's diary, soldier-class demon

Nimue's soul was a roaring storm of raw magic, ancient grief and murderous fury. Two halves of her—body and soul—-were at war; fire and shadow, each ripping her apart from within, demanding complete dominion. As Titania and Claudius poured their power into her, trying desperately to mend her demonic soul, burning agony cleaved through her mind. The fire raged against the new power, snarling and clawing.

Just as the damage was repaired, her dragon side tore into it, shredding her soul to ribbons. A scream tried to force its way from her lips, but she slammed her mouth shut, gritting her teeth, and focused on the fire, driving it back into the single flame at her core.

The flow of power ebbed, and her eyes opened wide, latching onto Titania and Claudius.

"Don't stop!" she cried hoarsely.

"It's too much. You're hurting!" Claudius snapped.

"It didn't stop you before! Keep going! I can take it!"

"She's right, Claudius. We stop now. She dies," said Titania.

The pair fell silent as their hesitation bled away, and a surge of energy pushed in. The fire retreated at her command. It lifted her from the dark abyss and out through the portal that hovered above them.

A storm erupted around her and a tidal wave of emotion and memories crashed in, flooding her mind in a cacophony of noise and color. Some passed too fast to recognize, but others lingered. One caught her attention, nearly sending her spiraling back into the darkness below.

That accursed room with the scent of new life.

She shoved it away, focusing on the magic, clinging desperately to life. She would not lose herself. By the Gods, she was a survivor and she had a mission to finish. Come hell or high water, she'd find her people and bring them home, even if it was the last thing she did.

The three of them shot up through the raging clouds as the cruel memories tumbled away. A new warmth filled her, a wave of love and pleading bursting through her chest. More magic spilled in, the warmth growing hotter, the feelings sharper. Someone was calling her home, a golden thread piercing through the chaos.

"Come back to me. Please, just come back to me!"

Lorca.

She took hold of the thread as Titania and Claudius drove more magic into her soul, stitching it back together. Her grip tightened. Fire poured down the golden line and into her.

High above, she spied the end, vanishing into a glowing sphere.

"I still have so much to show you, to share with you. Come back, Nimue, just come back!"

She roared upward through the light, and the world fell silent.

Nimue sat up gasping, the white light yielding to the bedroom. Thoughts tangled together. Her body hummed with magic, the two opposing sides restless but, for the moment, not at war. She closed her eyes, waiting for the dizziness to pass.

"Nimue?" Lorca whispered.

His face sharpened into focus, worry shadowed his eyes, the dark lines making him look exhausted. It melted away as he lifted her hand, kissing it reverently. Warmth thrummed down their bond, tugging her mouth into a smile.

"I heard you, Lorca. I *heard* you calling for me."

He pressed his forehead to hers, his emotions wrapping around her, anchoring her to the mortal plane. The scent of pine and clove, and something distinctly reminiscent of the mountains, filled her breath. She closed her eyes, allowing her body to steady once more. Though the echo of pain ached through her bones, and her demonic soul whimpered, she was okay. At least for the moment.

"Hey, we saved you, too, remember?" Titania's teasing voice drew her gaze away.

Titania swayed on her feet, sweat glistening on her face. Claudius didn't look much better. The man was still as maddeningly handsome as he had been the day he'd walked away from her. Fury prickled in her chest, venom pouring into her mouth. Heat inched up her neck, warming the tips of her ears. Lorca's hand on hers stayed her temper, for the moment anyway.

"Thank you. Both of you," Nimue said quietly, though giving Claudius any praise chafed at old, festering wounds.

Mercifully, he said nothing as Titania swayed into him.

He looped his arm around Titania's waist. Glancing back, his gaze dropped to Lorca's hands in hers, then up to her face. "I need to get Titania back to my mansion. It'll be hard to explain why we're here."

Nimue nodded. "Good."

"Nimue I—"

The tentative hope in his voice snapped something already broken within. She glared at him coldly.

"Know this, Claudius. I am thankful you saved my life, but that doesn't mean we're as we once were. You are *not* forgiven."

He flinched, saying nothing. As he stared back, she could see the war of emotions across his face and guessed what he wanted to say. Even after so many years, she read him like a book—and she hated it. He nodded before raising a hand and snapping his fingers. Titania and Claudius vanished into a plume of smoke, which dispelled as quickly as it had appeared.

She sank back into the pillows, closing her eyes.

"Nimue!"

She looked over at Lorca who was kneeling beside her bedside. "That can't be comfortable. Get into this bed. I'm not dying right now and don't want to sleep alone. I'll explain everything later, I promise. Just, not now, okay?"

He nodded and lifted the covers, slipping into the bed beside her. She didn't complain as he drew her into his chest, gently stroking her hip as she finally slipped into a deep, dreamless sleep.

When she stirred awake, Lorca was no longer curled at her side. She sat up sharply, stilling as she saw that he'd taken his dragon form and was curled protectively around her bed. The soft morning light spilled over his glossy black scales.

With the world outside momentarily silent, he seemed at peace. For that, she envied him. A restlessness lingered in her blood, and the pain of old, twisted memories hummed just beneath the surface. She crept from the bed, changing quickly into a loose shirt and pants, then padded out of the room.

She needed to feel fresh air on her cheeks and to re-orient herself in a world that felt out of balance once more.

Sounds came from downstairs and led her to the bustling hallway. As she continued to the front door, it swung open with an echoing groan.

Sybilla appeared, a golden cloak set about her shoulders. She smiled at Nimue. "You're awake."

"I just needed some rest. Are your men okay?"

Sybilla stepped forward. "They're doing as well as one can expect. However, I was wondering if you feel up to talking? I have a proposal for you."

Nimue tried not to look longingly at the door, at the promise of fresh air. Knowing she still needed Sybilla's help, she nodded. Sybilla bid her men goodbye, then set off up the stairs to her office.

Sybilla took a seat behind her desk and gestured to a chair.

"Please take a seat, Wren. I wanted to let you know I've sent spies to the temple construction to find out what's happened to your people."

Nimue tensed at hearing her old name from Sybilla's lips. She'd almost forgotten that Sybilla wasn't aware she was no longer merely Wren the climber from Fenware. At some point, she'd have to let her know, but now probably wasn't the time. Not when she still needed her help to rescue her people.

Deep shadows showed under Sybilla's eyes and her shoulders drooped with weariness. A slender hand lifted. "And before you assume this is merely a manipulation I want to repay you for what you did at the square. Looking back on how I handled things, I know I made a misstep with you. I could spin an excuse that I've done it with everyone else in this rebellion, but that doesn't make it any better."

Nimue sat mulling over Sybilla's words. It made sense, annoyingly. That didn't mean she enjoyed being played any less.

"Thank you," she eventually said. "For the use of your spies."

Sybilla shifted on her seat, glancing away. "You saved my neck out there. That attack could've gone much worse."

"You mean it could've ended your rebellion before it had a chance?"

"It still might," said Sybilla, rubbing her temples with a pained expression. She sighed and looked cautiously at Nimue. "Which brings me to my proposal. You don't have to agree because of the spies. I know my word means shit right now, but I'll change that. You'll see."

Unease prickled the back of Nimue's neck. The demon attack replayed in her mind. Those creatures had borne *her* mark, yet they had been summoned and controlled by someone else. Even though she'd managed to get one to realize who she was, the fight still unsettled her.

"Your proposal?"

"The army isn't at our walls yet, which means for the moment, we're able to get supplies from neighboring villages and towns. We're expecting support from the North, but winter is nearly upon us, and the lords are reluctant to march. This means we need to hold through the winter. I'm concerned if this demon issue escalates, it will create chaos in the city. I need to know what exactly is going on and who is behind it, and how to stop it before it becomes a bigger issue."

"And how do Lorca and I figure into this?" asked Nimue.

"I want to create a team and I would like both of you to join it if you're agreeable. You have talents that will be useful in hunting the threat and ending it. I know I don't have any right to order you and blackmail sits ill with me right now. So, you are free to say no and go wherever you please. But I'm asking for your help to save my people. I'm sure you can understand that sentiment."

It might've been the vulnerable, pleading look in those amber eyes or perhaps because Sybilla knew exactly which string to pluck.

Nimue rose and felt a rush of pain pulse sharply behind her eye. She clutched the back of her chair, hoping Sybilla hadn't noticed how unsteady she still was.

"I can't commit until I talk to Lorca. If he doesn't accept, I won't push him. We both say yes, or neither of us joins."

Sybilla nodded, exhaling deeply, relief bleeding the tension from her shoulders. "That's more than I could ask. Thank you."

"Don't thank me yet. You underestimate how deep old wounds run."

CHAPTER 14

"Power is not given. It is taken. So, I bide my time, listening to all that Titania teaches me. I wonder if she knows what I have planned, what I hunger for."
—Excerpt from Nimue's diary, soldier-class demon

A fae clad in flowing white robes approached, his golden eyes latched onto Flynn. Two women and a young man shadowed him, the latter staring with open suspicion. They stopped, all bowing to Castille.

The older man, with cropped black hair flecked with gray and hawkish features, smiled. "You grace us with your presence. I must confess, Claudius, Spirit of the Wind, only spoke of the half-blood and the girl. He didn't mention your arrival. Had we known, we would've prepared your chambers."

Castille laughed. "You flatter me, but Claudius didn't send me. I swooped in to save the day just as the sirens were attacking their vessel. It was quite heroic, if you ask me."

Flynn wasn't sure what to make of that. How *had* Castille known they were in danger? Had he been following them? Or was he the instigator—and if so, to what end? The questions continued to fill his mind, all lacking answers until frustration coiled tight like a snake ready to strike.

"Indeed, and very fortuitous timing!" The older fae's voice snapped Flynn back to the present.

Castille shrugged with that easy smile, but this time his eyes glinted with humor. "I wish I could take credit for that, but the warning of an attack came from my darling wife. It is to the Spirit of the Seas that my presence is credited. She wishes she could be here, but times are troubling and she is busy."

"Another time, perhaps?" the man said with a hopeful expression.

"Perhaps. But you know how she prefers her sanctuary, even though I tell her often how wonderful this place is. Truly, Atlas would be proud."

The man's cheeks reddened. "You flatter us. Now, enough chatter. I am too old for it. Please, introductions are in order." He turned his focus to Flynn and Mira. "I am Head Guardian, Mathias. These are some of my guardians, Ellery, Sypha, and Tobin. You must be Flynn and Mira."

The guardians dipped their heads, though Tobin's gaze lingered on him. A trickle of awareness prickled down his spine. Flynn swallowed hard, trying to ignore the intensity of that honey-gold stare, the slope of that strong nose, hard mouth, and high cheekbones.

Flynn knew at that moment he was in trouble.

Tobin murmured something to the women who snorted derisively. The only show of emotion on their unnervingly ethereal faces. His gaze never moved from Flynn as he straightened up.

Flynn didn't realize that Castille and Mathias were speaking when the former nudged him. He blinked, realizing the pair of them were looking at him. "Apologies, you were saying?"

Mathias smiled. "I was asking if you and your woman wished to see your quarters? You must be tired and wish to bathe?"

Mira blushed. "I'm not his woman! We're friends, nothing more!"

Castille pressed a hand to his mouth, smothering a laugh.

When he composed himself, he said, "I believe there is some confusion. These two are not lovers."

Fire flooded Flynn's cheeks and a rebuttal rose to his lips when the man turned and smiled at him.

"Forgive me for the assumption. We will arrange separate chambers. Ellery and Sypha, can you take Mira to one of the bathing chambers?"

Mathias gestured to Mira. "Go with them. They will ensure you are settled. Any concerns, please come see me."

Mira opened her mouth to say something, but Castille set a hand on her arm. Flynn didn't miss the warning look or the way he gently nudged her forward. Biting her lip, she glared at him before trailing after the women.

Once they were gone, Mathias turned to Tobin. "Please take Flynn here to his room to freshen up. I must speak with Castille."

Tobin stepped forward and flicked his hand, gesturing for Flynn to follow before he set off. Flynn hurried after him, scarcely keeping up as they headed straight for the temple built into the cliff face. As Tobin stalked up the steps, Flynn slowed by the pillars and gazed up at the one with his father's image. He swore he felt Atlas's gaze on him as he passed.

"Hurry up!" Tobin snapped.

Flynn scurried after him through the golden doors.

They entered a cavernous rectangular room. Flynn fought not to stare at the ceiling towering high above and painted with a mural of a bloody battle. Tobin didn't stop, forcing him to wrench his gaze away from the scene. They hurried through an archway and into a long hallway, lit by lanterns at regular intervals on the wall. Their footsteps echoed in tandem, the only sound as they moved along. They passed more hallways, branching off in several directions, and doors that were all shut.

Flynn wanted to ask Tobin about the temple, but the fae made it clear he was in a hurry and in no mood to answer Flynn's questions. The endless hallway sloped down and they came to a stop at one of the doors. Tobin pushed it open to reveal an enclosed courtyard. In the center, a glowing crystal hung, illuminating the interior with white light. Thousands more crystals speckled the domed ceiling and ran down the walls, throwing light on several other doors.

Tobin strode over to one and opened it for him. "This is your room. There is a bathing chamber inside."

Flynn stopped at the doorway, peering inside. Lanterns lit a spacious room, ornately furnished with a large bed and a tall dresser. He looked back at Tobin. "This is mine?"

Tobin rolled his eyes. "Of course, it's yours. This chamber is reserved for the spirits when they visit the temple...and now, it seems, their half-blood spawn."

He'd copped plenty of insults growing up, especially when knowledge of his preference in bed partners trickled through the village. Those that knew whispered cruel things in the shadows, threatening that at any moment they might expose him. No, cruel words weren't foreign to him, but after everything that had happened, he was determined not to take any more.

He pinned a hard look at Tobin. "Have I insulted you?"

Tobin stiffened. "No. Now, can you go inside already? I have a mountain of work to do and limited daylight to do it. One of the trainees will probably grab you for an evening meal, or perhaps Mathias will when he's finished speaking with the Spirit of Life and Order."

Flynn opened his mouth to ask again, but Tobin had already stalked out of the room. When the door clicked shut behind him, the sound of his retreating footsteps echoed, trailing off until silence gripped the chamber. Shaking his head, he made his way inside. After looking around at the opulent furnishings, he was about to disrobe when he spotted a portrait on the wall.

It was of a young couple, adorned in white and gold robes.

Wren's mother and Atlas.

He'd always assumed the pair had lived their whole time in Fenware, but it seemed they both had a life no one knew about. Had Wren known? Or had she, too, been kept ignorant? He hoped the latter, not enjoying the idea of someone else he'd trusted so deeply lying to him.

A shiver ran down his spine. He felt so far out of his depth, drowning in a sea with no land in sight. Sharp breaths quickened over his lips, and the walls felt as if they were closing in around him. His vision blurred and he staggered, sinking to the cold stone floor.

Just who the hell was he anymore? And had he bitten off more than he could chew?

Just as Tobin had said, there was a bathing chamber attached to his room. The pool was sunk into the ground and as he dipped his feet into it, he groaned in delight at the warm water. He lowered himself gingerly until he was submerged up to his neck. It was unlike anything he'd ever felt before. On the side was a small plate of soap, which he used to scrub himself clean. It was coarser than he expected, leaving a pinkish glow on his skin when he eventually hauled himself out.

Back in the room, he wrinkled his nose at the filthy clothes stinking of sweat and salt. He padded over to the dresser and found some clothes folded inside. Including the same fine ones from the portrait. He lifted out a fresh set of pants and a linen shirt, the simplest he could find, which still felt too nice to wear. Luckily, they fitted him well enough.

Exhaustion and the effect of the bath pulled him to the bed. He lay on top of the furs, staring up at the ceiling until sleep dragged him under.

It was impossible to know how long he slept. He awoke to the sound of knocking. Blinking blearily, he shuffled to the door, rubbing the sleep from his eyes. He pulled it open to find Mathias outside.

Mathias greeted him with a smile. "Did you sleep well?"

"I was more tired than I realized. Thank you for well, all of this."

"Nonsense. Nothing but the best. I was hoping to speak with you before the evening meal. There are lots of curious fae eager to meet you, and once they start chatting, we won't have time to talk!"

He thought of Tobin's sour mood. Not everyone was eager to meet him, which was fine by him. He didn't like crowds all that much, and the idea of a busy evening meal left his stomach in knots.

"What did you want to talk to me about?" he asked.

"About your trials, of course. You may be the son of a spirit, but we must know whether you are worthy to wield the powers within you. If you survive, then I will personally release you from the binding."

Flynn's eyes widened in alarm. "If?"

CHAPTER 15

"I met with Claudius today. He came to me with an interest in forming an alliance. He worries the King is weakening. He left after I assured him this wasn't the case, but I saw the look in Nimue's eyes. It was the same one she had when she crawled from the pit."

—Excerpt from Commander Titania's diary

Nimue's hand hovered over the door handle to Ellie's room. Her thoughts tangled together as she tried to find the words to express the turmoil within her. Ellie's world had already been torn apart. Now the knowledge that she wasn't entirely human wouldn't leave Nimue alone. She told herself that Ellie had lived nineteen years perfectly normal and happy until the attack, ignorant of what she was. That she didn't need to become a warrior, but...

Her fingers brushed the handle.

The door swung inwards. Ellie greeted her with wide eyes, silent for a moment before she flung her arms around her. "You're awake!"

Nimue returned the hug and pulled back, hating the shadows under Ellie's eyes. That once glowing, golden skin and luminous blue eyes were now dim. It was as if a fire had been snuffed out, leaving her fragile and unsure.

Was it right to shatter what little self-control was left?

Ellie stepped back. "What brings you here? Should you not be resting?"

"I've rested enough," was all she said as she slipped past Ellie and into the room.

Books lay scattered across the floor. The bed was untouched, but a pile of furs and blankets was tangled in a heap next to the fire. The stubby end of a nearly melted candle sat on a holder, the wick blackened and curled. The scent of old paper and smoke lingered in the air. Ellie hung back, arms around her tiny waist, glancing between the mess and her sister.

Nimue sat down and picked through the ones nearest to her. "Any favorites so far?"

Ellie hesitated before she moved closer. "I wasn't great at reading at school, so some of them are beyond me... but I like the distraction."

A basic literary skill had been required in Fenware. The elders had insisted it was for an understanding of trade, of knowing their history and documenting it properly. Something that had always struck her as odd growing up. In hindsight, she wondered if it was to maintain their connection to the Dragonirs, whom she suspected had forged Fenware in a desperate attempt to stay close to the mountains.

She shook off the thought, turning back to her sister. "How are you? Are you sleeping?"

Ellie's gaze shuttered, and whatever joy had sparked in her sister's face sputtered out as she retreated to the edge of the room. "I'm fine."

"Ellie—"

"I told you *I'm fine,*" Ellie snapped. Fire flashed in those fathomless pools, vanishing as quickly as it had appeared.

She sat there, unsure what to do next.

That room might as well have been a vast ocean, a storm raging between them. She was adrift on those turbulent waves, fighting to reach her sister and destroy the monsters torturing Ellie's mind.

But that fiery glimpse from before told Nimue that her sister wasn't broken. Withdrawing the dagger sheathed at her hip she stood and set the blade on the bedside table. Ignoring the way Ellie had flinched, she kept her back to her sister.

"You might feel lost and broken, and I can't promise that healing will be easy. But Ellie, you're stronger than you know." Nimue retreated to the door. Before leaving, she turned. "When you feel ready to talk, I will be there, open and without judgment."

Her room was silent when she returned. As she carefully pushed the door open and stepped inside, a shadow fell over her. Hands slid around her waist and an earthy scent filled her lungs. Nimue closed her eyes as she felt Lorca's lips drop to her neck, trailing feathery kisses up her jaw.

"You're awake." She leaned into his embrace.

"Where have you been? You should be resting," he grumbled.

"Are you going to carry me off to bed and tie me there?" she teased, twisting in his embrace as she slid her arms around his neck. "Because I'll have you know, I much prefer to be the one doing the tying."

His face flushed. "Now you're the one making promises."

Sybilla's proposal pushed its way up to the front of her mind, cooling her ardor. She slipped away from him and began to pace back and forth, arms around her waist, trying to find the right words.

She felt his eyes on her, tracking every movement.

"What happened?" he asked. "I can tell something has put you in a bad mood."

"Sybilla."

He stilled. "What did she do?"

"She says she's sent spies to the temple to find out if my people are still alive," Nimue said, pausing as she looked at him. "It's an attempt to redeem our trust—or so she claims. I'm not sure whether to believe it, though, because the next thing she talked about was a proposal to join a team of hers."

"To do what?" He sank onto the bed and leaned back against the pillows. "Wait, let me guess? Because of the demon attack?"

She nodded and sat beside him. "I told her I'd speak with you before I gave a response."

His piercing gaze betrayed nothing at first, then he sat up and cupped her chin in his hand. "You want to do it."

"Right now, I need more time to figure out a plan to save my people. Besides, you saw that attack. If things get worse, and this city falls then we're back where we started. Without allies and limited options...and I'll be frank, I'm not as strong as I used to be. The old Nimue could've vanquished an army, and brought this empire to its knees." A hiss of frustration pushed through her lips. "But now I'm just..."

She stared at her hands, annoyingly mortal. It wasn't a body hardened by conflict.

Lorca released her chin and slid his hands over hers, squeezing them softly. "Then we stay."

"You want to join her team?"

His lips tightened into a thin line. "Not to help her, but I saw those demons and what a few of them can do. The city will be massacred if it escalates...and if that happens, I'll also lose my only chance for answers."

What he didn't realize was that in her dying moments three hundred years ago, he had already witnessed what she could do—and the utter carnage she was capable of.

Sybilla appeared surprised when Nimue informed her the following morning they were accepting the proposal. She said there was a meeting later that evening, as the other members were already out in the city. That left several hours to kill before they were required. As Nimue returned to her room to grab Lorca, she paused at the threshold.

He stood in the middle of the room, shirtless, wielding a sword, gliding through his movements. The sunlight glinted off his muscles, shimmering over the faint sheen of sweat on his skin. With every shift and flex of his muscles, she was so entranced by him it took her a moment to notice the blade on the table close by.

Her blood turned to ice.

Since waking up, she'd forgotten about it, that she'd left it behind on her mission to rescue Ellie. As Wren, she'd felt drawn to the sword but hadn't understood why. Standing there, vaguely realizing that Lorca had stopped, the pieces clicked into place.

Oh, Gods, I remember everything.

The world was silent as her eyes refused to part from his sword. He must've misunderstood her expression, because in the next moment, he strode over, her blade in hand—and she flinched back with a hiss.

"Get that thing away from me!"

He froze. "What? Nimue, what's wrong?"

Sharp breaths scraped over her lips, blood roaring in her ears. Her chest tightened, darkness nudging the edge of her vision. She had to get away from the memory, pushing its way up to her mind's eye. Panic clawed at her chest, tearing her apart from within. Lorca threw the sword away and pulled her into his arms, rubbing her back. He said nothing as she heaved in gulps of air, clinging to him as if she was dying.

Demons below. She certainly felt like it.

Her heart thudded, every beat a dagger being driven deeper in. Closing her eyes, she sank into his embrace. The images of her death at Litania's hand filled her mind and threatened to overwhelm her; the sword jutting from her chest, slick with blood; the metallic stench in the air; the stinging agony that radiated through her chest.

She pulled on other memories; her people, her sister, Lorca, and the taste of his mouth.

Forcing her eyes open, she looked up and slid her hand to his neck, hauling him down. Their mouths collided, shock coursing through their bond. He pulled back, his hot breath fanning her lips, tasting of spices and mulled wine.

"Nimue—"

"Don't ask, please. I *need* this. I want to feel something good right now, not..."

His gaze bore through her, piercing her to the bone. She felt his curiosity nudging at her mind.

"We *will* talk about this," he vowed.

She barely nodded when his lips met hers once more. His hands dropped to her ass, lifting her. Rolling her hips against him, her legs hooked around his waist, she deepened their kiss. His soft curls felt like silk tangled between her fingers.

They stumbled deeper into the room and onto the bed. In a flash, he was over her, raining molten kisses on her neck and mouth. A fire burned through her veins, lighting up every inch of her skin. She lifted her hand, tugging at his shirt until he groaned, and pulled it over his head. The fabric vanished out of view.

He kissed her hungrily as she raked her fingers down his back.

He shuddered beneath her touch. Heat coiled tight between her legs as he tugged her shirt up and off, breaking their kiss for a moment.

She pulled her mouth away, trailing kisses to his ear. "*Lorca, pants.*"

He chuckled hoarsely, dropping his mouth to the crook of her neck. "Demanding little creature, aren't you?"

A wicked smile pulled at his mouth, his hands dipping to his belt as he tugged it free.

She sat up, molten liquid pooling at her core. "Slower."

Heat flared in his eyes. He kept his gaze on her as he got off the bed, letting the pants fall, his arousal on display.

Demons below...

"Now, you." Desire dripped from his lips.

She grinned and slowly undressed. Feeling bold, she lay back and spread her legs, watching as his gaze fell, devouring the sight of her hot and ready for him. "Are you planning to stand there all day?"

He moved quicker than she thought possible, his body covering hers. As he kissed her, she hooked her leg around his hip, drawing him closer before flipping over on top of him. She pinned his arms down, straddling him helpless beneath her. His cock brushed her stomach, the length of it larger than anything she'd had before.

In this body and her last.

"You're *mine,*" she whispered.

"Then let me pleasure you," he growled. "Release my hands."

She laughed breathlessly. "You get *one* hand."

His hand slipped between her legs, finding her nub and pinching it lightly between his fingers. Gasping, she dug her nails into his chest as he went to work, swirling, teasing, reducing her to a hot and wet, writhing mess.

"That's it, Nimue, *let go.*"

One finger slipped into her, then another as she rolled her hips, throwing her head back. A scalding heat roared upward from the depths of her soul, flooding her limbs, and sending her hurtling to the edge. All sense of control tumbled away. Cries spilled from her lips as she ground harder against his hand, chasing the oblivion that called her name.

He called her name like a desperate prayer.

An inferno exploded inside her. A hoarse cry broke from her lips and she slumped forward, sweat glistening on her skin as she took a moment to breathe, all rational thought gone. The world outside had gone mad, and now so had she.

She rolled to his side, his arm looped around her, drawing her to half-lie on his chest. The evidence of his release lay smeared on his chest and hers.

Her chest still heaved as she said, "Not quite how I planned the afternoon."

"Oh, you didn't picture having your wicked way with me?" He fell silent again, his hand tracing the length of her back as if he were savoring her.

For a moment, all was peaceful and the outside world was forgotten.

With a sigh, Lorca asked, "So, what happened before?"

"Hmm?" She looked up.

"My sword. You acted as if I was going to attack you with it."

Cold water dumped on her. She huddled in closer to him, seeking his warmth, his steady presence. It felt like an eternity before she discovered her voice, and the truth spilled out from the carefully walled prison she'd forged within herself.

"That's the sword Litania used when she killed me."

CHAPTER 16

"Peace has been broken between the four demon courts. I worry for our future. We are the smallest, the weakest...and our King? He is but a shadow of the great warrior he once was. Whispers in the court stir. Someone must challenge him soon, for all our sakes. The problem is those who have lived long enough, are aware of the curse linked to the throne. What we need is a puppet."

—Excerpt from Lord Claudius Dellabore's diary

Aziah staggered out of the portal, her head pounding. The world lurched forward, sending her crumpling to her knees. She hit the ground, promptly emptying what little food she'd eaten that morning onto the grass. Her gut twisted into knots. She closed her eyes with a groan, pressing the back of her hand to her mouth.

The world stilled, and her stomach finally settled. Wincing, she opened her eyes and looked about. Furrowing her brow, she realized she wasn't at her planned destination. She'd appeared in a forest, the ancient trees towering above, their limbs entangled, blocking out much of the light. Thin bands of sunlight pierced the canopy, scarcely illuminating the sparse undergrowth and brown leaf litter on the ground. The air was cool, touched with a heavy scent of damp earth.

The sound of rushing water was close by.

She pushed herself up, taking in the relatively flat landscape. It was hard to pin exactly where she was. Snapping her fingers, she called on another portal.

Nothing.

Frowning at her hand, she snapped her fingers, summoning a small orb of light. Sparks crackled in her fingers, knitting together. With a wave, the energy was dispelled. So, her magic wasn't gone, only the portals. Which meant Alexandria had taken precautions after realizing Aziah had defected. A way to ensure her old spy couldn't just slip in behind enemy lines like she once did.

No matter.

She had her mission. Pulling her hood up, she set off. The first thing she needed to do was figure out exactly where she'd ended up. Then she'd head to the temple and find those slaves.

Leaf litter crunched underfoot as she trekked toward the rushing water.

As she crested a small hill, the trees thinned. More light spilled through, illuminating the tree line, and beyond it, down a shallow embankment, the river. Water crashed and tumbled in white, frothy foam over rocks. Aziah paused, eyeing the position of the sun in the sky. From the shadows, it cast along the river bank and distant horizon. She had a fair idea of where she was.

She'd landed at least a week's walk from the temple. Maybe five days if she pushed hard. Less if she found a horse.

Her stomach rumbled, reminding her it had been some time since her last meal. She hauled out her small waterskin and carefully picked her way down the bank, taking care as she dipped it into the rushing water. She took a hasty step back as the icy water splashed over her feet. Once the skin was filled, she pressed the wooden cap back on and hauled herself back up to safer ground.

She might know how to swim, but that didn't mean she was about to tempt fate.

After a hurried meal, she stashed her supplies and stood. She turned to follow the river when a low growl echoed from the trees. Aziah spun, light erupting from her fingers, tendrils wrapping up around her arm. She scanned the tree line, then stilled as glowing red eyes stared back from the shadows.

A beast emerged from the tree line, followed by another and then one more. The three demons prowled closer; their wolf-like forms encircled by ribbons of black.

Aziah burst forward, hurling bolts of light. They leaped out of the way and charged at her. She yanked out her daggers, and at the last second, she rolled, driving up one blade into a demon's chest. Hot blood sprayed over her hair and cloak. A fetid, sticky black.

With a howling scream, the demon hit the ground.

The other two launched at her. She scrambled to her feet, calling light to her daggers. One beast leaped up. She side-stepped, slashing down its side. A savage scream split the forest's gloom. The other demon was already mid-air as she spun to face it. It slammed into her, bringing both of them crashing to the ground. Energy burst from her hands, sending it flying.

She jumped up, shifting her stance as the demons staggered up to their feet. Blood dripped from their wounds. One paused, tipping its head to emit a chilling howl.

For a moment, silence followed; then came an answer.

Dozens more joined in from the tree line behind her. Aziah froze as red eyes sparked through the darkness. Their low growls were a steady, menacing hum. She stepped back. Her foot slipped, and she tumbled back down the river bank. She cursed as her daggers fell from her hands. In desperation, her fingers clutched at the sodden soil, seeking something to stop her descent.

Icy water crashed over her, feeling as though a thousand daggers plunged through her skin at once. Her mouth snapped open as cold water flooded in. Aziah slammed her lips shut as her foot hit the bottom, and she pushed upward through the raging torrents.

Her face broke the surface and the water she'd inhaled sputtered from her lips. Coughs racked her body as she scrambled to use her magic. But no magic sparked in her fingers. Her energy was rapidly fading.

She battled to keep her head above water when she slammed into a rock. Something sharp sank into her back, scarcely dulled by her leathers. Waves of bitterly frigid water crashed against her, pinning her to the jagged surface.

As she felt herself slipping, it was Gabriel's face she pictured. The promise of a long life together, where they might find peace beyond the war, sparked like lightning in her chest. Screaming in defiance, she reached up until her fingers found a little ledge. It was the leverage she needed. With the last vestiges of her strength, she clenched her jaw and hauled herself up.

Her limbs throbbed in agony as she slumped across the rock, coughing wearily. She lay there gasping until some energy slowly returned to her body, and she could sit up without collapsing.

The fiery sting lingered at the small of her back. She gritted her teeth as she gently tugged her saturated shirt free and pressed two fingers to the throbbing wound. As she snatched her hand away, blood glistened on her fingers.

That was the last thing she remembered as the world spun around her and she hit the stone once more, surrendering to the darkness. And in that void, she heard Gabriel call out to her.

Hold on, Aziah. Just hold on.

When she woke next, a blanket of stars stretched far across the cloudless sky and the biting breeze pinched her cheeks red. Her head throbbed viciously as she pushed herself to her knees. The river still raged relentlessly on, leaping over jagged rocks and plunging in a foamy white cascade.

The grassy banks were absent of demons and she didn't sense any nearby. Small mercies, she supposed, and as she touched the wound on her lower back, realizing it had healed. The skin remained a little tender, but it was nothing she hadn't endured before.

She got shakily to her feet, eyeing a path of rocks when her gaze alighted on the tree line. A familiar figure lingered in the shadows, a band of moonlight catching the side of their face. Her breath caught as she took the first step and leaped for the closest rock. Her boot skidded across the slick stone. She wobbled for a moment and jumped again.

Aziah landed heavily on the bank, scrambling up the loose soil and pulling at the grass until she reached the top. Heavy breaths shuddered through her chest as she staggered forward, her legs nearly buckling out from beneath her.

Gabriel rushed toward her.

Tears burned her vision as she stumbled into his arms, burying her face in his chest. Their mate bond roared to life, glowing like the morning sun, full of warmth and hope, and all that she swore she'd lost.

"You're alive," she cried, clutching him so tightly in fear that he might vanish at any moment. "How? How are you here?"

When he stiffened in her arms, she pulled away, searching his golden eyes. A shuttered look fell across his face and the happiness chilled in her chest.

"I felt you were in danger...and I had to come," he said. "What are you doing out here? I thought you were with Sybilla."

"It's a long story." The icy wind lashed against her sodden clothes and she shivered violently.

The hard expression softened and he reached for her again, even though she wanted nothing more than to demand answers. As his fingers brushed her numb cheeks, he pushed the strands of hair out of her face.

"Come with me. We need to get you warm before you freeze to death."

CHAPTER 17

"Six challengers and the King still lives. War looms ever closer. Villages on the outer edge of our territory are attacked, yet we do nothing. This is our claimed land, not the land connected to the throne. This sacrifice sits ill with the people...nevertheless, we wait. Who will challenge him next?"

—Excerpt from Captain Atlas's diary

Titania paced the library, her thoughts twisted into knots. Bright sunlight spilled in from the narrow windows above the towering bookshelves. The scent of old memories lingered in the air, threatening to pull her into the past. When the main door groaned open, she stopped walking and lifted her gaze.

Claudius filled the doorway, an air of uncertainty about him. He'd been that way since they'd gotten back from the mansion, brooding in his office. It was the first time she'd seen him since then.

"Am I interrupting something?" he asked.

This side of him was unnerving. She hadn't seen it since he was a young demon in court before he rose to political power. Shrugging, she sat on the window seat and smirked at him. "You seem less moody."

"I wasn't—" He caught himself and sighed, taking a seat beside her. "I knew she'd still be angry, but the way she looked at me..."

"If you're expecting sympathy, I'm the wrong person."

Claudius glared. "What?"

"Did you not feel her pain?" she asked, leaning back with her hands behind her back. "I think the only reason she didn't eviscerate you was because of Lorca."

"The Dragonir," he said disdainfully.

"Oh, no, you don't get the right to be pissy that she moved on—or is it the fact that she looked at him the way she never looked at you?" she admonished.

"You don't know what you're talking about," he muttered as he pushed to his feet. "Gods, I don't know why I came to you to talk. Why I thought you might understand."

She knew exactly why. "Because you wanted someone to make you feel better, to ease your guilt. Well, you know what would help with that?"

A heavy silence hung between them. Tension tightened in Claudius, his hands curling into fists. He'd never been good with his emotions, less so where Nimue was concerned. Titania had been there to help Nimue pick up the pieces after their fallout. She'd watched the strongest woman she knew *break* and he never came back. Never once reached out to explain why he ran. For eight hundred years.

Now, seeing Nimue alive again had reignited the bitterness and anger she felt toward him.

His jaw twitched. "She wasn't the only one who lost a child." He looked away as if he had more to say, but then thought better of it.

"No, but she stayed and grieved. Do you know what might help your case? *Tell her why you left.*" She pushed off the table. "Now, I was sent to this city for a purpose, but I'm sure it's not to coddle you. We both know you will never have Nimue's heart again, but if you do the hard work, maybe she'll forgive you."

She didn't stick around to listen to what he had to say.

He's a big demon. He can figure it out for himself, she told herself as she headed to the front door.

Grabbing her cloak from the hanger, she slid it on and stepped outside. Amara had sent her to the city for a reason. She just needed to find out what it was.

The silence was downright unnerving as she wandered along the empty streets. A soft breeze stirred listlessly between the buildings, rattling shuttered windows and tattered flags. The city was quiet in the twilight hours, poised in a moment of eerie peace, as though the war wasn't about to set it all ablaze.

At that moment, she envied Nimue's mortality. How delicate her life was now, so easily snuffed out. As she passed through the gates into the Merchant Quarter, the air shifted and she saw people gathering in crowds and talking together in low, uneasy voices. Their whispers swirled through the air, wary eyes tracking Titania as she walked past them.

Sybilla would've sent word to her aunt by now, declaring the city was hers. An army was no doubt on its way. A battle of wills was being played out, the city waiting as the next move was decided. Meanwhile, the people grew restless, unsure of their new master. How would she buy their support? Because, right now, the people saw Sybilla as an occupying force, a threat to their peaceful lives. One that was about to bring madness and war to their doors.

She moved into a small market square, crammed full of tents and sheets with bodies laid upon them. The scent of death lingered in the icy air. Healers hurried about, baskets in hand, tending to the wounded. Shouts ricocheted over the chaos, bouncing off walls.

"You!" a woman shouted, striding over. "Have you been sent here to help?"

Titania blinked, pushing back her hood. "Sorry?"

"Or are you just here to gawk at the dead?" The woman thrust a basket into Titania's hands. "If you want to stay, make yourself useful and head to that big tent. They need help."

Titania opened her mouth to argue, but the woman hurried off, kneeling beside an injured child, a small boy. One of his hands was a bloody stump. Bandages wrapped around his head and torso, with patches of blood staining through. His skin glistened with sweat, eyes barely staying open. The woman took his hand, talking gently to him.

Drawing closer, Titania kneeled, setting the basket aside. "Was this a demon attack?"

The woman started, a scowl pinching her face. "You're still here? I told you—"

"Did demons do this?"

"Yes. The rich used to keep them as pets or fight them in pits. I guess they must've gotten loose in all the chaos, not that the Princess leading this damn mess seems to care." A frown deepened the woman's brow.

The boy gave a feverish cry. Her face softened as she pressed a hand to his cheek, murmuring kind assurances. Titania felt a stab of shame. Old memories stirred. Demons had done this, her kind.

"Has anyone tried to stop them?" Titania asked.

The woman sighed, a look of bone-deep exhaustion on her face. "Yes, but it didn't work and the attacks are getting worse. Look, any help would be appreciated. We need to get the wounded tended to, then move them into safe houses before dusk. Then we must pray the demons don't come back tonight."

Titania nodded, grabbing the basket. A sense of purpose sparked in her chest. Maybe, just maybe, she'd found what Amara had sent her for.

CHAPTER 18

"The army marches. I accompany Titania to the front lines. The time has come for my plan to begin."

—Excerpt from Nimue's diary, soldier-class demon

They were late for the meeting. Nimue pushed the door open and Lorca followed her inside a large study with several people seated around a long wooden table. Sybilla sat at its head. She glanced at Nimue, then gestured to them to sit. Nimue slipped into a chair while Lorca found an empty chair beside her.

The two fae seated near Sybilla wore guarded expressions. A male and female both strikingly beautiful, clad in matching black tunics. The woman had long, flowing white hair, while her partner's obsidian locks framed his face. Opposite them sat a small woman with cropped hair and a jagged scar stretching up her neck and over one cheek. Her lip curled into a smirk as she met Nimue's curious stare.

Sybilla started to speak. "I'm pleased you've all agreed with my proposal. Everyone, this is Wren and Lorca, dragon and Dragonir respectively. They will lead this mission. Wren, Lorca, the quiet couple are Dorian and Sylvie, and the prickly looking girl is Nora."

The fae dipped their heads, silent. Nora muttered an awkward hello. Nimue didn't know what to make of the three of them and had no idea what their skills might be.

"The situation outside the mansion is escalating, so we must move quickly. Time is not on our side," said Sybilla. She drummed her fingers on the tabletop,t a frown on her face. "There was another attack last night in the Merchant Quarter, close to where you fought the demons. Fifteen dead, around thirty injured. The number of dead is expected to rise."

Nimue stiffened, her blood cooling. "How many demons?"

"Reports suggest over fifty."

She fell silent. Surely someone hadn't built a Hell Gate? No, it was impossible. She would've felt a demon portal of that size. Her connection to the demon realm would've grown a thousand-fold. So, if not that, then were they taking advantage of a crack somewhere in the city? But pulling that number of demons through one would be tricky. It could destabilize the crack and cause it to close.

Unless they were mostly shades, like the ones she'd fought. It would mean the number of realm demons in the city would be lower. But to what end?

"What are you thinking?" Sybilla asked.

Nimue set her hands on the table, frowning. "Some of the demons we fought weren't real. They were simply shades. They can cause damage all the same, but they're weaker and easier to kill. It means the number of actual demons we're facing might be much lower."

"Know a lot about demons, do you?" Nora asked, one brow quirked.

Nimue flashed a smile. "I'm a well-traveled dragon."

The fae woman beside her leaned forward, steel-gray eyes lit with interest. "Do you have any idea why they're attacking?"

"No," Nimue said, shaking her head. "All I picked up during the fight was that someone was controlling them, but I couldn't figure out who. The first thing we need to do is find out where they're coming from. My guess is there is a large demon crack hidden somewhere in the city."

"A demon crack?"

"A portal to the demon realm. Don't worry, only weaker demons can come through. Anything too powerful would instantly destabilize the crack, which would then vaporize them. Besides, whoever is controlling the ones in the city wouldn't want a powerful one coming through. They wouldn't be able to control it."

The room fell silent. Nimue watched as Sybilla's new team glanced between each other, sharing silent exchanges.

"As you can see, Wren and Lorca's knowledge of demons is going to be helpful. Once you determine the source of the demons, destroy them and the crack. We need to crush this before the army arrives. When that happens, there are going to be a lot of frightened people, and I need them to feel safe within these walls."

At this, Lorca leaned forward. "How long until the army arrives?"

"It set off from Midlan two days ago. We have a few weeks if we're lucky. Now, I've sent word to our allies in the North to send support, but it's likely reinforcements won't arrive until after winter. Which means we will need to hold this city for four or five months," said Sybilla with a heavy sigh. "Time is not on our side, but we must hold this city."

"Then why did you take the city now? Why not take it after winter when your allies could come to us?" he retorted.

Nimue was curious as well. It seemed a poor tactical decision to take the city right before winter. There probably wouldn't be much in the way of snow to hinder the Empress's army from marching on the city. Why not wait until Sybilla had the army she needed to hold the city? The Princess smiled and stood up.

"The first acts of this war are a game of strategy. I took this city now for several reasons. It won't snow here, but the weather will not be kind to the army outside our walls. It will beat them down and demoralize them. I don't plan on just defeating this army. I want to *break* them. Everything I do has more than one purpose. Spirits, even the day the bells first rang out to show we'd claimed the city."

Nora cackled. "You took the city on the anniversary of your parents' murder."

Sybilla grinned, but it didn't reach her eyes. There was something cold and vindictive in those amber depths. It was the first glimpse Nimue had of what lurked behind that mask Sybilla wore so well. "She took something precious to me, so I took her prized city, the heart of her economy. Five months of holding this city will deal a harsh blow to her coffers. I plan on making the Empress bleed during this siege. When I'm finished, her own people will betray her."

The level of ambition was quietly impressive...and unnerving. It was as though Nimue was looking at her younger self, back when she was a soldier hungry for power. Before she knew how much that terrible desire would cost her. Maybe this girl had what it took to win a war.

And perhaps that would be enough for Nimue to get her people back.

She leaned back in her chair, mulling this over. "We should start tonight before there is another attack."

"Agreed," Dorian said. His voice had an accent Nimue swore she'd heard before. "Might I advise we start at the sight of the latest attack? We should see if we can pick up a trail from there."

"Wonderful, a hunt!" Nora exclaimed, clasping her hands together, her white teeth flashing a predatory grin. "How exciting!"

The sun dipped beyond the horizon, plunging the city into darkness. A savage wind hissed through the streets, bitingly cold, piercing through Nimue's leathers. It didn't seem to bother their three new friends, who fanned out in an arrow formation, with Nora moving swiftly ahead of the main group.

A small flame hovered in Lorca's hand, chasing back the shadows.

When they reached the market square, a few ragged tents fluttered softly in the breeze. A fetid, rotting smell lingered in the air. Death. It mingled with the echo of demon magic, dancing over her skin, calling to the darkness within.

Nora's voice split the silence. "I have something!"

Nimue broke into a jog, heading off to where Nora was kneeling by an upturned wagon. Dorian and Sylvie stood by the young girl, their hands resting on the hilt of their blades.

What's so special about Nora?

Tearing her gaze away, she looked at what the girl was pointing at. A chunk of flesh covered with matted black fur sat in a small pool of black demon blood. Nimue bent down and picked it up to examine it.

"Well, that's disgusting," said Nora. "Do you have any idea what happened?"

Nimue brought it to her nose, inhaling its smoky, acrid stench. There was another scent, lingering just beneath the surface. Something familiar. Struggling, she tried to draw on her memories as Wren.

Then she realized. "It came from the underground. I remember the scent from the tunnels."

"That makes sense. The tunnels are a good place to hide the crack from the demon's realm," Lorca remarked, holding out a hand. "Can I look?"

Nora handed over the chunk of fur. Wrinkling his nose, he sniffed it. With a look of distaste, he handed it back.

"It will be easier to catch a scent in dragon form," he said.

Lorca stepped back, his form flashing white for a second. In the nearly moonless night, his emerald eyes glowed from the shadows. He lifted his nose to the sky, nostrils flaring then without warning, he shot forward, leaping over the wagon.

I have a trail. His voice hummed through her mind.

"He's found something," called Nimue to the others.

Nora released a low whistle as she dashed around the wagon. "I like this one!"

Nimue hurried after her, followed by the two silent fae. Thick shadows crowded in close, leaving Nimue to wonder how the hell the human girl could move so confidently.

She spied Lorca racing ahead, leaving them all to run after him.

How many do you scent?

Just one for now. It feels close.

He vanished around a corner. Nimue hurried to catch Nora as they came to another narrow street. On one side was a small graveyard, cluttered with hundreds of stone markers. A few stone crypts stood among them, with ghouls crouching on their roofs, their swords brandished.

It reminded her of when she'd fled through the tunnels with Titania. They'd exited somewhere similar to this.

The groups paused at the threshold as Lorca's form flashed again, shrinking back to his human form. He pointed to one of the crypts. "The scent leads inside that one."

Nimue stepped into the graveyard, a cold breath brushing against her neck. Something wrapped around her heart, giving it a sharp squeeze. Magic brushed over her skin, ancient and demonic. But this was not from her throne. This felt different, sharper.

Was another demon king at work here? Had they somehow left their realm and come into this world? And if so, why?

Sylvie stalked past and slammed her fist into the metal door. It flew back, crashing into a tomb with a thundering crack.

"So much for entering with surprise," murmured Nora.

Sylvie stepped through the entrance, seemingly indifferent. "These tunnels run deep beneath the city. If someone is hiding demons down here, they won't be close enough to know we've arrived."

Let's hope she's right, Nimue thought.

Inside the crypt, a staircase descended deep into the dark. Lorca snapped his fingers, summoning flames to one hand, and headed down first. Nimue stayed close on his heels, with the others following in single file.

Lorca froze, forcing everyone to come to a sudden stop.

From the darkness came the sound of screaming.

CHAPTER 19

"The Battle of Tersim Falls is an unmitigated disaster. We lose half our forces in a single blow. Gods, I told the King not to advance when he did. That man is going to get us all killed."

—Excerpt from Captain Castille's diary

They rushed down the tunnel, following the screams. The path widened and Nimue took the opportunity to sprint ahead of Lorca. Her legs burned, the mortal body she now occupied a dim echo of her demonic one.

She pushed on, driving herself to go faster. The screams called to her, the demonic energy humming stronger with every stride. Like a moth to the flame, she raced on, flinging herself around a corner and down another flight of steps.

When she reached the bottom, the screaming ceased. A crossroads lay in front. Without hesitating, she headed down the right side, following a sensation that pulled her onward. Her limbs burned and sweat ran down her face. The screams came again, but this time, they were closer.

The tunnel narrowed, forcing everyone into a line. Her shoulders brushed the cold stone, that was damp with moisture. They passed more tunnels leading off into the darkness, but she knew the call. A demon crack was nearby, summoning her home.

As gray light trickled into the tunnel from up ahead, the screams choked off with a gurgled cry. Nimue raised a hand, signaling the others to halt. She withdrew her blades out and inched forward. Through the gloom, she could make out a doorway.

"How many?" Dorian asked, silently appearing at her side.

"Can't say. Be ready and aim for the heart." She eyed his fighting stance and the way he held the sword. He had the look of a warrior. "Watch yourselves, all of you. If you see a portal, stay away until I shut it down."

He cast a glance at her, as if curious about how she planned to do that. Ignoring him, she focused ahead and inhaled deeply, forcing her heart to slow. A steady calm flowed into her veins as she tightened her grip on her weapon. This was what she knew best. Death, the thrill of a fight. The darkness within her soul hummed in anticipation.

At the entrance, she paused, surveying the large cavern that lay beyond.

Her brow furrowed.

The inside resembled a temple with smooth, straight walls, that were supported by pillars adorned with faded murals. A walkway ran around the top level, and a staircase descended from it down to the floor below. She crept forward, crouching low as she took in the chilling scene.

A glowing crack lit the center of the room, bathing everything in swaths of blue light. It hovered like an open wound over a shallow pool of blood. The metallic stench filled her every breath as she studied the demons slumbered on the ground.

Drawing back, she turned to the others. "I need you to create a distraction for the demons. Once they're away from the portal, I can shut it down and stop any more from coming in. Nora, Lorca, do you feel up to causing a little chaos? Dorian and Sylvie, you attack them from behind. Move swiftly and don't hesitate."

Everyone nodded. Lorca's gaze lingered on her as the others moved into position, and his voice whispered through their bond.

Are you ready?

Don't worry about me. Keep an eye on Nora. She's the only human here.

He nodded. *Let's see why Sybilla chose her.*

He pressed a kiss to her mouth. Surprise flashed in her chest as he pulled away, moving off before she could respond.

Tease, she sent and then turned her focus to the portal.

On either side, the others fanned out, weapons drawn. She inhaled and opened her mind, using her magic to nudge the demons awake.

They stirred, lifting their heads.

She stood and cried, "Now!"

Lorca cast a blast of fire into the pack as Nora threw her dagger at the closest one. As the demons jumped to their feet, snarling, Lorca and Nora sprinted for the stairs. The two fae launched arrows at the demons' backs, causing two of them to fall lifeless to the ground.

Now, only one remained. Nimue vaulted over the railing, dropping to the floor below. She hit the ground with a roll and jumped to her feet. The demon spun to face her but was too slow.

She leaped, landing on its back, and driving the blades deep into its flesh. A savage cry filled the air as the beast sank to the ground. Yanking the swords out, she ran to the portal. Demonic energy poured out, washing over her. A feeling of euphoria filled her being and her throne called out to her.

Come back to me!

Shaking her head to dispel the voice, she sheathed her swords and inched forward. At the edge of the pool, she hesitated. The coppery tang of human blood infused every inhalation.

"What are you waiting for? Close the damn thing!" Nora shouted.

Nimue stepped into the pool and called on her powers. This time, they answered. As the magic flowed through her limbs, a sharp pain erupted through her skull, driving a thousand knives into her head at once.

Darkness exploded from her fingers, colliding with the portal.

The Azradan throne, so attuned to her soul, must've sensed her plan. A voice roared from the crack; inhuman, furious. *You will not leave me! You belong with me!*

Nimue snarled. *I belong to myself!*

Her voice thundered as she channeled the power to a single point within her—and then let go. The energy ripped from her palms with a deafening roar. The ground trembled beneath her and the remaining demons ceased their pursuit of the others to face their new prey.

The demons prowled closer vicious growls emanating from their drooling mouths, but Nimue kept her focus on sealing the crack. She clenched her jaw, forcing more power out. With a last burst of energy—it snapped shut.

The world lurched, leaving her teetering for a moment. Nausea welled up in her throat, bile burning the back of her tongue. She winced as a dull throb quietly intensified behind her eyes.

A black mass leaped at her and gnashing teeth came flashing straight for her throat. Just as they nearly collided, fire slammed into the demon, sending it screaming. Another blast finished it off and Lorca sprinted over, stretching one hand out to haul Nimue to her feet.

"Thanks. Let's finish this?"

"Are you sure you're okay?" he asked.

She opened her mouth to answer when she spotted a demon preparing to attack. In an instant, her blade was in her hand as the demon leaped for Lorca. Shoving Lorca to the side, Nimue plunged the blade into the creature's chest, the force sending her staggering back. Lorca darted around, slamming his sword down, slicing the beast through the neck.

Stepping back, she met his gaze and winked. "Try to keep up."

She spun as he did, their backs pressed against each other. Calling on the darkness, she cursed as her hands remained bare. A metallic taste pooled in her mouth, and the throbbing behind her eyes intensified.

There was no time to think. Several more demons rushed at them, snarling and hissing, with feral hunger glowing in their blood-red eyes. With blades in hand, she struck blow after blow until she was drenched in sticky black demon blood.

Nimue and Lorca moved in sync, the bodies piling up. Harsh breaths broke through her lips, but she pushed on. From the dark corners of the room, more demons emerged.

"Where are the others?" she cried. "We could do with their help right now."

A cold feeling swept over her. Had they been abandoned? Had this been Sybilla's idea all along?

A sudden flash of green light erupted. The room shuddered. A wave of energy slammed into Nimue, dropping her to her knees.

The light dimmed, and silence descended.

Her head swam and try as she might, she was unable to stand. Lorca appeared at her side, his arm sliding around her waist to help her to her feet. Shudders ran through her body and she leaned against him until the dizziness retreated. Opening her eyes, she saw a faint green glow flickering from the staircase.

Nora.

The girl offered a quick smile, swaying on her feet. Dorian moved behind her, as if ready to catch her. Sylvie's hand tightened on her sword as she stared back defiantly at Nimue.

That wasn't spirit magic, nor was it demonic. It was *primal.* And there was only one race who had ever wielded it.

She stilled. "You're a *Druid?*"

CHAPTER 20

"The King believes the loss of the battle results from a traitor. The poor fool doesn't realize how right he is."

—Excerpt from Nimue's diary, soldier-class demon

A Druid, alive and breathing before her.

Nimue had read about them in texts, one tragic story among many. Their numbers were already limited when she and her kin had arrived from the demon realm two thousand years ago. Systematic slaughter had killed off what few remained, and so she'd never dreamed she'd have the chance to meet one.

Until now.

Nora straightened up. The prickly child fell away and wiser, older eyes stared back. The look of a girl who had seen more misery than most; As she spoke, there was a fire in her voice. One that had been hidden before.

"So now you know."

"I thought you were human," Nimue said. "A good tracker, but nothing more."

"Well, to your credit, I *am* human—sort of. Anyway, we should check this place out and make sure there are no more demons." Nora's grin widened. "Sorry about before. I didn't know my magic would affect you like that. Although it's strange. Lorca seems fine."

Because I'm not a real dragon, unlike Lorca.

To give herself time to think of a reply, Nimue wiped the demon blood from her swords before sheathing them.

"I guess it was because using my powers weakened me, but you're right. We should be sure this place is secure."

Dorian and Sylvie stared at her with their golden eyes, as if they saw right through Nimue's lie. She'd have to be careful with those two.

Turning away, she opened her powers again. She swayed as Lorca caught her. He looked down at her, worry tightening his face.

"Are you sure you're okay?"

"Closing that portal took a lot out of me." The lie tasted like poison.

She carefully pulled from his embrace, closing off her magic. There would be time to figure out why her demonic magic felt agonizing to use. She had her guesses, though fewer than she liked the idea of.

Lorca shadowed her closely as they broke away from the others to explore the temple. The cracked stone showed it was far older than the city above. What little flecks of paint on the pillars remained were almost completely faded. At one end of the room was a black metal door, a lone symbol emblazoned in the middle.

Oh, Gods. No.

A shiver rippled through her as she inched closer. Reaching up, she ran her fingers over the demonic symbol. No power returned through her hand. It was a dead spell. Frowning, she grabbed the handle. It yielded with an echoing screech, swinging inwards. A rancid stench slammed into her.

Rotten flesh.

"Lorca, can you give me some light?"

He snapped his fingers, fire crackling to life in his hand. The amber glow cut through the shadows like a knife, illuminating the interior.

A pile of corpses was heaped in the middle. Nimue kneeled by the body of a young woman with long blond hair. Her skin was shredded to ribbons, hanging off her skeletal frame. A collar dangled loosely off her neck, soaked with dried blood, the flesh above it torn open like a bloody smile.

Nimue stood, glancing over at the rest. All wore a collar or had a noticeable brand. Many had their throats cut cleanly, showing they died from a blade and not from a demon's bite. She spun and headed out of the room, unease knotting her gut. This made no sense. Who was behind this? The blood was obviously used to strengthen the portal, but it still wasn't enough to bring more than a dozen demons through.

Dorian strode over. "What did you find?"

"Bodies. Slaves. It explains all the blood," she said numbly, staring at the pool.

"Spirits above, why? Why would someone need so much blood?" He stared at her. "You know, don't you?"

"Blood strengthens demonic magic, but it's a forbidden practice. What troubles me is that a portal that size doesn't explain all the demons we've seen. They can't have all come from it. Something doesn't add up." She looked around the room with renewed interest. "I wouldn't be surprised if there were more of these beneath the city."

Nora and Sylvie came over, the latter, frowning. "Should we try to find the source of these slaves?"

"The priority is finding any remaining demon cracks."

Sylvie's mouth tightened, as though she wished to argue. Then she nodded, her expression unreadable. "Very well, but can you tell me what that symbol on the door is? I saw your reaction."

Nimue gazed at the black door. "It means 'blood through sacrifice, power through death.'"

When they returned to the mansion, whispers stirred from the guards as they strode through the front door. Lorca glared at them, and they ceased muttering.

As she turned to the stairs, Nora called out, "I shall go with Sylvie and Dorian to brief Sybilla on what we found tonight. Goodnight to you both."

Nimue nodded a brief goodbye and was silent until she stepped inside her room where a glimpse in the mirror made her stop in her tracks. Black demon blood sticky and cloying clung to her hair and clothes. On every exposed part of her body, scratches and bruises were visible. The deep lines of exhaustion etched on her face spoke volumes of the toll the battle had taken on her.

She sank to her knees.

"Nimue!" Lorca dropped in front of her, gently lifting her chin. "Do you need a healer?"

"No, I just need to get out of these bloodied rags," she forced out.

He gently helped her peel off her clothes before leading her into the bathing chamber where a tub filled to the brim was waiting. He moved forward and plunged his hand into the cold water, his fingers glowing with heat. Soon, steam swirled across the surface and he stepped back.

"Get in. I'll grab you some clean things," he said, leaving her alone to sink exhausted into the tub.

Lowering herself into the water, she groaned as the heat sank into her bones. She dunked her whole body under, holding herself there for a moment. The world grew quiet, broken only by the steady thumping of her heart. For the first time, she could hear her thoughts clearly, and a sense of peace washed over her.

Soon, her lungs burned and she surfaced, gasping as the cold air hit her cheeks. Leaning back against the porcelain, she closed her eyes, almost drifting into sleep. Footsteps signaled Lorca's return, with a robe, soap, and a comb in hand. Wordlessly, he sat behind her and began massaging the soap into her hair. Setting it aside, he took the comb to ease all the tangles out.

"Do you often comb women's hair?" she teased softly.

He chuckled. "When my sister was young, she got up to all kinds of trouble and her hair and clothes were always a mess. To ensure my mother didn't find out, I learned to tame her hair. In return, she never told our mother about my adventures."

Her heart ached at the wistful tone, even as she loved the fact he was sharing more of his past. It was one thing to have watched it from afar as the Spirit of the Mountain; it was another to hear it in such gentle, intimate words.

"She probably knew of the adventures," she whispered.

He laughed softly. "I think you're right. Little escaped my mother's attention. She was an incredible queen." He set the comb aside, pressing one lingering kiss to her shoulder. "She would've loved you."

In the companionable silence, her mind drifted.

There were so many things occupying her mind. Her mission was to rescue her people, by convincing Sybilla to march her army to them—once the city was secured. Finding an army herself, which in her current condition, appeared increasingly unlikely.

As for the matter of identity, she knew she couldn't avoid it forever, even if she wished to do just that.

But the portals, symbols, and the demon attacks left her unnerved. That kind of power was reserved for the demon kings, but they'd shown no interest—or ability—to cross realms before. What had changed? And if it was a demon king, was it one of her usurpers?

"It makes me wonder if the Empress is behind this because it would be a hell of a way to sow chaos in Sybilla's ranks," Lorca said softly as he started to braid her hair.

She mulled this over. The answer danced just out of reach, a maddening puzzle. "Maybe, but the mark on that door was old. It could be just a coincidence that the sacrifice was done there, but..."

"That's not what your gut is telling you?"

"I don't know what my gut is telling me anymore," she confessed. "I thought getting my memories back would make me feel better, but honestly I just feel more lost than ever."

"But you're not alone, Nimue."

She couldn't reply to that, not unless she wanted to lie again.

"Now, get dressed and then sleep. You still look half-dead with exhaustion," said Lorca tenderly.

Nodding, she couldn't disagree. The events earlier had drained her to the point of collapse.

The next morning, like the one before, Lorca lay curled in dragon form around her bed. Taking care not to wake him, Nimue changed into some new clothes and headed to Ellie's room. As she drew closer, a woman rushed past, then spun back and grabbed her by the hand.

"You're her sister, aren't you?"

Nimue frowned. "Yes? Why? What happened?"

"Come with me!"

They broke into a run, worry erupting through Nimue. A sickening feeling twisted inside her gut.

As she reached Ellie's door, whimpering and shouting could be heard from inside. Ice flooded Nimue's veins as she threw the door open, stopping at the threshold. Two women were attempting to pin her sister down as she thrashed wildly on the bed.

"Get your hands off her," yelled Nimue, striding forward.

The women jumped back, fear lighting their eyes as they scrambled away from the bed. The one who'd grabbed spoke up. "Your sister was hurting herself. They were only—"

Nimue's hand shot up, cutting her off. She sat down on the bed as her sister thrashed, muttering pleadingly under her breath in a language she knew all too well. The ancient demonic tongue spilled effortlessly from Ellie's lips as if she'd been speaking it her whole life. Reaching out, she took Ellie's hands and a rush of energy exploded up her arm. A gasp broke from her lips as her sister stilled and was silent.

"Thank you for helping her, but I'll take care of her now," said Nimue.

With a hurried goodbye from the servants, their footsteps retreated and the door shut.

Exhaling steadily, Nimue clenched her jaw as Ellie's energy poured into her, filled with fear and anger. As she let it flow in, she bent over, her lips brushing against Ellie's ear. Using her sister's power to sustain her, she spoke a single command, laden with magic. "Rest."

The power retreated. Nimue let go of Ellie's hands and stood up on shaking legs. She grabbed the blanket from the floor and draped it over the pale, sleeping girl. Nimue pressed a palm to Ellie's brow, peering inside at the bind on her sister's demonic side.

Swirling black energy was concealed by a glowing translucent wall with a crack running right up the middle. And from within that void whispered an ancient power, a quiet voice that slipped into Nimue's mind. Ice flooded her veins, plunging her into a freezing tundra until all she perceived was darkness and frost.

She stood in ankle-deep water, an endless expanse of it stretching out into the dark, with a blanket of glittering stars above. A figure stood with its back to her, swathed in a shimmering black gown flecked with gems like starlight. Long blond hair billowed down an exposed back, revealing an intricate web of tattoos, symbols of a language she knew.

The loose curls danced over the words, stopping her from reading them fully, letting her catch snippets; *sister, traitor—death.*

A scream erupted from within, savage and roaring with ancient power. It ripped through her body like a storm unleashed, tearing at her insides. The scene shattered like shards of glass tumbling into the abyss.

She yanked her hand back, staring at her sister. *What the hell was that?*

CHAPTER 21

"The King hunts for his spies but he is blind to those closest to him."
—Excerpt from Nimue's diary, soldier-class demon

For Flynn, dinner was an unnerving affair.

The main hall was crammed with several long tables running its length, and another across the dais. Simple platters were heaped with fermented vegetables, roasted meats, small pies, and freshly sliced fruit. Jugs of honeyed wine were passed along, the golden liquid glowing as it was poured into delicate glasses. Soft laughter and low conversation flowed freely, leaving him feeling increasingly like an outsider.

He sat beside Mathias, acutely aware of the curious looks shot his way. Though, when he dared to meet a few, they averted their gazes and returned to hushed whispers. It made him wish Mira could sit close to him, but she'd been relegated to the other end of the room. He spied her in the fray, talking animatedly to a group of women.

"Flynn?" Mathias's voice lured him back to his table.

He blinked, tearing his focus to the fae leader. "I'm sorry. Did you say something?"

"You have scarcely touched your food," Mathias remarked, gesturing to Flynn's plate.

A fae had brought it to him before he could utter anything, and scurried off, leaving him with food he barely had the appetite for. It was more than he'd ever seen before, even during the feasts at Fenware. At the thought of his home, his gut clenched.

"Might I be excused? I need some air," he asked abruptly.

Mathias frowned, then nodded. "Tobin can escort you back to your room if you like?"

It was the last thing he wanted. He needed silence. Managing a gentle shake of his head, he pushed his chair back, wincing as it scraped across the stone. A few faces jerked his way, leaving his cheeks red, his ears burning.

"I'll be okay. Let everyone enjoy the meal," he murmured.

He slipped away through a side door, hurrying along a long stone hall with open windows on one side. The moonlight guided him outside, where he picked his way past several stone huts. The silence was his companion as he walked. No destination in mind. When he came to a small stone bench beneath a flowering red tree, he figured it was as good a place as any to think.

As he sat beneath the gently swaying branches, he tipped his head back. Stars glittered through the leaves dancing in the soft sea breeze, the moonlight dappling his cheeks. Right at that moment, he ached for the biting breeze of the mountains and the snow drifts eddying across the village. He wished he was sitting out the front of his home, side by side with Wren as they watched the snow fall.

At last, he could think, could *breathe.* Floral scents tickled his nose in the humid night. A warm breeze nudged against him, rustling the leaves above in quiet song. In that instant, he could pretend the world was normal.

"Figured I'd find you here, kid." Castille's soft voice danced over the rustling leaves.

Flynn's eyes flickered open. Standing in the moonlight, Castille paused a few feet away, regarding him with a fathomless expression. The corner of his mouth twitched as if he was remembering something.

"I'm not running away," said Flynn, straightening up.

It wasn't what he intended to say, but his mind was a mess, his nerves frayed at the edges.

Castille laughed. "Where would you even run to? You're on an island and ships only come here when Mathias, myself, or one of our kin comes."

"Not home, at least. That's all ash now." He fell silent as Castille sat beside him. "What do you want from me?"

"Would you believe me if I said I was concerned?" Castille arched one brow at him.

Flynn laughed bitterly. "Why? I'm nothing to you. I'm just the son of someone you once knew."

Castille didn't flinch. "Your father is like a brother to me. Besides, you don't know how much your existence means to us. That you're even alive is a damn miracle," he replied softly, releasing a heavy breath before he continued. "We believed for a long time we couldn't have offspring. One of us tried many years ago, but it didn't end well."

"What happened?"

Castille's gaze shuttered. "That's a story for another time... You should know, your existence gives us hope, and that's something we haven't had in a long time. It means we may have a future."

Flynn had no idea what to make of what Castille's words meant and right now, he felt more confused, more isolated than ever. He leaned forward, pressing his palms onto his knees.

This future loomed before him like a storm he couldn't run from. There was no shelter, no protection. Only the knowledge that he would be someone—*no, something*—completely different when the clouds parted. All he could hope was that he was strong enough for whatever came his way, and that it would be enough to get his people home.

"Castille?"

"Hmm?"

Flynn turned his head. "Do you know much about these trials I'm going to face?"

"Sorry, kid, no. I heard your father talk about them once. They're a way to test and prepare you."

"Prepare me for what?"

Castille shrugged. "I never found out. Whatever it was, it made him sad."

The next morning, Flynn crept from his room. He had barely slept, tossing in the furs all night, playing over Castille's words. He guessed they were meant to comfort him, but they'd simply left him feeling confused and alone. No one was about as he passed through the main hall and out through the huge golden doors. The first strokes of dawn painted the sky. The songs of birds drifted across the trees, but thankfully, it appeared the rest of the fae were still asleep.

Good.

He wanted to go for a hike, maybe find something to climb, so he could get a better view of the island he was to call home for the next few weeks. As he passed the last hut, a shadow shot out from behind and a hand landed on his shoulder. He spun around. It was Mira. She threw her hood back, holding her hands up in apology.

"Sorry, I saw you leave."

"Couldn't sleep?" he asked.

She shook her head. "No. Haven't been able to since we got here. Where are you going?"

Then why did you look so damn comfortable last night? He nearly asked, catching the words before the damage was done. They'd been through hell together. Mira was allowed to have a good meal and enjoy the kindness of others.

He shrugged. "A walk. They're probably going to have us pretty busy soon, so I want to take advantage of what time we have to explore," he said, reluctant to confess he hadn't slept either.

She snorted. "Busy? You'll be training for those trials, but me? They still won't say what they want me to do. I don't want to be a burden, but I don't have any special blood. I'm just...me. A boring old human. About as out of place as someone could be here."

"Mira, you're not a burden. Not to me, at least and who gives a damn what those fools think? It's not worth it. So, come on, let's get out of here for a bit. I'm itching for a walk."

Her soft laughter danced through the trees as they set off into the woods. Shadows still crowded the undergrowth, making it slow going as they trekked uphill. The songs from the early morning birds filled the easy silence that fell between Flynn and Mira. Flowers bloomed around them in every shade, stretching high toward the morning light spilling in through cracks in the canopy.

The path sloped up sharply, slowing their pace. Heat burned in Flynn's legs as they picked their way over fallen logs and scrambled up rocks, blocking the path. Rivulets of sweat ran down the side of his face. He wiped them off with his sleeve, then squinted up the path, wondering how much further it was to the peak.

He relished the harsh breaths that squeezed through his lips. It made him feel like a climber again, even if it was just for a few hours.

Eventually, the path evened off, curling around the side of the hill. Eventually, the trees thinned and morning light burst through warming the air.

A little way ahead, some stone structures emerged. Ruins of a long-destroyed village, half consumed by vines and flowers. The macabre scene was one of haunting beauty, an eeriness that sent shivers down Flynn's spine. He passed what might've once been homes, stores, and a market square. A place someone called their own.

"What happened here?" asked Mira, as if the forest might reveal the truth about this tragedy.

"Nothing good," he answered, eyeing the hints of destruction that remained; charred stone, broken doors and windows, shattered pottery jutting from the grass like jagged teeth. There didn't need to be skeletons to say what happened there.

They picked their way through the ruins until they came to a sprawling field above a cliff's head. Dozens of stone markers lined the field, each neatly cleaned. Wild flowers bloomed around them in shades of blood red and pale pink. Mira stilled, wrapping her arms around her waist. He stopped beside her and tried not to think of their village. The bodies that would've been left to the elements and the ruins that marked their grave. If there were gods, he hoped they'd taken pity on his people and didn't care they hadn't been buried according to tradition.

Such fragile, naive hopes were all he could muster.

"Gods, couldn't you two have gone somewhere else?" Tobin's sharp voice cut the air like a knife.

Flynn jerked around, his heart thundering against his ribs. Tobin emerged into the sunlight, the golden light catching the hard planes of his face. Flynn's stomach flipped, and as his pants tightened he realized belatedly he'd been holding his breath.

Out of every man he'd met, why was it this one that caused him to feel something?

And why was his heart still slamming so hard against his ribs?

Flynn released a shaky breath, hoping he sounded steadier than he felt. "We were just exploring."

"Is that not allowed?" Mira added.

Tobin stopped in front of them with a frown. "It's not forbidden, but we believe in not disturbing sacred grounds."

"We didn't know," said Flynn. "I'm sorry."

Something softened in Tobin's eyes. "Obviously, but had you shown some patience, someone would have explained where you could walk," was all Tobin said as his attention drifted to the ruins. A cloud covered the sun for a moment, casting a sudden chill over the area.

"What happened here?" Mira asked.

Tobin laughed, but it was a cold, brittle sound. "The Empress of Danomir happened. We were a threat to her, so she sent her armies. It was a long time ago and I have little interest in giving you both a history lesson. Not when you have to prepare for your trials and you," he paused, his gaze moving to Mira. "You are requested to see Mathias. You have your own training to begin."

"*Training?*"

A heavy-winded sigh broke from Tobin's lips. "Yes, or did you think we'd permit you to be idle? Mathias seems to know what you might be useful for."

"And what's that?"

Flynn bit back a smile at Mira's question, enjoying Tobin's jaw twitch, his patience thinning. There was something damnably enjoyable about watching that man battle to control his temper.

Without bothering to answer her, Tobin headed to the trees. "Now, come along before I drag you back there myself."

CHAPTER 22

"I think we have been betrayed...We shall know by this evening's meal. The King has said he has an important message."
—excerpt from Commander Titania's diary

Aziah stared at her mate as he gazed into the flames, as if they were speaking to him. His bare chest, mottled with scars from another life, glowed in the burnished light. She itched to run her fingers over them again, to lose herself in his embrace. But even as she sat there, clad in little more than his shirt, her bare legs peeking out, he hadn't said a word.

A wooden bowl with some plain stew steamed away in her hands, untouched. She'd been starving on their walk, but as she waited for his explanation, the appetite vanished. What she hungered for were answers.

Eventually, impatience got the better of her, and she set the bowl down. "Are you going to explain where you've been?"

His words had implied he'd known where she was the whole time, that it had been his choice not to reach out. It was like a knife to the heart. How many nights had she ached for his touch, prayed to the spirits that she might find him? Desperate for hope.

Gabriel's gaze jerked upward, flickering in the firelight. An eternity passed before his lips moved. "After the cottage was attacked, I scarcely got away. I was on the run for days when a spirit appeared to me, commanding me to go on a mission of theirs."

"What mission?" she asked.

His face shuttered. "I cannot say."

Which meant he'd been bound to secrecy. No amount of pressuring on her part would change that.

She sat back, mulling over this with an air of unease. Spirits typically kept to themselves. The fact they were involving themselves in mortal affairs boded ill. Had it something to do with the increased demonic activity?

"This mission isn't finished, is it?" When his face reddened and he lowered his gaze, she understood. "You defied them to come to me."

"I was close...and I could sense you. I couldn't stand by. If that earns me punishment, then so be it—"

"Gabriel—"

Fire flashed in his eyes. "*No,* I will not be scolded. You are my mate, Aziah. My lover, my heart, my *wife.*"

Heat fanned her cheeks, rendering her silent for a moment. By the time she untangled her tongue, he was looking at her with a molten gaze that sent awareness prickling down her spine.

"Is there anything you can tell me?" she asked, a little breathlessly.

Gabriel straightened up, his muscles flexing in the glow. He walked over with a singular focus, a wicked promise in those endless pools. When he kneeled in front of her, one hand rested on her bare knee. Sparks skittered up her leg.

"Is that what you truly wish to do? Talk?" he teased, pushing his hand higher.

Her heart beat like a frantic bird in her chest. She leaned in close, their faces inches apart. "When this night is over, you won't be here, will you?"

His hand stilled, just inches from her heat. "It will not be forever."

"Don't make promises you cannot keep," she whispered.

"Have faith, Aziah. Nothing will keep me from your side."

She knew there was no way to prevent him from leaving after this night. No demand for truth would yield any answers. The call of a spirit was one no fae could deny. For the makers of their kind held a power that would not be ignored.

So, she leaned into his kiss, knowing that every second that crept by brought their parting closer. It was gentle at first, two souls reaching out, re-forging the bond that had weakened in their absence. But it grew until his hands lifted to the edge of the shirt, tugging it up.

The silken material brushed over her skin, sending sparks dancing down her limbs. A shivery breath rattled her chest as she pulled away to let the shirt be removed. And as it tumbled to the grass, she rushed forward, crushing her lips to his.

Heaven exploded within her whole being.

All sense scattered to the wind as they collided together in a tangle of limbs, desperate kisses, and breathless pleas. Aziah landed atop him, her thighs straddling his hips. His arousal pressed low against her belly. She reached out, but in a flash, he flipped her, and she was pinned, his mouth hard against hers.

She wrenched free. "Let me taste you."

"After," he replied hoarsely, dropping fiery kisses down her neck, chest, belly, and, finally, to her core.

Aziah threw her head back with a cry as his lips descended on her heat. His tongue teased, sucked, licked, plunging her into ecstasy. She writhed, breathlessly crying his name. Molten heat scorched through her limbs, burning her from within. It sparked and flamed her blood, leaving her reaching for his head, sinking her fingers into his hair.

A low moan of pleasure rumbled through his lips.

Higher she rose, throwing herself to his mercy, racing toward the edge of oblivion. A thousand suns blazed behind her eyes, and she threw her head back with a primal scream. The evening birds scattered into the sky, and Aziah slumped back, body trembling and slick with sweat.

"All done?" Gabriel's teasing lilt brushed her ear as his shadow fell over her.

Those eyes that had stolen her heart all those years ago burned with a hunger that had never faltered or faded. She reached up, tracing the lines of his face, committing it to memory.

She didn't know how long it might be until they saw each other again, and though she ached to follow him, she knew that whatever his path was, it wasn't with her—for now.

"I love you," she whispered.

His lips parted for a moment, softening and curling to a tender smile that stole her breath. “I love you too.”

When she woke the following morning, she knew she was alone. The fire was already cold. A bristling breeze stole through the trees, whipping up wisps of ash into the air. Gray flecks hovered before her as she sat up, her skin still mottled with marks of passion. Flashes of their night together warmed her body as she donned the clothes folded close by.

As she reached for her cloak, a small parchment tumbled to the grass. For a moment, she stared before she plucked it up, her brow furrowing. Gabriel’s messy scrawl greeted her.

Take care at the temple, my love. Chaos slumbers within those walls.

CHAPTER 23

"Nimue has been captured by the King's men for interrogation. I expect she'll crack by the day's end. Such a waste."

—Excerpt from Lord Claudius Dellabore's diary

Bells tolled across the city, rousing Nimue from her slumber. As she sat up, the door was thrown up. Lorca's head snapped up, a warning snarl greeting the intruder. Nora stood in the doorway, clad in leathers, with a short sword at her hip. A thin sheen of sweat glistened across her brow, and her eyes glowed green in the morning light.

"Get up! Both of you! Attacks are happening across the city. Sybilla wants us to head out now. We'll meet you both out front," she said in a rush before shutting the door.

Nimue jumped up from the bed. She hadn't changed after returning from her sister's room. Lorca shifted to his human form and strode past her to the dresser, where he grabbed his belt and sword. Nimue hurriedly slid her two short swords into their sheaths and slipped on her boots before following him out of the room.

True to her word, Nora was waiting out front with two horses. Dorian and Sylvie were already mounted. Seeing Nimue and Lorca arrive, they nodded silently.

Nimue grabbed the reins and leaped up into the saddle.

Lorca glanced at the horse, hesitating for a moment before he slanted her a wry look. *I could fly.*

"No point. It's only two streets over. Now get on!" Nora said urgently, wheeling her horse around.

He muttered something under his breath as he leaped up onto his horse. Nimue grinned at him as they shot off out of the compound, and his grimacing had her fighting back a laugh.

"Still don't like horses, I see," she teased.

Hooves clattered across the stone, echoing like thunder as they galloped down the street. She hunkered down low, squeezing her thighs to the saddle as the wind whipped at her hair. Anticipation roared through her blood like a beast ready to be unleashed, snapping for blood.

A flame kindled low in her belly. A thread that pulled outwards from her body, reaching for something scarcely a street away.

"Lorca, can you feel that?" Before he could answer the chaotic cries of men spilled into the air as they rounded a corner.

A dozen wolf-like demons were tearing through the soldiers. Swathes of smoke twisted through the fray, and the air hung thick with blood. Ringing metal rattled off windows and walls, the men scarcely holding their own as more beasts poured in from the shadows.

Nimue jumped down from the horse, unsheathing her swords

"Lorca, don't use your fire. We need to find one of the real ones, and ensure it doesn't get away. We can use it to track where these came from," Nimue ordered, slipping into her old self easier as the chaos raged around her. "Now, fan out and kill the bastards!"

She exploded forward, dashing past the line of soldiers as one of the wolf demons charged at them. She dropped low at the last second, driving her blade open and slicing it clean down its belly. It burst into ash overhead as she rolled over and jumped up to her feet, racing to the next beast.

It leaped at her. She darted to the side, pivoting sharply as she rushed as it turned. She jumped onto its back, driving both swords into its fur. Instantly, it erupted into smoke and she dropped to the ground.

Lorca appeared at her side, swinging his blade in tandem with hers. They left a trail of smoke in their wake as they cut through the horde of demons.

"Gods! We have to find a real one soon or these shades will overcome us!" Lorca cried as lunged at another of the beasts.

"Tired?" asked Nimue through gritted teeth.

Lorca rolled his eyes.

There was no time to talk as two more wolf demons launched at them from the side. Breathing hard, lungs burning, she cut one of them down. Sweat dripped down her face. Her strength was slipping fast. She had to find a real one soon, and end this fight before she ended up like the last time.

Desperate, she tried to summon her demon magic. A dagger of pain slammed through her head, nearly forcing her to her knees. She slammed the power back down and called on her fire, but only a sputtering flame made its way to her fingers.

A string of curses fell from her lips as she pivoted on her heel, dodging another attack. Lorca lunged forward with his sword and the demon turned to smoke.

She turned to the others, fighting their way through demons across the street.

"Keep trying to find one of the real ones. There must be one of them here!"

There had to be. The shade demons hadn't vanished.

Dorian yelled, "Behind you!"

Nimue pivoted, yanking up her swords as a demon crashed into them, vanishing into a plume of smoke. The force sent her staggering back. Cursing, she had but a moment to breathe as the other demons continued their onslaught.

A dozen more demons spilled from a nearby alley, sprinting straight at them. Nimue brought up her swords when she spotted something—a woman a few doors down, half-hidden in the shadows. Her gaze met Nimue's, and a wicked grin twisted her lips. She winked.

"Lorca, blast them with your fire."

"What?! But you said—"

"Trust me."

He dropped the sword and raised his hands. Fire shot forward, slamming into the demons.

She darted forward through the plumes of smoke to where she'd seen the watching woman. Footsteps hit the stone behind her—Lorca.

"Keep looking for a real one! I've got this," she shouted over her shoulder.

Not waiting to see if he listened, she headed down the alley. The woman darted around another corner with Nimue in hot pursuit.

A dead-end greeted her.

The woman stood facing a wall her back to Nimue. Dark laughter, like shattering glass, cut the air, echoing around them. Slowly, she turned. Demonic energy rolled off her in thick waves, shadows swirling around her feet. An ancient power filled the air.

Nimue hesitated. This was possession...but the only ones capable of that were the demon rulers. She tightened her grip and stepped forward.

"Is that you Eldrick? Or is it Ronan? Sirius?"

"They're dead, Nimue," she crooned. "I killed them all. Just like I'm going to kill you."

"Not in that form," retorted Nimue.

"We'll see." The woman shot forward, faster than possible for a normal human.

Just as they were about to collide, she threw her hand forward and a bolt of darkness ripped from her palm. Nimue dropped low, the blast sailing inches above her head.

Whoever this was, they were good.

But they weren't her.

She darted around her attacker, slamming her foot into the woman's back. The woman staggered and Nimue surged forward. A wall of shadows appeared. Nimue swung her swords, tearing through the darkness. When the smoke dispelled, the woman was gone.

Dark laughter erupted behind her.

A burst of magic shot over her head. Spinning on her heel, she leaped up and drove both blades into the woman's chest. Surprise flashed, twisting into a scowl. They hit the ground together. Nimue wrenched her swords up and jumped back. Black blood bubbled from a gaping wound.

The woman smiled bloodily at Nimue as if she was the one who'd won the fight. "Hello, old friend."

Nimue froze, those words cutting straight to her heart.

A choked laugh made its way through bloodied lips. "D-don't worry. We'll see each other soon enough. I'm not done with you yet."

PART 2

TRUTH

CHAPTER 24

"It's been weeks since Nimue was taken away for interrogation. Fenrys's army continues its path to the capital, burning our villages in his wake. We are running out of options. Tomorrow I will lead my men in a final assault."
—Excerpt from Commander Titania's diary

Since the ominous warning from the possessed woman, Nimue had barely slept, sitting for hours curled up by the open window or pacing the library in silence. Though she knew Lorca watched her with concern, she'd kept him at a distance, lost to her wandering thoughts. The memory of Litania murdering her haunted her every waking moment.

One morning, she sat in one of the rear gardens, pouring over a pile of texts trying to learn more about the Gray Army. A missive rested on the bench beside her. Dorian had requested a training session. He'd been absent for a few days, though he hadn't mentioned where he and the others had been.

Which left her in the garden, waiting.

Lorca was sitting against one of the trees, the shade stretching over him, with a book in one hand. It was one of the historical texts they'd been poring over in the last few days. His sword lay beside him on the grass.

"I can feel you staring," he remarked.

Heat fanned her cheeks as she held back a smile. "Perhaps I enjoy the view."

He set the book aside and looked at her with a heated gaze. Wicked thoughts burned through their bond, sparking a heat low in her belly. Her fingers itched to reach out and close the distance between them.

"*Nimue*," he growled.

She took a step toward him. Damn the training.

The doors leading into the garden swung open, the screeching metal dragging her gaze away. Nora jogged over, followed by Dorian and Sylvie. The pair were strikingly beautiful, their every movement poised and graceful. They moved in step, as if intimately aware of the other. Sylvie scanned the garden, while Dorian kept guard at her side, maintaining a watchful distance from Nimue and Lorca. These were a pair that had fought together in battles, trained and bled, trusting each other to know what the other needed.

"We're here to train," Nora announced with an excited grin. "I've only ever done this with Dorian and Sylvie, so I think it will be fun."

Fun? Something inside of Nimue hardened, and though she knew the girl had no idea what Nimue had endured of late, the anger bubbled up anyway. It heated her body, flaming her cheeks red.

"Fighting demons isn't fun. If you want me to train with you, show me what you can do," Nimue replied.

Nora's mouth opened and shut, looking away. For a moment, a flicker of guilt wormed through Nimue's gut. An apology danced on her lips, but she swallowed it away.

Sylvie approached, arching her brow. "And will you also be demonstrating your talents? Beyond what we've already seen?"

Nimue squared her shoulders. "What exactly are you trying to say?" she said, giving Sylvie an unflinching look.

"Some of the powers you've shown are not those of a dragon. I've seen demons display the same ones. What exactly are you?"

"I am Wren from Fenware *and* a dragon. I struck a deal with a demon to get additional magic. I hoped to use it to save my people. I failed," Nimue said tightly, then pushed on, saying in a low voice, "Something I have no intention of repeating. Now, do you need to know any more, or can we continue with the purpose of this visit?"

Sylvie stared at her with an unreadable expression. It was a war of defiance, one Nimue would not lose. Another beat of silence ticked past. Sylvie bowed her head, something quick flashing in those fathomless depths, and the fae stepped back.

"You're not what I expected," was all she said as she returned to Dorian's side.

Nimue didn't know what to make of *that* remark, so turned her attention to Nora.

"Step forward. Let us see how well trained you are with that sword."

Nora's eyes widened. "You don't want me to use magic?"

"That's up to you. I want you to pin me to the ground. If you can do that, you win the fight. Easy as that." Nimue reached over her head, withdrawing her swords. A soft metallic hiss cleaved the air. Sylvie stiffened but didn't move, leveling a warning look at Nimue, as if to say, *don't you dare hurt her.*

She took up her position in a clear area in the garden, shifting her feet into position. After a quick flex on the hilts, she waited with poised limbs while Nora shed her cloak, passing it to Dorian. He murmured something into Nora's ear, then stepped back, taking up beside Sylvie with a hawkish expression. Neither of them trusted Nimue, and for that, she was glad.

It was foolish to trust a demon.

When Nora drew her sword, Nimue lifted her own. A cold calm slid into her chest, her heart steady in its cage. Her magic was a mess, but she'd long since learned how to fight without it. Titania had beaten that lesson into her when she was little more than an arrogant soldier-class demon, long before her rise to claiming the Azradan throne. Nora might be stronger at that moment—there was an unknown element with a Druid's magic but Nimue had fought against stronger enemies—and won.

"When do we—"

Nimue exploded into action, swinging both blades. A startled cry came from the Druid as Nimue dropped low, sweeping her leg, and the girl hit the ground. In an instant, the point of her sword was at Nora's throat. From the corner of her eye, Nimue glimpsed Sylvie take a step forward, only to be stopped by Dorian's hand on her wrist. He gave her a warning look before the pair stepped back, rejoining Lorca.

She moved back, permitting Nora space to stand. "Again."

Nora's hand pressed against the earth and she pushed up to her knees. A green light flashed beneath her fingers, so quick Nimue almost missed it. Instinctively, she took a step back. Her foot caught a dip in the earth and she staggered to the side, then looked upon what had tripped her up.

A tiny hole in the ground. One she swore hadn't been there before.

She shot a startled look at Nora. "Did you do that?"

Nora stood with a smile. "Perhaps. I think you'll find I am full of secrets."

Nimue didn't wait for the girl to speak. She rushed at Nora in a flurry of blows. The girl yanked up her sword, parrying her attack. They danced across the grass in a dizzying clash of ringing metal. Harsh breaths followed, but neither yielded, not even as the sweat dripped from Nimue's skin and every muscle burned.

Nora held her own, but didn't come at her with any offensive attacks. Nimue knew that piercing gaze well. She was studying her opponent, testing every response, and Nimue responded with a series of unpredictable attacks.

She moved forward, breaking through Nora's desperate attempts to block. Blades clashed until mere inches separated them.

"You're looking tired there," Nora taunted.

Nimue's brow lifted. "And you talk too much."

She stepped back suddenly. The weight threw Nora off. The girl stumbled forward. Nimue saw her chance and rushed in again. This time, she side-stepped and pivoted. In a flash, she was at Nora's back, one blade lifted to her throat, the other pressing lightly into her side. She leaned in close to Nora's ear.

"You're good and you watch closely. The first lesson though, if you don't know your enemy, *keep your distance.*" She stepped back, sucking in a deep breath.

"Who taught you to fight like that?" asked Nora.

A thousand training sessions in sparring yards beneath a burning hot sky, and the sand stained with black blood, flashed through her mind. She blinked the memories away, sheathing her swords. "One of the best warriors I've ever met, and my oldest friend."

"Can she teach me?" Nora's eyes widened. "Sorry, I don't mean—"

“Am I not enough?” Nimue teased. Even as the echoes of her past stirred at the fringes of her mind, she held the smile.

“I—”

“It’s okay. I’m jesting,” Nimue said. She turned to Sylvie. “Care for some sparring?”

One perfectly shaped brow lifted in response and a short nod answered. Sylvie’s slender hand withdrew the delicate blade at her hip. The polished metal gleamed in the sunlight, its sharpened edge deadly. It was a fine sword, forged by fae metal smiths if Nimue had to hazard a guess.

As they build, I destroy.

She shifted into position.

They sparred for a few hours, then transitioned into lessons about demons. None of them knew she was the worst of those she described, or that she had left a trail of carnage in her long history. As they reclined under the shade of a tree, Nimue shared her knowledge.

“The two types we’ve so far encountered are true demon wolves and shades. The latter are fabricated by magic. I guess you could say they’re echoes of the true demons. However, don’t be fooled by this. They can—and will—rip your throat out. Usually, these shades wouldn’t be able to pass through a demon portal, so that means they’re forged here, and anchored by a real demon.” She paused, considering how to best explain her concerns. “These were organized attacks, and that worries me. It makes me think someone may be behind this, rather than just beasts lashing out.”

It was Dorian who spoke first, leaning forward, his brow furrowed. “Can a mortal do this? Or a fae?”

She hesitated. “No.” It took her a moment to find the next words, choosing them carefully. “A woman was observing us. I think she was the one who brought the demons and shades there. My guess is that she is a demon, likely a powerful one, using the cracks as a conduit, controlling them whilst she is safely back in the demon realm."

Sylvie looked up. "A woman? Why did we not know of this?"

Nimue shook her head. "She was possessed by a demon and attacked me. I had to kill her. None but a select few demons have the power needed to possess someone from the demon realm."

As she spoke, she didn't miss the way Sylvie watched her. That piercing gaze, questions burning in those ancient depths. It stripped her bare, her tenuous lies crumbling with every word. Dorian, at least, appeared satisfied, nodding. Perhaps the threat was enough to distract him from examining her too closely.

"And this woman did you—"

The mansion doors burst open. A soldier strode through and hurried over. After a curt bow, he spoke. "Princess Sybilla requests the presence of your team. We've discovered some more bodies at the entrance to the underground tunnels a few streets away."

CHAPTER 25

"They say that Nimue has not broken, but it's simply a matter of time. No one has withstood the King's interrogators for long."
—Excerpt from Captain Castille's diary

Bodies littered the courtyard, torn to ribbons. The looming shadow of an abandoned temple, with its leaning wooden walls and dilapidated roof, presided over the grizzly scene. Statues of spirits, half consumed by tangled ivy, were splattered with blood and remains. The air reeked of decay, the metallic notes saturating every breath, and beneath it was the familiar stench of demons. The lingering brush of dark magic prickled across Nimue's skin.

She inched forward ahead of the others, swords drawn. Halfway across the carnage, she came across the remnants of a soldier's tunic, stained dark with blood. Had they been on patrol and stumbled across the demons? Or had this been an intentional attack?

"Can you sense any demons?" Dorian asked, appearing beside her with silent steps. That unreadable gaze slid over her, studying far too intently for her liking.

She didn't know what to make of him beyond that he was a little less hostile than Sylvie. He was quiet, never too far from Nora, but always seemed to watch Nimue. If she had to hazard a guess, he hadn't yet made up his mind about her.

"No," she said after a pause, then stepped forward, following the trail of bodies to the open door of the temple. "This way. Keep your eyes and ears sharp."

The stench of death lured Nimue deeper into the tunnels. Silence reigned over the group as they descended, guided by Lorca's fire. At the bottom, the path diverged into two. Metal cradles for torches hung along the walls at regular intervals. Nimue followed the pull in her gut and headed down the left tunnel.

"Let us see what's down here first, okay?" she called.

What do you think? Lorca sent silently from the front of the group.

That we've barely scratched the surface of what's going on and an army is due here any day now.

They lapsed into a long silence, doing little to still her tangled thoughts. Descending further into the shadowy depths, a cold feeling stole through her chest.

Demons were close.

"Look, up ahead," whispered Nora.

A black metal door blocked their way. Nimue held up her hand for everyone to stop, giving her time to inspect it first. The door was slightly ajar, allowing a faint blue light to squeeze through. Demonic energy trickled out, brushing her skin. Squaring her shoulders, she drew her swords. A faint metallic hiss cleaved the silence.

Lorca moved behind ready to back her up as she pushed the door open.

Metal screeched, announcing their entrance. Snarls erupted from within.

Shit.

Nimue hurled herself through. A surging wave of demons flooded her vision. She wrenched up her swords, as one of the beasts crashed into her, metal sinking deep through matted fur and fetid flesh. Black blood sprayed, splashing her skin. Tearing her blade free, the beast hit the ground.

Others were on her, but she edged forward, cutting them down until bodies were strewn across the floor. Yet for every one she tore apart, another took its place.

Shouts and snarling filled the air. The others ripped into the demons, cutting down with vicious efficiency. Even Nora, though Dorian shadowed her, left a train of bodies in her wake, impressing Nimue.

A demon leaped at his back. Nimue's hand jerked up, shadows exploding from her palm. She dropped to her knees. A stabbing pain ripped through her head, and darkness clouded her vision. Someone called her name. She felt a hand on her back and sensed someone shielding her.

"Nora, can you—" Lorca was cut off as a green light erupted.

Her eyes slammed shut.

Demons screamed, their panicked cries choked off abruptly.

Silence descended. A few moments passed before she pried her eyes open, the throbbing ache in her eye fading a little. The floor was strewn with wolves, ripped apart by whatever Nora had done. The girl stood in the middle of the room, her arms wide, breathing hard. A thin trickle of blood dripped from her nose. Their eyes met from across the room, a faint smile tugging across that youthful face.

Nora swayed. Sylvie cried out, sprinting over, catching her as she nearly hit the ground.

Nimue watched as the fae's hardened mask fell away, leaving only tender concern in those fierce eyes. A thumb on a cheek, hushed whispers, a tender embrace. The look of a mother fretting over a child. Her heart squeezed at the sight and she forced herself to look away.

Lorca's arm slid around her waist as he helped her up, casting her a lingering look. Refusing to let him see the old wounds open once more, she smiled reassuringly. A muscle in his jaw twitched. He didn't appear convinced.

Pulling her gaze away, she studied the space.

Her blood ran cold.

Across the room, a large ring was etched into the stone, nearly worn away by the passage of time. Half of the symbols had faded, but she recognized the ones that were left.

The symbol of a Hell Gate. The very thing that had ripped her and her kin from the demon realm. Things were worse than she'd imagined.

"A hand with this door!" Dorian's shout carried from across the room.

The fae was trying to pry open another black metal door. She hurried over followed by Lorca when she spotted the symbols etched into the metal. Her heart froze, and the air rushed from her lungs.

"No!" She exploded forward. "Get back, it's a trap!"

The second the door cracked open, a force ripped outwards, sending them flying. Nimue slammed into the wall, the back of her head hitting stone. Bone shattered on impact. Stars flashed across her eyes. She dropped to the ground, *hard,* and darkness hauled her under.

Nimue awoke with a groan, her temples thumping. Pain lanced down her spine as she pushed herself up to her knees, her body fighting the movement. Something wet and sticky glued one eye shut, and when she wiped it, realized it was blood. She cleaned her face and squinted across the room, the world tilting for a moment. A dull ache throbbed through her head as her gaze alighted on the others. She glimpsed no obvious wounds, and she still sensed a hum of life through her bond with Lorca. A thread of tension eased within her as she looked at Nora who was closest to her.

She dug her fingers into the stone, hauling herself across to where the girl lay. Fire blazed through her limbs, but she continued, gritting her teeth. When she reached Nora, she pressed two fingers to her neck. With a sigh of relief, she felt a flickering heartbeat nudging her finger.

Clenching her jaw to stop herself from crying out, she forced herself up. The world lurched as she scanned the room for Lorca, finally seeing his prone form by the far wall. Ice flooded her veins as she stumbled over and crouched beside him. Her hands flew to his neck. A delicate beat answered.

A sob choked in her throat as she rolled him onto his back, grabbing his shoulders as she shook him. His eyes fluttered beneath his lids before a groan fell from his lips. Groggily, he stirred awake, looking around in confusion.

"Nimue?"

She kissed his forehead, her heart eased. "I'm fine. How are you?"

He sat up stiffly. "I feel like shit. What happened?"

"A trap."

"That's right. I heard you. How did you know?"

She pointed to the door that hung on by a single hinge. "The symbol. I've seen it before. A long time ago."

His gaze lingered on hers as if he knew she wasn't telling him everything. She cupped his face, hoping the tenderness would distract him. His mouth opened a question poised on his lips when a shadow fell over them.

Nora stood at Nimue's side, eyeing the open doorway. "Is that...?"

Nimue rose and moved around Lorca. "Let me go in first."

"But—"

"Help Dorian and Sylvie."

Nora huffed, but walked off without further complaint.

Nimue entered the room. Blood and entrails clung to the walls. Torn limbs lay across the stone floor. Whatever bodies had been in there had been ripped apart in the blast.

The darkness inside her hissed awake, unfurling in her chest. Power trickled down to her fingers as she surveyed the damage. In the center of the room stood a stone table, soaked with blood. Shadows crowded in as she approached, the glow of the crack struggling to pierce the gloom. A message had been etched into the stone, written in her tongue. It stared back tauntingly.

Hello, old friend.

The mansion was a flurry of activity when they returned. Soldiers poured out of the courtyard, marching off down the street. Shouts ricocheted across the courtyard. Nimue strode through the gates, past the wagons being loaded up with crates.

Lorca seized a soldier who tried to rush past. "What's happening?"

The man opened his mouth to answer, but the front doors swung open and Helena swept out, clad in fighting leathers. Seeing her hard face, he hurried off, rejoining the line of men loading up the wagons.

Helena stopped in front of the group, giving them a searching look, lingering on Nimue, and the blood dried on her arms and hands. Worry creased her brow.

"What did you find?" she asked.

The words died in Nimue's mouth, nothing adequate rising to her lips.

Demons below. How can I tell them that evil is about to descend on them all?

Luckily, it was Dorian who spoke first, his expression serious. "It was a trap."

Helena's face crumpled. Whatever hope there had been that the mission might yield information died. She pinched the bridge of her nose. "I see."

A feeling of despair washed over Nimue. *No, you don't.*

The cacophony from the soldiers grew louder, drawing her focus to the panicked fray. "What's going on?"

Helena laughed bitterly. "The army was sighted on the horizon. We've run out of time. The siege has begun."

CHAPTER 26

Nimue's appearance in the court meeting sent shock waves throughout the court. She stood at his side; her gaze on the floor. At that moment, she looked broken. Later, I caught her gaze from across the room, and she smiled. It seems our plan has worked.

—Excerpt from Commander Titania's diary

The Empress's army had arrived at the City of Slaves.

Stopping at the cusp of the distant tree line, the force was mostly concealed by the ancient woods. The vast clearing that stretched between the city, once dominated by sprawling markets and festivities, lay barren. A low, mournful wind rolled in from the storming seas, whipping dust across the empty battlefield.

Distant plumes of smoke billowed high across the horizon. Sybilla knew a dozen small villages were dotted along the coast, running all the way to the next major town of Calthorn. They had already secured plenty of supplies from there before taking the city, which she assumed the town had likely suffered for.

Her grip turned white on the stone as she leaned forward to get a better view. The city walls were already bustling with men, finishing up the final preparations for the siege. Boulders and casks of oil had already been hauled up and positioned ready to be launched when the time came; crates packed with arrows and pikes stretched along the top of the walls, and heavy coverings soaked with water lay ready in case of flaming projectiles from siege engines. Men stood by, polishing their weapons and talking in low whispers, roused only by the occasional bellowing command.

General Galen appeared at her side, clearing his throat. "Your Highness, a report."

She kept her gaze on the army. The bitter wind bit through her clothes but she didn't care. "Go on."

"All requested positions have been manned. We've also begun moving all residents from the Merchant Quarter deeper into the city. There's been some resistance, but once we explained the threat, the majority moved without complaint." Galen hesitated.

"But?"

"A few resisted. There have been injuries. Healers have been dispatched but some of the nobles don't like the idea of leaving their homes. Do you want us to force them?"

"Not yet." She massaged her temples. What little sleep she'd gotten last night had been piss poor and now she was paying for it. "What else?"

"We've moved our food supplies to the guarded sites. Fortunately, we have slightly more than expected, which should serve us well if this winter turns cruel. Spies have been posted around all water supply points, watching for anyone who might attempt to poison the wells, as per your orders."

"Marshall all the horses and any other animals. If anything happens to the food supply, we'll have to slaughter them to feed the people."

He bowed and retreated to the others. She cast one final look at the army before she turned and set off along the wall. Oren fell into step beside her, the rest of his men in position.

Once they were out of earshot, he cleared his throat. "Take heart, your Highness, this city is well-prepared and the men have little interest in making this an easy fight."

"Do all truly share that sentiment?" she asked as they passed into a tower and descended the steps. Halfway down, she paused. "I saw the state of the city; the disease, the conditions of the Merchant Quarter, the way the slaves were treated. This city may have been falling apart, but some prefer familiarity over change."

"The city shall not revolt. For now, anyway," he replied.

"For now?"

He leveled a grim look at her. "Hope for a better future is a tricky thing to cling to in a long siege. When hunger and disease come—and they will—that is when the real fight begins."

Out on the street, their horses awaited them. She swung up into her saddle, pulling her hood over her face. The wind was bitter that morning, biting through her leathers and fur-lined jacket. A shiver racked her body as she nudged her horse onward, breaking into a trot. Her mind moved from the army, returning to the mission at hand.

In the folds of her dress, a medallion glowed warmly. Blood howled in her ears as her stomach twisted into knots. If she were alone, she would've thrown up.

Bile burned up her throat. Once she returned to the mansion, the next phase of her plan would happen.

Forgive me for what I am about to do.

Hours later, Sybilla stumbled into her room from the balcony, barely making it to the empty chamber pot before emptying her stomach. Once the last remnants of the morning meal lay at the bottom of the porcelain bowl, she straightened up and wiped her mouth clean.

"Your Highness? Are you well? Shall I send for a healer?" Oren's voice came from the other side of the door.

It took her a second to reply. "I'm fine. Let the healers rest."

She sat there until her breathing slowed, and she was at last able to stand. She took off her bloodied clothes with shaking hands. When she finished, she tossed them into the empty fireplace and snapped a finger, summoning a small flash of light. All it took was a little coaxing and a small flame slowly crackled to life, the amber glow chasing back the evening shadows.

As the traces of what she'd done turned to ash, she padded over to where a few simple night shifts were hanging.

A bowl of clean water sat on the table beside her bed. Dipping her hand into it, she rubbed the stain away. The tiny amount dissolved into the water; the last trace of her act erased. Once she was dry, she stared at the fire, the last remnants of the clothes nearly consumed. Wisps of ash floated in the air.

A knock at the door broke the silence. She flinched. "Who is it?"

"Helena."

"Come in."

Helena slipped inside, closing the door softly behind her. That unreadable gaze slid over the clean dress, then drifted to the fire. "You got what you were after?"

"Yes."

The pair shared a long look, but Helena didn't inquire further, which Sybilla was grateful for. She inclined her head for Helena to continue.

"Lord Delmont has arrived. He's waiting for you in the sunroom."

"What? Did he say why?" The smug bastard had been ignoring her summons for the past two weeks. All he had said through a runner was that he was busy aiding her mission. Whatever *that* meant.

Helena's mouth tightened. "No. He's determined to see you, and won't say a word to me. Shall I have him removed?"

It was sorely tempting, but she shook her head. "No, better see what he has to say. I cannot afford to alienate *all* my allies."

She followed her adviser out, wondering what had brought Claudius Delmont to her door. What had changed his mind?

They walked in silence down the hall to the sunroom. Helena gestured for the guards to open the door but remained outside as it closed behind her.

All the furniture had been removed to make space for a private sparring room. It was one of the last few places of privacy she had left, and now that too had been interrupted.

Claudius stood in the middle of the room with his back to her while looking out across the private garden. He appeared to fill the room with a presence that rivaled any highborn, that air of power and position rolling off him. Though she knew he was of merchant blood, he had risen to power, dominating the markets and swaying favor with the nobles. He would've been a threat to be removed, but months ago, Helena had approached him and offered him a place in the rebellion. Reports had indicated he had no love of the Empress and appeared desiring of change. He had accepted Helena's offer, though since the city had been claimed, his silence had only deepened Sybilla's caution with him.

At the sound of her entrance, he turned.

"Lord Delmont," she greeted.

He bowed. "I must apologize for my delayed presence. Personal matters arose, requiring my presence."

"More important than the present situation?" she retorted archly.

The edge of his mouth twitched. "Unfortunately, yes. But that is for a later discussion. Has your team made any progress with the demon threat?"

"It's being resolved," she replied.

She knew he had a spy network that ran deep into the city and beyond and was aware of everything that had happened in his absence. Though he claimed to be an ally, she refused to trust him implicitly. Out of all futures she'd glimpsed before, his remained elusive to her, and she didn't like that at all.

He cocked his head to the side, a smile teasing his lips. "I see."

She was exhausted and in no mood to play games. "What do you want, Lord Delmont?"

He smiled. "Please, in such privacy, call me Claudius. May I call you by your name?"

"Your Highness will suffice," she replied. "Pray tell, what has brought you to my mansion? I am a busy woman."

To her irritation, his smile deepened. "What would you say if I told you there were several ships on their way here from the Mithra Archipelago?"

Supplies she had...but men? That was something she feared she didn't have enough of.

"And what is on these ships?" she asked carefully.

"Oh, men, weapons, a few little gifts to aid and protect the city."

Warning bells chimed in her mind. Claudius was not one to give help without wanting something in return. Reports might show he was generous, but he was still a businessman. Nothing came for free.

She schooled any interest she had. "Why would you help me?"

"The Empress has sent the Midlan army, which is around five thousand men I believe. We barely have that, and I would like to survive this conflict."

She rolled her eyes. "Enough games. Tell me what you want?"

He pressed a hand to his chest. "You wound me."

"*Lord Delmont.*"

"Claudius," he corrected with a serene smile.

Fire flashed through her chest. "*Claudius.*"

"Oh, how I love the sound of my name on your lips," he drawled.

Heat flooded her cheeks and anger snapped like a whip through her chest. She scowled, hating how easily he could rile her temper. "What do you *want*?"

His smile lingered for a moment, then fell, as if a mask had been pulled away. A coldness replaced it and his eyes looked empty of any human emotion.

"I offer you the goods and men. You may call it a peace offering, an apology for my behavior of late. As for what I want, it is simple. I want this city."

When she returned to her office, Sylvie was waiting for her, cloaked in the shadows of the room. The woman stepped into the flickering glow of the fireplace, pushing back her hood.

"I have found those involved in the experiments. It's all on your desk for you to read."

A stack of letters was piled neatly for her, each bearing the marks of the noble family responsible. She picked up one after another, leafing through them, devouring the words etched there. Rage burned through her, threatening to escape as she set the last letter down. The murdered slaves had been referred to as *things,* something disposable—little more than a means to an end.

She stepped back as her heart pounded, trying to pry its way from her chest. The blood roared in her ears. She was going to drag those bastards from their home and interrogate them.

No one got away with that shit and lived. Not under her rule. She would not become her aunt, permitting such heinous atrocities.

"Oren!" she thundered.

The door flew open, her guards rushed in.

"Yes, your Highness?" Oren glanced between her and Sylvie, lingering on the latter with suspicion.

"It seems we have found those responsible for the experiments. It's time we bring them to justice."

CHAPTER 27

King Barden came to our aid today, helping us rid King Fenrys's army from our home. As we celebrated tonight, I could not help but glance at Nimue as she sat beside Titania. There was a quietness about her. She ought to have been happy. Our plan worked. So why did she look so ill at ease?

—Excerpt from Lord Claudius Dellabore's diary

Demons below. What am I doing?

Nimue shivered in the pouring rain outside Claudius's mansion. It was garishly ugly in her opinion, but she remembered his room in her palace. Heated memories stirred, pushing to be seen. She shoved them back down, calling on the rage that had fuelled her for hundreds of years.

The deafening rain drummed against the cobblestone as she strode to the door and rapped her knuckles against it. Time crawled by, every messy thought scraping its talons down her mind. What was she thinking? She turned to go. A single thought roared.

Leave!

The storm raged on, lashing her with stinging droplets, and yet she hesitated, staring at the ground contemplating whether to stay or go. All the pain that threatened to overcome her was stayed by three little words.

Hello, old friend.

She stepped away from the door. How was she to face him?

The door opened with a low groan she heard even through the cracks of thunder and lightning. Her breath caught in her throat and her heart pounded.

Looking up, she saw first the polished boots, the strong legs, the hands that had touched her with such tenderness once, the broad chest...and *his* face.

His blue eyes burned with shock.

"Nimue, you're here..."

She forced herself to face him, squaring her shoulders. "I need to see both of you. Something has happened."

It took him a moment to speak as he stepped aside, holding the door open for her.

"Come inside."

She didn't trust her voice as she swept inside. A wave of fragrant spices lingered in the air, tugging at old memories, luring them up from the darkness that she'd banished them to. In an attempt to calm down, she inspected the grand foyer, stilling as she spied one of the paintings dominating the walls. Her portrait stared back, the old her, the strong her. The Demon Queen.

"Nimue—" Her name was a hoarse prayer on his lips.

She forced herself to look at him, saying, "I'm not here to talk about us. That will have to wait."

He nodded and gestured for her to follow. Many paintings were portraits of people she once knew. Several times, she glimpsed the others that had come to the realm with her two thousand years ago; Titania, Castille, Amara, Claudius...Atlas.

Her demonic family.

As he slowed, she jerked to a stop, nearly colliding into his back. Claudius pushed open a door, holding it for her as she swept past him.

The room was unexpectedly furnished well. Ornate furniture, golden threaded rugs, the wooden floor polished and dark. She shed her cloak and started to fold it.

"May I?" he asked with his hand outstretched.

She handed it over and watched him warily as he hung it up. By the door, he paused once more, casting her an unreadable look with a burning gaze. One hand gripped the door frame. "I'll fetch Titania. She'll be glad to see you."

And with that, he was gone.

After a few moments spent inspecting the room, she realized it belonged to Titania.

Two crossed short swords hung on the wall. On either side was a mounted spear, Titania's weapon of choice. Carved animals made of polished stone were placed on the shelves. On a bookshelf were dozens of medical books, jars of dried herbs and flowers, and even a handful of trinkets.

The door swung open. Two sets of footsteps entered, one hurried, the other slower. As she turned around, she was yanked into Titania's arms. The scent of weapon oil and earthy notes swirled around her. Nimue closed her eyes and for a moment, the worries gnawing at her were silent.

But such mercies never lasted. Titania pulled away. "What is it?"

And just like that, the past few weeks tumbled from her lips. As she told them about the message from the possessed woman, the color drained from their faces. When she finished speaking, she sat on the couch and waited for their questions. But they only glanced at each other, a silent conversation she wasn't privy to playing out.

Titania spoke first. "Do you know who it might be?"

Nimue stared at her hands. "I've thought about every powerful demon I have ever known, but none of them strikes me as strong enough to beat *three* demon kings. Hells, once you become a ruler, you learn of the damn curse we're all gifted with. It's why no one has tried to take more than one throne before."

It was why neither of them had ever challenged her to the throne, why she was the one who took it. Because they knew what the price was.

Claudius frowned. "That kind of power would drive them mad."

"Suppose this is to open a Hell Gate here," ventured Titania. "Why? That's a bold move, even for someone with three thrones and their armies under their control."

That was what scared her. "Find out what you can about this, before things get worse—far worse."

A grave silence descended on the room, gripping all of them in its tight embrace.

Claudius had left, and she was alone with Titania who sat down beside her. One assuring hand slid over Nimue's knee, squeezing it.

"You look like shit," Titania said.

"There's another reason I'm here." She leveled a grim look at her old friend, mustering the courage for what she had to say next.

"Ellie?"

Her hands gripped her knees tightly, the knuckles turning white. "I need someone to train my sister, and I'm not in the best condition to do so. You're the smartest demon I know, and you were my teacher. I know this is a lot to ask and I certainly do not order this—"

"I'll do it."

Nimue's head jerked up sharply. "You will?"

Titania's hand slid over hers, squeezing it softly. "She's one of us and we protect our own, even if we want to kill each other some days. How is she feeling, though?"

"About as well as expected after what she went through. I've tried talking to her about what happened but..." Her voice choked off with emotion.

Titania's hand covered hers. "Your sister is *alive.* Take heart with that. Her recovery won't be easy, and it will take time. But Nimue, you are going to have to tell her the truth soon and Lorca too."

Nimue sat up and looked at Titania in surprise. "How do you know I haven't told him?"

"How long have we known each other?" Titania retorted.

She sat up with a groan. "Far too long, but that isn't the point. He knows I'm a demon. Does he really need to know everything? We never reveal ourselves to anyone. Not truly."

Titania looked away. "*About* that..."

"What?"

The mask slid from Titania's face, and naked grief burned through. The weary smile turned sad as Titania stroked her cheek. "It was a long time ago. I'll tell you about her someday but, for now, think about it. We shouldn't bear our secrets alone, Nimue. I've seen how he looks at you. He will understand."

Claudius escorted her out of the mansion, passing her cloak over as they reached the front door. The rain had ceased, and puddles of water glimmered in the moonlight like pools of silver. Overhead, dark clouds still churned, heavy with the promise of another storm, but for now, the city had settled into a moment of perfect stillness.

She didn't realize Claudius hadn't left until his hand brushed hers. She flinched.

"Nimue, I—"

"Why didn't you come back?" There, she'd said it.

When he didn't answer, she stared at him, trying to read the lines of his face and those eyes she once knew so well. But he was just as elusive as he had been all those years ago.

"Nimue, I—" His voice cut off and he stepped back. "I cannot...I wish..."

The silence enveloped her heart in a blanket of ice. All those bitter and lonely years aching for his return, for any kind of explanation, crashed into her.

She laughed bitterly, refusing to cry. "I don't know why I bothered asking. Goodbye, Claudius."

When she returned to the mansion, her thoughts were no clearer.

She went upstairs, stopping by Ellie's room. Her sister was fast asleep, curled up soundly in her sheets. When she reached her bedroom, Lorca was absent.

Lorca?

Nimue? You're back? The relief in his voice was like a balm to her aching soul. She nearly sank to her knees after hearing it. *Where are you?*

Outside in the gardens. Come find me, he teased.

CHAPTER 28

What are they waiting for? The time for victory is now.
—Excerpt from Lord Claudius Dellabore's diary

Sybilla stared at the mansion from astride her horse, her stomach twisting into knots. None of the windows were lit, and the front door was wide open. A cold breeze whipped at her hair. She tucked it behind her ears, heart racing as she dismounted and approached the front door. Oren fell into step beside her, the remainder of his men fanning out around her.

A dozen soldiers strode ahead of her, murmuring among each other.

Oren gently held her back as the others went inside. She wrapped her arms around her waist, trying to warm herself from the cold. An eternity passed as they waited there, silent in the shadowy night. A lump formed in her throat. Why were they taking so damn long? Was something wrong?

Her mind churned over a multitude of possibilities when shouts sounded from within. She took a step forward when one man rushed out and threw up all over the stone. Moments later, others appeared, pale-faced.

"What is it? What did you find?" she asked.

The young soldier raised his head, wiping his mouth before speaking. His face glowed white in the moonlight. Taking a shuddering breath, he said, "They're dead. They're all dead."

She moved away and hurried inside. It wasn't difficult to follow the sound of the other soldiers, their horrified voices luring her down a shadowy hall and into a drawing-room. The door gaped open, splattered with blood.

At the threshold, a bloody handprint stained the floor, smearing into a trail that ran back into the room.

"Maybe you shouldn't—" She cut Oren off with a sharp look.

She had to see it. Two steps into the room, and she froze. Her blood turned to ice. Nothing could have prepared her for what awaited her.

The noble family of Renomir had been torn apart, reduced to strips of flesh and bone. The walls and ceilings glistened with wet blood. None of the bodies remained intact, their limbs lay scattered across the floor. Scraps of once fine clothing showed the lord and lady of the house were part of the carnage.

Sybilla staggered out of the room with trembling steps, barely making it to the hallway before sagging against the wall. Her mind howled with white noise. From the pit of her gut, a fiery rage sparked and grew.

"*Fuck!*"

Oren stepped forward. "Your Highness—"

"Who did that to them?" she seethed. That someone had butchered the family to cover up their tracks twisted in her chest. Which meant they were more likely in charge of gathering resources, rather than the ones who were behind the experiments

She was back where she started. Failing the people who needed her.

"I don't know, but perhaps your spy can find out," Oren said.

A bitter laugh tumbled from her lips. "That's just it, Oren. Sylvie is thorough, and even getting the information she did was hard." She sighed. "We're no closer to finding out who started those experiments or why. And our only damn leads are dead in that room."

"Are you sure?"

She managed a nod. "I saw both the lord and lady. I imagine the other remains were of their children and servants."

He had no more words of comfort, nothing to say to make the situation any better. All that was left was the stench of blood and her growing fury.

CHAPTER 29

"I watch and I wait. Timing is everything. Soon, though, I will rip that man from his throne and drive my sword into his heart."

—Excerpt from Nimue's diary, soldier-class demon

Found you, Nimue thought.

The skies opened and rain fell in a thundering roar, fat droplets splashing the silvery grass of the private garden. Lorca basked in the storm, his face tipped to the sky. Rivulets of water ran down his face and body, soaking his clothes.

She lingered in the open doorway. His shirt clung to the tight lines of his long, hard body. Muscles shifted as he straightened up, pushing the damp curls from his face. Slowly, he turned, his gaze near black as he stared at her.

We shouldn't bear our secrets alone, Nimue. Titania's worlds propelled her forward.

Even as fear seized her tongue, her feet carried her closer. He walked toward her, slowly, each step measured, controlled.

Thunder rumbled above, lightning exploding across the sky. White light splashed over his face, illuminating his green eyes.

She met him halfway, grabbing his shirt, yanking his mouth down to hers. Their lips collided as thunder erupted above. Heat tore through her, melting the icy chains around her heart.

She tore her mouth away. His hands locked on her waist, keeping her close. Hot breath mingled in the cool air, white clouds swirling, tangling together.

"Nimue—"

"Promise me something," she whispered urgently.

Worry chased the heat from his eyes. "Anything."

"Promise me you will always look at me the same way you're looking at me right now." When he stared at her with a puzzled frown, she tightened her grip. "*Promise me.*"

He reached up, pushing her wet hair from her face. With aching tenderness, he kissed her cheek, lips lingering before he kissed the other. Then her nose, each eyelid, her forehead. As he pulled away, his thumb drew small circles on her face. "I promise."

"I—" The truth froze on her tongue.

"You can tell me. I'm right here and I'm not going anywhere."

Maybe it was the way he looked at her at that moment or the way he uttered that quiet promise.

"I didn't tell you everything about me. I am not *just* a demon. I am also a Queen. To be specific, Queen Nimue of the Azradan Court."

"Well, that certainly confirmed a few things," he answered with a dry smile.

A breath lodged in her throat. "What! But how?"

"You don't think I didn't realize you were someone special after seeing how Titania and Claudius defer to you? And the way you take command so easily. You have the bearing of a queen, my love."

"Why didn't you say anything?"

"Because I wanted you to tell me when *you* were ready," he replied.

She didn't dare to ask how that affected his feelings for her. Who was to say what he might think when he truly witnessed the darkness she was capable of?

"You should be afraid of me," she whispered against the roar of the rain.

When his forehead rested against hers, her stomach flipped nervously.

"The only fear I have of you is that you shall realize that I am not worthy of you." His aching confession pierced right down to the depths of her soul, rendering her silent.

The rain softened, misty droplets dusting her cheeks. All the fear and doubts that had crowded her mind in those last few weeks shattered. Shards of hesitation tumbled to her feet.

She hauled him close, crushing her mouth to his.

Something inside her broke free as he kissed her back. His hands slid to her waist, pulling her in, chest to chest. Groaning, he lifted her. Wrapping her legs around him, she pressed him into her heat, gasping as his cock pressed hard against her.

There are too many damn layers, she thought as she tried to pull his shirt free, but it clung to his body.

She wrenched her mouth free as he shoved her into the stone wall. She grabbed what fabric she could and tore his shirt off his body. Her lips dropped, tracing kisses along his skin.

"*Nimue,*" he groaned breathlessly.

Heat surged through her. She wrenched her lips away and pulled her cloak back, leaving it pinned against the wall. Before she could blink, he lifted her shirt over her head. The icy rain hit her naked chest. She gasped at every drop that ran down her skin.

His mouth dropped, taking her breast into his mouth as hands moved to her pants, releasing her belt. It came free, and he lowered her back to her feet, kneeling as he peeled the leather pants from her skin. Inch by inch, they came down and he pressed heated kisses along her thigh, inching closer to her core.

"Get your damn pants off," she moaned.

Chuckling, he looked up, heat burning hungrily in those eyes. "Patience."

"Lorca."

He grinned. "Demanding little demon, aren't you?"

A smile rose to her lips as she grabbed him, pulling him back up, crushing her mouth to his.

Her hands dropped to his waist. His hard arousal pressed against her belly, drawing her gaze down, hunger roaring between her thighs.

"Stop looking at me like that," he warned. "I don't want to finish *on* you."

Her mouth parted. He took his chance and kissed her. A battle of wills erupted between them. Her nails raked down his back, hauling a bloody trail. A hiss tore from his lips as his hand slipped between her legs, finding her heat. She bit back a scream. Liquid fire poured straight down to her core as she buried her face into his neck.

"Please, Nimue, say it. Say what you want me to do."

"Lorca, fuck me."

In a flash, he plunged into her. She groaned in pleasure as his cock filled her.

Demons below...

"Nimue—"

"*Move,*" she commanded.

"With pleasure." He pulled back slightly before thrusting himself deep within her.

A cry ripped from her throat as she met him thrust for thrust, bare skin scraping on the stone. She welcomed the pain as it rose, sending her into oblivion, and she surrendered to his touch.

His thrusts grew frantic, harder, driving her closer to the edge. Breathless pleas fell from her lips as his hand dropped between them, rubbing her again. Something inside her yanked tight, coiling tightly. His lips tore away, trailing along her jaw, nipping at her ear.

"*Let go,*" he growled.

"Make me."

"Gladly." His fingers rubbed her faster, sending her hurtling over the edge.

A savage scream tore from her throat, scraped raw with desire, as she exploded. Seconds later, he sank into her, calling her name. Liquid heat flooded her as he stayed there, dropping his lips to her shoulder. Ragged breaths shook his body as she leaned back, gasping for air.

Laughter bubbled up from her gut, spilling out. She wiped the rain from her face as he looked up, that dizzying smile meeting hers. This time, he kissed her, slower, lingeringly as he let her back down, slipping from her.

Drawing back, she couldn't hide her smile.

He pressed his forehead to hers, closing his eyes. "Now, *that* was something."

CHAPTER 30

"The time has arrived for me to undertake the trials to join the King's Guard. I must be patient, for the chance will come."
—Excerpt from Nimue's diary, soldier-class demon

It had been a week, and Flynn was no closer to understanding what his trials would entail.

None of the jobs he'd been assigned gave any clue. In the morning, he assisted Tobin in sweeping out the temple and dusting off the rugs before moving into the library. He transcribed texts in the ancient fae tongue, though Flynn had no idea what he was writing. The job took them to lunch, which he wasted no time hurrying off to attend.

It was the only time he could talk to Mira. When he asked her what she was training for, she avoided answering and instead asked about his chores.

In the afternoon, Mathias took him for private lessons. Flynn learned about the history of the fae and the temple's origins. If he was lucky, he learned a little more about his father. He also covered philosophy, riddles, and hypothetical situations.

He stayed there until the evening meal, which Mira was always absent for. Whatever she was up to, he had no idea, and was never left alone long enough to find out. On the rare occasion he was able to pin someone down to talk, they offered no explanation as to what she was doing.

Once the meal was finished, he was taken to the stables for lessons with the stable master, Fyoran. There he worked the horses, cleaned them, and learned to ride without a saddle. Every day was the same, and he began to wonder if the trials even existed.

One afternoon, while he was brushing down one of the horses, Tobin wandered over. Flynn's heart gave a traitorous little flip when he spotted him. Sweat gathered on his brow, so he tugged his shirt up, using it to wipe down his face. It was then he caught a whiff of his stink.

Spirits above, I need a wash.

He smiled at Tobin, but it wasn't returned. Flynn didn't care. He'd make Tobin smile one day, somehow. "Where am I being summoned now?"

Tobin didn't immediately answer; blinking, he shook his head, as if clearing a thought. "Your first trial. It begins now."

Blue fire lit the torches in the main hall. The haunting hue danced over the white robes of the assembled fae. A walkway was cleared down the middle, running to the main dais. Mathias awaited him there. Tobin walked with Flynn, the stoic fae a strange comfort.

All eyes tracked his approach, the silence deafening, broken only by the soft footfalls of his boots. At the dais, Tobin left his side. Flynn's heart thumped hard, uncertainty and fear trickling ice down his back. Doubts corralled in his mind, sending his panic flooding through his veins.

He forced in a deep breath, then eased it out to calm himself. A low table was set out next to Mathias, a single goblet with a clear liquid inside. Was it water? Or poison? Tearing his gaze away, he found the older fae watching him, silent.

"Step closer," ordered Mathias.

There was no backing out now, no return to his former life.

Mathias turned to the crowd. "The son of the Spirit, Atlas, has come to us, seeking his birthright and power. In accordance with our customs and the law written by his father, he has been summoned for three trials; a test of the soul, body, and mind. The first of which begins now." He turned back, seizing the goblet. Holding it out to Flynn, nodding with a flash of assurance in those fatherly eyes. "The Trial of the Soul. May you be deemed worthy."

Flynn grabbed the goblet before he could think, staring down into the clear contents. "What is it?"

"Taboran Root. It will guide your soul to a place where it shall be judged. Trust yourself and you will pass. Now, drink."

He brought it to his lips, then tipped his head back, downing it in one go. The bitter liquid rushed down his throat, warming his stomach. At first, there was nothing. Then his gut grew hot, as if fire was erupting within his body. His legs buckled as he hit the ground, hands shooting to his throat. A hoarse cry tore out, darkness nudging the corner of his vision.

Desperation flooded him as he looked around, trying to call for help. The fae stared at him, unmoving, unyielding. Tobin met his gaze, then looked away. Flynn felt his limbs grow cold, his thoughts scattering. Bit by bit, he slipped into the darkness.

What had he been doing again? Where was he? What—

He fell back, a cold abyss swallowing him whole, and then he felt no more.

He sat up with a gasp, his throat scraped raw. A sprawling meadow surrounded him. Overhead a cloudless sky, the warm sunlight bathing him in golden tones. Pushing himself up unsteadily, something materialized in his hand. A short sword.

What the—?

"Nice of you to appear, Flynn," called a familiar voice.

His head snapped up. Wren. She stood a few feet away, dressed in her furs, as she withdrew the sword from a sheath at her hip. It was the one she'd come back from the mountains with.

The air rushed from his lungs as he stared at her, looking just the same as the last time they'd spoken. That hard edge in her eyes, that same quiet smirk, the wildness that he'd found startling the first time they'd met. Only this wasn't Wren.

"You're going to test my soul with a sword fight?" he asked, frowning.

Wren rolled her eyes. "Spirits above, no, why would I need to do that? No Flynn. I'm going to kill you."

She charged forward, swinging her blade. He yanked up his own and metal clashed. The force sent him staggering back when she swung again. Clumsily, he parried the attacks where he could, desperately dodging her blows. But she was fast.

Inhumanly fast.

"Why Wren?"

A wicked grin lit her face. "Why not? You are pathetic. You don't *deserve* the power you seek. It would be a waste."

Hot anger stoked in his chest. "You're wrong! I'm doing this for our people!"

Fury twisted her face. "Half of our people are dead because of you! When the attackers came, what did you do? Nothing. You did nothing!"

"That's not true!" he argued as she charged at him again.

His foot snagged, sending him teetering. Metal flashed. He darted to the side, but it wasn't enough. As he scrambled away, something hot dripped from his skin. Touching his cheek, he looked at his hand. Blood glistened on his skin.

Wren laughed coldly, swinging her sword idly. "How is it a lie? Your soul *festers* with shame. You know you could've done more. The signs that an attack was coming. You had the ear of the council. Why didn't you say anything? Why didn't you *do* something?"

"I tried!" he protested.

It was true. He'd wanted to talk to his father for days leading up to the attack. Convince him that maybe they should retreat further into the mountains, just for a few days. Camp somewhere until the threat was gone. But he'd stayed silent, afraid of being shut down, of seeming like a fool.

He should've done more. Spirits above. Wren had never stopped looking for a way to save their people. Then, when the attack had come, his thoughts had been on his own family. He'd run by homes as his people were captured, cut down in the street, and their village burned.

Even when he'd tried to save Mira, it hadn't made a difference in the end. Flynn's knees buckled, shame roaring in his mind. Who was he kidding? He was nothing, no one. Nothing but a failure.

"I..."

"There it is. The acceptance. Just as well, your soul would never have been able to bear that power." Wren prowled closer, standing over him with a cruel smile. "Whatever Wren saw in you, I don't know. Perhaps she was blind or stupid. She had to be to think you could ever be a leader, that you were stronger than you looked."

His gaze dropped to his hands as he closed his eyes, waiting for the killing blow. In his mind's eye, he saw Wren—*his* Wren, the one who teased him about his failures in love. The one who had picked him without hesitation and had commissioned a set of daggers for him. Because she'd believed him, steadily, without hesitation.

Their first meeting materialized in his mind. She'd come to the school, a newly made leader, and walked straight into morning class with swaggering confidence. She hadn't been intimidated by everyone's stares as she spoke to the teacher. He remembered she turned and pointed right at him.

"You, with me. You're one of us now."

When he'd asked her why she chose him, she'd smiled and said, "Why not you?"

He looked up as Wren swung the sword. "You're wrong about me."

The blade stopped at his neck; the metal pressing lightly on his skin. Fury darkened her gaze. "I am never wrong."

"I was ashamed I didn't do more, that I didn't somehow stop the attack. But there wasn't anything I could've done. The past is the past. Dwelling on it won't save my people. So, I'm done feeling ashamed, like I'm not enough. You're right. I'll fail, make mistakes, and doubt myself. But I'll be damned if I let you or anyone else tell me I'm not strong enough." He stood, ignoring the blade at his neck as he stared Wren down. "I. Am. Enough."

That cold fury slipped from Wren's face. She stepped back, warmth softening her face.

"Perhaps there might be hope for you yet."

He sat up sharply, blinking as his bedroom came into focus around him.

Tobin was asleep in the chair beside Flynn's bed, curled up awkwardly. A blanket had been draped over him. His raven-black hair was tousled, curls falling softly over his face. Flynn had so many questions burning his mind but exhaustion hauled him back into the pillows.

He rolled onto his side, wondering what had brought Tobin to his room. But as he fell asleep, he realized he didn't care. He was glad, that someone wanted to stay by his side, to watch over him. He fell asleep smiling.

One trial down. Two to go.

CHAPTER 31

"Titania's new shadow, Nimue, is an intriguing character. I watched her during training today. She spent much of the class watching from afar or sparring as little as possible; then, at the end, she challenged the best student and had him on the ground in seconds, her sword at his throat. I believed myself hidden as I watched this, but she looked up, as though she sensed me, and smiled."

—Excerpt from Lord Claudius Dellabore's diary

Dawn had yet to break as Sybilla entered her sparring room. Gray light spilled in from the windows, catching the wisps of dust that floated lazily through the air.

She shed her cloak, and hung it on a hook on the wall, then pulled a sword from the rack. The familiar weight eased her darkened mood, the troubling thoughts from a restless night of trying to sleep dispelled.

Hard as she tried, she could not shed the memory of what she'd done from her mind. It hadn't mattered that those folks had already been dead when she ripped their hearts from their bodies. Nor that it had been asked of her by a damn spirit of all creatures.

If she was to beat her aunt's army, getting her hands bloody was simply a price to be paid.

She slipped off her boots and pressed her bare feet onto the polished wooden floor. As she eased through her sets, warming her muscles up, the chill ebbed away. A thin band of sweat gathered on her brow as she upped her pace, spinning, slashing, thrusting, and weaving her across the room. Heat burned in her legs.

Ribbons of magic flowed from her fingers, dancing up her arms and tumbling from her shoulders to create a trail across the room. It eddied about her, bathing the room in swaths of glowing light, chasing back the shadows.

Her magic sang louder inside, swelling up and spilling out of her hands. The room tumbled away, and all she felt was the power singing within.

Another wave of magic swept through her, roaring in her ears. She lifted higher until she tumbled headlong over the edge. Her eyes flew open, a gasp tearing from her lips as magic erupted from her chest. The light dimmed, and the sword was at her feet, her hands wide. Ragged breaths racked her chest. Rivulets of sweat ran down her skin.

"Well, that was impressive," drawled a familiar voice. Claudius.

She spun sharply, her breath hitching. "Lord Delmont, how long...?"

Claudius bowed deeply. "Not long. Lady Adara knocked and let me in, but you were lost in your training. You're quite good. Who taught you?"

"My adoptive mother taught me the sword, the magic I was trained by another," she said, grabbing her weapon from the floor. "Now, to what do I owe the visit?"

"An update about the delivery of soldiers. The ships are being loaded and shall depart the Mithra Archipelago within the next day or so, weather permitting. Unfortunately, they may have to skirt some of the main islands. The Empress has sent additional ships to the seas upon rumors of rebellion," he said conversationally.

"Do you have any contacts in this supposed rebellion?"

"None of my allies are revealing anything, but these are dangerous times," he replied calmly.

"A shame. That could've been useful. Back to your report. The news is good. How long will it take for them to arrive?"

"Two weeks, if the weather permits. It would usually be a four-day journey, but with the increased military presence precautions must be taken. I've arranged papers if they're stopped and I trust the men handling it."

She didn't know what to think of his aid. He was honest that he wanted the city, but she couldn't help but wonder if there was more to the story?

"It is well appreciated. The more men we get, the better."

His gaze moved to the swords on the wall. "A fine collection you have."

Omi had once told her you could tell a lot about someone by how they fought. She smiled. "Would you like to spar?"

The corner of his mouth twitched. "Are you sure you're not too tired?"

"Is that fear I hear in your voice?" she retorted.

"Never." He stalked to the wall, grabbed a simple sword, and tested it in his hand before he turned with a grin. "Ready?"

She burst forward, surprise flashing on his face as she swung. He parried with his blade, metal colliding with a ringing cry. Pulling back her sword, she dropped low, sweeping her foot. He retreated, then pushed forward. He matched her every blow with equal speed, a burning intensity locked on her, stripping back her walls.

Refusing to yield, she watched his movements. He was better than she thought, faster too. But she wasn't deterred and called on her visions, just enough to predict his attack. This time, her powers answered. An image flashed in her mind. She dropped low as he swung and burst up, driving her shoulder into his gut. The air rushed from his lungs as he staggered back.

He recovered quickly, straightening up just as she collided with him. Metal clanged, their faces inches apart. She could smell him, male and primal, and taste his breath on her lips. Their eyes locked, a battle for dominance, the smile never falling. Her gaze dropped to his mouth.

What would it...

He hooked his foot around hers before she realized it. The world tilted and suddenly she was falling back, hitting the ground hard. In a flash, he had her pinned, wrenching the sword from her hand. His hard body pressed against hers, heat burning her skin. She breathed hard, staring up, still refusing to yield. Magic pricked her fingertips. His gaze snapped to them, then back to her. One brow lifted.

"Now, now, this is meant to be a—"

A blast of magic flew from her, smashing into Claudius's chest, sending him flying. No sooner had he hit the ground than he leaped to his feet. His face hardened for an instant before a smile claimed its place. Something inside of her loosened.

"You continue to surprise me," he murmured, staring at her in a way that left her breathless. It plunged right down to her toes, curling them. Though she'd been acutely aware of his looks, she'd never truly *looked* at him before.

How had she not noticed how piercing those deep blue eyes were? Or the way his mouth always carried a ghost of a smile.

It took her a moment to find her voice. "Likewise. Who taught you to fight like that?"

Something flashed in his eyes so quickly that she almost swore she'd imagined it.

"Many good teachers who probably charged me far too much," he replied with a lazy smile.

Just like that, the air of the practiced noble took over.

"Oh, I don't know. I should think their teachings proved sufficient. Perhaps one day you shall beat me," she teased.

Claudius smiled at her, but it didn't quite reach his eyes. "Who knows what the future will hold?"

CHAPTER 32

"Day by day, Nimue is tested and passes each one, but I see the look on the King's face. She is good—too good. I feel a sense of sadness now. Nimue will be dead by dawn."
—Excerpt from Lord Claudius Dellabore's diary

The hazy morning light trickled through the half-destroyed bedroom. Nimue sat up groggily, wiping the sleep from her eyes, wondering for a moment why she was on the floor. Her gaze lifted to the bed, untouched. Deep breaths labored beside her, drawing her focus to Lorca sprawled out on the bed. A blanket rested precariously over his hip, barely concealing anything.

She drank him in all the hard lines and taut muscle. Scratches and bruises mottled his skin, mirrored on her own.

Pride filled her as she rose and padded over to the wardrobe, pulling a robe from one of the hooks. She slid it on, feeling the delicious aches in her body. A lazy breeze whispered, ruffling the curtains, and lifting the hairs along her skin. She repressed a shiver, eyeing the open window.

The memories of their multiple rounds trickled back in. Heat coiled tightly at her core. *Oh.* That was right. Their clothes had been shredded, so he'd shifted and carried her up to the window. Then he changed back and climbed in after her. Which promptly resulted in them making it as far as the middle of the room before she had him pinned.

She rubbed her back, tender from the rug. "Next time, bed."

Lorca stirred, groaning awake. He sat up, rubbing his eyes blearily. "Agreed."

Snorting, she turned back to him, the blanket gathering at his hips. Her mouth dried, thoughts scattering for a second. The sound of his chuckling stopped her thoughts. She turned back to the window, looking at the rapidly clearing sky.

A shuffling of blankets and gentle footfalls signaled Lorca's approach. His arms slid around her waist, drawing her into his chest. He kissed her cheek, then rested his chin on her shoulder. "Good morning, my beautiful demon queen."

She'd never tire of hearing that. "Careful. You tease me too much and we won't leave the room."

He hummed softly as he pressed a string of feathery kisses along her shoulder, up her neck, lingering on her cheek. "That sounds terrible."

Rolling her eyes, she pulled from his embrace. During his kisses, he'd untied her robe and the morning's chill sent goosebumps along her skin.

"Are you sure you're not also a demon?"

"I am only a mere Dragonir," he said, bowing deeply. "And I am at your service."

Stop bowing at me, she thought, blinking away a flash of Claudius bowing at her, with the same wicked grin, over eight hundred years ago. "Lorca—"

A knock at the door cut her off. *Demons below...* Was there to be no peace for one damn moment?

"Good morning. Are you both clothed?" Helena's voice, muffled by the door, held a note of impatience.

"Hold on," said Nimue tightly as she grabbed Lorca's clothes from the floor, tossing them at him.

With a lingering look, proving their conversation was far from over, he tugged on his clothes and followed her to the door. Nimue opened it to see Helena with a look of impatience on her face. Her eyes widened as she stared at them both.

"So, I suppose I can let the guards know we didn't have a demon running loose in the mansion last night."

Nimue's cheeks reddened. "What do you need, Helena?"

"A messenger has come from Alexandria's army. They're to meet with Sybilla shortly and she would like you to both be present." Helena cast another look over the messy room, then shook her head as she slipped away.

Nimue shut the door softly, her thoughts tangling into knots when Lorca threw his head back and laughed. Frowning, she turned. "What's so funny?"

"A demon. The men thought it was a demon because you were so loud. If they only knew."

Nimue tried to fight it, but a smile lifted at her mouth.

"Come on," she said. "We can scare them again later. For now, let's see what our dear Princess wants."

Helena met them in the foyer and gestured for them to follow. She led them down a wide hall, flanked by guards, and pushed open a door, holding it for them to head inside. The room was crowded with finely dressed men and women speaking together in low whispers.

Sybilla sat on an ornate chair dressed in her battle leathers. Her long black hair was braided atop her head, supporting a simple golden crown. She met Nimue's gaze from across the room and gestured to the space on her right. Nodding, Nimue and Lorca made their way down the parted crowd and took up their positions.

Sensing what this meeting was really about, Nimue had slipped on her cleanest leathers and strapped on her short swords. Lorca cut a menacing figure, his tunic tight against his chest, with one hand resting on the hilt of his sword. Nimue took up a position within reach of Sybilla. Lorca stood at her side, casting a cool gaze over the room.

The Princess glanced at her. "Have you ever done one of these before?"

Far too many. "A few."

"Any advice?"

Nimue blinked, glancing down at the calm mask. Then she saw Sybilla's hands pressing hard into her thighs, her knuckles white. "Never show your feelings. *You* command this room, so act like it. That's half the game."

"And the other half?"

"Knowing when the time is to kill someone."

Sybilla's gaze snapped up, her mouth twitching. "What?"

"That will throw most people off, so you can then take advantage of the chaos," said Nimue calmly.

"You're insane."

You have no idea, she thought to herself ruefully.

The door swung open. Silence descended as four men swept inside, three of Sybilla's guards shadowing a young man wearing a green tunic embroidered with a silver bird on his chest. Nimue was surprised at his youth.

He stopped in front of Sybilla and stood without bowing until Lorca stepped forward, an inhuman growl rumbling from his chest. Flames danced on his hand. The messenger's eyes widened, his mouth parting as he stared at Sybilla accusingly.

"If you kill me, the promise of peace is off," he said in a trembling voice.

"Peace? Has my aunt come to surrender?" mused Sybilla. "My, that was far easier than I expected. Well, I should go tell my men that the war is over!"

Silence answered her. The messenger shifted restlessly as he dug out a scroll from his bag. His hands shook as he held it out and opened his mouth to read.

Nimue walked forward, grabbing his wrist, and forcing him to meet her gaze. "I have a personal message for your Empress. Tell her she missed one in the mountains."

She stepped back, taking the scroll with her, and handed it to Sybilla, who nodded in thanks.

I think you scared him more than I did, mused Lorca ruefully.

Did I hurt your ego?

He snorted softly, just loud enough for her to hear. Amusement buzzed through their bond. *Hardly, but I may have to spank you later.*

You can try.

Sybilla looked up as she lifted the scroll and tore it in half. "Does your general honestly think I'll agree to these terms?"

The messenger straightened his spine as if wielding a second rush of courage. "You cannot hope to win. Our resources are endless, our numbers growing by the day. The people you claim to love will starve. Is that what you want?"

A hush chilled the room.

Sybilla stood up from her throne and stalked forward. Magic kindled to life in her hands, wrapping itself around her arms and body. Ribbons of light danced around her frame. The messenger dropped his gaze as if she were a blinding sun.

"Look at me!" thundered Sybilla. The messenger shakily lifted his gaze. She grabbed his collar, hauling him off his feet. "I am Princess Sybilla Danomir, *rightful* heir to the throne. I claim this city as my blood right. I *claim* this city for the murder of my parents by that monster. I *claim* this city for every man, woman, and child she has enslaved. Tell my aunt and all who follow her, this. I am coming for them. I am coming for them all."

CHAPTER 33

"Nimue stood shakily to her feet, a fire blazing in her eyes as she pointed her sword at the King. 'I challenge you for the Azradan throne!'"
—Excerpt from Commander Titania's diary

Aziah walked for a day before she reached a small town. Slipping in under the cover of darkness, she stole a horse and some supplies, vanishing before dawn broke over the settlement.

As she rode through the ancient woods, following the lands she knew as intimately as the islands of her home in the Mithra Archipelago. A heaviness lingered in the air. A hum of magic pricked her skin and squeezed her heart. This was not spirit magic, nor primal. It had a sourness about it that lingered on her lips like venom. It stank of demonic power.

The endless stretch of gray clouds, heavy with the promise of rain, did little to ease the darkness from her mind. She was close enough to sense the power of the Gray Army. It left her gut in knots, and an ill feeling twisted like a knife as she drew closer.

The smell of smoke soon tickled her nose, acrid and tangling with the stench of an army. It stank of oil, of something festering and dying, and of demons. She paused at the dip of a hill, where the undergrowth barred any further advance on horseback, and the trees blocked out most of the light.

Reluctantly, she dismounted and removed its gear. The beast stared at her, ears twitching before it ambled away into the woods. Once it was gone, she shed her cloak. Left only in her dark leathers, she descended into the shadows and followed the call of death.

CHAPTER 34

"A new ruler has been crowned. All hail the first Demon Queen, Nimue, of the Azradan throne."

—Excerpt from Commander Castille's diary

After the Empress's messenger was escorted out of the makeshift throne room, and the nobility had departed, Nimue and Lorca retreated upstairs. When they reached the top of the stairs, Lorca paused, touching her arm. He said he was going to rest, that he had a headache.

"I'll summon a healer," she said, turning to head off when he grabbed her wrist, shaking his head. "Are you sure?"

"I am tired, that's all. Some rest in dragon form will do wonders, you'll see." He smiled reassuringly. "Go see your sister."

A quick kiss and she watched his retreating figure, all slow steps, and low shoulders. It wasn't a good day. She remained there until he vanished from view, then released a heavy sigh. Her health was a mess, and so was Lorca's condition, even if he didn't want to admit it.

What a pair they made.

She headed over to Ellie's room and pushed the door open.

Ellie was pacing in the middle of the room, a sleeping gown hanging off her painfully thin frame. Dark shadows lingered under her eyes. Despite Nimue's effort to get her to eat more, it was a losing battle.

Nimue frowned at the state of the room. The books had been tidied up, stacked in neat piles on the desk. The bed was made, the blankets gone from the floor. It was orderly, a far cry from the girl who stood among it all.

"Ellie?"

"I hate this room," Ellie muttered. She turned to the window. "I feel restless, like something inside of me is itching to get out. Yet every time I reach for the door, I freeze. I can't...I can't do it."

Anger and grief roared in those pale blue eyes. Ellie spun away from the window, scowling at the floor. Shadows stretched out from the corner of the room, reaching for her. The air chilled, clouds of breath swirling around Nimue's lips, but her sister didn't seem to notice.

Nimue moved forward and before Ellie could fight her, she wrapped her arms around her. Ellie didn't move a muscle. Demonic magic welled within her, thick with emotion, pounding until her walls cracked open—

The power from within Ellie slammed into Nimue's chest.

"Ellie—" The words died in her lips as her sister jerked out of her arms, eyes wide.

"What did you do?" There was a note of fear in those four little words, each one cutting deeper than the last.

A vast ocean stormed between them, as turbulent and volatile as any that had lashed the mountains. The two of them, staring—one demanding an answer, the other afraid of revealing the monster. Lorca had taken it well, but what promise was there that Ellie would be the same?

"Ellie, there is something I need to tell you," Nimue said.

"That doesn't sound good."

"It might be easier if you sit down."

To her dismay, Ellie remained where she was. "I prefer where I am."

Nimue searched for the right words, for the place to start. She sat down on the bed, not trusting herself to stand as she loomed on the precipice of the confession. But she knew it was only with the truth Ellie might stand a chance of moving forward.

"You're not losing your mind. That feeling you're experiencing? It's magic. Magic that was bound by your father." She paused and dared to look up. "I know that magic because it's part of me, too."

Ellie stepped back, white as death. "I'm a dragon, like you?" Nimue's reaction must've exposed her because Ellie's hand moved to her chest. "I'm not, am I?"

Nimue shook her head gently. "It's demonic magic. From your father, to be precise."

"*Demon* magic?" Ellie swayed, staggering back until she hit the wall, and she pressed the back of her hand to her mouth. Silence claimed the space between them, poignant, until she spoke once more. "Father isn't a demon. He's...He aged, got sick sometimes, broke his arm once. That's not—" Her eyes narrowed. "Wait, what do you mean 'your' father? He's..."

"He's still a demon, mortal maybe now, but that doesn't change what he is—who he is." Nimue still had no idea how he'd even done that. Atlas's lies would have to be answered later. She didn't dare to rise from the bed, but there was still more to tell. "His name isn't Alaric. It's Atlas, a demon general—my general."

There, I said it.

"But you're a dragon."

"In body, yes. My soul, however?" Nimue stared at her trembling hands. "I—"

"I'm not a demon!" Ellie shouted.

Her sister retreated further into the corner of the room, pulling the shadows with her. Nimue felt something inside her squeeze sharply. This was more than simple demonic blood in her sister's veins. This was...*older.*

Cracks splintered along the windows. Wreaths of magic spilled from her, eddying around her trembling form.

Nimue rose, reaching out, but Ellie flinched. Her hand fell. "It's okay. You're not alone. There are others like us."

The horror deepened in Ellie's eyes. A fragile world shattered around her. "I-I'm Ellie Dumare! I'm *not* a demon or a half-demon. I don't know why you're saying all this, but it's a lie. I'm just..."

Nimue tried to reach for her sister but stopped as tears spilled down her cheeks.

"Ellie, I'm not lying!"

"Shut up!"

Darkness erupted from Ellie's hands. Nimue tried to dodge but it was too late. The energy slammed her into the chest, sending her smashing through the window and out into the garden below. She struck the ground with a deafening bang, the air ripped from her lungs. Desperate gasps shook her body as she tried to breathe.

Nimue! Lorca roared through the bond.

She forced herself up to her knees, staring up at the window she'd broken. The soul-shattering grief tore through her soul, shredding it to ribbons.

Lorca appeared moments later, rushing to her side. He helped her up, looping his arm around his waist. Though she saw his lips move, all her focus was on trying to say her sister's name. But she couldn't get the word out, so she raised her trembling hand to the broken window and spoke down their bond.

Ellie. She...

Lorca nodded and helped her inside. They made it to the foyer where Nimue froze as Ellie ran down the stairs. Wreaths of black energy swirled in her wake.

"Ellie! Stop!"

Ellie didn't even slow her stride. The guards reached for her but her hands snapped up, energy exploding, throwing them as if they were little more than dolls. Nimue staggered after Ellie as she flew through the front door.

Her legs quaked with every step, threatening to give out, as she hurled herself out into the courtyard. Men and women screamed, scrambling back as Ellie rushed past. Nimue threw a hand up, a primal rush of power tearing up from the depths of her soul. The darkness howled for one of its own, sensing her sister's pain.

A savage scream spilled out of her throat. Magic flooded down her arm, brushing her fingers when her legs gave out. Molten pain ripped through her blood, pouring into her head until blackness edged her vision.

"Ellie!" The hoarse plea choked off as her body slumped forward, and the last thing she saw was her sister racing off into the city, vanishing into the night.

CHAPTER 35

"I can hear it at night, whispering to me, slowly devouring me. This is what drives kings mad. The thrones aren't just stone and spells. They're alive, relics of our gods. And now I am bound to mine until death."

—Excerpt from Queen Nimue's diary on the eve of her coronation

Titania was waiting for them when they landed. Her old friend was dressed in leathers and a black cloak, the picture of ferocity and grace. As Nimue slid off Lorca's back, Titania approached. "It's Ellie, isn't it?"

Nimue recounted everything, watching Titania's expression darken. When she finished, her friend glanced at Lorca. It was a look she knew well—assessing just what he was thinking, given he'd learned about their ancient secret, and that he seemed to be rather calm about the whole thing.

Titania's gaze narrowed. "You're handling all of this calmly. You knew, didn't you?"

"For a long time."

Titania opened her mouth to ask more, but the front door swung open with a deep groan. Claudius appeared clad resplendently in gold and black. His gaze slid over them all, lingering for a second longer on Lorca before finding Nimue. She felt the weight of that look, and the way he'd studied Lorca. Their last conversation played out in her mind, but she quickly buried it.

"What do you need?" There was no hesitation in his question.

She never thought she'd be there, asking *him* for help, but her sister was worth more than her pride. It made it a little easier to swallow the lump in her throat.

Lorca was at her side, his arm brushing hers, offering comfort. But she had to be strong, forcing down the memories and the pain, and all the demons that wanted to shake Claudius for answers. She took a step toward him.

"I need you—" She paused, glancing at Titania as well. "I need both of you. Please help me find my sister."

Even with Titania using her powers, hunting for any trace of Ellie's emerging magic had turned out to be harder than expected. Nimue's nerves were taut, near snapping as she jogged down the busy streets. Soldiers marched past them, all on their way to wall duty or to dig more trenches beyond the city. Nimue stopped them, asking if any had seen her sister.

No one had seen a blond girl wielding magic or otherwise.

She pushed on with Titania toward the Pleasure Quarter. As much as she hoped her sister hadn't gone back to the source of her pain, they had to check it out and be sure, at least.

Up ahead, the gates to the quarter were wide open. She knew that all the slaves had been taken from it, given shelter down in the Merchant Quarter. Why the area hadn't been burned to the ground already, she didn't know. If her sister wasn't there, she was sorely tempted to do it herself.

She stopped at the gate, glancing at Titania. "Do you sense her?"

Titania strode past her down the main street, still littered with debris from the battle with the demons earlier. "I don't know..."

First, they tried the brothel that Nimue had rescued Ellie from. The front door was ripped open. Nimue crept in first, the stench of old perfume and alcohol lingering in the air. Broken collars scattered the ground. Furniture was upturned and shredded as if done in a rage. Ripped paintings depicting lascivious scenes lay on the ground.

"I'm going to murder whoever did this to your sister," Titania snarled.

"It will be like old times, then."

They inspected every room but found nothing except empty spaces, full of ghosts. Nimue left each door open to let the dead leave, then headed back out onto the street.

The sun was dipping beyond the city walls, casting long shadows over the buildings. A sharpness bit the air, when the last remaining scrap of warmth the sun had given retreated into the shadows. Her sister had run out barefoot, wearing little more than a thin dress. Not the kind of clothes suitable for a night out in the cold.

"Where else could she be?" Titania asked.

"The only other place I can think of is the slave markets, where she would've been processed with the rest of my people," Nimue said. Closing her eyes, she reached down the bond to Lorca. *Have you checked the slave markets yet?*

There was a long silence before Lorca replied. *Yes. Claudius was thorough, but he didn't sense her. I couldn't catch any scent of her, so I went back to the mansion to track her from there. Nothing.*

Her chest squeezed painfully. A string of curses spilled from her lips. Her sister was somewhere in the city, but where? She'd sworn to Ellie that she'd keep her safe. At that moment, she was failing. Again.

"Nimue, this isn't your fault," Titania said.

Nimue rounded on her. "Isn't it? I failed spectacularly by trying to tell her. Gods, I should've kept silent." She stopped. Blaming herself would not find Ellie any faster. "Let's keep looking. We have a lot of ground to cover and it's going to be a cold night."

They searched for hours, calling down every street and asking everyone they came across. But no one had seen her sister. It was as if Ellie had vanished without a trace.

As midnight arrived, they met Lorca and Claudius back at the mansion. Once Lorca saw her, he shifted from his dragon form and she found herself in his arms.

Burying her face into his chest, she closed her eyes. His warmth steadied her mind and calmed her thoughts.

She turned to the others, grateful that Lorca's hand remained on her back when she spied a shadow emerging up the street behind Claudius. It was slight, wearing little more than a thin dress. Hope surged through her. Nimue burst forward, her feet pounding the stone. Behind her, the others called her name to stop her.

Nimue halted. Under the silver band cast by the moon, the girl's face was visible. It wasn't Ellie. Blackened eyes stared at her, bruised lips twisting into an empty smile. The stranger raised a trembling hand, and her legs gave out, sending her tumbling to the ground.

Nimue rushed forward to catch her. Blood trickled from the girl's ears and eyes, a crimson trail that stained her ashen skin. It was a host possession, and the body was dying...which meant the demon in control was acting from the demon realm.

Her nails dug into the girl's arms, dragging her up so that their faces were inches apart.

"Where is my sister?"

The girl smiled bloodily. "You should better protect those you love, old friend. I'm going to have a lot of fun with her."

"You touch her and I will come back to the fucking demon realm myself and tear you apart," snarled Nimue. "Now, *tell me where she is.*"

The girl sputtered again. Droplets of blood splashed Nimue's cheeks. "Where would be the fun in that? Don't worry, you and Ellie will be reunited soon enough. But for now, a parting gift."

Her hand shot up, slamming against Nimue's cheek. The second it touched, Ellie's screams tore through her mind.

Nimue *snapped.*

CHAPTER 36

"It does not take long for allies to become enemies, and for war to come knocking at our door. The other kings sense a new ruler, who is weak and inexperienced in their eyes."

—Excerpt from Lord Claudius Dellabore's diary

Night had descended over the island, stretching its shadowy fingers across the temple grounds. The birds ceased their songs and only the warm sea breeze stirred through the leaves. The cloudless sky offered a glittering blanket of stars and a full moon that painted the grass silver.

Once Flynn finished stabling the last horse, he stopped by Fyoran's room at the back, knocking softly.

"Yes! Come in!" came the brusque reply.

He pushed the door open, popping his head inside. The metal hinges screeched softly. He'd have to oil them soon.

Fyoran was at his desk, quill in hand, a pot of ink nearby. Impatience tightened his leathery face. Flynn bowed, as he'd been taught. "The horses are in for the night. Is there anything else you'd like me to do?"

"No, that'll be all. Good work today. You're good with the horses."

Flynn bowed again, then withdrew. A weariness weighed on his shoulders as he trudged out. As the door swung shut behind him, he rubbed his neck. It had been a long day and he still felt like shit from the trial. Even after being allowed to rest for nearly two days, he still hadn't fully recovered. He woke up tired, worked himself to the bone, then collapsed into bed, waking up just as tired as before.

"Flynn!" Mira's voice called to him across the quiet night.

He blinked as she jogged over. She looked different in leathers and a sleeveless shirt. There was a little more muscle back in her body again, an energy that hadn't been there since the attack on the village. What were they doing to her?

She offered him a sheepish smile. "How are you? I'm sorry I haven't seen you since the trials. The others kept me busy and said you were resting. Is this your first day back?"

"Second," he replied. "You look good. What are they teaching you?"

The smile slipped for a second. "A lot of stuff. I can't say right now. They've forbidden it, but I don't feel useless anymore. What about you, though?"

"I feel great," he lied. "It's just been a long day today, that's all. Keeping myself busy until the next trial."

"Oh, yes! That reminds me. I've heard something about it. That's why I wanted to come and talk to you—"

"Flynn!" Tobin's voice sent a shiver down Flynn's spine.

Mira's eyes widened. "Uh, I'm not meant to be here. If he asks, just say I was asking how you were. Bye!"

Before he could stop her, she hugged him and darted off. He looked at Tobin, arms folded across his chest. The moonlight danced off his bronzed skin, playing over the lines of his muscles. Flynn's fingers itched to reach out and trace every ridge and line to linger over the slight spattering of freckles. It was madness, truly wonderful *madness.*

"What did she want?" Tobin asked gruffly.

"We've spoken little these past few days. She was just worried and wanted to see how I was," Flynn replied.

"Did she?" A note of skepticism curled Tobin's words, making Flynn's stomach flip. "What a concerned friend."

"Is Mathias after me?" Flynn asked restlessly, resisting the urge to do something truly stupid.

Like reaching out and trying to kiss Tobin.

Tobin rolled his eyes. "I came here of my own accord."

A snort burst from Flynn's lips. He slapped a hand to his mouth, dropping it once he felt the smile finally go. "Sorry."

"Is that amusing to you?" Tobin's words lacked their usual bite.

"A little, but if Mathias didn't send you? Why are you here?"

Tobin fell silent, glancing away with a strangely shy expression. The tips of his ears turned red. "Meet me at dawn at the gates of the temple."

"What are we doing?" Flynn leaned in, curious.

Tobin looked at him, that burning intensity stealing the air from his chest. "You'll see."

He didn't have to worry about sleeping in. His body had always, without fail, woke him before the sun even peeked over the horizon. By the time he hauled on fresh clothes and hurried out to the meeting point, Tobin had arrived. He leaned against one of the pillars, the twilight glow catching the wisps of hair dangling around his face.

Flynn drank the sight in. Tobin in his sleeveless tunic, the muscled arms folded across his broad chest, a belt tied off at his narrow hips. His pants hugged those strong legs, revealing every muscle...and shape.

Spirits, I'm doomed.

"Do you plan to stare all morning?" Tobin slanted his head to the side, that gaze lazily lifting.

Heat pricked the tips of Flynn's ears as he cleared his throat and jogged over. "Where are we going?"

Tobin glanced about the quiet temple grounds before looking back at him. "Be patient."

It was all he got before Tobin pushed off the pillar and set off. Flynn trailed behind, biting back the questions as they left the grounds. The warm, fragrant air of the forest filled every breath, and soon he heard the quiet rustle of birds as they awakened. Gentle songs wafted through the leaves, and rabbits darted among the undergrowth.

They veered off the main path and onto a barely worn track. Tobin tramped ahead, giving Flynn a fine view from behind. Even as the air rapidly warmed and sweat gathered on his brow, he didn't mind. Curiosity fluttered in his chest, a little bird restless to escape. More than once, he nearly asked where they were going, but decided against it. Tobin likely would not say, anyway.

It was a short-lived concern.

The trees fell away, yielding to a clearing.

His jaw dropped. A sheer cliff cut off one section of the space, revealing a sprawling view of the island, stretching out in its jewel-green brilliance. In the distance, dotted on the glittering sea he spotted what looked like hundreds of islands running to the horizon.

The sun eventually emerged from the dark and painted the sky in rich shades of burnished orange and red. Shadows retreated, exposing the towering peaks of the larger islands, like hands reaching for the heavens.

"Spirits above," he murmured in awe.

A faint thud drew his gaze. Tobin had dropped the bag onto the ground and was kneeling to open it up. He dug out two wooden swords and stood back up, handing one to Flynn.

"Take this," was all Tobin said.

His fingers brushed Tobin's, sending shivers skittering right up his arm. He yanked back the sword, trying to quell the traitorous flip of his heart. Not that Tobin showed any reaction as he stepped back, tightening one hand on the hilt.

"What's this for?"

"Your second trial. The test of your body." Tobin paused, his gaze dropping for a split second, and Flynn felt fire heat his cheeks. It lifted as quickly as it had dipped, the moment gone.

Flynn swallowed the lump lodged in his throat. They'd come to the clearing under the cover of darkness, and he got a distinct impression it was so they weren't seen.

"Why all the secrecy?" he asked.

Tobin lifted his sword, and there was a spark of challenge in those sunset eyes. "There isn't much time until your next trial. Do you wish to talk or train?"

Sweat dripped from Flynn's body as he collapsed onto the grass. They'd gone through more movements than he could keep track of. Side by side, Tobin would move through a set first, then do it again slowly so that Flynn could try to mirror it.

Finally, he'd been given a break. Tobin retrieved a waterskin from his bag and handed it over, his shadow momentarily shielding Flynn from the sun.

Flynn grabbed the water and greedily gulped it down. As he handed it back, their hands touched, and like before, his heart thundered, and awareness rippled across his skin. Their eyes locked. Neither moved.

The wind whipped strands of Tobin's hair across his face, leaving Flynn itching to brush it aside so that he might stare into those eyes a little more. What secrets might he see? He wanted to ask why Tobin had been in his room after the trial, asleep in that chair, as if keeping watch. Why did the hardened edge in his voice seem softer than before? And finally, why did he cast lingering glances when he thought Flynn wasn't paying attention?

"Tobin?" Those very curiosities danced along his lips.

The spell shattered and Tobin stepped back, taking the waterskin with him and stashing it back in the bag. Flynn could only watch with bated breath as Tobin rose once more, slower, as if he were dragging out the moment.

"I thought you'd have more stamina," mused Tobin.

Flynn sputtered, coughing as a few droplets caught the back of his throat. "What?"

Tobin came back over. "Climbers. I know it's been a trying few weeks, but after a few hours of this, you look exhausted."

"I'm fine," argued Flynn, jumping up.

The world spun, sending him tipping forward straight into Tobin. Fire burst in his cheeks as his hands shot up, trying to steady himself, only to press onto Tobin's firm and very defined chest. Flynn pulled away, but Tobin grabbed his arm. Heart thumping, he swallowed hard, peering up slowly.

Tobin's molten eyes caught his, stealing the breath from his chest. All sense scattered. His mind scrambled, but rather than form any sensible word, Flynn's gaze dropped to Tobin's mouth.

Fuck.

CHAPTER 37

"War has descended on the Azradan court. All eyes are on the young queen, who sits with a quiet confidence in her eyes as if we are all right where she wants us to be. We might have schemed for a new ruler, but have we made a terrible mistake?"
—Excerpt from Lord Claudius Dellabore's diary

The afternoon was dedicated to Sybilla's patrol of the wall, shadowed by her guards. Oren said nothing at her side, though more than once she caught him glancing at her. She didn't know what to make of his attention, nor did General Galen make any remark on it, if he even saw it at all. The old warrior, with his flint-gray eyes and leathery face, was another who was difficult to read.

Galen marched beside her along the wall as they discussed the preparations being made to defend the city. She listened attentively, asking an occasional question. When they reached the end of their patrol, she paused and leaned against the wall. It was there, lost in her thought, shadowed by her guards, that someone called her name.

When she turned, a runner approached the guards first and stopped, bowing deeply. "A message from Lady Adara."

One of the guards moved forward, collecting the missive. The runner bowed once more, then hurried off. Oren glanced at the letter before handing it over. Their eyes locked, and she glimpsed the flecks of gold in his eyes. How had she not noticed that before?

Oren pulled away first, inclining his head in a slight bow before returning to his position. She returned her attention to the missive in her hand.

The girl, Ellie, has run off from the mansion. It seems she discovered she has magical abilities and was in a state of panic. Wren and Lorca have not found her yet. Reports have come that they went to Lord Delmont's home. Seek your advice on how to proceed.

Lady Adara.

Sybilla read the letter twice more, then folded it and tucked it into a pocket in her cloak. She turned to Galen. "Unfortunately, I cannot visit your men at the barracks. Please give them my deepest apologies. I am required back at the mansion."

Once it had been determined that no one knew where Ellie had run off to, and she'd sifted through the mountain of letters on her desk, Sybilla rose and donned her cloak. Night had fallen, and the fire in her office was sputtering its final breaths.

It was time.

Under the cover of the moonless night, she crept from the mansion, unseen by her guards. Hurrying down the shadowed streets, she took care to avoid the patrols of her men. A few blocks away from the mansion she came to an old, long-abandoned temple.

Slipping along the side, she came to the back door, almost hidden by a thick growth of ivy. Pulling the leaves away, she entered. Darkness met her, and cold, stale air invaded her lungs. Inching forward, she snapped her fingers, summoning a small orb of light. The shadows retreated to reveal what was once the main hall.

The wooden floors creaked as she walked over to a small wooden doorway and hurried through. A set of stairs descended into the basement and at the bottom, the light of a crackling fire illuminated a sprawling room. An old table, along with some chairs, was set off in one corner. They were the only furnishings within the otherwise sparse space.

Her gaze slid to the woman standing by the fire, wearing a flowing green gown. A sheer golden cape fell over her slender shoulders, sparkling in the firelight. The amber glow from the flames danced on her golden skin. It caught the stray strands of brown hair escaping from a neat braid. Although she was shorter than Sybilla, with a thicker shape, an ancient and immense power radiated off her.

The weight of it made Sybilla drop her gaze, and she bowed respectfully. "Spirit, I have come, but I have not gathered all that you asked."

The spirit turned slowly, luminous golden eyes staring back, unreadable. "There is a growing darkness in this city. You had vowed to end it."

"There were complications," said Sybilla, her cheeks reddening. "But the threat has already been reduced."

"No, it has not," said the spirit, turning back to the fire. "I can sense it. This evil is growing, reaching out. It taints everything it touches."

The spirit fell silent once more, a grimness pinched those ethereal features. Her lips opened, but then shut as if she was unsure how to proceed.

"If you have any insight into what I need to do."

"You know I can only help you so much. If I push too hard, I shall burn the tether we have created and the others will know I am here."

Sybilla shoved down the memory of her standing over the bodies, bloodied knife in one hand, a heart in the other. Desecration of the dead had always been one of the greatest taboos growing up in the caravan.

"Spirit, why did you summon me?" she asked after a pause.

"To hasten your work. This power grows in the city and if it is what I precisely fear it to be, then time is running out."

CHAPTER 38

"Queen Nimue is an unknown force and I find myself uneasy with the truths of our past that I must burden her with."
—Excerpt from Keeper Amara's diary

When Flynn finished his lessons with Mathias, he was surprised to find Tobin waiting for him outside. The maddening fae resembled a proud statue, with his strong hands clasped behind his back. He faced away from Flynn, and appeared to be gazing upon the murals of Flynn's demonic family with an unreadable expression.

It gave Flynn a moment to study him; the hard lines of his body, the severe expression always on his face, the tousled curls impossible to tame. He was otherworldly, and Flynn couldn't stifle the rush of heat coursing through his blood as he drew closer. It was as though he were inevitably drawn, enraptured by Tobin's very being and that even if he tried, he doubted he would be able to stay away.

Tobin turned abruptly, blinking quickly, as if dispelling a vision, and he levelled a fathomless gaze upon Flynn. His golden eyes darkened as if they were burrowing under Flynn's skin, peeling back all his defenses. "Come with me."

That imperious tone pricked at Flynn. "Where?"

"You have a new task," was all Tobin said as he set off.

Flynn sighed and jogged after him, falling into step as he followed him down the hallway. Shadows danced around them down the dimly lit path, the blue witchlights glowing as they drew nearer. As they passed, the lights sputtered out behind them. Only the soft sound of their footfalls broke the silence as they descended deeper into the temple.

They entered a prayer chamber with a domed roof. Several priestesses were kneeling before the statues of three unfamiliar figures, placing offerings and lighting candles. They were not the spirits on the pillars. These were different. The first was a woman with vines wrapped around her, and a blooming flower carved delicately in her hand. Flynn stopped for a closer look. Next to the woman, another woman stood wearing a warrior's garb and bearing a sword. The last was a man dressed in flowing robes, his hands spread wide, with a witchlight glowing in each palm.

A couple of priestesses sang softly, their ethereal voices like a siren's call. Flynn nearly asked to stay, but Tobin had already slipped down another hall, so he hurried after him.

"What were they doing?" he asked when the hall widened, allowing him to talk beside Tobin. "And who were they?"

Tobin didn't answer as they rounded a corner and came to a pair of dark wooden doors. He pushed one open, then held it open, shadows falling over his face, but those eyes found him, burning intensely once more. Flynn felt them on him as he proceeded into the room...and he stilled.

Witchlights flickered to life, chasing back the shadows, revealing the cavernous space level by level.

A dome-shaped library with an enormous hole in the middle, dropping several levels. Hundreds of shelves surrounded him neatly packed with scrolls. It was more books than he'd ever seen. He stepped to the railing, the chamber with the strange statues momentarily forgotten, and peered down.

He let himself breathe, savoring the smell of old books. Ancient knowledge whispered to him. He wanted to snatch up a hundred books and lose himself among them. It would be so easy.

"You like this place?" Tobin asked softly.

Flynn smiled over his shoulder. "I used to covet the few books my mother had. I must've read them all a hundred times. I tried to get my father to have the merchant bring some more, but he never did. Once I began my schooling, I found more books, but it was never enough. Here, I suspect that would not be an issue." Dark thoughts spilled into his mood. "But you didn't bring me here to appreciate this. You said this is for work."

Tobin drifted beside him, haunting in the blue glow. His hands slid onto the railing, clutching at it firmly, as he leaned forward, his shoulders flexing beneath his tunic. Flynn tried not to stare, but it was hard. He shifted uncomfortably, his pants tightening.

"We all speak the common tongue, courtesy of the Empress, but that is not our natural tongue. Mathias wishes you to learn our language and to learn of our history." He paused for a moment, his brow furrowing before he went on saying, "I have been tasked to assist in your lessons. You will still have some classes with Mathias, but now myself as well."

Flynn grinned. "Did you upset Mathias?"

Tobin blinked. "What?"

"This is a punishment for you, I'm assuming," Flynn said. "That's okay. I'll try not to be too frustrating a student."

Tobin opened his mouth as if to say something, then with a sigh, he gestured for Flynn to follow him. They descended two levels and walked over to an alcove. A table with two chairs stood in the middle.

"Take a seat," Tobin said.

Flynn did as he was told, watching Tobin drift between the shelves, running a hand along the books and scrolls. Every so often he plucked a book out, adding it to the growing number in his arms. When he had a pile so huge he could barely carry it, he returned to the table and set them down in front of Flynn.

"This should be enough to start with. It's all in the common tongue, so you should be able to read it easily," Tobin murmured, then stepped back, clasping his hands behind his back once more. "I must retrieve some other items for you, but I will not be long. Do not wander, for there are more than just priestesses moving about in the dark."

Before Flynn could ask him what he meant, Tobin had moved away, abandoning him to the pile of ancient texts.

An hour at least passed before Tobin reappeared, his arms laden with more books and a couple of scrolls. Flynn lifted his head, squinting over the pile of books, his mind momentarily lost in the history he'd been devouring. He rose to inspect the others Tobin had brought. More history texts. Excitement skittered through his veins, pricking his fingers.

"And here I thought you hated me," Flynn murmured teasingly.

Tobin blinked, his attention shifting to the opened book on the table. "You have read that much already?"

Flynn smiled. "Don't sound so surprised. I have some questions, though. I found several mentions of the old gods. When I was young, I heard a few stories in the village about them, but my mother never enjoyed talking about them. Were those the statues I saw?"

"Yes. Lyria, the Demon Goddess of Death; Aislynn, the Primal Goddess of Chaos and Order; and Ronan, the Spirit God of Life. It was a decree of the spirits that we have a chamber for them, and it has been a long part of our ceremonies to place offerings, though these gods have long since passed from the living."

Flynn sat back in his chair, mulling this over. All his life he'd worshipped the spirits, at least in a basic sense, but it wasn't so common in the village. He hadn't thought it strange until now. "But why?"

"It was the last command your father gave the temple before he returned to Danomir over thirty years ago," Tobin said with a shrug. "And why should we not offer the gods, even in death, some measure of thanks? Through their collective sacrifice, they divided the Chaos Realm, thus forming the spirit, demon, and primal realm. There are many lessons to be learned through their story, some that you should take to heart for your trials."

This information gave Flynn more questions, and his frown deepened. "But *why* did they split the Chaos Realm?"

Tobin shrugged. "That has been debated for years. It's hard to say where the truth is. Time has claimed much of it, and perhaps we will never know."

He didn't know what to make of that or of the burning gaze that was leveled on him. It made him restless, the hairs on his arms lifting. Tobin didn't look away...and Flynn couldn't either. The library air crackled with an undercurrent of tension. Something had shifted between them.

Clearing his throat, he returned his focus to the book and tried to lose himself once more. It was hard. Tobin didn't leave; instead, he slid into a chair and took up a book. Every breath Flynn took was thick with Tobin's scent; a spiced, earthy scent purfumed the air, and slowly nudged Flynn to madness. How was he expected to think clearly with Tobin sitting so damn close? He tried not to be so affected but it felt like a losing battle.

Hours passed between them, and soon Flynn realized he enjoyed the companionable silence. More than once he felt Tobin glance up, his gaze lingering until Flynn lifted his head, then Tobin would return his focus to the book. He didn't mind. It felt exciting, each glance a thrill fluttering in his chest.

Tobin set his book down. "You're wrong."

Flynn didn't dare to look up as his heart raced. "About?"

"This being a punishment." Tobin cleared his throat, then glanced away and rubbed the back his neck. "I offered."

At that, he looked up, his brow lifting. "Why? From the moment I arrived, you haven't...well, I thought you disliked me."

"I don't." Tobin clammed up again as he lifted the book. "I just wanted you to know that I chose this. To help, I mean."

"Why?" Flynn asked again. He wasn't sure why he suddenly had to know, why it mattered, but he couldn't stop the question from tumbling out.

At that, Tobin had no reply.

The following day, they trained with swords. Tobin had him working through set after set, though Flynn had the distinct impression he had scarcely improved. It all felt so awkward, and more than once he ended up on his ass. That he didn't mind because Tobin would loom over him, framed by the sun, and he rather enjoyed the view. Even though his pants tightened uncomfortably, he was grateful they were snug enough that he wasn't too obvious in his enjoyment of the moment.

Those moments never lasted long before they were sparring once more. Their swords crashed together in ringing songs, broken only by haggard breaths and Flynn unceremoniously hitting the ground. He parried as best he could, driving in whenever he glimpsed an opening. While sweat dripped down his chest, Tobin pressed forward, elegantly brutal and singularly focused. He was a predator of muscle, achingly beautiful and thrilling all the same.

Heat burned through his arms, his grip nearly loosening on the hilt. He had to figure out a way to get Tobin down—and fast. But how? The man moved so damn fast, his feet scarcely touched the ground. Any time Flynn thought he was close enough to land a decent blow, Tobin danced out of the way. He gritted his teeth.

Tobin sprinted forward, dropping low at the last second. Flynn had no time to react, as his feet were knocked out from underneath him, and he was sent careening to the ground. Stars crashed over his vision as his head smacked the earth, and the air rushed from his lungs. The sword was wrenched from his hands, and a weight suddenly bore down on him. He couldn't move. Tobin had him pinned.

He stared up his chest heaving desperately to rake in the air, straining to get free. Tobin remained as still as a statue, unflinching from his attempts to escape. Flynn stilled, hoping that might make the grip on him loosen. It didn't. A curse slipped from his lips.

"Now what?" he asked.

Tobin gave a small smile. "Now, you learn how to escape this. Watch closely."

CHAPTER 39

"War is a game I enjoy. It's a game, played out in blood, battles, and spies."
—Excerpt from Queen Nimue's diary

It was the last place that Nimue wanted to be, even as she sat there with her fingers threaded with Lorca beneath the table. The meeting room for this team she had found herself in was sparsely furnished and reminded her of the war rooms back at her palace. It had the same heavy air, thick with notes of ink and old maps and books dug up from libraries long ignored.

When Sylvie and Dorian swept into the room, moving with the predatory grace akin to a wyvern, Nora followed close behind. The young Druid flashed her a comforting smile before sliding into the seat between her guardians.

Nimue wanted nothing more than to be out in the city, but it was obvious her demonic abilities were pathetically dismal at the moment and she would be no good to her sister in her present condition. Instead, Claudius and Titania were on the hunt.

What she could do with the team, however, was something she was capable of. Sybilla might play the role of the manipulator well, hiding it beneath passionate speeches and good intentions, but Nimue had played it for much longer. It was time to use the team to her advantage, for the threat to her sister's safety was real.

"I know you have all heard what has happened to my sister by now. What you must know is that a demon appears to have her." She left out the connection she had, and some of the threats made. "That a demon is strong enough to possess someone is concerning, and I would hazard a guess is likely the one behind the attacks. It is at least an option I think we ought to consider."

Silence descended in the room, heavy with unspoken questions. She didn't miss the way Sylvie leaned back in her chair, casting Dorian a lingering look. A silent conversation played out between them, then Sylvie sat back up, her face once more unreadable. Did she suspect there was more to the story?

Nora cleared her throat, breaking Nimue's wandering thoughts. "We should return to the last site and see if there is anything we missed."

Dorian released a heavy breath. "There could be more traps."

The city is probably littered with them. She kept that thought silent. "We keep our guard up. Nora is right. We should return to the site and see if there is anything we missed. We're two steps behind this individual and if we want to stand a chance at beating them, we need to figure out their plan, and fast."

The tunnels were eerily quiet as the team retraced their steps. Nimue took the lead, with Lorca behind her. At the door, the darkness stirred deep within her soul. The air crackled with demonic magic, flipping her stomach into knots. The beast within her hissed softly, then retreated with a whining cry deeper into her soul.

Something wasn't right. She raised one hand, gesturing for everyone to stop.

"Nimue?" Lorca drew closer while the others held back. "What is it?"

"Watch my back," she said, pushing the door open gingerly.

"Always."

She entered first, drawing her swords slowly in a metallic hiss, and scanned the room choked with shadows. A warm firelight sputtered to life behind her, illuminating the surroundings in an amber glow.

Something she couldn't pin raked down her spine. It was a presence she swore she had felt before.

When no monster appeared, and a trap didn't immediately spring out to kill her, she called for the others to join her. As their soft footfalls echoed across the stone, Nimue moved deeper into the room. The demon crack was long gone, though the residual traces still lingered in the air, brushing her skin.

At the base of where the crack once burned, the symbol was still there. Carved into the stone, several feet wide, and etched with markings she knew as intimately as her broken soul. She'd glimpsed markings for it before, but finally, she was able to examine the marking she knew so well, and what it meant.

A Hell Gate.

More specifically, a strengthening spell for the crack. In its current spot, it was likely used to stabilize the smaller demon cracks dotted around the city, a way to ensure they didn't collapse after the demons came through.

Deep down, she knew why the demons were in the city. Someone wanted to claim the last demon throne and to do that, they had to kill Nimue. Once they had all four thrones under their power, they would possess all the magic of Lyria, the goddess who forged their realm. But what she didn't know was what they would do once they had achieved that.

The uncertainties loomed in her mind like a storm without end, set to devour her whole.

Tearing her gaze away, she studied every inch of the carved walls. Many were so badly faded that she could barely glean a few spells from them, and none offered any comfort. Either this demon had been in the primal realm for some time or they possessed enough power to manipulate the demon attacks from the demon realm.

With a heavy sigh, she followed the others into the room where the trap had been sprung. Nimue stared at the bodies, none of which had yet rotted.

She turned to the others. "They should have festered by now."

"I don't like the feel of this," Lorca murmured.

"In that, we agree." Nimue moved to the stone table, where the warning still glistened in glossy blood. "The markings on the walls and the floor tell me this was here long ago—perhaps when the city was built—but why now? Are they capitalizing on the rebellion?"

She cast him a long look. *Or is that the cause?*

Lorca's brow furrowed. *Do you think Sybilla might be behind this?*

At that, she shook her head. *No, but all of this feels far too organized.*

Just what the hell did this demon want? To conquer this realm, perhaps? Who knew what kind of effect bringing a whole army of demons through a Hell Gate would have? The imbalance of power would be downright destructive, perhaps enough to destroy the walls that divided the realms.

It would be carnage.

When the underground temple offered no further information, the group retreated to the surface. Beneath a cloudy gray sky, darkening with a whisper of a winter storm, and the air damp with moisture, the journey back to the mansion was a sombre one.

Walking along the eerily quiet streets, she cast a lingering look at Lorca. There was a tightness in his face that hadn't been there before, and she sensed a dull ache throbbing through his body through their bond.

"Lorca. Is anything wrong?"

"I'm okay," he said, perhaps a little too quickly, giving her a gentle smile. "Truly, I am. Once we're back, I just need to rest."

From how close he kept to her side, and that his gaze kept darting across the street, she knew he was reluctant to leave her. She chafed at the idea of being vulnerable, even as her own body betrayed her. But part of her loved that he was being protective, though she knew the foolish Dragonir was paying for it.

"You shouldn't push yourself," she whispered.

"A demon is after you—" He slammed his mouth shut, looking away.

She wanted to push him, but the hard look indicated the matter was over. At least for the moment.

"Wren! Lorca! Are you thirsty?" Nora called, drawing Nimue's focus from Lorca to where the Druid was leaning against one of the city's wells.

Like those common in the wealthier inner districts, it was ornate in its polished white stone, guarded with statues of what she suspected were spirits.

Her throat was raw and itching for a drink, so she trudged over. Nora had already filled one water skin and handed it over. Nimue took it gratefully, murmuring her thanks, and swallowing. The water wasn't as crisp as the mountains and had the faintest earthy taste, but it was fine. As she lowered the skin, her gaze snagged on the bottom of the wall.

Close to the ground, a circle of faded symbols sat around the stone. It was nearly invisible and as she kneeled, running her finger over them, something inside her turned cold.

Understanding dawned low in the pit of her gut, heavy like molten metal.

"What is it?" Nora asked innocently.

She was aware the others had wandered over, but she could not form a reply. The City of Slaves was an old city, and she had been unsure why the demon had chosen it. It wasn't the site of the Hell Gate, but it didn't need to be.

To open any gate or crack, one needed a shit load of power. For demons, that best came with blood...and what better source than a city about to be besieged? Run the streets with blood and you had all the power you required. All you'd need then was a portal to funnel all the energy the city created to wherever the Hell Gate was located.

She released a shaky breath. "I think I know what the demon's plan is."

CHAPTER 40

"There is madness in desire, which is the reason so few rulers take serious lovers. In this, I have erred. I have taken Claudius to my bed and I feel that this will not be so easily dismissed."

—Excerpt from Queen Nimue's diary

The hot sun blazed with a thick, oppressive heat. Every breath was a strain, and no matter how many Flynn took, it never felt enough. Waves rippled through the air around him as he tried to follow Tobin's instructions. Tobin glided through another set, a wooden sword in hand, graceful, poised as if he had been doing it all his life. His muscles shifted beneath a sleeveless green tunic, bare feet sliding soundlessly over the grass.

The sight nearly dropped Flynn to his knees.

Spirits above...

"The sword is an extension of you. When your back is up against the wall and your magic expended, it may just be what saves your life," Tobin said as he spun sharply, thrusting the sword forward.

The blade stopped at Flynn's throat, the point just touching.

His heart froze in his chest, the air growing still as if the entire world held its breath. As those golden depths studied him, sending a throbbing ache right through his body, he could barely think, let alone reply. The burning intensity in those eyes peeled back the walls Flynn carefully erected and peered deep into his soul. He felt stripped bare, a deer caught by a hunter's gaze.

Tobin stepped back, dropping his sword. "Now, your turn."

No other male had ever affected him the way Tobin had, and it was driving him utterly mad.

"Flynn?"

He tried to pay attention.

Flynn tightened his grip and shifted into the first movement, one foot slightly back, both hands on his sword. Drawing in a long, steady breath, the salt air sharp on his lips, he began the set. Hesitation gnawed as Flynn went through but, after a few slow swings of the sword, he froze.

Spirits, what was next?

Tobin stared at him; arms folded across his chest. "Don't stop."

Heat flooded Flynn's cheeks. Embarrassment clawed up his throat, rendering him mute once more. Every movement of Tobin's he tried to mimic felt so awkward. As a climber, that had been how he'd learned but this? Swordplay felt so unnatural to him. Even the weight of the wooden sword felt jarring. How he was meant to wield a metal one with enough confidence to win a fight he had no idea.

His hands dropped, the sword hitting his thigh. "I...I forgot."

Tobin's gaze hardened, his jaw twitching. Flynn braced himself for a scathing remark. It never came as Tobin released a long breath, then took up position beside him. He held up his sword, gesturing for Flynn to do the same. "Follow me and watch closely."

The hours stretched on agonizingly in the heat. Sweat poured off Flynn, enough that he'd stripped off his tunic and rolled up his pants to his knees. Even then, the humid breeze offered little in the way of relief. Tobin was several feet away, waiting as Flynn took a drink of water, a picture of composure in the sun. He'd tied his hair back to the nape of his neck an hour ago, which distracted Flynn to no end, who imagined pulling that tie loose and burying his fingers in Tobin's hair.

Which was an annoying fantasy to have, since he suspected Tobin wouldn't let him even touch him. Let alone get close enough to consider it.

"Are you rested enough?" Tobin asked, impatience edging his words.

Flynn plugged the waterskin, then set it back down in the shade and rose once more. The question that had been burning his lips rose without warning and spilled out. "Why are you training me?"

Tobin stilled. "I explained."

"I understand that this is for my next trial, but why are you the one training me?" He didn't know what to make of Tobin. Since their near kiss, things had been *strange.* Not hostile, but whatever gentleness had been there briefly was gone. He was just so damn *confused.*

A heavy silence fell between them. Tobin spun on his heel, stalking out of the clearing. "Grab your things. There is something you must see."

Flynn barely had any time to grab the water, their satchel of food, and his wooden sword before he had to chase after Tobin. The man set a brutal pace as they cut down a barely worn path through the dense foliage. A few times Tobin held out a hand...and the bushes *moved.* They descended the mountain in silence.

The bird's warbling cries echoed through the ancient forest. Their tunes were softer than the shrieking cries of those back home. But he whistled along to the melody all the same.

The dense canopy above cooled the air, offering the first bit of relief all day. Finally, the trees thinned, yielding to a rocky beach fronting a small bay. Cliffs covered by thick foliage encircled the beach, with a tiny mouth opening to the seas beyond. A rock, taller than the cliffs, jutted from the middle of it.

He was staring at it before he realized Tobin had shed his tunic and pants, down to his loincloth, and was wading into the water. Flynn froze, the sunlight glinting over Tobin's back...and scars. Faded white lines mottled the hardened muscle. Dozens of them. His stomach clenched at the sight. Who had done that to him?

"Can you swim?"

Flynn blinked, realizing that Tobin had turned and stood waist-deep in the water. "Uh, no."

"Very well. Shed your clothes down to your cloth and leave the rest by the shore." Tobin turned back to face the rock but didn't move.

Was he offering Flynn some privacy?

Flynn took off the pants, then tucked them in the satchel with the wrapped food and tunic. He pulled off his boots, throwing them aside before he waded nervously into the water. It had been a little easier on the boat. Something solid beneath his feet. Though whenever he'd looked over the railing and looked into the depths of the seas, the bottom out of sight, he shivered.

Give him the towering cliffs any day.

At least that was something solid to hold on to.

His feet slipped over loose pebbles, sending him staggering forward and throwing his arms wide as if that might save him. A string of curses tumbled from his lips as he straightened up, meeting Tobin's...*smile.* Yet as quickly as it had appeared, it slipped beneath a frown, as if he'd caught himself smiling and hated it.

Tobin held out a hand. "Trust me."

There was warmth in those two little words that had Flynn reaching out, taking Tobin's hand. With more gentleness than he'd expected, Tobin led him deeper into the water until his feet lost the ground completely. Terror squeezed through his heart like a thousand daggers stabbing him at once. He lurched back, desperate to feel the land again. Tobin tugged him forward and to his relief, he floated.

Tobin launched himself forward, still holding Flynn, and began to swim. Flynn was pulled onto his belly through the water and after a bit of fumbling, he figured out how to keep his head up. Somehow, Tobin was pulling him along and swimming with one arm, and kicking easily. Flynn focused on him, and not the deep water beneath him and what was probably swimming around him.

To his relief, it was soon over, and Tobin pressed Flynn's hand onto a rock. Instinctively, Flynn hauled himself onto it and scrambled up. The faster he was out of the water, the better. The past few weeks restored some condition to his muscles, but he was still weak. Halfway up the cliff face, his legs and arms burned, though he relished the heat. Closer to the top, he let go with one hand and looked back out across the water.

It felt good to be climbing again.

"Do you plan on hanging there all day? There's further to go," Tobin asked.

Tobin climbed up past him. The sight of his back and arms working as he powered up made Flynn breathless. He hung there for a moment, entranced. A man had no right to look *that* good climbing shirtless.

He twisted back to face the cliff and climbed after him. When he reached the top, he hauled himself over the edge. Tobin was waiting for him, framed by the midday sun. Some curls had come free of the tie and clung to his skin.

Flynn pushed himself up to stand and moved to Tobin's side—there, he followed that unreadable gaze across the glittering ocean to the next island. A thin band of mist swirled around its shores, yielding to a pebbled beach and steep hills of dark green foliage. It looked almost normal until his gaze snagged on a section of gray stone. Then more came into focus and he realized what he was looking at.

Ruins.

Not just a village, either, but a small city. A stone castle was built into the side of a cliff and stretched down into the forest below. Walls had chunks missing, towers long destroyed. Black marks charred the stone.

"What is that?"

Tobin's hands curled into fists, his gaze darkening. "Home. Well, what's left of it. My people thought that when our capital fell to the Empress's Gray Army, they would stop there and we'd be safe." His gaze dropped to his hands. "We were wrong."

Flynn's heart ached for the fae who stared at the ruins of his home. He was afraid to ask what happened to his family when none in the temple appeared that close to him. Tobin always stood apart or just watched from the shadows, there but never quite present.

"When did it happen?" Flynn asked gently.

Tobin's gaze slid to him. "Ten years ago." There was a pause, and Tobin spoke again, his voice low and gravelly. "You're wrong, you know? I don't hate you."

"You could've fooled me." The corner of Flynn's mouth nearly tipped up. "So, if not hate, then what?"

But that seemed the wrong question to ask. Tobin's gaze darted away, as though a part of him was retreating. "My people tried to fight back in the beginning.

For a time, it worked, but whenever it got too big or threatening, the Gray Army returned. They'd burn anyone who defied them, or who was considered a threat." He sat down on the stone as if the past was too heavy on his shoulders. "We used to have so much magic, but after that first attack, something changed. Now, every year we grow weaker and weaker. More fae are being born without magic. We were losing hope for anything—then you appeared."

Flynn dropped beside him. "Me? But I can't be...well, I'm doing this magic for my people. I have to save them."

Tobin twisted to look at him, a wildness flaring in his eyes. "That's *why* I was so mad when I saw you. We finally had someone with strong magic, but they had no interest in our struggle. It felt like a final cruel blow by the spirits."

"So why train me? Why the change of heart?" Flynn replied heatedly.

There was a heavy silence before the reply came. "Because I don't want you as my enemy."

Flynn's mind whirled with Tobin's words until his soul ached, tearing itself in two. How could he save Fenware and the fae? He was just *one* man, and he still had two trials to survive. It was a long road before he was ready to save anyone.

"Tobin, you know I can't stay. Once I have the power I need, I have to return to free my people. I can't..." *I can't be the hero you want me to be.*

He expected an angry response for Tobin to lash out, but only silence filled the void between them. Resignation darkened Tobin's face as he drew his knees up, resting his chin there. It made him seem younger...and yet so very tired.

But I could return, he thought. After his people were safe. He *could* come back. Perhaps that was his purpose, once the dust settled. The life of a climber had felt right, but he'd always wondered if he could be more. But that desire had been so absurd and selfish given the state of their crop. Why look elsewhere when his people needed him?

Tobin sighed. "Do you want to know what reason the Empress gave us in the end?"

There was a deep agony in that question. It filled the space between them, poignant. Shadows close in around Tobin, as though he were falling into an old memory. Flynn wanted to reach for him, but couldn't move.

Instead, he asked, "what did she say?"

Tobin smiled bitterly. "One of her officials said we'd committed an act of rebellion, that our work was treasonous. Which was absurd. None of my family's work was against the throne, but they murdered everyone anyway."

Flynn leaned in. "What was your family's work?"

"They had spent generations looking into the stories of the gods. They're long dead now, but we know they existed and that the three of them split the Chaos Realm to form the three realms we know." Tobin laughed harshly, the bitter smile not touching his eyes. "Apparently, *that* was enough to have my family butchered. It made no sense. None of it was critical of the crown."

And then I came, with the promise of power but no interest to help, thought Flynn guiltily.

That promise to help nearly rose to his lips but was cut off. He just couldn't say the words, even though his heart spoke them.

"You belong with your people. That I can respect, as I belong here, with mine." The hollow note in Tobin's voice clawed at Flynn's heart. "That is how things must be."

Later that night, Tobin led him back to the temple grounds. Everyone had retired for the night and all the lanterns were snuffed out. Silver moonlit lit the sprawling grounds, catching on the portraits painted on the pillars. His father's eyes stared him down as he walked with Tobin back to the main temple.

As they neared the steps, Tobin stopped. "I have something I must do, but we will train again tomorrow. After the evening meal."

"Is there anything I can help with?"

Tobin blinked. "Uh, no, no, it's fine."

Before Flynn could press further, Tobin hurried off toward one of the huts. When he was out of view, Flynn wrenched his gaze away and started toward the temple. His foot touched the first step when a shadow flashed in the corner of his eye. He spun, but a hand was slammed against his mouth, silencing him.

Mira's blue eyes met his. She held her hand there for a moment, then stepped back, flashing a grin. "Impressed?"

"A little. Is that what they're teaching you? To fight?"

"I can't say, but I will when I can. So, tell me, where were you? I went to your little training area, but you weren't there." Mira leaned in close and touched his hair. "Have you been *swimming?*"

"No, well, yes. I didn't swim. Tobin helped, but that doesn't matter." He flushed a bright red and looked away. "Did I miss anything?"

"Some of the fae were on edge today, kept talking in their tongue around me. I think something has them spooked, but they wouldn't tell me what. I'm trying to learn their language but it's difficult," Mira said, frowning. "Has Tobin said anything?"

"We didn't talk about the present. Do you think it's something serious?"

She shrugged. "Maybe. I'll keep my ears sharp but, back to you, how *is* training going?"

"Woeful. I can't swing a sword to save myself," he confessed. "I have no idea how I'm meant to win this second trial or even the third. I feel as though I beat the first by chance." He felt the sting of her punch in his arm before he saw it. "Ow! What was that for?"

"For doubting yourself," she replied. Her fiery expression softened. "You're stronger than you think, Flynn. So am I. We're here for a reason: to gain skills so we can save our people. You have your magic, and me? Well, I'm figuring that out, but we won't save anyone if we doubt ourselves."

"When did you get so wise?"

The corner of her mouth lifted, pride glimmering in her cerulean eyes. "I've always been wise and clever, if I do say so myself. It's time for you to realize the same about yourself."

CHAPTER 41

Today we face King Fenrys in battle. This is our first test of strength. We must not lose, lest we risk all that we've built. I lead my soldiers into battle. We will arise victoriously and lay waste to his army.

—Excerpt from Commander Titania's diary

As the sun retreated beyond the horizon, plunging the land into darkness, Aziah slipped into the Gray Army's camp. Concealed by magic, she dashed unseen past a patrol of soldiers and behind a row of tents. The ashy scents of crackling fires carried on the bitter breeze as it swept through the camp. The chill cut through her clothes, sinking its talons deep into her bones.

She jogged past the tents, slowing as she passed fires where soldiers gathered, holding her breath until she passed out of earshot. These weren't just regular men. The Empress had gifted them with demonic magic, forging an army of nearly immortal soldiers. These were the same men who had burned the fae capital, Toranelle, to the ground.

Though she cursed the magical wards that prevented her from using her portals, she relished moving among the shadows once more. Just as Gabriel had taught her all those years ago.

Her heart ached at the thought of her mate, and though she prayed to the spirits that they kept him safe on whatever mission he was on, experience had taught her better. All she could do was trust that they would meet again—in this life or the next.

She moved past the last row of tents reserved for the lower ranks. A wide path met her, a clear separation from the rest of the camp where the higher ranks dwelled, along with the tents for supplies and meetings. She moved swiftly into the next section. There were fewer soldiers around, save for the patrols that marched past.

Just as she moved to cross another path, she jumped back sharply as a patrol marched past. Her heart slammed into her ribs, the blood roaring in her ears.

Eyeing them from the shadows, she watched them march on...until one of them stopped dead. The rest followed. The first man turned, dark eyes peering out through his gray hood—the uniform of this army. He stared in her direction as if he could see her. Aziah held her breath until the man turned once more, murmuring something to the others.

They marched on.

She set off again. Her heart raced until she was deeper into that part of the camp. Fortunately, there were no more close calls with patrols, and she glided like a wraith through the labyrinth of tents. At the edge of the camp, she arrived at a wooden wall guarding the slave quarters. A walkway ran along the top, manned with roaming guards.

One gate marked the entrance. More guards stood watch at the bottom, armed to the teeth with swords and daggers. It wasn't a matter of a distraction. Chances were, given it was after dark, the gates would likely remain closed.

Mulling over her options, she edged her way along the length of the wall, hunting for a way in. The posts used were smooth, with no holds for her to climb.

She reached the other side of the slave encampment and discovered another heavily guarded gate. One stood at the front of the temple construction, the face of which was carved into the cliff face. Scaffolding still covered most of it, rising high. How many had fallen from it in order to carve all the intricate markings on the pillar?

Tearing her gaze away, she studied the gate.

She'd have to wait until the guards changed. From her reconnaissance before entering the camp, most appeared to rotate on a regular four-hour watch. There was a slight delay across the camp as this happened. She'd hoped to find a way in without having to use the rotation as her entry. Plenty of things that could go wrong if she made a mistake.

Some things were worse than death.

It was a long, bitter wait before the guard rotation occurred. Aziah stood at the side, poised for action. Her heart leaped as she spied the change coming. A couple of dozen soldiers approached the entrance. One of the guards by the gate shouted to the ones on duty, and moments later, the gates scraped open.

Aziah took her chance, slipping in just as a group of men came out. She didn't dare to look back as she ducked to the first slave quarter, wasting no time as she carefully pressed her palm against the lock on the door. It clicked open.

With a deep breath, she stepped inside. Only a thin band of moonlight squeezed in through a narrow open window at the top. A cold breeze spilled in, a white breath swirling around her face as she took in the row of bodies huddled together. All were men, collared and chained together. They whispered together in fear, having seen the door open but no one enter.

She slowly dispelled the surrounding magic, materializing before them. Their whispers grew louder. Pressing a finger to her lips, she let a flicker of magic dance over her hand. They fell silent, watching her with wide eyes. Aziah scanned the men.

"Who here speaks the common tongue?"

Slaves were taken from across the territories that Alexandria had attacked, from remote islands and the fringes of distant kingdoms. There wasn't a guarantee that the men spoke the land's common tongue.

To her surprise and relief, a couple raised a hand. She crept to the first one and kneeled before him. "I'm looking for a group of slaves brought here a few weeks ago. They wouldn't have been split up. Do you know where I might find them?"

The man hesitated, the others around him watching him with owlish eyes. "You're not here to rescue us?"

"I wish I could, but I am alone. I seek a group of slaves that would've arrived a few weeks ago and that I believe them to be kept separate." She described them as best she could from what Sybilla had given her and watched the men for any sign of recognition.

He paused once more before he spoke. "Are you freeing them?"

"No."

That answer seemed to appease him. He leaned in close. "They're being kept inside the temple itself. Wish I knew more, but that's it."

Shit. The last thing she wanted to do was enter the temple. It had been unnerving enough when she'd gone in with Alexandria. The walls whispered with dark magic, and she swore the dead watched her from the shadows. Misery soaked every inch of the temple.

"That is more than enough, thank you," she replied and rose without another word.

She slipped from the slave quarters, relocking it with a stab of guilt. It felt sickeningly wrong to leave them, but trying to free them by herself would only end in bloodshed. Help would come with an army.

Refusing to look back, she made her way up to the walkway via a set of wooden steps. Treading silently, she shadowed a patrolling guard, noting where his foot stepped. As he turned to continue along the next wall, she leaped over the edge, hitting the ground below with a roll. As she surged up to her feet, she ducked into the shadow of a nearby tent and let herself breathe.

Lifting her gaze to the towering structure of the temple, she felt a chill slither down her spine.

May the spirits protect me, thought Aziah. *And may those poor souls inside be alive...*

CHAPTER 42

"I will show them all—I will break King Fenrys. Soon they will all fear the name, Queen Nimue."
—Excerpt from Queen Nimue's diary

Flynn's mind repeatedly returned to the ruins Tobin had shown him as he tried to finish the mind-numbing work set for him. Candlelight sputtered, then steadied, the light dancing over the pile of books.

Tobin had asked him to catch up on the written translation work he'd begun before their training sessions. That was all he got before he was, once again, left alone in the darkness and silence.

Pinching his nose, he shoved those thoughts away and returned to the dreary effort. He'd finished a few more pages of translations by the time Tobin strode into the space, a gray cloak set on his broad shoulders. He swallowed as Tobin stopped beside him, his spiced scent filling his nose, the hairs on his neck lifting.

Tobin leaned over him, eyeing the work with a hum of approval. "You're improving."

Flynn glanced up, a smile threatening. "You sound surprised."

"We weren't sure of the level of education you might've had in a mountain village," Tobin said.

He shrugged. "Our elders encouraged education, at least in reading and writing, as well as focus on the trades required for the village. I liked it, the learning, the challenge—I used to, at least."

Tobin leaned in closer, his shoulder brushing against Flynn's. "Used to?"

His heart kept thumping hard on his chest as if it were about to jump right out and bounce across the table. All he wanted to do was grab Tobin and kiss him. Forcing away the urge, he straightened up. The effort made him press just that bit harder into Tobin's shoulder. It should've made Tobin move away.

But the damn male stayed right where he was.

"But what of you?" Flynn asked, and he twisted in his seat to look at Tobin. "Were you a scholar?"

Tobin smiled. "My family were artists and scholars, which was a skill that I, unfortunately, did not inherit. I had much more interest in men, women, parties, and gambling dens. They were simpler times..."

Shadows crowded his gaze. But in just one little confession, he'd learned more than he had about Tobin since his arrival. And damn if his heart didn't flip excitedly at Tobin remarking he *enjoyed* the company of a man.

Before he realized it, he'd touched Tobin's hand, who jolted at the touch, looking down in surprise. Flynn kept his hand as he spoke. "Thank you for telling me."

A look of surprise and confusion warred in Tobin's eyes, as if he wanted to say more. Whatever he'd been planning, Flynn would never know. Tobin nodded slowly in the end, saying nothing.

What Flynn would remember most of that moment was that Tobin didn't pull his hand away.

When they emerged hours later into bright daylight, there was an uneasiness about the temple grounds. It hit him as abruptly as a mountain storm, dimming whatever lightness had lingered in his soul after his time with Tobin.

Flynn felt the tension in the air as others hurried back and forth between huts. No one smiled or laughed, and gazes were lowered and unreadable. He glimpsed Mira being ferried into one of the larger halls where some of the hooded female fae lived and worked. Tobin was cagey about what went on there, saying nothing except that it was a partial offshoot of the main temple. They didn't worship Atlas there; instead, they prayed to another.

Titania, Spirit of the Night.

Tobin didn't elaborate, and Flynn gave up after a few days. As he watched her vanish into the hall, he wondered what she'd been up to. Every time they'd spoken, she looked bright and cheery. There were no bruises or shadows under her eyes. Hells, she'd filled out and he swore she was even building muscle. She was becoming something new; stronger, leaner, a force to be reckoned with. He only wished he could change that quickly.

"I wonder what's going on?" Tobin said.

Flynn scanned the faces, looking for Mathias, who'd left earlier that morning for business down by the docks. He spotted him at the tree line, shadowed by one of his attendants whose face was hidden beneath their hood.

"I see Mathias—there!"

Flynn headed over to the older fae with Tobin at his side. He could have sworn he stood just a fraction closer than usual with their hands nearly touching. Desire pooled low in his belly, flaring through his veins, and he shifted uncomfortably, trying to ease the tightness in his breeches.

Spirits above, he can probably smell it. Flynn shook off the thought and went to speak, but Tobin beat him to it, asking, "What news do you bring?"

Mathias frowned, glancing between Flynn and Tobin for a moment; then he spoke in another tongue. A couple of words Flynn managed to catch, but the rest was lost on him. He studied Tobin instead, hoping to read the answers in those golden eyes.

To his grief, they revealed nothing.

The two fae continued talking. Tobin grew visibly angry, his replies becoming short and waspish. In the end, Mathias snapped something and Tobin flinched back, silent, his gaze falling to the grass.

Tobin finally snapped something heatedly, and Mathias flinched back.

The temple leader's eyes widened at the first, then softened at the following two pleas. He leaned in, whispering something in Tobin's ear, squeezed his shoulder, and then left them. Flynn watched the older fae walk away, his attendant shadowing close behind, and vanish into the same hall Mira had gone.

When Tobin turned to Flynn, his face was ashen.

Flynn reached out, daring to touch his hand for the second time that day, snapping Tobin from his trance. "What is going on?"

"The Empress's forces just docked in Ruden," said Tobin distractedly; then, as if realizing Flynn had no idea where Ruden was, went on saying, "It's a few islands away from us."

"Are we in danger?" His stomach twisted into knots.

Tobin never replied as he looked back at the temple. Flynn held his hand while his mind descended into chaos.

CHAPTER 43

"The drums of war ring out from the palace. The army marches out to face its first battle, while the rest of the court watches on. All eyes are on the new Queen."
—Excerpt from Claudius Dellabore, newly appointed Prince of the Court

Ellie's screams tore through the darkness.

"Save me, please! Make it stop!" Her sister cried, panic and fear thick in her voice.

Nimue sprinted through the dark. The screaming grew louder. It shredded her soul, reducing it to ribbons. Panic welled within her, hollowing her chest with every jagged breath.

"Ellie, where are you?" Nimue called. "Answer me, please!"

The screaming continued.

Desperation consumed her. She called on her magic, straining for any hint of Ellie's location. Pain erupted in her head, throbbing hard behind her ear. Gritting her teeth, she pushed on, refusing to yield.

The darkness bled away, yielding to a stone cell. Stagnant, damp air invaded her lungs as she looked about the room, freezing as she saw Ellie on her knees. A woman loomed over her, a mouth twisted to a wicked smile. One hand raised high, ribbons of black energy pouring into Ellie's hunched form. Her sister screamed again, tears spilling down her cheeks.

Nimue strode forward. "Get your hands off my sister!"

She tried to slam her hand onto the woman, only to tumble through as if Nimue were little more than a specter. Ellie's screams choked off as she crumpled, hitting the ground with a muted thud. The woman turned to Nimue and smiled. A chill ran down her spine.

"Soon, Nimue, soon."

Nimue roared in fury, driving her fist forward, but this time it collided with skin. The woman staggered back, her eyes widening. Anger pinched her face. Recovering, she moved forward with magic swirling around her hands when a hand grabbed Nimue's shoulders.

"Wake up, Nimue, wake up!"

Nimue gasped awake. Blinking slowly, the world sharpened. The faint echo of Ellie's screams lingered in her ear. She pressed a hand to her face. Had that been real? Or a nightmare her mind had conjured? The throbbing pain behind her eye sharpened, and a sudden wave of nausea hit her. She twisted sharply and promptly retched onto the floor. The hand on her shoulder moved to her hair, pulling it from her face.

"Easy now, I'm here." Lorca's voice drew her back to reality as she emptied what little was left in her gut.

She hated feeling so damn weak, the damnable echo of what she once was. Shame burned her cheeks scarlett.

His hand traced small circles on her back, meant to offer comfort, but instead stoked a bitterness in her chest.

She flinched away. "I'm fine."

"Nimue—"

"Leave me," she hissed.

His hand jerked back. "What?"

"Just leave me!"

When he offered no answer, she shot a fiery look over her shoulder, daring him to leave. The stubborn ass just stared at her, then sat back on his haunches.

"Where is this coming from?"

A bitter laugh tumbled loose. "*Where?* I can barely make it through a damn day without wanting to throw up or pass out. In recent times, I have come far closer to death than I'd like, and I am failing at everything I do. Hell, even my sister is off god knows where, being tortured!"

"That isn't your fault," he argued, and stood, stalking halfway across the room. "None of this is your fault. I understand that things have changed—"

"No, you *don't.*" She rose with trembling legs, refusing to falter any further. Anger fuelled her, hardening that broken, furious thing within her. "I was powerful. Armies kneeled to me. Cities fell because *I* commanded it. Now, what am I?"

"You're Nimue, clever and fierce, a storm that will not be contained," he argued back heatedly. "You will save your sister and bring your people home and finish any task you choose. I know this because I *know* you."

"You don't *know* me," she threw back. "You fell in love with a mortal, a stupid girl who naively thought she could take on the world."

He threw his hands up with a hiss of exasperation. "And I'm still in love with the demon in front of me! Is that really so bad?"

"Why are you so damn accepting?"

"Because you haven't shown me anything I do not like! You are fire and chaos and passion." He stepped towards her, brave against her rage, stubborn against her ire. "I may struggle with what I learn about you, with your past and your nature, but I do not shy away from it. You have trusted me this far. Why not a little more?"

All those old fears bubbled to the surface, cooling the anger that flowed like liquid fire through her blood. As she stared at him, trying to formulate the words to say, to explain that yes, she *did* trust him; silence held her captive instead. It was her fear and anger and all those bitter demons snarling away at the pit of her soul that made her lash out.

He moved in front of her and this time; she didn't flinch from his touch. Even though she felt little better than a caged beast, snarling and ready to swipe, she remained still.

"I do trust you," she murmured.

"Then let us move forward—together."

She pressed her forehead to his, barely trusting herself to speak. He returned the touch in kind, wrapping his arms around her. Perhaps she could delude herself into believing that once he saw all the horrors she was capable of, he might actually stay and remain in love.

"Lorca, I—"

He jerked back with a cry, dropping to his knees. White light flashed, blinding her for a moment. She threw up her hand, shielding her eyes, when it dimmed a second later and his dragon form stretched out across the room.

In a flash, she was at his side, reaching out. "Lorca? Lorca? Talk to me!"

He blinked groggily, looking up with an unfocused gaze. It took a moment for awareness to flicker through their bond.

I'm okay. I...I think I just need to rest.

"Are you sure? I can send for a healer," she said.

There aren't any healers for Dragonirs who were stupid enough to spend hundreds of years in dragon form, he replied wryly. *I'll be fine.*

Nimue wasn't convinced.

She stayed with Lorca for another hour until she was satisfied his condition wasn't getting worse, and that he was actually resting. Content he was okay for the moment, she left the room.

Downstairs, she asked around for the runners' room, and a healer volunteered to take her to the west wing. The woman knocked, earning a muffled reply beyond the door and she held it open, gesturing for Nimue to head inside.

The room was large, cluttered with desks and a dozen men and women behind them, hastily scribbling out messages. A line of gray-cloaked runners stood waiting along one wall. When one of the seated workers raised a hand with a missive, a runner dashed forward, snatching it up before darting out. Every so often, an empty hand was raised and a runner came over. A verbal message was exchanged, and repeated twice before the runner headed out.

Nimue took her chance and moved to a desk. A woman looked up, shadows under her eyes, irritation lining her pinched face. It softened quickly, her mouth parting in a smile. "You're the dragon?"

"Yes, I need a message sent," said Nimue, reaching for her purse.

But as she pulled some coins out, the woman waved a hand. "No money. You work for the princess. What's the message?"

"Could you give me your quill and a sheet of paper?"

A frown knotted the woman's face but she did as requested. Nimue scribbled out a message in ancient demonic, a script only Titania and Claudius would be able to read. When she finished, she handed the missive to the woman, who eyed the message, then looked up, affronted. "Our runners are trustworthy."

"Your fastest runner, *please*." The pleading note worked.

The insulted expression softened as the note was folded; then, one hand shot up and she called out a name. "Cale."

A young boy, who barely touched Nimue's shoulders, approached and took the letter. He was out the door before she could raise any concerns.

"He's our fastest. If there is a reply, he will deliver it to your room."

Satisfied, Nimue murmured her thanks, and headed out, praying the message arrived soon. Until the reply came, there was a meeting to attend. Alone.

Any hope that there would be no questions about Lorca's lack of appearance was quickly dashed. Nimue strode into the room, the conversation trailing off as Dorian, Sylvie, and Nora looked at her.

Nora frowned. "Where's Lorca?"

Nimue stiffened. "He's resting. Recent days have taken a toll, but he shall be fine." She lowered herself into the chair. "There's much we need to discuss."

"This is about what you found at the well?" Sylvie inquired, one brow lifted.

As the explanation tumbled from her lips, a stillness chilled the room. Sylvie and Dorian shared a quiet look, their brows furrowed, and eyes soft. It was the first time that Nimue had seen genuine worry in their eyes, and as Sylvie's gaze slid to Nora, she understood the motherly look.

Throughout her talk, the Princess had been silent, but even she, too, appeared a little pale when she eventually spoke. "To what end?"

"A Hell Gate. Like the cracks we found, it's a portal to the demon realm, but bigger, *much* bigger. Enough to bring an army through to this realm." She paused for a moment, ignoring the flash of old memories that nudged her mind before she continued. "I saw one a long time ago, though it failed to bring anything through from the demon realm before it leveled an entire city."

"Why have I never heard of such a thing?" asked Sybilla. The others murmured in assent.

Nimue gave her a grim look. "There wasn't anyone—or anything—left after the blast. Time took care of the rest."

Sybilla's gaze darkened as she leaned back in her chair, drumming her fingers on the table. The sound echoed eerily in the quiet, each tap like a crack of thunder. "Those symbols that you've found are old, so how can you be sure the plan is happening as we speak?"

There was silence for a moment while Nimue tried to think of an answer that would satisfy the others. None came.

"I don't think we can take the risk that I'm wrong," she finally said.

Sybilla's hand stilled on the table, pressed flat, fingers sprawled. Those glowing amber orbs remained fixed on Nimue, unreadable. After an agonizing silence, she drew her hand back, dropping it under the table. "How sure are you?"

"I'm staking my life on it."

A heavy breath fell from Sybilla's lips. "Is the gate here?"

"No, it's outside of the city. If it were, it would be impossible to miss...I would sense it. This city would be saturated with demonic energy, even if it wasn't activated."

Sybilla rose to stand, the others following suit. She smoothed down her dress, as if by habit. "Do you know what this gate might look like?"

"Its designs might vary, but I can sketch my best guess, along with all the markings that would need to be on it."

"Good. Deliver it to me personally tonight." Sybilla moved her gaze to the others. "Speak nothing of this beyond these walls."

Nora froze. "Is this not something our men should know?"

"Until we know *where* it is and we have a plan to destroy it, then no. This city is already on the verge of panic. If the people hear of a world-ending demonic portal and an immortal army coming to slaughter us all? It would shatter what little peace we have left." Sybilla's tone brooked no argument from anyone. The warning was clear. "Your missions will continue as before. Find all the cracks and seal them. I assume this will slow down the opening of the gate?"

Nimue nodded. "It will help."

CHAPTER 44

"In the chaos, the Queen was separated from our forces. When we returned, there was chaos in the throne room. As the nobles bickered over succession, the door opened and Nimue strode in, soaked with blood, carrying in her hands the heads of Fenrys's generals. She threw them at the nobles, who fell silent and then took her seat. At that moment, the throne glowed, *as though it were singing. Nimue was no longer just a queen but a Goddess of Death."*

—Excerpt of Castille Dellabore's diary, Prince of the Court

Sweat dripped from Flynn's brow as he and Tobin circled each other, swords drawn. Sunshine beat down on their naked torsos, glistening with sweat, light dancing over every shift of their muscles. Flynn tightened his grip, studying Tobin, hunting for an opening. Those golden eyes mirrored that same intensity, an acute awareness prickling across Flynn's skin.

He itched to throw the weapon aside, grab Tobin, and kiss him.

Like he'd been dying to do a week ago, right before he'd panicked and withdrawn. Tobin had said nothing about it and acted as if it had never happened.

Flynn's heart beat like a frantic bird, trapped in a cage, yearning to be free, to accept his desire. But, like a God's damned coward, he did nothing.

Nothing but stare, dream, *hunger.*

Tobin shot out, swinging his sword. Flynn yelped as he narrowly deflected the blow. Mere inches separated their faces, and as their eyes locked, his mouth dried. Heat blazed between them as the world fell away. His heart pounded.

"Good," remarked Tobin, his voice low, heady. "Now, what will you do?"

Flynn's gaze dropped to Tobin's lips, and all rational thought fled. What would he taste like? Salty from the sea breeze? Or spicy from the teas he knew Tobin enjoyed?

Tobin's eyes turned black. The air crackled with magic. Bumps rippled along Flynn's skin, and the hairs lifted. A breath caught in his throat.

Time slowed to a crawl. Flynn blinked.

Tobin's lips pressed against his.

Flynn's mind froze. Tobin dropped his sword, then wrenched Flynn's one from his grip, tossing it aside. Flynn only hesitated a second before pressing himself against Tobin's already firm cock. With a groan, Tobin shuddered and pushed Flynn back against the tree. He grabbed Flynn's face, kissing him like he was the air he needed to breathe.

Flynn ran his hands over Tobin, drawing him in, tracing those sweat-slicked muscles, committing it all to memory. Tobin's hands dropped, cupping his ass. His hardened cock strained through his pants, digging into Flynn's belly.

Spirits above...

It was...*heaven.*

Flynn's thoughts scattered as he lost himself in Tobin, his soul *singing.* A smile split his cheeks as he returned every devastating kiss.

At that moment, he felt like a god. Immortal. *Powerful.*

Tobin wrenched his mouth away, harsh breaths fanning Flynn's lips. His molten gaze betrayed a war of emotions. It dropped to Flynn's mouth again, hunger flaring, his gaze darkening. Flynn reached for Tobin again, fingertips grazing the skin softly. A shuddering breath stole from Tobin.

"Flynn—" His name was a whispered prayer from those swollen lips, heady with the desire that pulsed between them.

"Don't you dare say this was a mistake," cried Flynn.

Surprise widened Tobin's eyes. "What? Why would I—"

The sound of bells tolling cut him off. Tobin stepped back, panic draining his face. He turned to the path, still as death. The bells continued, echoing through the forest. Tobin shot him a grim look, one that brooked no argument.

"Gather your things. We have to go *now.*"

They raced back down the path, Tobin setting a brutal pace that Flynn could barely follow. By the time they arrived at the temple, his heart felt like it was tearing itself from his chest. His legs wobbled and he doubled over, breathing hard, sweat dripping from his face. He straightened up, to see the fae spilling from every building, gathering at the threshold of the temple grounds.

His gaze moved to Tobin to see him striding over to Mathias. The older fae was marshaling several of the assembled fae, barking orders in their natural tongue. Flynn, who had been taking lessons from Tobin, caught a few snippets.

Coming now.

No time.

Hide them.

Flynn caught up with Tobin as Mathias turned to them.

He stared first at Flynn, then at Tobin. A silent conversation seemed to play out before he spoke in the common tongue. "You need to hide him *now.*"

"Is it them?" Tobin asked.

The Empress's men? Flynn remembered the worry only days before, how the men had been sighted a few islands over. Why had they come here and why was he to hide?

Mathias nodded. A woman hurried over from the tree line, a rush of words tumbling from her lips, too fast for Flynn to translate. Mathias paled, glancing at Tobin. "No time for the temple. The bakery, *now.*"

Tobin turned and grabbed Flynn, hauling him over to the closest hut.

"Tobin, what's going on? Is it the Empress's men?" Flynn asked as Tobin shoved the door open, then thrust Flynn inside. He was dragged into the back-store room, where Tobin let go, dropping to his knees and yanking open a hatch.

"Tobin!" cried Flynn. "Tell me what's happening."

"I'll explain later, but you have to hide," Tobin blurted out, urgency tearing at his voice. "*Please.*"

It was that single word that moved Flynn. He moved to the hatch and began to lower himself down, questions roaring in his mind when he met Tobin's gaze. The *fear* was loud in his gaze, raw and bare. Flynn reached out, cupping Tobin's cheek. "Tell me, is it them?"

Tobin closed his eyes, leaning into the touch. "I'll tell you everything after, but you have to hide. Now, no matter what you hear, you must stay. You cannot come out."

"Why? Why the secrecy?"

"*Flynn, please,*" Tobin begged, and something cracked in his voice; that hard, prickly voice was gone, replaced with a raw vulnerability that stole the air from his lungs as Tobin spoke again. "I can't lose you."

Flynn opened his mouth but Tobin grabbed him, kissing him hard. It felt like all Tobin's desperation poured into that kiss, and he held Flynn as if he were his whole world.

In a blink, it was over, and Tobin pulled away. Flynn reached out, but Tobin's hand fell to his shoulder, gently pushing him down the hatch. As his feet touched the bottom, he drew in a shaky breath. All the things he wanted to say suddenly dried on his lips, and he could only stare in fear for Tobin, for the unknown, for—

"Mira! Is she—"

"She'll be hidden, too. I swear it, she will be okay. Do not come out until I come for you, okay?" Tobin hesitated again, casting him a final look before he stepped back and closed the hatch.

Flynn was alone once more.

He waited there for hours; the silence warring with his thumping heart. The air at last cooled, and he guessed it was now nightfall. Still, no one came, and he was painfully alone with his thoughts. He sat there imagining every terrible possibility, even the one that had destroyed his life.

Have the slavers come and taken everyone away?

More than once he stood, reaching for the hatch. It was Tobin's pleading voice that stayed his hand. But, by the spirits, it was *hard.*

Where was Mira? Was she okay? Was Tobin?

Their last kiss returned to his mind; the way Tobin had held him. Reverently, desperately. It had almost felt like a goodbye.

Surely not...

He stood again when footsteps thumped against the wooden floor. His mouth filled with dust. Silence fell, broken seconds later by the panel above his head being lifted. Powdery light spilled in, blinding him for a moment, silhouetting a figure.

Ice slid down his spine.

The figure was too slender for Tobin. The shape was all wrong, the scent too soft. A hand reached down, the fingers sloped and delicate.

"Flynn, it's okay, you can come out." Mira's voice filled the darkness like a warm blanket, full of comfort.

He scrambled up the ladder. His eyes adjusted to the lamplight. Mira was draped in a gray cloak, peering at him beneath her dark lashes. She studied him as he looked beyond her to the open door.

"Tobin said he'd come for me—what happened? Why was everyone panicking?"

Mira bit her lip. "I don't know. I was hidden in a room and told to be quiet until someone came. When they did, I came to fetch you."

"And Tobin?"

She shook her head. He strode past her, heart pounding. Dozens of fae filled the main path, but none were Tobin. His mouth filled with ash. Where *was* he?

He stumbled on, calling Tobin's name as tears threatened to spill from his eyes.

By the main temple's towering pillars, Flynn spotted Mathias talking with two women. A cut was visible above his eye and dried blood stained the side of his face. Flynn stumbled forward.

"Mathias!" he called out; as Mathias turned, he swallowed a lump in his throat. "Where is Tobin?"

Mathia's eyes softened. "We didn't know they'd come this early."

"Who came early?"

"The Empress's men. They come every year to collect new men for their army." Mathia's gaze shuttered. "They weren't due for months, but something has changed."

Flynn's legs buckled. "*Where's Tobin?*"

Mathias shook his head, eyes raw with grief. "I'm sorry, my son. They took him."

CHAPTER 45

"King Fenrys retreated. The other courts are silent. They underestimated me and paid dearly for it. It's inevitable they will come for me again. So, I will plan and wait. Now, I must attend the ceremony—the new Keeper is to be revealed."
—Excerpt from Queen Nimue's diary

In the afternoon, Nimue sparred with Nora, who got in more than a few good hits. The garden was quiet, far away from the chaos in the mansion. Nimue used to love that noise, the thrill of anticipation before a battle. Now, it gnawed at old memories and made her feel unsettled.

Lorca's collapse played over in her mind. She wanted so badly to help him, but he was right; there were no healers who knew how to treat his condition. His time spent in dragon form had thrown out the balance between his human and dragon side, causing serious damage. A problem to which there was likely no cure.

"Looks like I'm going to beat you again," said the girl.

As Nimue lunged at Nora, the ground beneath her feet shook and a hole appeared. Unable to save herself, Nimue sank to her knees. It was just as before from their first training session. But she was embarrassed to be caught unaware a second time. A smile pulled at her lips as she fought back a laugh.

Nora laughed and reached a hand to haul her up.

"Nice trick."

"My people have always had a deep connection to the earth. Long ago, we once built great cities beneath the ground—or so my mother used to tell me." She laughed again. “Perhaps one day I shall be able to do more than a hole. For now, I practice.”

Nimue brushed the soil from her clothes. “Could be a rather handy trick given what we face.”

The smile slipped from Nora’s lips. “This truly has you bothered? This whole Hell Gate threat?”

“It doesn’t bother you?”

“I’ve faced the extinction of my people my whole life. There aren’t many of us left, so this doesn’t truly change much for me.” Nora shrugged as she sheathed her weapon. “That may sound cold and don’t think I would not grieve to lose Dorian or Sylvie, or that I don’t care about the people in this city. I do. Truly. But this situation is familiar to me. It’s a companion I’ve had since birth.”

Nimue hadn’t wanted to ask about the relationship between the three. Yet, she was also wary about forming new connections. Friendships and alliances were easily broken by time, death, or betrayal. Old wounds cautioned her from reaching out with an open hand.

But curiosity was never a trait she could ignore forever. “What is the story with Dorian and Sylvie?”

Nora wandered over to the wall, plucking up a folded towel, and wiped her face. She shrugged. “After my village was destroyed, I was alone. They found me, took me in. The rest is history.”

There was clearly much more to that story than that, but Nimue refrained from asking.

A shadow passed over Nora’s face, and she blinked, forcing a smile that didn’t quite reach her eyes. A feeling of kinship came over Nimue. They were both outcasts in a world that didn’t want them, had suffered and lost.

Nimue gently set a hand on Nora’s arm. “I’d like to hear more one day if you ever wish to share.”

Nora smiled and picked up her weapon.

“Shall we begin?” she asked.

The sparring left Nimue aching and weary. She emerged from her bath's tepid water and grabbed a cloth to dry herself. When she emerged, Lorca was back in his human form, and pulling on a loose shirt. She closed the distance between them. As his head poked through, she wrapped her arms around his waist, burying her face into his chest to inhale his scent.

Lorca's arms encircled her and he pressed a kiss to the top of her head. She softened. They were both a mess, but for that moment, they were okay.

When sleep proved elusive, Nimue left the mansion, seeking some solitude from the turmoil raging within.

Few people were out on the streets and those who were avoided her gaze. Their silence was broken only by the murmuring wind and the distant cawing of crows.

Nimue wandered through the twilight, calling on her powers as much as they would permit, and soon her head throbbed mercilessly. Sometimes, she swore she caught the tiniest fleck of her sister's emerging powers, but it darted out of reach, lost before she could track it.

As the sky turned into a canvas of luminescent purple and burnished orange, she entered an area where more people were about. Men boarded up windows, securing their homes. Women gathered in small groups with children playing nearby. They were likely seeking a brief escape from the fear of the impending siege.

Patrols strode down the street, some offering nods of respect as they passed. Otherwise, she was left to her own devices, wishing Lorca was with her. She'd considered asking Nora to join her, but she had left after their training session, saying she was off to meet Dorian and Sylvie in the Merchant Quarter.

Nimue had wanted to ask why they were going there, but beyond their teamwork, their interactions were few and she was not sure she could call herself their friend. She hated the uncertainty twisting in her chest. The doubts crowded her mind. Her time living as Wren had left her with a human connection she barely understood.

What exactly *was* she anymore?

She passed through a few little meeting squares, each with a well with the same damnable symbol emblazoned upon it. Each one was a reminder of the threat that hung above them all.

As the sun dipped and the night stretched out its shadowy fingers across the city, Nimue turned to head back. An aching weariness threatened to overwhelm her. Lorca was right. It was not just her magic that was becoming weaker.

Every day felt harder.

A shiver of fear trickled down her spine. Her dark magic stirred, hissing softly in her mind. Something cold and unnervingly familiar slid over her skin. Old magic. She stopped and turned slowly. Her breath caught in her throat. A few feet away stood a young man, a letter in one hand, a dagger in the other. She moved to him when his hand snapped up, plunging the blade into his throat. Hot blood sprayed as he yanked it across, opening his neck like a bloody smile. His body buckled, sending him crumpling to the ground, dead before he hit the stone. A pool of crimson welled around him, tendrils racing between the cracks in the stone to the letter in his hand.

Nimue dashed forward, snatching it up as the first droplets touched the edges. She opened it and read her heart racing. The demonic script staring back at her sent shivers down her spine.

Come to where I left my first message for you by midnight tomorrow. Come alone or else your half-breed sister dies.

CHAPTER 46

"Her name is Amara. As the tattoos of the Keeper are marked into her flesh, she watches me from across the room. Those dark, watchful eyes. Even then, with her power emerging, I felt as though I were in the presence of our goddess. And this one knew all my darkest sins."

—Excerpt from Queen Nimue's diary

Unease lanced through Sybilla's chest as she slipped into the shadowy confines of the old temple. The long days of preparation had left her strung out, and Nimue's confession about the demonic threat had pushed her over the edge. All her planning suddenly useless, a child's defiance against a god. As she reached for the door leading downstairs, the darkness moved.

She froze, her breath freezing in her chest.

The spirit emerged from the shadows. "I did not summon you."

"I know, but I had to come. Wren discovered something troubling about the demon threat in the city."

The story spilled from her lips like a storm that would not be contained. A look of concern deepened the spirit's face, her lips pinching into a thin line. Finally, the spirit moved from the shadows and Sybilla noticed the limp. Each step seemed slow, pained, and that usually unreadable mask tightened in flashes of discomfort. She moved to what was left of an old pew and lowered herself down onto the wooden bench.

"What happened?" asked Sybilla. "Have the spirits learned of your involvement here?"

“No. Do not trouble your mind. The others will know once we reach the final phase of our agreement. Are you truly sure you wish to put yourself in such a position? They may not be forgiving,” the spirit murmured.

Sybilla laughed softly, not for joy but for the consequences she had long accepted. Omi had warned her that using her prophetic abilities would eventually lead to madness. But in the end, if her mission was achieved and her people saved, what did it matter if her fate was grim? She danced on the edge of a knife her whole life.

“I’ll be okay, but we are not here to discuss me. What are your thoughts about what I have told you?”

The spirit frowned. “I’m aware of the symbols but haven’t yet determined what they meant. If Wren is correct, then things are worse than I feared.”

What hope there was for Wren being wrong crumpled. “What do I do?”

She’d planned for so many futures, but she hadn’t even *glimpsed* a hint of a demon threat. How had she been so damn blind?

The spirit said nothing, her focus on the ground. It was as though she’d forgotten Sybilla was there at all.

At last, she spoke. “Our deal remains. We continue on with our plan.”

Hours later, Sybilla paced the sparring room, restless, her mood darkening with every moment. She hoped her training might at least wear herself into such exhaustion that sleep would come to her without its usual nightmares.

The door cracked open, breaking her wandering thoughts. Familiar footsteps trod softly over the floor, marking just who had come. Her heart gave a traitorous flip as she turned and Claudius swept into the room, slipping off his cloak. He, too, appeared as if he’d slept little. Shadows hung under his eyes, and he moved a little slower.

“Glad to see I’m not the only one not sleeping,” she said conversationally as she grabbed their swords and returned to him, offering the blade.

He took it with a tired smile. “Suffice to say I am grateful for the distraction.”

She swung her sword, but didn't come at him. "We don't have to spar. I have a nice bottle of aged spiced wine if you'd prefer?"

"Is that from Lady Adara's collection?"

"I will neither confirm nor deny," she retorted, then shifted her stance to spar. "So, what will you choose?"

He hesitated for a moment, then groaned and got into position. "I'd rather not make an enemy of Helena."

"Coward."

"Of course. Have you seen her mad?" He shuddered.

She let the magic flow to the surface, wrapping around her arms in glowing ribbons. "You should see me mad. I am told I am quite terrifying."

The corner of his mouth tipped up, a real smile peeking out. "Consider me warned."

This time, she kept her visions at bay and trusted her gut as she moved about him, parrying off his blows. She studied the sleek shift of his muscles, how his feet moved as he came in to strike, and how he moved back, shifting his weight as he went. There was something practiced, like a well-honed warrior, and nothing was betrayed in those fathomless depths. It was maddening and thrilling, and she wanted to beat him.

She dropped one hand, firing a bolt of energy, slamming straight into the middle of his chest. He staggered back with a gasp, his back hitting on the wall. She shot forward and in seconds the point of her sword was lightly pressed at his throat. He stilled. Shadows passed over his stony features, unreadable as he drew ragged breaths. His piercing gaze never wavered from her, sending her heart racing nervously.

"I win," she said softly, stepped back, and turned.

His hand shot out, grabbing her, spinning her back. In a flash, he had her against his chest, his gaze bearing down on her. He leaned in, his lips hovering inches above hers.

"Tell me no and I will go no further."

"I—"

Her mouth moved, a reply summoned when the door was flung open. She jumped back, Claudius releasing her, and she smoothed down her dress. Steadying her pounding heart, she turned to face Helena, whose face was darkened with worry. Blue eyes slid to Claudius, lingering until he got the unspoken message, bowed, hung his sword up, and left.

Oren lingered behind Helena, shadowed by his men, with an unreadable expression leaving her shifting restlessly on the balls of her feet. Had he seen how close she'd been to Claudius?

Spirits above... She'd gotten so carried away and nearly crossed a line with terrible consequences. From Helena's tight-lipped look, it was obvious her advisor knew what had nearly happened—or suspected, which was even worse. A mind could conjure many stories to fill in absences.

"Don't say it." Sybilla hung up her sword. "I know."

"Then why did you call him here?" Helena challenged.

Sybilla closed her eyes for a moment. The headache was returning with a vengeance. Cursing internally, she opened her eyes, staring at the wall. "A moment of weakness, that's all."

Truthfully, like some fool, she'd craved the excitement he'd given her the last time they'd sparred. It let her forget of the pressure bearing down on her. By the spirits, she knew she couldn't afford it, but, in an act of pure need, she'd caved.

"The messengers aren't perfect—such things will be noted," said Helena reproachfully. "The nobles will not—"

"*Stop.*" Sybilla turned, squaring her shoulders. An iciness slid into her heart, hardening it. "You didn't come here to scold me like a child. I would advise you *not* to continue this. Now, what is it you want?"

Helena's nostrils flared, anger flickering in her jeweled depths. When she spoke, her voice was hard, controlled. "I came because some healers have arrived, seeking an audience."

By the spirits, my work is never done...

CHAPTER 47

"There is a traitor in my court. Half a dozen convoys of supplies, their routes secret, have been attacked by our enemy. One I might dismiss to chance, but now that the number has grown, I turn my gaze inwards. It is time for a hunt."
—Excerpt from Queen Nimue's diary

The scent of the death clung to Titania's skin as she moved about the injured. She kneeled by the beds of women and children, dressing their wounds. An old memory stirred, nudging her mind, demanding attention. Shaking it off, she forced herself to focus on the task at hand.

A young boy, his arm a mess of deep gashes and mangled flesh, was her latest patient. A thin sheen of sweat gathered across his brow as he slept with shallow breaths, his eyes darting rapidly beneath his eyelids. She gently peeled his bandages, wincing at the skin beneath. It was red, angry, and warm to the touch.

She cleaned the wounds as best as she could, applied a healing salve, then redressed them. Hopefully, his fever would break soon. Titania had seen the supplies dwindling in the storeroom. If he got worse, there wouldn't be much she could do.

She was a demon. There was no healing magic in her veins, only darkness and death.

Without a plethora of fae at full strength, if disease struck the city, it would be carnage. But no fae truly possessed the level of magic they once had—not since the fall of Toranelle, when some strange spell weakened their kind.

Sighing, she cleaned the boy's face, then propped him up as she trickled some water through his lips. The healing tonic would help keep his fever down and aid his body fight the infection ravaging his system. Time would decide his fate.

As she stood, the matron healer, Savira, approached. Weariness dragged her narrow shoulders down, mirroring Titania's own exhaustion.

"How is his condition?" she asked.

Titania recognized the motherly glow in those warm depths, and it made her ache for the future she never fulfilled with her beloved.

"His wound remains the same, but his fever has yet to break. I've done what you've instructed. Now we wait," she replied.

Titania knew Savira hadn't just come to check in on the boy. Her gaze dropped to a letter in Savira's hand. "Is that for me?"

"Another runner. The poor boy looked exhausted, just like the last one. Must be urgent." Savira held out the letter.

Titania took it with a quiet thank you and opened it. Ice flooded her veins as she was met with a single symbol, a bloody chalice. The demon had made its move and the plan to save Ellie was in motion. Good. No one attacked one of their own—for that was exactly what the half-blood girl was to them now—and got away with it.

The armory Claudius had deep within his mansion was stocked with a plethora of weapons. Blades hundreds of years old, yet all still deadly and well-maintained hung from the walls. The finest weapons forged. They were proof of all the bloodshed and pain they'd endured.

As she moved to the armor hung on the wall, she smiled. Claudius had kept hers, though it was unpolished and scratched. He knew how she liked it kept. Lifting it off, she savored the weight of it. It slid onto her body with ease.

The healer was gone as she fastened the last piece into place.

The warrior emerged.

She plucked her spear from the wall. It felt steady in her hands. A familiar friend. Stepping back, she glided through movements, shifting with the weight of the weapon. On the last pose, she turned and thrust the spear.

The point stopped inches from Claudius's chest.

He threw his hands up. "Mercy!"

Rolling her eyes, she straightened up. "Your servant found you then. Good."

As she turned and placed the spear against the rack of weapons, she reached for the daggers hanging on the wall. She selected two and slid them into the sheaths on her thigh.

"It's time?" Claudius moved to the wall where his polished armor gleamed in the lamplight. "So, what's the plan?"

As she turned to him, she grabbed her spear. "The Bloody Chalice."

"*What?*"

Titania grinned. "This should be fun. Time to go on a demon hunt."

CHAPTER 48

"My birds are on the hunt. The traitor will be found—lest our queen's wrathful gaze descends upon us all."

—Excerpt from Claudius Dellabore, Prince of the Court's diary

Nimue's boots thudded softly on the cobblestone as she jogged down the street. A faint burn warmed her muscles. It was a welcome heat as she navigated the twisting streets. Her destination wasn't much further.

A heavy fog rolled in from the sea as night descended over the city. It drifted about the quiet streets, broken only by the striding patrols of soldiers or Sybilla's runners. Their shadowy forms left swirling clouds in their wake. All around, a chill tightened its icy grip on the air.

She rounded the last corner and closed the distance to the graveyard. There, she slowed and stopped at the threshold. One final look at the sky as she forced herself to steady her breathing. Soon, she'd be with her sister again. Dropping her gaze, it locked on the crypt. And the open door.

The invitation was clear.

Nimue shivered. Demonic energy crackled in the air, stirring the slumbering power within. Even with the offending demon still in its realm, the power bled through. The power of all four demon rulers.

She pushed on, half-expecting a trap to spring up at any second. Warily, she entered the crypt, slowing at the top of the stairs. A row of torches was mounted on the wall, illuminating the descent.

For her sister, she played along. She'd do whatever she had to. The plan was in place.

She hurried down the steps, pushing on down the lit path. When she came to the black door, it gaped open. A blue glow hummed from within. A new crack from the demon realm to this one. Demonic energy choked the air, saturating her senses. It sunk deep, like talons, refusing to part. She inched toward the door, peering inside. A new crack cleaved the air, four times the size of the last.

And through it, a room she knew as intimately as the mountains.

There her throne sat, gleaming in polished obsidian and veins of gold.

It stared back at her, and a presence she'd once fought to escape reached out. The shadowy hands made their way into her mind, for no wall she might construct could keep it out. The bond she forged when she claimed it certainly ensured that.

The throne was alive, and it wanted her back.

Have you come home to me? It crooned.

It took all her will to refuse a response, even as the words lodged in her throat. Part of her wanted nothing more than to return and sit upon it once more. Of course, she knew it was a certain death sentence if she yielded.

"You still feel the pull, don't you?"

Nimue wrenched her gaze from the portal to the woman who pushed off the wall, advancing with slow, graceful movements. Her glassy black gaze was steady, piercing her to the bone. Ancient magic rolled off her as she prowled forward, her tattered dress brushing the floor. Bare feet made no sound against the stone, every step forward matching the hard thump of Nimue's heart. The possession of this body felt more concrete.

A shadow passed over the face. "You're going to die here today, Nimue. I will finish what I started."

"Confident, aren't you?"

"I beat the others and they were at full strength." The demon cocked its head to the side. "But you're a mere shadow of your former self. Do you even have any of your powers left?"

Nimue itched to prove the demon wrong, but the throbbing behind her right her stayed her hand. She reached up, drawing her two short swords from her back. Lowering them, she shifted her feet apart.

The demon smiled, but it didn't quite touch its soulless eyes.

"I don't need magic to defeat you," Nimue said. "I'm a warrior who has slain countless on the battlefields simply by using my sword. Men and demons shook at my name. But I guess you're afraid to try my sword."

The demon laughed. "Afraid of *you?*"

Nimue burst forward. The demon's palms snapped up, and darkness flooded out. Cursing, Nimue jumped out of the way. The shadows parted as the demon leaped through. A sword glinted in their hand, the black leather hilt glowing with white symbols.

Nimue barely got her swords up as the demon bore down on her. She dodged as the demon's blade missed her chest by a hair's breadth.

"You think you can beat me? I have spent *centuries* preparing!" the demon snarled.

Nimue snorted, saying nothing as she lunged at her foe swinging her blade. The demon parried and sliced clean through Nimue's armor, cutting into her chest. Blood welled, trickling down.

The demon rushed forward.

Nimue danced back, dodging the blows. The throbbing behind her eye sharpened, darkness pressing on her vision. Forcing it down with a shuddering breath, she pressed her heels in and let the demon gain ground. Victory gleamed in those hellish eyes. They darted to the side, missing Nimue's sword; at the last second, they twisted back and drove their foot into her chest.

The air rushed from her lungs as she staggered back. Her legs buckled, threatening to give out.

Just a bit longer.

The demon burst forward to deliver the killing blow.

Nimue winked. A flash of alarm shot across the demon's face, but it was too late. Nimue side-stepped as the demon surged past. They tried to turn, but Nimue had already swung her blades, crossing them down the demon's back.

She sliced through muscle, then bone. A savage scream tore from the demon as they staggered forward, sinking to their knees. Blood dripped onto the stone, running down the cracks in the floor.

Soon.

She pressed forward and drove the blades into the shoulders, forcing the demon facedown onto the ground. They thrashed, opening the wounds wider. More blood spilled, saturating the remnants of the ragged dress. Nimue didn't give a damn. Immune to the demon's screams she drove her foot into their spine.

"And *you* were a fool to think I've been idle in this realm."

The screams cut off, laughter bubbling up, like glass shattering on stone. Confusion chilled Nimue's soul. Darkness erupted and slammed into her chest, sending her flying. She hit the wall with a sickening thud. Bone crunched, and she crumpled to the ground with a cry.

Waves of nausea rolled through her. Panic flared down her bond with Lorca, his worry pushing through. Desperately, she shoved a wall back up. If the demon sensed him...She forced herself to her knees.

The game wasn't lost yet.

The world swayed and blurred, the throb in her head sharpening. Pressing her palms down, she pushed up to her feet. This body she had was failing—and fast. Death whispered to her soul.

Blood dripped in the demon's wake as they strode forward. "I am going to enjoy killing you."

A metallic taste pooled in Nimue's mouth. She spat it out, the glistening red splattering the stones, and she forced a bloodied grin. "I will not die today."

The words she'd said to Wren stirred through her mind. *The price will be your life.* The war wasn't ending today, or even in the City of Slaves. It was only the beginning. Nimue knew her inescapable fate. It had haunted her since she claimed her throne. Death was coming for her.

But just not at that moment.

She wiped the blood from her mouth. "I never got your name."

"Does it matter?"

"Well, if I'm to die, I'd like a name—so, what is the harm?"

The demon paused. "You truly don't recognize my magic, do you?"

"Was I meant to?"

Heat flashed in that hellish face. "It's *Mirena.*"

Shock thumped Nimue's soul, but she schooled her face.

"Mirena, you say? Can't say I remember that name. Were you someone important in my court?" Nimue forced an air of indifference into her voice.

"I was your *student,* your *only* student. You cannot pretend to forget me," Mirena snarled.

Nimue's brow lifted. "Sorry, I don't remember you."

Fury darkened those inhuman eyes. Mirena burst forward, swinging her sword for a strike. A gasp tore from her lips as Nimue dropped one sword, then slammed her fist straight for Mirena's throat. The demon stepped back, the blow missing. But it was enough. Nimue grabbed her remaining sword and slashed Mirena's arm as she tried to dart away. Blood dripped down to the floor.

They broke apart, both breathing hard. Sweat glistened on Nimue's brow. Every part of her burned, exhaustion threatening to consume her. The second sword lay on the ground, just out of reach. Could she dive for it? Make a move and spin back? Her gaze slid to the blood staining the floor, at the small puddle gathered in a crack in the ceiling. That *had* to be enough blood.

She slammed down the walls in her bond to Lorca. *Now!*

CHAPTER 49

"The screams of those interrogated fill the castle for days. Nimue spends much of her time in the dungeons. She will not keep her hands clean—if this task must be done, then it will be her hands that are stained."
—Excerpt from Keeper Amara's diary

The door behind her shattered into splinters, and a shockwave crashed into Nimue, sending the pair of them flying. Mirena hit the wall first, Nimue a second later. The world spun as she tried to get up. Her hands screamed in defiance, heat roaring down her limbs. Something hot and slick ran down her arm. A metallic stench filled the air.

Nimue! Lorca's voice burst into her mind like a crack of thunder.

She tried to raise her head, but it hurt so damn much. Chaotic thoughts tangled into knots, an assault on her senses. Bile burned her throat and as she opened her mouth to cry out, she emptied her stomach all over the stone.

Nimue!

Again, she tried to answer, but her head throbbed. She worked the reply to her lips, but no sound spilled out. Bit by bit, she felt herself slipping; the darkness wrapping around her. Warmth, comfort. She had a mission...she was trying to...

Nimue! Lorca's desperation clawed at her mind. *Stay with me! Just hold on!*

Magic surged down the bond like a burst of light. Her eyes flew open, a gasp tearing from her lips. The pain dimmed a fraction, the edges of her vision still touched with shadows. She jolted upright, clutching at her chest as she tried to suck in whatever air she could.

A cacophony of roars and cries and ringing metal crashed through her head as her vision cleared.

Across the room, demons spilled from the crack. Claudius, Titania, Nora, Sylvie, and Dorian carved their way through the chaos. A blur of strikes and dodges, flashes of white and green light erupting among the fray. Savage howls echoed in the air.

And in the middle of the chaos was Lorca.

Fire raged from his hands as he rushed toward her, a god reborn in mortal flesh. Fury roared in his eyes, a burning determination hardening on his face. A demon leaped at him. Lorca twisted, hurling a burst of fire at his attacker. It slammed into the beast's side, turning it to ash before it even hit the ground.

She had to help him. She had to—

Pressing her hands to the ground, she tried to stand. Her body rose a few inches when a force slammed into her right shoulder, pinning her back down. Nails dug into her skin, biting through flesh. Liquid fire lanced down her arm. A scream slammed against her lips.

"Stop!" Mirena's voice exploded over the fray.

Silence slammed down, the demons freezing. Lorca stopped mid-stride, his hands raised with flames coiled around his arms. Sweat glistened on his brow as he stared at Nimue, breathing hard. His gaze dropped to her neck.

Nimue felt something cold and sharp pressed against her throat.

"Let her go!" Lorca thundered.

"No."

The blade cut into her skin, and warm blood trickled down her neck. Nimue tried to move, but she was slipping once more. Magic flooded down the bond, but it wasn't enough. Her eyes rolled back in her head.

Don't you dare let go, Nimue!

Nimue was so damn *tired*. Her soul ached, her body stripped bare. All she wanted to do was sleep and never wake, to surrender blissfully to the abyss.

Why shouldn't she just rest? Had she not fought enough? All she'd ever done was fight...and what was she fighting for anymore? There was someone...wasn't there? Her mind frayed, all the memories bleeding away.

Death clawed at her.

She closed her eyes, surrendering to the void when a single voice cut through the chaos.

"Let my sister go!"

CHAPTER 50

"The Court was summoned this morning. Nimue was not there when Lord Camden arrived. A few minutes later, Nimue strode in with a severed head of a soldier in her hand. She tossed it at the feet of the nobles, then took her throne and looked at us with a steady gaze. 'Know this. I will always protect my court.'"

—Excerpt from Claudius Delmont, Prince of the Court's diary

Titania watched in shock as Ellie strode through the doorway that she'd just ripped open. Broken chains hung from her bloodied wrists. Ribbons of shadows raged around her, as her hair whipped up, as though she were a goddess. Her eyes were bottomless pits, all the white devoured. Fury darkened her face.

With every step forward, all traces of her torture faded away, as if they'd never been there at all.

This wasn't Nimue's mortal sister anymore. No, she had become something else—and it was downright terrifying. Titania dragged her gaze back to Mirena as the demon cried out in ragged fury.

"No, it can't be!"

There was only a quiet pause before Ellie spoke again, and Titania looked upon her, shivering at the wrath blazing in those nightmarishly dark eyes.

"I *said,* let my sister go!"

"How did you get free? I broke you!" Mirena demanded.

Harsh laughter bubbled from Ellie's lips as she eyed the demon venomously. There was no human warmth in those eyes anymore. The demon side had taken over. Power rolled off her in thick waves. "You can't break what was already broken."

The blade in the demon's hand didn't waver from Nimue's neck. "You were human!"

Ellie's hand snapped up. Darkness burst from her hands. "Not anymore."

The demon released Nimue, throwing up a wall of shadows as Ellie's bolt slammed into it, devouring it instantly. More bolts burst from those slender hands.

It was breathtaking.

Ellie advanced, just as Nimue used to prowl ahead of her armies, a creature of death unleashed.

Beside Titania, Claudius stepped forward. Titania's hand shot out, stopping him.

"Let's see what she can do."

Titania was curious to see how much of Atlas's magic the girl could wield... and whatever else was flowing from her. Because it certainly wasn't just from her old friend. It felt...older.

Ellie held up both of her hands. "I am the daughter of a demon. You shall not harm what is mine."

Magic burst from her, slamming into the wall. The roar of her raw power filled the air. Lorca moved forward.

"Stay back, Lorca!" cried Nimue. "Ellie could hurt you!"

Lorca's gaze snapped to her a look of desperate defiance on his face. It seemed like he would ignore her entreaty, but he stopped, closing his hands into tight fists, fury rolling off him.

"I said, let her go!" commanded Ellie.

Titania didn't like it. *This is more than Atlas's power. This is...something else.*

Ellie's power roared louder, the darkness raging around her like a small storm. But she wielded it with confidence, steady hands bearing down on the wall, determined to shatter it.

"What the hell is she?" whispered Claudius harshly. "That isn't..."

Titania was silent, keeping her eyes fixed on Ellie.

Ellie drew her hands back to her chest, pressing palms together. A low murmur spilled from her lips. It was a language Titania knew all too well. The question was, how the hell had Ellie learned it? The air prickled.

Waves of magic tumbled from the girl, whirling across the stone floor beneath her feet. Shadows took shape atop her head. A crown. Black jewels glittered at the thorny points. A dress forged of pure darkness formed on her body, and demonic symbols covered her exposed skin. Any trace of Ellie was being erased...and someone new was pushing through.

Someone Titania had seen before, once long ago, a mere drawing in a crumbling text. Her jaw dropped. Surely it wasn't possible? It couldn't be... There was no way.

Ellie lifted one hand and stepped up to the wall, pressing her palm against it.

The wall shattered.

The demon stood there, white-faced, clutching the knife to Nimue's neck. "*You!*"

Ellie cocked her head. "Yes. Me. Don't worry, Mirena, I will deal with you soon enough. For now, *run.*"

The demon's eyes rolled back in her head as she crumpled. Nimue swayed and started to fall. Ellie dashed forward, catching her before she hit the ground. Lorca raced over and dropped beside her. The three of them fussed over Nimue, but Titania couldn't stop staring at Ellie.

Already the shadows were bleeding away, revealing Ellie's human form. Worry was clear on her face as she huddled close, tending to Nimue while Lorca lifted her into her arms. She seemed so human, infinitely mortal and fragile.

Ellie's eyes rolled back, and the girl dropped like a stone to the ground.

Titania was beginning to understand what she had just witnessed...It sent shivers right down to the pit of her soul. Their troubles in the City of Slaves were about to get a lot more complicated.

Titania remained with Claudius to seal the demon crack while the others went to Helena's mansion, seeking a healer for the sisters. Claudius had wanted to go, but Titania gently reminded him to stay with her. She knew she could close the crack, but for the moment, Nimue needed to be with her sister and lover.

By the time they finished up and headed back to the mansion, the sun was already stretching out over the city. A biting chill lingered as they walked among the quiet streets. It pinched her cheeks red and bit through her furs. She loathed the cold, cursing it as she yanked her jacket tighter on her body.

In the end, Claudius returned to his home with their weapons so Titania could check on Nimue at the mansion. She slipped through an open door at the side of the building, drifting through the shadows until she found the room she was after.

Nimue lay on her bed, in a deep slumber, with Lorca curled at her side, holding her close to his chest. His head was buried in the crook of her neck. Even in her sleep, Nimue held him and curled into his embrace. Titania watched them for a few moments, satisfied that, even though Nimue was sickened, tonight wouldn't claim her.

After leaving them, she found Ellie's room. The girl slept soundly, even as Titania brushed the hair from her brow. Moonlight tumbled in from an open window, falling gently over her fine-boned face and gold-spun hair. She looked so human, so achingly mortal, that Titania wondered if she'd imagined what she'd seen. But as she gently brushed her powers against Ellie's mind, a chill stole down her spine.

A burst of power shot up, plunging into her head.

In the corner of her gaze, a figure emerged from the shadows. That cold, familiar power slid over her skin, dropping her to her knees. She bowed her head, as if by instinct.

"Curious," the woman murmured, a voice resonant with ancient power. "I did not expect anyone to recognize me...especially a demon not bound by a throne or the Keeper's curse. Rise, child, and meet my gaze."

Titania's heart was a raging storm of nerves in her chest. Instinct screamed at her not to rise, to keep her gaze lowered. This was no mere demon. She swallowed the lump in her throat and rose shakily to her feet, lifting her eyes. A shiver rippled through her as she looked at the woman standing before her.

No, not a woman.

A goddess. A mirror image of Ellie, though her hair flowed black and loose over bare shoulders. Thin straps held a tattered black dress to her flame and a black crown glittered in the moonlight.

"You know who I am." A note of amusement rang through the room.

Titania swallowed. "Lyria, Goddess of Death, Mother of Demons."

"Hello, General Titania of Azradan." Abruptly, Lyria's gaze flickered to Ellie, her jaw twitching. "It seems I do not have long. A shame. I had hoped for more time."

"Time? What do you mean?"

Lyria reached out to Ellie, caressing the girl's cheek. "Promise me you will train her. A darkness is brewing. My power passes to her now. It's time for the new gods to rise and the old ones to sleep."

Titania was still trembling when she returned to the mansion. The quiet halls did little to distract her from the tangled mess of her thoughts. Part of her questioned whether the encounter with Lyria had been real, but the lingering touch of ancient magic told her it hadn't been a dream.

Ellie.

Gods, what would Nimue think? The sister she was determined to protect, chosen to be the new Goddess of Death?

She stumbled into her office and wandered over to her desk. Still in her armor and splattered with blood, she sank into her chair and closed her eyes. A familiar pressure tugged at her head. Before she could react, it vanished as quickly as it had begun, and standing in front of her, clad in a flowing green dress, was someone she'd been hoping to see.

Amara.

Her somber brown eyes met Titania, softening with warmth. Her long flowing hair and soft, fine-boned face looked the same as they had weeks ago, but there was a note of exhaustion set in the dark lines under her eyes.

"About bloody time you reached out," grumbled Titania. "We need to talk. There's a lot to catch up on, and I have some questions."

CHAPTER 51

"The attacks at court have stopped. Peace has returned to the court. For now."
—Excerpt from Queen Nimue's diary

Flynn stalked toward the temple.

"This is madness!" Mira snapped, trailing after him.

His mind was made up. There was no turning back now, and nothing that Mira could say would deter him. She didn't feel what he did, what he'd experienced when Tobin kissed him. When he'd looked him in the eye and pleaded for Flynn to hide.

There was no more time for further training.

The hot midday sun beat down on the temple grounds as the rest of the fae went about their usual work. It was hard to believe that mere hours before, several of their own had been stolen. None of them dared to look at him. After he'd learned Tobin was gone, something inside of him snapped.

"Flynn! Just stop and talk to me. Please." Mira grabbed his upper arm.

He spun, wrenching his arm free. "I won't lose anyone else. Not again."

The fight dropped from her shoulders. "You're really going to do this, aren't you? I'm just worried you're not ready. You barely trained for the second trial and you have done nothing for the third. What if it kills you? Then all of this is for nothing. You'll be dead and I will be alone to save our people."

Anger flooded his veins and flushed his cheeks. "You think I'll fail?"

She threw her hands up. "That's not what I mean, and you know it!"

"Do I?" he threw back.

Mira stared back at him defiantly before the fight bled from her eyes, and she threw up her hands. “If you want to follow this path of madness, then do it alone. I won’t stand by and watch you die.”

A fiery retort rose to his lips, but she twisted on her heel and stormed off. He watched her, angry, ready to run after her, but his feet refused to move. His instincts were pulling him back to the temple, to Mathias.

Scowling, he headed into the temple. A few fae scattered out of his way as he made his way to Mathias’s office. At the door, Mathias awaited him, shoulders drooped, and shadows aging his face a thousand years. A heavy sigh fell from his cracked lips and he stepped aside, gesturing for Flynn to step inside.

Bowing, Flynn hurried inside and waited for Mathias to take his seat.

With a look of resignation on his face, Mathias said, “I know why you’re here, my son.”

“And will you refuse?” Flynn’s heart pounded in his chest.

Mathias lifted those steady golden eyes. “You will be afforded no rest then, even if you change your mind. Are you sure? There will be no turning back.”

For Tobin, he had to try.

“Yes, I understand. But Mathias, a ship will come in a week to take Tobin and the others away,” said Flynn. “I can’t let that happen. Not when I may get the power to do something.”

Mathias said nothing. He stood and walked over to a cold fireplace. Sparks leaped from his fingers to the pile of logs. A steady fire crackled to life, the ashy tones spilling into the air.

“They will retaliate. This act will not go unpunished,” Mathias warned.

The Empress’s soldiers. The woman who had taken everything from him and sold his people into slavery. Mathias’s warning was clear. There would be consequences.

The fight nearly fled him, but a dark voice stirred deep within his soul. A single word rose, taking hold.

Fight.

His hands closed into fists. “Then let them come. I’ll be ready.”

If he had to sell his soul to the old gods, then so be it. If he had to become a god, *then so, damn, be it.*

Mathias gave a sad smile. "Then say the words."

Flynn relaxed his hands and bowed. "Temple Master, I formally request to undertake the remaining trials without delay."

CHAPTER 52

"Wars come and go, losses and victories, death and rebirth. I believed myself prepared for the demands of ruling. I have never been so wrong in my life. Five hundred years of this throne and I can no longer ignore its whispers. Day by day, I feel myself slipping closer to madness."

—Excerpt from Queen Nimue's throne on the anniversary of her coronation

Shadows danced among the torch-lit halls. A breeze stirred in from some unseen source, carrying with it the stench of blood and death. The acrid note filled Aziah's lungs as she crept silently through the long hallway. Every sense strained for a sign of guards, and every breath and fall of her foot felt too loud, calling out to anyone who might be close by.

Locked doors and tapestries of ancient battles accompanied her walk through that cursed temple. When she came to a cavernous hall flanked by polished pillars, she paused. A towering statue stood watch at one end. It was of a woman with one golden crown atop her head and two others in her hands. Aziah had seen nothing similar in any of the common drawings of known spirits, which often had temples erected for them.

So, who was this temple built for?

As she emerged from the shadows, the sound of approaching footsteps echoed nearby. She jumped back and pressed against the wall. Two hooded figures appeared, each carrying a basket full of bloodied bandages. Their hands were stained red.

"Let us pray," the older woman murmured.

Her companion stopped. "We should not waste time. There is still more to drain and the Empress is growing impatient."

A younger woman, by the sounds of it. There was a familiar twang to her accent. Aziah's brow dipped. It sounded oddly like her old accent, back when she regularly spoke Torenellan, one of the fae dialects.

"There is always time to pray." The older woman sat her basket down. "To Mirena, Goddess of Chaos, we give thanks and offer the blessing of blood. May you favor this temple with good fortune."

She bowed her hand and murmured a series of lyrical prayers. Her companion cursed, snatched up her basket, and hurried off. Aziah waited until she was out of earshot then glided from the shadows, silent as a wraith. The woman started to rise, but Aziah yanked one of her daggers out, holding the blade to her throat, before she could even react.

"Scream and I'll slit your throat," hissed Aziah.

"Do it. Blood spilled here serves the goddess Mirena." The woman was still as a statue, with no tremor of fear in her words.

Aziah brushed her lips against the woman's ears. "A shame. Now, tell me what I wish to know and I may spare you. Where are the mountain slaves being held?"

"I do not fear death," the woman said.

Why were all the martyrs so damn stupid? Aziah pressed her dagger in until a trickle of blood welled and trailed down the pale throat. The woman remained steady. Even her pulse beat without hurry.

"Then you cannot help me."

Aziah pulled back, and plunged the dagger through the back of the ribs, up into the heart. The woman gasped as she slumped forward.

There was a small space behind the statue, but it was enough to hide the body.

Aziah slipped out of the room and headed off in the direction the other woman had taken. She knew that there were cells at the bottom of the temple. For sacrifices, the Empress had claimed. Traitors to the crown whose blood could be better served to the spirits.

Aziah had kept her mouth shut, knowing full well the affront of blood sacrifices to the spirits. It had been those times when she knew the Empress was testing her, baiting her to respond. After eighteen years at that murderess's side, lying came easily enough.

The hall ended at a staircase that descended into shadowy gloom. The stone pressed in so closely on either side her shoulders nearly touched it, and she didn't consider herself particularly broad. With one hand resting on her the hilt of her dagger, sheathed on her thigh, she descended swiftly.

As she moved from the last step, a distant scream split the silence. Her breath caught in her throat. When the air fell silent once more, she exhaled and pushed forward.

She inched along the gloomily lit hall until she came to the first cell, empty and stained with puddles of blood, shit, and vomit. The stench burned her eyes and twisted her stomach. Dozens more like it followed.

By the time she came to a cell with a man inside, his empty eyes scarcely lifted from the ground. Tattered cloth hung off his skeletal body, mottled with bruises and cuts in various stages of healing.

The following cells held more people. A few looked up, but none said a word. They watched with blank faces. She tried to talk to a girl who appeared nearly lucid when a soft plea stirred the air.

"Y-you're not one of them," a man whispered.

Aziah followed the sound. A slimly built young man pushed himself up from the filthy floor, eyeing her warily. "No, I'm not. Are you from the village of Fenware?"

Surprise widened his gaunt face. "Y-you know of my village?"

"I have been sent to determine whether you all still live. My lady sent me at the behest of one of your own," she explained. "But please, tell me of your name? How many still yet live? Why are you here?"

The distant screams of someone dying—tortured, perhaps—arrested his reply for a moment. Only once the silence returned its heavy grip did he speak again. "My name is Vaughn Cardan. I am not sure exactly how many of us are living, though I think no more than eighty. We're here for them to experiment on. They believe that our consumption of the red flower we grew, which we consumed in small doses once a year, has changed us. They torture us, then when they're done, bleed us dry." He paused for a moment. "Have you seen a blond girl, slim, a little freckle on her cheek, and a scar on her neck?"

Aziah said that she'd not—neither in the dead that she'd seen, nor the few living that she had passed. But the unsaid truth piled like stones on his bony shoulders. The fate of the woman he asked was likely not a promising one.

A look of hopelessness darkened his face. "You didn't come to save us today, did you?"

"I'm afraid not. We had to be sure you were alive first. That was a condition, I suspect, Wren must have given. She's journeyed far to save you."

Something in his eyes sparked. "Did you say, Wren? As in Wren Dumare?"

As he rattled off a description, she nodded. "That certainly sounds like the girl I saw. Given the fact you're all still here, I presume no others of you are dragons?"

"Dragons? Wren isn't a dragon. You must be confused."

Aziah's brow lifted. "I doubt that. She is the reason I'm here, after all. She and her Dragonir were on a mission to save your village."

He sunk to his knees, staring at the floor, laughing mirthlessly. "She always was different and apart from us. I suppose it makes sense...But if she's a dragon and has a Dragonir with her, why are we still here?"

"Probably something to do with a magical army standing between her and you." She had lingered long enough. There was more to see. By her count, she had a few more hours before dawn. Reluctantly, she stepped back from the cell. "Spread the word. Help is coming."

She felt his eyes locked on her as she walked away.

CHAPTER 53

"Once more, war is declared, but I feel disinterested. I send Titania and my other generals out, though this time I remain behind. I'm just so tired. So damn tired."
—Excerpt from Queen Nimue's diary

A white mist rolled in from the sea across the empty battlefield as a lone rider shot from the city, carving a path through it. The listless sky had dumped a deluge of rain over the night, and the morning offered only an endless stretch of cloud.

Nimue felt a flicker of anticipation curl in her belly. The fight that Sybilla hungered for was coming. The final refusal on the fourteenth day would be answered by the drums of war.

She pushed off the stone wall, her legs wobbling for a moment. A wave of nausea welled up, and the morning's breakfast threatened to appear. She squeezed her eyes shut, waiting for the weakness to pass. Eventually, it ebbed away enough for her to move.

The past two weeks had been hell on her body. She'd woken after being out cold for a few days, but improvements since then had been minimal. Most mornings she vomited blood, and during the day, could scarcely keep food down at all. Lorca kept pushing more at her, worry in his eyes, between the hours he spent in the library, hunting for a cure, and sitting with her in Ellie's room.

Her sister hadn't woken yet, much to everyone's confusion.

A shadow fell over her as a gust of wind hit her. She teetered for a moment as a bright light flashed behind her, dimming quickly.

"I thought I'd find you here," Lorca murmured.

"How's my sister?"

His arms slid around her waist as he gently drew her back to his chest, pressing a small kiss to her cheek. "Resting, as you should be."

"I've rested enough. It won't make much difference for me," she replied.

He snorted softly. "Were you always this stubborn?"

"Before I was Wren?" When he hummed a wordless reply, she sighed. "If you asked my court, yes. I suppose I am slowly becoming who I was before." She dared to meet his eyes, searching for his thoughts. "Does that bother you?"

She held her breath as his hand rose, brushing a strand of hair behind her ear. "I'm not going to change how I feel. What I fear is that you will fall out of love with me because you'll realize you deserve more than I can ever give you."

The raw honesty in his eyes sucked the air from her chest. For all her fears of him fleeing at the sight of her nature, she'd never considered that he might feel that she would be the one to walk away. She leaned into his hand that caressed small, tentative circles on her cheek, as if he were afraid even at that moment she would walk.

"I have lived thousands of years. I have loved and lost, grieved and raged at the fate I have endured, but never have I met anyone like you." She stared into his eyes and smiled. "I do not plan on going anywhere. You and I are fate, and if anyone tries to change that, let them know my fury."

Hours later, Nimue crawled from her room after a short sleep. She followed the thread of their bond down into the library where she found Lorca seated by one of the tables. Piles of books were heaped around him like a mountain range forged of forgotten stories.

"Found anything interesting?"

He closed the book in his hand. "Nothing of worth." As he dumped it on one of the piles, he glanced up. "The messenger returned for Sybilla's response. You can guess what her reply was."

"Refusal?"

"So it would seem," he replied.

She closed the distance to him, running a hand over his shoulders. Knots of tension met her fingers and she dug in, earning a low groan that rumbled from his chest.

"She's baiting them," she remarked.

The girl was up to something. She claimed to be transparent about her plans, but Nimue sensed there was something she was keeping from everyone. Lorca stood watching the distant army with the same shuttered expression he'd had all week. The approaching battle was unnerving him.

She peered over his shoulder at the books. "How is your research going?"

He pulled away from her touch and rose, turning to her with a sombre expression. "I've scoured so many books, but found nothing to help you."

"I wasn't talking about my problem. You were reading about Litania for a little while. Don't tell me you've stopped?"

"Of course, I've stopped, you're—" He looked away, his gaze shuttering.

The unspoken word carved the room out.

Dying.

She gave him a searching look. "And yet this may be your one chance for answers."

Lorca looked away and his hands tightened into fists. Tension ratcheted through his muscles, as though he were withdrawing into himself further from her. It made her heart ache. He was hurting for her, and there was nothing she could do. Nimue moved to him, pushing on as he tried to edge away from her. She reached out, cupping his face until he looked her in the eye. Raw grief met her.

"You think I could ever live with myself if something happened and I had been spending my time looking for answers about my sister? I can do that after you're saved," he replied harshly.

But what if there is no saving me? She wanted to ask, but the words felt too cruel, so they remained bound on her lips. She'd wanted so badly to save her people, but with her fading condition and an army outside the city, she didn't fancy their odds.

"You're a fool," she whispered.

"For having hope? Is that a demon thing? To give up?"

Heat flashed up her cheeks and she pulled away. "You believe I've given up?"

"You're certainly much more accepting of your condition," he replied, and she didn't miss the note of accusation in his voice.

"No more than you! Is your condition not growing worse or am *I* to ignore that?" she said heatedly, then folded her arms across her chest. "Is that a *Dragonir* thing?"

His nostrils flared. "That isn't—"

"*Yes, it is,*" she cut in, taking a step forward, reaching for him even as anger burned her blood. "I am not ignorant to my body failing and I am not giving up. But being Queen has meant that I have had to learn to prepare for the worst. It is the only way I ruled as long as I did, the only reason I yet still draw breath. This threat goes beyond my desires. If Mirena comes through with her army, and she certainly appears to have that attention, it will be to conquer. *That* is where my focus must be, not trying to solve a problem that might not have a solution. As long as I still breathe, I will fight. To defeat her, to live, to bring my people home and to spend whatever years I am blessed with, *loving* you. Even if you are a stubborn ass."

She wrapped her arms around his waist, burying her face in his chest. He offered no argument, no darkened looks, only his touch and presence. As she listened to his heartbeat, his grip tightened as if he was terrified that if he let go, she would be gone from his arms forever. So, for a selfish minute, she held the man she loved and pretended the world wasn't falling apart.

When Nimue visited her sister's room, Titania was by the bed, holding Ellie's hand. Those dark, fathomless eyes, black like the night itself, lifted and for a moment, she felt like a young demon again.

Silently, she sat down on the side of the bed, brushing a stray strand from Ellie's face. She appeared at peace, even as demonic magic eddied in the air, much of which appeared to be radiating from her.

Magic far older than anything Nimue had experienced before.

Titania straightened up. "How much of the fight do you remember after that demon had hold of you?"

Nimue winced at the memory. "Very little—why?"

Titania didn't answer immediately answer. She reached out, brushing some hair behind Ellie's ear tenderly. Her hand lingered for a moment, then she spoke again. "Ellie shattered the binds on her magic."

Which meant she'd broken down the last remnants of the spell Atlas had created to contain Ellie's magic. No doubt the vicious shattering of the spell would release all that magic, an amount that might potentially completely consume her sister.

The power she'd witnessed had been something else. Ancient, vicious, vengeful. It was a power she'd read about long ago.

A knife twisted in Nimue's gut.

"How the hell did the essence of the demon goddess end up in my sister?"

Titania's head lifted, and their eyes met. "Lyria appeared to me."

Air rushed from Nimue's lungs. "What?"

Her old friend told her what Lyria had said, and then about her visit with Amara. When silence claimed the room once more, Nimue's gaze fell to her sister. Her heart ached. All the promises of a normal life for Ellie were reduced to a thousand broken shards at her feet.

Nimue mourned as she found her voice. "I hope Amara is right, otherwise we may not stand a damn chance at what comes next."

When the sun dipped beyond the horizon, Nimue slipped into the library. Shadows crowded the quiet refuge, with only thin bands of moonlight spilling in from the narrow windows to shed any light. Dust floated iridescently in the air, settling gently on the wooden desk, cluttered with books from her late evening research. It had been left undisturbed, perhaps at Sybilla's command, or by Lorca, who she'd caught among the books in the twilight hours, buried among numerous magical texts.

Trying to save her, if such a thing was possible.

Sitting down, she picked up the journal, which contained all the information she'd learned about the kingdom. There were many notes about the Gray Army and its campaigns on the Mithra Archipelago nearly two decades ago. She carefully notated the rise of Alexandria, including how the Empress had maintained power in Danomir and the territories across the sea.

All of it she kept neatly written in her ancient demonic script, half out of habit, the rest in caution of Sybilla. The Princess might correctly assume the contents, but without the ability to read that would be all she had.

She plunged into another book. Minutes stretched into hours. Clouds shuffling across the sky concealed the moon several times, forcing her to pause, stubbornly refusing to go fetch a candle. She tried, of course, twice to light her own, much to a dismal failure. Even her ability to create fire was growing weaker.

"Nimue?" Lorca's voice whispered through the dark.

She squinted through the gloom. High above behind her, the clouds parted. Moonlight spilled into the space, striking his face. Those piercing eyes slid flicked over the books, then returned to her.

Her heart slammed hard in her chest as she waited for him to speak. Gods, even in the dark, wearing a loose white shirt and leather pants clinging to his thick legs, he was maddeningly handsome. Desire heated her blood. She itched to pin him to the floor, strip him bare and ride him in the moonlight.

"Want a hand?"

She blinked. "What?"

His gaze darkened as he moved forward, prowling closer, each step agonizingly slow. "Something on your mind?"

The words died in her mouth as he picked up a history book, idly leafing through the pages. Her gaze locked on the deft movements of his hands, recalling vividly exactly what those hands could do. On her. *Inside her.*

Her core tightened. It was a dangerous trail of thoughts.

But demons below, her mind wandered anyway. She tightened her grip on her quill, which then snapped.

The sound broke her thoughts. She looked up to discover Lorca smirking. Her cheeks flushed and to distract him from her embarrassment, she pushed back from her chair and attempted to school her features. Lorca's molten gaze lifted from the book and lingered on her face as he walked slowly around the table.

"I've been curious to ask what this says," he murmured, lifting her journal.

She blinked, realizing she'd lost herself again. "It's about this kingdom. Nothing too exciting."

His presence affected her more than he knew. She stared into those deep eyes, a shiver rippling across her shoulders, then pulled away, returning to the notes in her hand. The words spilled from her lips.

One page bled into another, then another, and he didn't stop her. She felt him inch closer, his warmth falling over her, his woody scent invading her senses. Her heart raced faster, and her voice trembled.

His hand brushed her cheek, tucking a stray strand of hair behind her ear. "Nervous?"

She stopped, swallowing the lump lodged in her throat. "Why would I be nervous?"

"Why, indeed?" He stooped low, lips brushing the shell of her ear. "Nimue, you need to tell me to stop."

"Why?" she asked in a voice scarcely above a whisper.

He pulled back slightly. "Because I am trying to be good. You—"

She stood up sharply, chest to chest, meeting his gaze, a stubborn fire sparking in her chest.

"I'm *alive.* Stop treating me like I'm going to break."

Heat flashed in his eyes. "You nearly *died.*"

"Do I look like I'm dying now?" She inched closer, their breaths mingling as she nipped his lips. "And what about you? Still pretending as if you are fine?"

His hands snapped to her hips, pulling her closer. Warning darkened his face. "Careful, Nimue."

"*To hell with careful.*"

She grabbed his collar, pulling his mouth down to hers.

He froze. Doubts whispered in her mind. She pulled back when his grip tightened, hauling her back in. A storm erupted between them. Desperation burned across her skin.

His hand slid to her ass, lifting her onto the table, her legs wrapping around his waist. Their lips danced together, breaths becoming one, hands entangling, moving over clothing, removing it. Her shirt went first, then his. His hands dropped to her pants, tearing at the strings, before pulling them down her legs to discard them on the floor.

Losing his lips had her reaching for him, desperate, hungry. But he dropped to his knees before she could stop him, his mouth descending on her. All thought left her. She threw her head back with a groan as he devoured her, savoring every inch. Licking, teasing, sucking, and drawing her higher into oblivion. Wordless cries tumbled one after another.

Pleas for him to—

Stop? No, demons below, no, *not that.*

She hurtled over the edge with a scream. Heady desire flooded her limbs, stringing out all thought and sense. She stood and pulled him up to meet her mouth, her lips finding his. This time, she grabbed his pants and tore them off, the scraps of material pooling at his feet.

His hardened length bobbed, all ready for her, the tip glistening.

"Nimue—"

He never had a chance to finish as she kneeled and took his cock into her mouth. This was his turn to lose his mind, to be hers to command. He shuddered as she moved over him, moving her mouth and hands in sync, listening to every breathless movement.

She wanted to be his madness, his hope, his future.

Even as his grip tightened on her hair, as if that might arrest some control back, she pushed on, taking him in deeper, harder. Teasing him with bliss. His body shook, then he threw his head back with a groan as he let go.

She licked him, savoring it all, and then stood slowly, running a satisfied hand over his length and his chest. Harsh breaths filled the space. The stench of their desire consumed every sense, roaring to life a new wave of hunger, as she pushed him back to lie on the table.

Their gazes remained locked as she climbed up, moving over him. Her hands pressed flat over his slick chest, the erratic thud of his heart matching her own. It spurred her on as she raised herself over him, teasing him with her heat until he became hard for her. She sank down, throwing her head back with a low groan.

"Feel me," she commanded, rolling her hips. "I'm alive."

He groaned, nails biting into her hips, nearly piercing her flesh. The pain was nothing as she felt him thrust up, meeting every demand she gave him.

"I feel all of you. Gods, Nimue, don't stop."

"Don't command me," she said heatedly. "I am your Queen."

His hips thrust up hard. "And I am yours, all yours."

Those words sent her hurtling to the edge.

She forced herself to slow, taking back the pace. A low snarl rumbled from his chest in response as he yanked his lips back, fire sparking in his eyes. But he didn't let go and met the deeper roll of her hips. A battle of wills raged between them. One she would not lose.

His hand dropped between them, stroking her.

Her control slipped.

She took him even deeper, leaning close as her lips brushed his ear.

"Mine," she murmured, flooding their bond with her desire.

He let go, sinking his teeth into her shoulder, a thundering groan shaking through his body. She let herself go with a savage scream, falling against his chest. Closing her eyes, she trailed lazy kisses along his neck and shoulder.

"You are mine, Lorca," she whispered. "In this life, and the next."

He hummed softly. "I like the sound of that, my Queen."

CHAPTER 54

"Nimue sits at night in the garden, staring up at the stars. I approached her once to ask if she wished for company, but she replied she did not. She is becoming distant, which is often the first sign. Even Claudius cannot reach her. More than anything, I grieve, anguished that I will lose my friend—but this course I know cannot be prevented."

—Excerpt from General Titania's diary

Candles flickered gently in the library. Their sweet, waxy fragrance hung heavy in the air. Nimue sat with her knees drawn up, scribbling on her journal. Lorca was stretched out beside her on the table, shirtless. The buttery light danced over the scratch marks lining his back and arms, and the bruises her lovemaking had left behind. He was leafing through a book, seemingly unaware of her stare, and had an air of contentment about him. As if there was nowhere else, he'd rather be.

As she thumbed through another book, her gaze kept straying. Desire coiled again low in her belly, drawing her thoughts to dangerous waters.

His molten gaze lifted, the corner of his mouth sparking to a wicked grin that did nothing to slow her racing heart. "Nimue..."

"What?" she replied breathlessly.

A silence stretched between them. Lorca rose, setting the book aside. The smile fell from his face as he moved across the table and gently cupped her cheek. "How are you feeling today?"

Her desire cooled in an instant. "Honestly, I'm a mess. All I want to do is leave this damn city, abandon this whole accursed rebellion, but I can't."

"Can't we?" He had no idea how damn tempting it was.

She laughed coldly. "No, we can't. Well, I can't."

"You act like it is your responsibility alone to stop that threat," he replied, his brow dipping.

"In a way, it is. A long time ago, I convinced the others that we didn't need to return to the demon realm, that we could stay here. It didn't matter that our arrival had caused the barriers between the realms to weaken. What did we care if a few beasts slipped through? I didn't want to return. I liked it here." She pulled away. Being close to him was hard as all those ugly truths tumbled from her lips, one after the other. "Because of my selfishness, we now face a threat that could destroy us all. So, I have to put aside all my feelings with my people, with...with how much I struggle to be around Claudius."

He drew a sharp breath, silent for a moment, before asking, "What is your history with him?"

She pushed off the table, itching to move for distance. His piercing gaze burrowed through her defenses. "I don't want to talk about him. I can't. Not tonight."

But she knew she owed him the story with Claudius. It had been buried within her for so long, festering like an open wound. Her blood ran thick with poison from it.

Why couldn't she find the words to tell him?

Lorca stood and moved closer. His shadow fell over her, but he made no sound, nor attempt to touch her. The space between them felt vast, like an ocean.

"What happened?" he asked once more.

"I—" No, I can't, no, not now. She wrenched herself away, the wound of her past ripping open once more.

She made it halfway across the room when a hand clamped around her wrist. "Just tell me. *Please.* You are hurting. Let me help—"

"We had a child!" She spun around, tears burning, threatening to spill down her cheeks.

Lorca's eyes flew wide, but he said nothing, his lips parted. Nothing but the roar of her own heart filled her ears, drowning out all else. She was stripped bare, all her sins exposed. Ragged breaths rattled from her body.

She took a step toward him. "She died and I broke. I broke into so many *damn* pieces and he *left.* He just left and never came back! He abandoned us...and you know what I did? I *burned.* I screamed and raged and tore the mountains apart, chasing every fae out. And then I waited for *five hundred years!* He never came back, he never—"

She was pulled into his arms, and in that warmth, she felt her heart crack wide open. The tears broke through, tearing her apart like a vicious storm until she slumped forward. An inhuman cry tore from her lips as she sank to the ground. Lorca dropped with her, never letting go, but holding her as steadfast as always.

"I am right here, Nimue." He pulled back, framing her face with his hands, their eyes meeting. "I love you, scars and all."

#

Morning light trickled in through a slit in the curtains as Nimue sat up in bed, rubbing the sleep from her eyes. A delicious ache lingered in her legs and core. Peeling back the blankets, she inspected the marks left by Lorca's grip on her hips. They'd heal soon enough.

Beside her, the bedcovers nearly consumed Lorca's slumbering form. Only the tiniest hint of black curls peeked out near the pillow and a single arm stretched out to her, where he'd been holding her in his sleep. She carefully uncovered his face. Asleep, at peace.

As if sensing her stare, his eyelids fluttered, then lifted. Green eyes met hers. "Is it morning?"

"Maybe, hard to say. Do you want to rest in your dragon form?"

He groaned as he sat up. "Later. Let me enjoy this moment."

His hair was ruffled, chaotically hanging around his face. The beauty of him left her aching. Without realizing it, Nimue reached out, cupping his jaw, and caressing his smooth skin.

She was edging closer to a place where he could not follow her. The thought made her pull away, but his hand snapped up, catching hers. He pulled her into his chest and buried his face in the crook of her neck, breathing her in deeply.

"You smell like me," he mumbled approvingly.

She snorted and pulled away, climbing out of bed before he could stop her. "Possessive man."

Her clothes lay on the floor, torn to ribbons in his need. Frowning, she dug out a fresh change of clothes, wincing a little as she hauled the pants over her bruised hips.

"Sore?" Lorca.

She tugged the shirt down over her head, glancing his way. "Are you?"

He grinned wickedly, opening his mouth to reply.

The city bells tolled, a long, heavy sound. Unease cooled her blood. It meant only one thing. Spinning sharply on her heel, she grabbed her boots, slipping them awkwardly on as she hopped across the room. The back sheath for her two short swords was hanging over the back of a chair. She slid it on and, turning to Lorca, saw he had already gotten out of bed and was pulling on his clothes and weapons.

She put a hand on his chest. "Stay close to me."

"Nimue..."

"I've fought many battles. I need you to have my back, okay?"

Truth was, part of her thought she might shield him from the horrors that were about to descend on the city.

Suddenly, his mouth was on hers, hard and fast, then gone all too soon.

"I will always have your back."

Nodding, a wave of emotion threatening to overwhelm her, she pulled away and they headed out.

CHAPTER 55

"The end lays before me, my only option clear. I have decided to inform Claudius. The time for him to become King has come. This will be my final command to him, and then I will have my peace."

—Excerpt from Queen Nimue's diary

Sybilla moved like a wraith as she slipped into the old temple. The spirit awaited her below, standing by the low burning fire, framed by its amber glow. Only as she moved closer did the spirit turn, an unreadable mask staring back.

"It's time—are you ready?"

She wasn't, but she nodded anyway, doubting there would ever be a time when she was ready. "Yes."

The spirit nodded, then walked to Sybilla. "There will be no turning back beyond this point. You understand this?"

Truthfully, that point had long since passed. "Yes."

Even though their deal terrified her, she battled on. What was her soul worth anyway when the war would inevitably demand the price of her mind? Using her prophetic abilities would consume her, eventually. She might have twenty years—or she might have five.

All the more reason to finish the war quickly and choose a suitable heir, if she could not produce one of her own.

She fished out the dagger from her hip and slashed it across her open palm. Blood welled in a thick line before trickling down her wrist and onto the ground. She sheathed the dagger and held out her bloodied hand. "The price."

Something unreadable flashed in those dark eyes. The spirit didn't move.

Blood pounded in Sybilla's ears, drowning out the crackling fire and harsh sound of her breathing. Something coiled tight in her gut and her vision clouded.

The spirit's hand shot out, taking hers.

A blinding flash of light and molten heat flooded her limbs, surging inwards to devour her. Her head jerked back as she screamed in agony. The darkness surged in, crushing the light, and swallowed her whole.

A sharp throbbing behind her eye hauled her from oblivion. Groaning, she sat up, trying to ignore the pain in her limbs, fighting every movement. Drool dripped from the corner of her mouth. She glanced around the room blearily.

The spirit was nowhere to be seen.

The pain in her hand was gone, and the wound was healed, not even a scratch left behind. Had she imagined it?

She pushed herself up to her feet, swaying a little. Enough time had passed. She had to return to the mansion before a search party was sent out. Forcing one foot forward, then another, she dragged herself up the stairs and out of the temple.

But as she walked out onto the street, she froze.

The city bells were ringing. The attack had begun.

PART 3

SIEGE

CHAPTER 56

"She believes I will yield to this command. I will not. I cannot stand by and just let her—no, I will not. I…I. Demons below, I love her…"

—Excerpt from Prince Claudius Dellabore's diary

Watch out!

Lorca sent a desperate warning as a ball of fire hurtled toward them. Nimue's wings snapped in, diving sharply, the wind screaming in her ears. The city below rushed to meet her. At the last second, she threw her wings wide and shot across the rooftops.

Fire split the sky, tearing open the thundering clouds. Gusting winds swept embers across the city, falling like glowing red snow across the streets teeming with terrified people. Screams ricocheted from windows where people stared in horror as fire rained down.

Lorca shot past her, and powered upward, flying high above the city walls. Nimue followed close behind. Soldiers scrambled out of the way as she burst past, shouting and snarling.

The air was heavy with the stench of sweat and dirt and oil, infused with the coppery tang of freshly spilled blood. She gazed across the sprawling field littered with traps and pits, to the distant tree line, and what she saw turned her blood to ice.

A row of trebuchets—each one hurling enormous fireballs straight at the city walls. One after another, a steady rain of fire tore across the sky, ripping through the low blanket of clouds.

Hell had arrived at the City of Slaves, bringing with it the wrath of the Empress.

We need to take out those trebuchets. Follow me and watch for archers. She gave him a searing look. *If you get yourself shot, I will drag your soul back to this realm and rip it apart.*

His head pricked up, and amusement bubbled through the bond. *As you command, my Queen.*

Nimue flew high, flinging her wings wide until she entered the churning storm clouds. Darkness surrounded her, the howling wind lashing her scales, blowing her in every direction at once.

Lorca soared into view, his throat already glowing with the promise of fire.

Ready? she asked.

With you, always.

And in sync, they plunged toward the battlefield. For a moment, their roars silenced the war cries and drums until the carnage began. Dragon fire collided with the trebuchets, exploding them on impact. Wagons and equipment were destroyed as soldiers on horses attempted to flee. Blood and smoke followed, but she didn't stop, the fire pouring from her without end. Men screamed, desperately attempting to escape the raging infernos she and Lorca had unleashed.

This was what she was born to do, what sang in her veins and fed her soul. She was no hero, no creature created of heroism and kind ideals.

She was Nimue, the Demon Queen.

CHAPTER 57

"A terrible disaster has occurred. Even now, I cannot make sense of it. Every part of me hurts, even as I write this. One moment I was walking at the edge of the sparring yard with Claudius, arguing over my decision to lose at the next throne challenge. The next moment a blinding light and rush of pain came followed by darkness. When I woke, I was with five others, and we stood in a field of bodies and ruins. I knew we were no longer in our realm."

—Excerpt from Queen Nimue's diary

The Merchant Quarter was burning.

Pillars of smoke billowed high into the sky, turning day to night, and chasing off the bite of winter. A raging inferno stained the clouds a burnished amber until it appeared as though the city itself had been devoured by the demon realm.

For Titania, as she sat on the back of a wagon of healers as it raced through the burning streets, a dozen injured already onboard, it felt like being back home.

The ash-choked air dried her lips, nearly burning her lungs with every breath. Waves of heat bore down, leaving sweat dripping from her skin as they barreled around the corner.

"Halt!" one of the healers shouted and pointed across the fray. "Over there!"

The wagon jerked to a stop. Several whimpers sounded from the injured at her feet as two of the healers leaped from their seats, dashing over to where a woman was hunched over a man lying on the street. One healer knelt, took one look at the man, then glanced back at the wagon, shaking their head. They murmured something to the woman before they came back.

The driver clicked his tongue and flicked the reins. The wagon jerked forward, and they were off once more, the horses breaking into a brisk trot. Hooves thumped heavily over the winter-hardened earth.

Titania squinted ahead as they continued through the winding streets. Luckily, the fire hadn't yet spread but, if they couldn't control it, then the whole Merchant Quarter would burn.

The same healer who'd shouted before carefully clamored over the injured, dropping next to her.

"There are so many wounded and not enough of us," the healer said, her voice nearly consumed by the roar of the fire.

"There will be many more," said Titania, glancing skywards. She noticed the healer was shaking, her arms wrapped around her middle. The pitiful sight touched her and propelled a question from her lips. "What's your name?"

"Rell, short for Aurelia—and yourself?"

A lie nearly rose to her lips, but she pushed it aside. "Titania."

"That's a beautiful—"

A huge fireball roared overhead, cutting off the reply as it crashed with a thundering bang onto a nearby house. The horses reared up in a panic, jolting the wagon and making the injured cry out in terror and pain. The wagon dropped back down, and the driver calmed the horses into order.

They took off again, racing down the streets as hell rained down.

Titania felt the shadows call to her, the dark magic within answering. It lifted the hairs along her arms, sending shivers right down to her fingertips. She drew in a deep smoky breath, forcing the power back down.

The wagon slowed as it clattered into the market square near the merchant docks. Tents were erected along the wharves, as far from the water as they could get. But the bitter wind made the cloth structures flutter precariously.

Titania jumped down as the wagon drew to a halt. More healers approached from the fray, carefully lifting off the injured and ferrying them away. The smallest was a small child who clung to a dead woman. Titania stiffened, old memories threatening. Ugly emotions twisted in her chest like a knife. She jumped as Rell came forward and carried the child away.

Don't think about it.... Don't go there. But try as she might, as she headed to the nearest tent, her mind inevitably wandered. She'd hoped by staying with the healers that the sound, and the *stench* of the army beyond the wall, wouldn't trigger things. As her heart raced faster, she realized she was a fool.

A stupid fool.

She pushed through the curtains into the first tent and set to work, hoping the activity would banish the memories that threatened to consume her once more.

Patient after patient, she worked methodically, dealing with what wounds she could, and setting bones. More than once, someone came in too far gone and all she could do was hold their hand as they died, whimpering in agony. She itched to grab her dagger, to ease their suffering.

Soon, she was in another tent when Rell reappeared, her dress splattered in blood. Shadows lined her eyes. "There's more coming in and the fire is getting closer to the docks. What the hell are we going to do?"

To that, Titania had no answer. She *knew* she ought to be at the wall, commanding forces, leading the fight, defending the city. Claudius had men at his command, those who would follow her. It wouldn't be much, but she'd led with worse odds before

As she went to reply to Rell, a man approached. "Both of you, come with me!"

Titania followed him back to the wagons that were filled with healers clutching their supplies. They clamored up and sat next to the driver.

"Where are we going?" she asked.

The driver flicked the reins, the wagon surging forward. "To the wall."

CHAPTER 58

"We are alone in a strange land. These folk bear no powers and look at us as though we are gods."
—Excerpt from Atlas's diary

Sybilla sprinted down the street toward the mansion. Her legs burned, every breath stinging as if she was swallowing knives, but she pushed on. She had to get to the wall—and fast.

As she rounded the corner, a squad of soldiers marched in her direction. Just behind them was Captain Oren astride a horse. She twisted sharply on her heel, dashing to him. His eyes widened at her approach.

"Your horse, now!"

Stupefied for a second, he stared, but as she grabbed the reins, he jumped down and she swung herself up. "Get all your men to the wall, *now!*"

The horse took off with a neigh, its hooves clattering across the cobblestone. She hunkered down low, urging every bit of speed from the creature. Dropping her hand to its side, she pushed the magic into its skin. Her magic was pure energy; it might be wielded like a blade, or it might provide a last rush of strength. A second wind flowed through the horse as it thundered down the street. The surrounding buildings blurred as she rode faster than ever before, spurred by the new power roaring through her veins.

Passing through several city gates, she arrived at the Merchant Quarter. No one dared bar her as she barreled through, the light streaming off her skin like luminous starlight. Magic spilled from her lips with every harsh breath, as if it were seeking release from her body. She was ready to fulfill her mission.

Pillars of smoke clouds billowed high, blocking out the sun. Darkness swept across the city, distinguishing any remaining pockets of light. It was as though hell itself had descended.

A thunderous roar came from overhead. Red flashed. Sybilla's gaze lifted right as a fireball flew straight toward her. Cursing, she yanked the reins, moving aside just as the inferno shot past and crashed into a building. Her terrified horse reared up, nearly unseating her. A string of curses tumbled out of her mouth as the horse dropped back down with a jolt and tossed its head, panicked by the growing chaos.

She leaned down, running her hand along its neck, pushing more magic into its coat. Pitching forward, she whispered into its ear, and slowly, the horse steadied. She remembered Omi telling her that the horses could smell her fear, so she tried to calm her racing heart. It would do no good to be thrown from a horse now and snap her neck.

There was too much to be done.

With a flick of the reins, the horse galloped off down the street. Several more fireballs blazed overhead, one slamming into a building behind her.

The city burned in pillars of flame and smoke.

Doubts crowded in, thick and fast, and whispered how foolish she'd been. Imagining that with a bit of planning and scheming, she could overthrow her aunt or even protect the city.

No!

She shook her head to dispel those thoughts. This city would be hers and she would strike such a blow to her aunt. If she had to slaughter thousands upon thousands of Alexandria's men and make her cities bleed, then so be it. She would burn them all.

The stench of ash thickened as she neared the looming shadow of the wall. The distant glow of fires raged across the Merchant Quarter as fireball after fireball slammed into the wooden buildings. Explosions shook the ground, sparks leaping high into the sky, sending embers into the howling wind. Flames whipped up, racing on across the streets, devouring more homes. Screams followed; desperate and unanswered pleas for help lost in the cacophony.

At the last stretch to the wall came the tolling of war drums and chant from her aunt's army.

Yanking on the reins, Sybilla slowed the horse to a trot before she leaped down, taking off to the men taking up position around one of the city's main gates. Sweat glistened on their sooty faces, and desperate eyes stared at her as she raced past, glowing like a sun.

She spied General Galen bellowing orders and dashed over to him. His eyes widened. She stopped, chest heaving, but before she could speak, a look of anger darkened his face.

"Where in the spirits have you been?"

The bite in his voice pulled her up sharply. Her shoulders squared. The man had forgotten who he was speaking to. Calm flooded through her, the light growing brighter around her, ribbons of magic swirling around her limbs.

"Calm the men. I have come. They will not break through."

She took off past him, darting into an open door to one of the towers. Men crowded the stairs as she shoved past, throwing some into walls by accident. But her mind was set, her body throbbing with power. The spirit was with her.

At the top, she crashed through the door and sprinted out onto the wall.

It was time.

She slowed her breathing, trying to calm herself. If the other spirits hadn't sensed the betrayal of the one now bound to her, then they were certainly about to sense what she did next.

All she hoped was that this effort was enough. Just one step closer to winning.

Ready, little Princess? The spirit murmured.

She squared her shoulders. "Ready."

At once, the power over her own body slipped away, reducing her to a passenger. Her arms flung wide, light erupting at her fingertips. Orbs that blazed brighter, growing rapidly until the nearby archers scrambled away. The power continued to expand, and she stepped forward, slamming her palms onto the wall itself.

The world exploded into light.

The spirit's soothing voice slid into her mind. *As per our agreement, my name. You may call me Rhea.*

CHAPTER 59

"These mortals call us gods and build temples in our names. We use our powers and bring them a good harvest, calm winds, and safe homes. For a time, we are power, absolute and final. But Amara worries that there is some tragedy to come."
—Excerpt from Nimue's diary

The battlefield was awash in flames and smoke, and the agonized cries of men ringing in her ears. Nimue flew like a blade, cutting down all who stood in her way. She turned her gaze to the soldiers retreating to the trees. They ran like ants escaping the flood, but as she sent her fire to rain death upon the forest, an agonized roar split the air. Her jaws slammed shut and she tore her focus from the screams of the men to Lorca—

As he fell from the sky, a dozen arrows sunk into his side.

Nimue's wings flared wide, driving hard and fast, propelling her faster than she'd ever flown before. The ground blurred, becoming a stream of ash and charred earth. All the carnage she had wrought was obliterated from the forefront of her mind.

Her soul roared down the bond, clinging desperately to the flickering thread. Heat burned through her wings, but she didn't care. All focus was on Lorca. She would not lose him. Not now.

She threw her claws into his body, colliding mid-air. For a split second, they tumbled through the air, the wind screaming against her. Nimue pushed upward as an arrow shot past her head. A yelp of alarm broke from her lips as she banked sharply. Dozens of arrows shot hissed straight at her. One cut across her wing, tearing the skin. Heart pounding, she headed for the city.

Billowing smoke twisted high from the burning city. It was an ominous sight, and yet, atop the wall, a single bright light. It blazed like a dawning sun, growing brighter with every second.

Familiarity sparked deep in her soul. *A spirit.*

Another volley of arrows cleaved the air, falling short as she raced toward the city walls. Curses ripped through her as she realized she was too low. She dug deep, drawing on her last reserves of energy, and surged up barely making it over the top of the wall, where she dropped Lorca onto the walkway. The soldiers scattered out of the way, bellowing as she crash-landed.

As every inch of her body howled in agony from the crash, she lifted her head.

The world erupted into a blinding light.

Silence reigned even as the light dimmed, and she could see once more. A shimmering shield glowed just beyond the wall, rising until it arched over the city in a protective dome. Pillars of smoke still sailed harmlessly through, joining the storm overhead.

Pulling her gaze away, she glimpsed Lorca, and in a flash, she shifted back and staggered forward. She dropped to find his side riddled with arrows and a trail of blood staining his glossy scales. Shuddering breaths racked his body. Her heart stopped dead in her chest.

"Help him!" she screamed.

Healers emerged from the chaotic fray of soldiers and jostled her out of the way. She could only watch as they carefully removed the arrows, whispering among themselves. A single word caught her attention, freezing her blood.

Poison.

A hand touched her arm. She spun around sharply, heart pounding. Sybilla threw her hands up, a strange glow lighting her skin. The ancient magic rolling off her caught Nimue off guard, for she knew it well. Spirit magic.

"I need your help," Sybilla said urgently.

"With what? We stopped those attacks," Nimue replied.

Lorca let out a whimpering groan, his body shuddering as the healers worked on him. She couldn't leave his side. Not when he was so sick. What if something happened to him?

"The fires. My men can't stop it, but you can." As her mouth opened to protest, Sybilla pressed on. "If we don't stop them, hundreds or even thousands will die. *Please.* I'll make sure Lorca is saved. I will save him, but for this I need you. This city needs you."

Nimue wrenched her gaze to the burning district. The thick smoke billowed high into the sky. Screams tore through the air, panicked as people ran for their lives.

"I don't know if I can stop that. My body...I'm not—"

A hand pressed on her back, and a rush of energy ripped through her, flooding her veins. The pressure faded, allowing her to turn. Sybilla stepped back, swaying on her feet. The guard behind her rushed forward, catching her as she fell.

"What did you do?" she asked.

Sybilla smiled weakly. "Gave you the help you need. Now, please, save this city."

People screamed, scattering as she landed with an awkward trot.

Tucking her wings in, she shifted back and burst into a run. The chaos was frenetic along the docks as healers rushed about, desperately attending to the scores of wounded that stumbled in from the hazy streets. The ash-choked air whirled and howled in the chaos, pressing the oppressive heat down across the docks like a smothering blanket.

Beads of sweat ran down her face as she pushed through the fray, side-stepping between the wounded and groups of bloodied healers. She emerged at the mouth of a street, the flames rapidly approaching, barely a couple of buildings away. Several children were sprinting down the middle, the flames close behind.

Nimue darted forward, throwing her hands up as the flames licked closer to the kids. Barely a few feet away, a building exploded, the shockwave sending her flying.

She threw her hand out, catching on the pressed earth, as she landed. Driving back up to her feet, she dashed toward the children, who had been thrown into a stack of crates. Their terrified sobs reached her ears as she dropped beside them, throwing up her hands as the fire came down.

Twisting her hands, she worked the fire into a wall, then pushed it back away and stood up, the effort burning her arms. Her body shuddered, but she pressed her heels in. In the corner of her vision, she saw the kids stumble off, heading for the docks.

A presence brushed her mind, the same one she'd felt back at the wall. Warm, comforting. Familiar. It slid in with ease. She knew a spirit when she felt one, and yet she wasn't afraid or wished to fight it.

Draw the fire into yourself. The same voice, feminine, humming with ancient power.

And do what with it?

Release to the sky. You can do this.

Nimue frowned. *Who are you?*

There was a pause, then a soft chuckle. *We've met before and we will meet again.*

Questions threatened her control, but she shoved them back down. She stretched out her hands, reaching for the raging inferno surrounding her. The heat licked her cheeks, embers dancing across her skin like sparks of sunlight. Closing her eyes, she focused on the flames and summoned them inwards.

The fire leaped in response, a beast sparked with interest, and reached out. She dragged it in closer, but as the first of the flames brushed her fingertips, forging the link, everything erupted. The fire roared into her. Heat blistered along her skin, a thousand daggers piercing her all at once. Tears burned her gaze as a metallic taste pooled in her mouth.

More fire crashed into her, waves of it filling her with more magic than she'd felt in years. Not since her time as Queen in the demon realm. The world fell away, all sound and sight gone, only the cacophony of the fire, and the rush of raw magic pooling in.

Pain lashed up her back and down her limbs, but she held on, clenching her teeth, as tears streamed down her face.

Keep your hands up, she screamed to herself as her arms trembled, fighting to keep up.

She tried to pry her eyes open, to see how much was left, but all the strength she had left was keeping her standing.

Another wave crashed into her, sending her staggering forward. The connection wavered. Cursing, she threw her hands up with a savage scream, and opened herself fully, letting another wave pour in. Her legs wobbled, threatening to give out, but she dug her heels in.

She clenched her jaw tighter until pain throbbed through her whole head, and the blood squeezed through her lips, dribbling down her chin. Sticky wetness ran down from her eyes and her ears. Thicker than tears.

Blood.

The fire began to slow. Her control tightened, nearing breaking point. Ragged breaths racked her chest as she clung on for dear life.

A final surge collided with her hands. She threw her head back, screaming. The presence from before flooded her mind again.

Do it now, Nimue!

Throwing her palms upward, she turned the sky to fire.

CHAPTER 60

"Claudius believes he can hide his affections for Nimue, but I see how he looks at her. With longing. It is a tragedy waiting to happen. His heart is too wild and fickle for Nimue, whose soul yearns for a peace he can never give her."

—Excerpt from Amara's diary

Fire streaked across the sky and slammed into the Merchant Quarter. War drums and distant chants sounded beyond the wall, growing closer. The song of war.

Titania's blood roared in response. This should've felt like home, but instead a sense of dread coiled tightly in her gut, a snake poised to strike. Flashes of another time and city, far beyond this glittering sea, threatened to come once more. A woman's face appeared in her mind. Ocher skin, luminous dark eyes, tightly curled black hair. Titania's breath caught in her throat, and she blinked the woman's face away.

The wagon rattled over the damaged roads. Beside her, a healer cried out in alarm. But Titania couldn't offer any words of comfort. All she could do was clutch tightly at her knees, tension ratcheting her body until her bones ached and a headache throbbed behind her eye. A wave of nausea pushed burning liquid up the back of her throat.

The wagon jerked to a stop. Men marched in a formation past them toward the gate. A few glanced at her as she climbed down and helped the other healers down, along with their satchels laden with supplies.

Rell shot her a worried look. "I've never been this close before...what if the wall falls?"

Titania shouldered her satchel. "I will let nothing hurt you, understand?"

"You speak as if you can fight?" Rell laughed nervously.

"I've got a few talents," was all Titania said before a soldier shouted for them to follow.

They followed him through the marching chaos, nearly getting knocked down twice before they made it across the street. The cacophony of shouting, ringing metal, the approaching army, and the thump of a thousand boots grew even louder.

They were led into a warehouse, already brimming with the injured and dying. The familiar coppery stench washed over her. No time was wasted as they set to work. Under the direction of another healer, Titania helped set out more makeshift beds on the ground and moved the less injured men to them. Their grateful smiles, bone-tired and innocent, tore at her, but she pushed away from the ugly well of old memories.

This isn't Toranelle, she reminded herself.

But it was hard to not think that as she tended to a myriad of minor injuries by the door, watching uncomfortably as more injured men spilled in. Fireballs had devastated a section of the wall, one told her, and dozens of soldiers had already died. A few moments later, the same soldier went into shock and died. A healer had missed the ugly bruising underneath his whole torso. For a moment she just sat there, numb, cursing her stillness and the roar of her blood.

Move dammit!

But her body refused every command. She stared at her trembling hands, and could only listen to the chaos outside. Her mind kept hauling her back to the past, back when she'd been rushing through the streets, sprinting toward the citadel.

A hand fell on hers, shattering the memory. Rell knelt, worry clouding her face. "Titania?"

"I'm okay," she lied, pushing up to her feet.

Rell's mouth tightened to a thin line as if she wanted to argue. Mercifully, she gave a brief nod, and the matter was dropped. Which was just as well. Titania was barely holding it together. She felt herself sliding closer to the edge, the dark oblivion looming, whispering to her cruel and malicious things.

And all of them were true.

"Titania!" shouted a healer from the door.

She stood wearily, wiping her hands clean. "Yes?"

It was a woman, her hair veiled, with pale skin and dark eyes, rushing over. "You and...oh, what's her name again? Rina? Rani?"

"Rell?" Titania offered.

"Yes her, I was told I'd find you here. Both are you to come with me now," she ordered.

Titania looked back at the scores of injured men she had to tend to. Healers were in short supply. They couldn't just *leave.* These men needed her. Hell, they needed as many healers as they could. She returned her focus to the woman, shaking her head.

"We are needed here."

Rell had been brought over by a soldier and stood frowning deeply at the conversation. Blood splattered her frock and face. "Titania is right. These—"

"One of Sybilla's dragons has been injured. They're just outside. Matron Rona said both of you had more training than most—"

Titania was out the door before the healer could finish. Rell shouted her name, but Titania didn't stop until she saw a familiar figure limping toward a wagon and the relief flooded her. It wasn't Nimue. She slowed her pace as she jogged over, and Lorca looked up, wincing. Bruises mottled his skin. He doubled over, crying out.

"Everyone, back off!" she shouted. "He's going to shift."

Men and healers scrambled back. Lorca staggered blindly away from the wagon. He barely took a few steps before his form flashed a blinding white, fading rapidly.

For a moment, he appeared fine, but his legs buckled out from underneath him, and he hit the ground hard.

"Rell, with me!" she shouted at Rell who stood at the doors.

They rushed to Lorca's side. Titania got to him first, moving straight to his head, and one eye cracked open. A warm presence brushed her mind, and she let him in.

I feel shit, he sent weakly.

They split up, inspecting every inch of his body.

"I found something!" Rell shouted.

Titania vaulted over Lorca's tail, dropping next to Rell who was inspecting a small wound by his hind leg. If she had to hazard a guess, it was an arrow wound. As she reached for it, Rell snatched her by the wrist.

"What—?"

"Poison." Rell frowned, as if considering something, then spoke again. "I think I can fix it."

"How?" The question was out before she could stop it.

Rell lifted a hand, a flickering tendril of light dancing through her fingers. "I have only a little magic, but it may be enough to help. Let me try."

If Lorca died, she didn't want to think about how Nimue would react—the loss of her daughter had been...destructive. There was no telling what she'd do if she lost Lorca.

"Do it."

Rell pressed a hand to the wound, closing her eyes. A faint light sparked through her delicate fingers, flaring for a second before tapering away. The young healer sat for a moment, pressing her palm against the now sealed wound. Then she smiled and nodded. Titania sighed, the tension bleeding from her. Disaster had been averted—if only momentarily.

Lorca released a shuddering groan as he shifted back and sat up, wincing. "Well, I advise against being shot by poisoned arrows."

Laughter ruptured from Titania, catching her unawares. She sobered quickly, schooling her face. "I am pleased you're okay, as will Nimue be once she sees you."

His eyes opened wide, and he pushed shakily to his feet, swaying as if he might fall. "Nimue, I have to—"

The words cut off as his eyes rolled back and he crumpled. Titania caught him just before he hit the stone. Rell was already calling for help as Titania laid him down, and soon, a wagon was trundled over. They had to get him back to the mansion. Once Nimue was done doing...whatever she was up to, she'd go straight there.

The glowing shield around the city hummed with spiritual energy, doing little to stem Titania's darkening thoughts. In her experience, when the spirits were involved, it never ended well. They were slippery bastards, so high and noble in their vague little ambitions. She never forgave them for their role in driving Nimue and Claudius to the fae nearly eight hundred years ago. That damnable quest of theirs had ended in heartbreak and death and carnage, all of which might've been fixed if the spirits hadn't been so damn prickly.

It's in the past. But that thought barely stemmed the rage simmering in her veins.

On the way back to the mansion, Lorca reverted to his dragon form. When they finally rolled through those iron gates into the courtyard, she roused him awake and coaxed him into human form so they could haul him up the stairs. They barely got him into his room before he shifted back with a low groan and slumbered once more. Rell kneeled, checking him, and rose with a satisfied nod.

"He's okay, just worn out. The poison battered his body, but his healing is already helping. I think he does better in this form." Rell asked questions about Lorca, but Titania had no answers to give. She resolved to pick Nimue's brain later.

There was a lot they had to discuss.

They were out in the hall when Titania felt something pull her to Ellie's room, and she turned to Rell, gently touching her upper arm. "You head back. I just need to check on someone here first."

"Do you need a hand?" Rell asked, lingering with that same concerned expression.

Titania felt a flash of familiarity in her mind, an answer nearly rising to her lips.

You worry too much, my dear, an old voice whispered from the fringes of her mind, drudged up from a memory she was sure she had buried.

Where had that come from? An ugly tangle of memories churned through her mind, darkening her mood. She had to get some space and clear her head. Yes. That would do nicely.

"No, it's okay. I'll be okay."

Rell gave her another searching look before giving a slight nod and slipping away. Titania kept telling herself those words, though she scarcely believed them. She hadn't been okay in so damn long. Not since...

Ellie slumbered in eerie stillness, her mind a fortress that barred Titania from entry. Dark magic swirled and eddied invisibly around the bed, seen only by her. It brushed her skin, sending shivers rippling through her bones. Instinct told her to leave, but she forced herself to sit beside the girl, taking her still hand, cold as ice. Were it not for the steady rise and fall of her chest, and the heartbeat that pattered against her thumb, she might've mistaken the girl for dead.

She wished she knew what was going on with Ellie. The fight to save Nimue had changed her, awakening some ancient magic and Lyria's essence. Though how it came to be there, she had few guesses and nothing in the way of answers. Why had Ellie been chosen? And what would she be when she finally opened her eyes?

A threat to them all, or the salvation they so desperately needed?

The room answered with deafening silence.

By the time she hauled herself back to Claudius's mansion, she was bone-tired. Her immortal body could keep going, but her soul *ached,* her mind shredded at the edge. She stumbled through the foyer and grasped the banisters to the grand staircase, numbly lifting one foot after another.

Entering the library, she sank into a chair by one of the arched windows, the fading light on her back. The talons of sleep had almost dragged her under when the doors flew open. Claudius strode in, staring at her.

So much for being left alone.

"I'd hoped for a nap. What do you want?" she asked grumpily.

He stopped. "It's chaos out there. The men are in tatters. I think some of the archer captains were killed when the fireballs hit the wall. The Merchant Quarter is burning—or rather was. I had a report it's been extinguished."

"How?" *By Lyria's grace, just how much had that damn Princess bargained with the spirits for?*

Claudius slumped into the chair across from her. "From all reports, Nimue."

A heavy silence fell between them. She knew he wanted to talk, and that his conscience was at war. It had been since Nimue had reappeared. But she was tired and irritated. Why couldn't he just leave her alone for a moment?

She closed her eyes when she heard him give a deep sigh.

"Will you remain a healer in this fight, Titania?"

Her heart froze in her chest. Slowly, she forced her eyes open. "As opposed to what?"

"A general. You still fight. The demons—"

"That's different," she said tightly. Old walls slammed up, shutting off the memories she'd so carefully buried. Her voice was brittle with frost as she spoke again. "Why not you?"

His eyes never even flinched. "I was never a general, not like you."

"That time is over for me," she replied, standing up and heading for the door. "Now, if you'll excuse me—"

He stood and placed a hand on her arm. "Titania, please just tell me why you won't fight. Have we not been through enough together for that?"

She spun back to him, cheeks heated. "Then why not tell me why you abandoned Nimue? Why you didn't speak to *any* of us for decades after that?"

The blood drained from his face. Finally, a reaction. "It's not that simple."

"Then I owe you no answers."

She turned to leave when his voice cut through the air like a knife. "I *want* to tell you, but I *can't.* I physically cannot tell you."

Perhaps it was the agony that dripped from his words or the phrasing, but she turned. The naked grief raging in those eyes, how broken he looked, and understanding dawned. She never would've considered the answer that rose to her mind. The last few days had changed that. There was only one person who might place a command on Claudius stronger than Nimue.

"Lyria?" His silence was all she needed. She staggered back, sinking against the door. "All this time?"

All he managed was a jerky nod. "I will tell you when I can, but not now. All I can do is to serve in the way I know best—as a politician. I'm not the warrior you are. You might not be able to lead Sybilla's armies, not without questions, but you could be more than just a healer."

The walls within her crumbled. She closed her eyes. It was a story she couldn't tell if she looked into his eyes and saw pity. It would cut deep—and she was already hurting again.

"When I left Danomir to learn about healing arts, I found myself in Toranelle. It soon became a home. I made friends, learned so much and I fell in love. I..." The words choked in her throat as a face bloomed in her mind. It took her a minute to find her voice. "I married, had a wife..."

Claudius gasped. "Why did you never tell me? Where is she?"

"This is not a happy story, Claudius."

The tears burned her eyes, even as she forced them shut, trying her best to hold on. It was a losing battle. Iron talons raked through her chest, tearing it apart from within.

"I had all that I wanted, and I yearned to grow old. But when the royal family of Danomir was murdered, everything changed. We knew an attack was coming, so there were measures in place to spot the approach of ships. But no one ever imagined a damn army emerging from the mists just beyond the city walls, conjured as if from thin air. We never stood a chance."

The tears broke free and spilled down her cheeks. "I was across the city that day, helping train some recruits. Then all hell broke loose. I tried to fight, but when word came that the citadel where...where she worked was under attack, I ran to her. I never made it in time. All that remained was charred stone and ash."

The stench of death filled her chest, as if she was right back there, screaming into the ruins.

Claudius held her tightly and murmured in her ear, "I'm sorry, Titania. I'm so very sorry."

Titania sank into his arms and sobbed.

CHAPTER 61

"We have become too soft. Castille has taken a human mate, as well as Titania and Atlas. I warn them of their love's mortality and of the war that now threatens the land we currently call home. They do not listen, for fools in love are tragic fools indeed."

—Excerpt from Claudius's diary

The crowd gathered in the main hall of the temple, watching Flynn as he kneeled before Mathias. His knees pressed onto the cold, hard stone, but even as the ache throbbed in his bones, he remained still. He tried not to think of Tobin who was only the spirits knew where; or Mira, who stood several feet behind him, hooded among her new sisters. By doing this, he knew he risked her life. He risked everyone's life.

But how could he stand by and let more people be taken? For Tobin to be sacrificed? He shook off the doubts crowding his mind, turning his attention to the trial. He'd only been training a short time and was by no means a champion. Against any decent opponent, he'd lose.

No!

There had to be time. Tobin had been convinced that two weeks would suffice, so perhaps in their training, the required lesson had already been instilled.

But Tobin had been taken a week early. What if that lesson hadn't been taught yet?

Mathias cleared his throat. "Rise, Flynn, and drink the chalice of the second trial."

A shiver slipped down his spine. A golden chalice was held out to him. Warily, he reached up, taking it in hand. The liquid was clear and odorless, though he doubted it was just water.

For my village. For Tobin. And for all those taken.

Flynn downed the drink.

He waited, all senses focused, hunting for the first sign of delirium. None came. Silence hung over him like a blade. It felt as if the air could've been cut with a knife. They were waiting, but for what? His brow furrowed as he lifted his gaze from the chalice.

Mathias gestured for him to stand. As he got up, uncertainty crept back. Had he somehow failed?

"For your second trial, you must follow the mountain path to the village ruins at the summit. There, you will face your opponent." Mathias paused for a moment before he continued, "if you survive, on your return you will begin your third and final trial."

If.

The word boomed like a crack of thunder, quivering through his soul. He knew the ruins and the path. He'd been there with Mira.

Not trusting his voice, he bowed deeply and turned. All eyes rested on him, peering out beneath the fringes of hoods. Did they all know what he had planned? Why he was doing two trials? If they did, were afraid he would bring disaster to their door?

But as the crowd parted neatly down the middle and he strode the opened path, none reached for him. Their eyes followed him and as he made it outside, he swore they were still watching him. He glanced back at the pillars of the temple, swathed in the moonlight. The dark eyes of his father bore down into his soul as if to say, *lift your head. You are the son of a demon.*

He bowed, then set off into the night.

The ruins emerged from the trees, betraying no sounds of life. Flynn's heart thumped in his chest as he neared closer to the treeline. Every step closer sent his nerves skittering in every direction.

His stomach tightened as he stopped at the threshold. The memory of his burning village flashed in his mind and the desperation on Tobin's face as he begged Flynn to hide. He crept onwards. A breeze whispered over his skin, doing little to cool the humid night air.

Flynn glanced behind at the path, but it was already lost in the darkness. There was no turning back.

He continued into the village and drew his sword with a soft metallic hiss. The empty ruins were crowded with shadows, each so thick he imagined ghosts within them, watching him with curious eyes.

A sudden movement caught his eye and he spun, sword at the ready. He relaxed when he realized it was just the tattered curtains and scraps of cloth entangled in the overgrown foliage fluttering in the breeze.

He wasn't sure where to go as he wandered, glancing around every corner for who his match might be. Why did he have to come to the village to fight? Perhaps it wasn't someone from the temple...As he reeled his thoughts as he emerged at the field of stone markers. There, blooming flowers swayed gently, their pale leaves turned silver beneath the moon, like thousands of tiny blades.

A field of death.

"You aren't what I expected."

Flynn jerked around, yanking up his sword.

Several feet away stood a man clad in a simple tunic and loose pants. He was barefoot and unarmed, both hands clasped behind his back, studying Flynn with a curious sort of expression.

"You're my opponent?" Flynn asked.

The man smiled, flashing a row of white teeth. "Indeed."

"Where's your weapon?"

"I don't need one."

Warning bells chimed in Flynn's mind. He didn't *need* one? Just what kind of power did this man wield? Tobin trained him for a sword fight...not *this.* He gulped, trying to pick apart every detail about the man. Beyond his oddly normal facade, there was a strangeness about him that pricked at Flynn's nerves. He couldn't explain it, but it made him tighten his grip on the sword, not sheath it. This man wasn't to be underestimated, but should Flynn start the fight?

Or was he meant to wait?

"Then let's begin, shall we?" said the stranger.

In a blink, he stood before Flynn, his hand shooting out. Flynn jumped back, feeling cold fingers brush his neck. Pain lanced down his body. He cursed and swung the sword, the man vanishing as the metal cut the air where he stood.

Dark laughter echoed behind him.

He pivoted sharply, thrusting the sword forward. The man slapped the blade away, then stepped back, grinning wolfishly. Flynn burst forward, trying to drive an opening, find a weakness. There had to be something. There had to be a chance for him to win, right?

His foot caught, throwing him off balance. The man vanished. Movement flashed in the corner of Flynn's eye. He threw himself forward, then spun, and swung. Metal hissed through the air, striking something solid.

The man caught the blade. "Is this all you're going to do?"

Rolling his eyes, the man ripped the sword from Flynn's hand and an iron grip snapped around his throat like a vise, squeezing hard. The air rushed from his lungs as he was lifted into the air.

This couldn't be the end. Not when he was so damn close to getting the power he needed. He couldn't fail them, not again. Fury roared up from his gut. Thrusting his feet up, just as he might do on the cliff, he drove them forward into his attacker's chest.

The man's eyes widened and Flynn burst free, hitting the ground hard. Scrambling to his feet, he hunted for his sword, but it was too far away. The man was on him in a flash, driving him back onto the ground, cold hands once more around his throat. Stars flashed across his vision as he struggled to breathe.

The man's lip curled. "You are weak. Why would the spirits choose you?"

The *spirits?* They hadn't chosen him. He'd been born with this power, the son of a demon.

Right?

"T-they didn't choose me," wheezed Flynn.

"Yes, they did," the man replied, and he gave a deep sigh. "Poorly, it seems. How could you ever be deserving of my gifts? A half-blood demon, no less! It's insulting."

"I'm not weak!" To fail his people once more was a fate he would not endure.

"Then *prove it.* Show me your strength!"

But *how?*

His hands flailed on the ground, reaching for something. *Anything.* But what? He tried to twist his head, to see something, but the hands held firm. He was pinned. A hand tightened around his throat, driving out the air.

Every half-breath burned his lungs, the strength bleeding from his body. He didn't have much time. He had to do...something... His chest shuddered, trying frantically to expand.

In his delirium, he imagined Tobin was kneeling, whispering in his ear. *Fight, dammit, fight!*

How? He wanted to scream back, but it was pointless. Tobin wasn't there and—

His thoughts froze, snagging on a memory that burst through his mind like a clap of thunder.

The man leaned down, those cold eyes cutting right through Flynn. "Time to die."

Flynn stilled his body, willing his thoughts to steady, even as his heart thumped viciously, and his mouth was full of ash. Blood roared in his ears, drowning out the world. All focus was on the man. He raised his hands to those arms, working his lips to mumble a reply. A frown flittered down the man's brow, and his grip slackened.

Idiot.

He thrust his hips up. The man jerked forward, letting go. Flynn twisted sharply and rolling, had the man beneath him. The victory was short-lived, as he was thrown to the side. He barely had time to react before they collided in a tangle of blows. Blood filled his mouth, and his body burned from every punch and kick.

The man was behind him again with one arm across Flynn's neck. Hot breath brushed his ear. A low, mocking laugh rumbled through.

"You aren't strong enough to beat me, so *give up.*" Lethal promise coated every word.

Flynn knew at that moment he was dead if he stopped. Any chance of rescuing his people would be over. *No.* His hands snapped up, grabbing the man's arm, and flinging him over his shoulder. The man crashed onto the ground with a sickening crunch. The world fell silent, holding its breath in dizzying anticipation.

Air flooded into his chest as he stood there, heart pounding, staring down at the still figure crumpled on the ground. The fight wasn't over. He felt that deep in his bones, even as a newfound rush of strength roared through his body.

The man groaned as he moved. Flynn's breath lodged in his throat. The sword wasn't too far away. Could he make it in time? Probably. He spun on his heel, striding toward it when the sound of gentle laughter carried across the clearing from the trees. He stopped dead.

The man was on his feet, regarding Flynn with darkened fury. He stalked forward.

"No, it cannot be! *You? You're the one they chose—*"

He cut himself off. Whatever he'd been about to say, Flynn had no idea.

A shadow moved at the treeline. A woman emerged, pale as the moon, with hair like a blazing fire.

One brow lifted, her mouth twitching. "Ronan...you knew this day would come." The ghost of a smile fell, and she moved between the two. "You can see it now in the boy. He has your essence running through his veins."

"You told me the day I gave my essence over was so that we might be reborn, *not replaced,*" he said scathingly.

The woman glanced back at Flynn, her eyes shining with unshed tears. She returned her focus to Ronan. "Our time is over. I'm sorry for this trickery, but I knew you would not agree if you knew of our true plans."

"*Lyria* was in on this, too?" Betrayal dripped from his words. "You both conspired against me."

"Long before we forged that final spell to split the Chaos Realm, a decision had to be made. We were facing an enemy we could barely defeat. The price of success was always going to be a steep one. I'm sorry we did not tell you, but you were so insistent on a plan that had no chance of success."

"It might have worked, but you never gave it a chance—"

"That would have required more strength than we would have had after the spell," Aislynn snapped.

Lyria? Ronan? He'd heard those names before, and as he stood, things clicked into place with a terrifying chill down his spine. All his expectations about what the trials meant—what he'd become from them—blew away like ash in the wind.

Aislynn moved closer, her ethereal face softening. "Brother, we are but ghosts in this world, echoes of what we once were. Even these bodies are mere illusions. Aren't you tired? We can at last rest, after so many long years."

Flynn watched Ronan, the war of emotion playing out in ancient eyes, and he wondered what Ronan would do. A bolt of understanding shot through him.

He knew them, though mostly from stories, and felt the call of their power in his veins. One by one, the names rose to the forefront of his mind, singing loud and clear.

Aislynn, The Primal Goddess of Life.

Lyria, the Demon Goddess of Death.

Ronan, The Spirit God of Balance.

These were three founding gods that had split the Chaos Realm, forging the three realms. The creators of all that was known.

Ronan appeared in front of him, shadowed closely by the goddess. She offered a comforting smile.

Ronan held out his hand. "Take my hand. You passed the second trial and have earned my gift to you."

Questions erupted from his mind, or would've, had his mouth obeyed the command to move. Instead, silence arrested him as he took the offered hand. Ronan yanked him in close. Over his shoulder, Aislynn stepped forward, but then stopped as Ronan's lips brushed the shell of Flynn's ear.

"Let us see if you can pass the next trial."

Pain crashed through Flynn, buckling his knees. Ronan vanished, and Flynn hit the ground with a gasp, liquid fire tearing through his veins. Darkness sank its talons into him and pulled him under. He couldn't scream. The pain was too much.

Oh, spirits, make it stop!

As in answer, the pain rushed away. Flynn slumped forward, landing on all fours. Ragged breaths clawed out as a shadow fell over him. It took him a moment to find the effort to look up.

Aislynn stood over him. "Rise, Flynn. It is time for your final trial—then you will be as the spirits wished you to be."

"But I'm a demon's son!"

She nodded as if this were obvious to her. "No demon can create life, but your father sought the spirits who commanded a price. Atlas believed that by binding the power they infused with your demon side you would be safe."

"What did they ask?"

"For whatever children he sired to take on the last of our essence."

His head dropped to the ground, to one of the stone markers half-buried in the grass. "*Why?*"

"To forge new gods, of course, and should you complete the last trial, you will be reborn. For the evil we had sacrificed so much to defeat was not fully destroyed. The Goddess of Chaos is rising once more. So, you see, you have a new future. Not as a demon but, as Flynn, the Spirit God."

CHAPTER 62

"War has erupted across this strange land. Men fight for land, power, and revenge. The village where Castille lived was burned to the ground. He was absent on a hunt, returning to find his wife butchered and their home in flames. This was the first lesson we demons learned of this world. There is no rebirth here. Death is final. Absolute."

—Excerpt from Claudius's diary

Aziah picked her way carefully from the cells to a staircase that descended into the shadows. Just as she began her descent, she heard the footsteps of someone coming up. She hurried back up the steps, ducking into an open room full of crates. The stale air closed in around her.

Only the dim light from the hall came under the door, leaving her concealed in darkness. The footfalls inched closer until they stopped outside the room.

"Damn idiots. Can they not just lock the doors behind them?" The man muttered curses as he drew the bolt across, sealing Aziah inside.

Her heart thudded hard in her chest, every beat a war drum in her ear. She breathed deeply, forcing it to calm, even as her magic skittered nervously. The deeper she ventured into the temple, the more unsettled her magic became. As if something truly horrifying lurked within its shadowy depths.

The footfalls ebbed away, but she remained there, still as a statue, until satisfied she was alone. Then she rose. Cursing the age which had crept up on her without her consent, she edged cautiously to the door. She held her ear against the wood, listening carefully for a moment. Silence greeted her. Satisfied no one was coming, she thrust a bolt of light through the lock.

It wouldn't be long until the body of the temple worker was found, so a broken lock wasn't of much consequence.

She stepped outside and cast a spell so that its broken status would only be revealed when another worker went to unlock it. Enough time for her to slip away into the night.

This time, no one interrupted her as she descended the steps, following the thickening stench of death and torture. A metallic tang sharpened on her lips, bitter with every breath until she reached the bottom. Luckily, the enchanted witchlights lit as she neared, then sputtered out in her wake.

The deafening silence made her feel like a child again, terrified of monsters lurking just out of view. Foolishly, she glanced over her shoulder twice, then pressed on, weaving her way through a labyrinth of twisted halls, locked doors, and antechambers full of empty tables.

No, not tables.

Aziah drifted closer to one, stilling as she glimpsed the blood-stained wood and the leather straps. Her stomach twisted and she moved away, pushing on until the sound of a girl's sobs brushed her ears. She followed it down another twisting hall to a locked metal door.

She had to figure out what they were doing with these people. The Empress had bought them all as one batch, which was unprecedented, then had them taken to the temple. The branding and processing in the city had been a political move, keeping any unwanted attention away.

Pressing her hand to the lock, she fired a bolt through it and pushed it open. This room was filled with tables. Only, these weren't empty. People lay strapped down, their bodies cut and pinned open, some missing limbs. One woman hung from a contraption by her ankles, her throat cut open to a bloodied smile. Her ashen skin and all too still body said enough.

Aziah crept across the space, studying the myriad of broken bodies and the desks cluttered with books. She picked up a couple, leafing through the pages. From the notes inside, it appeared they were testing the people for magic because of their prolonged use of Hellis powder. There were also questions concerning whether these people could be used as hosts. For what exactly would inhabit them, the notes were unclear.

She selected the most detailed book, then lashed it to the strapping on her back. With it secure, she turned to leave, when a hand shot out, catching her wrist.

Aziah stopped, glancing down. A girl, barely a woman, with pale skin stretched thin over her gaunt and bruised face, eyes staring up through milky irises.

"Kill me," she whimpered.

Her stomach was mottled with stitched wounds. Black lines spread out from them across her skin, showing signs of infection. Sweat drenched the tattered remnants of her dress, clinging to her frail body. Aziah's hand dropped to one of her daggers and pulled it free, bringing it up to the girl's chest.

The killing was easy but, even at that moment, as she stared into those blank eyes, she felt a pang of grief. She'd served the woman who'd done this for eighteen years. Swallowing the lump in her throat, she drove the dagger in. Shock jolted the girl's face wide, her mouth parting in a silent cry. The agonized face slackened and a look of peace took its place.

Aziah yanked the blade out and stepped back, letting the blood drip onto the floor.

"Who are you?" a voice thundered.

Aziah spun, magic sparking to her fingers, skittering along the edge of the dagger.

A woman marched into the room, clad in flowing red robes, splattered with dried blood. Her leathery skin stretched into a look of fury. Behind her came two men, armored guards, and seeing Aziah's bloodied dagger, they drew their swords.

"*Intruder!*" the woman yelled.

Aziah hurled the dagger, light sparking across the air. The men ducked, but the woman was too slow. It slammed into her chest with a muted thud, and she dropped to the ground. Aziah burst forward, leaping over a table, throwing another bolt of magic. She landed with a roll and unsheathed two more daggers. One man rushed at her, but she darted around him, slashing the back of his neck.

A spray of blood fanned the air as she shot forward, launching herself at the next two men, ducking the arcs of their blades.

She ducked in close, then drove the blade into the nearest man's chest until he slumped. Yanking it free, the other man approached from behind. She spun sharply and thrust the dagger forward, driving her blade into the nape of his neck.

He hit the ground soundlessly.

Two more men entered but kept their distance, circling closer like sharks. Snapping her fingers, she summoned light to one hand, then to the other, imbuing it into her dagger.

"You have no idea who you are dealing with," she said.

"And who is that?"

She grinned. "I am Aziah, the White Ghost, the Empress's once-fabled assassin."

Their bodies stilled. Even in the shadows, she had collected a reputation.

"But that is impossible," one of them spat. "They said you were dead!"

She straightened up and flicked her hand, gesturing them in close. "And yet here I stand!"

Their mouths opened for a response, but she shot forward to the closest one, dropping low at the last second and sweeping her leg, knocking him to the ground. The other snapped into action, rushing at her, but she leaped to her feet and hurled the dagger before he took another step. It landed with a hard thud in his throat. She didn't watch him fall as she spun back to the last man as he staggered to his feet.

He didn't stand a chance.

Her hand snapped up, magic shooting from her fingers. It tore right through his neck, spraying blood across the wall. He sank to the ground, eyes wide in shock as he died.

Aziah looked back at the victims on the table. She should put them all out of their misery, but as she took one step closer another shout rang out from up the hall.

She wrenched her gaze from them. Time to run.

CHAPTER 63

"Death has left a gaping void between us all. Those who dared to love mortals have learned the bitter truth—there is no resurrection. For those who remained hard-hearted, we are in a state of confusion. We told them, but Atlas insists love knows no sense. I think them utterly mad."

—Excerpt from Nimue's diary

Nimue landed in the mansion's courtyard, shifting quickly to stride through the front door, her heart thundering. Men and women rushed about; orders bellowed through the echoing space. No one paid her any attention, nor did any guards attempt to stop her. Dizzying chaos propelled her forward, one destination in mind.

Helena stood in the hall, commanding those around her with the confidence equaling any general. The men listened to her, and Nimue finally understood the real power she possessed. Sybilla may have had the blood, but it was Helena who had spent the past eighteen years sculpting alliances. All without garnering the attention of the Empress.

Helena spotted her as she headed up the stairs. "Lorca came in with a wagon of injured an hour ago, but he is now recovering, so we sent him to your room. A healer went with him and said she knew you. I believe she just left."

Titania. It had to be.

She mumbled a thank you, then hurried past, stopping by Ellie's room for a moment. Her sister still slumbered, oblivious to the madness outside her window.

For the best, really. The longer Ellie slept; the more time Nimue had to figure out what to do for how did one handle a sister becoming a goddess?

And if her sister's violent awakening had caused this deep slumber, she fretted over that unknown fate when Ellie awoke.

Her mood darkened at the grim reality that Ellie would face once she woke. Nimue shut the door gently and headed to her room. As she entered, Lorca was struggling with his shirt, caught halfway. His head was wrapped in the material. She laughed softly as she strode in.

"Stop laughing at me," he grumbled.

Another giggle escaped her lips before she could stop it. Rolling her eyes, she fished out a dagger and slashed his shirt. The two halves fell away, his arms and head released. He stared at her, trying to fight a smile but failing. She leaned up to kiss him, but paused as she spotted the wound at his side. It had mostly healed, but there was a faint scar where the arrow had entered.

"Lorca..."

"I'll be fine. The poison is gone. All I need is rest."

She pressed a gentle kiss to his chest, then pressed her ear to his skin, savoring the sound of his heart. It was a steady drum, a balm to wild thoughts and frayed nerves. "I hated seeing you hurt. I wanted to rip that whole damn army apart for that arrow."

He wrapped his arms around her. "I know."

"Are you sure that you're okay? Do you need more rest? I can summon a healer. They may have something—"

"My love, I'm well. Whoever healed me did something. I feel wonderful, better than I have for weeks."

A knot of tension untangled within her. He was alive, and so was her sister. She inhaled his scent, reminding herself that he was with her and wasn't going anywhere. It felt as though nothing could touch them at that moment, an illusion she savored, knowing full well it wouldn't last.

"Can I ask you something?" he asked.

"Of course."

"When you lived as the Spirit of the Mountain, why did you never reach out to me?"

She shrank back, a cold feeling washing over her. "I enjoyed watching from afar. Getting too close, becoming attached? I'd had enough of mortal experiences."

"What happened?" he asked softly.

"I told you I bore a child with Claudius," she said, then paused as she drew in a deep breath, as if that might offer her some courage for what she was about to say. "I suppose it is time I told you the whole story."

She turned away, her voice lost for a moment in the past. Then the words spilled from her lips like water broken free from a dam, crashing into that room.

The story of two demons seeking help to have a child, and the foolish trust that they placed in the fae who once called the mountains their home. She told him of the fae's betrayal, that they had no intention of ensuring her daughter lived for more than a few hours. That she had stared into her baby's eyes, so full of life, and could only watch as they closed and never opened again. The fae had wanted her broken and grieving, that at her lowest, they might strike them both dead and steal their magic.

There, she paused in the story, and her eyes closed. The vision of the destruction she unleashed upon the fae filled her mind. She could still taste the ash on her lips, hear their screams, and pleas for mercy.

She told him what she did, and at that the end of her wrath, she had stood in the ruins of a kingdom she had torn apart. Alone. Abandoned without reason or cause by a man she thought had loved her, and had yet to offer any reason for his actions. Even after eight hundred years.

When the silence settled, she waited with bated breath for his reply.

"Now you know what I did. The truth of what I am and the destruction I am capable of." She didn't realize the tears were falling until she tasted salt on her lips.

"You were grieving," he said, his voice soft and steady and comforting as it had always been. When his arms encircled her, she didn't fight him, nor when his hand tipped her chin up and their eyes met. "They took advantage of you both and hurt you deeper than anyone ought to be."

"I *destroyed* their kingdom, reduced it to ash!"

"And yet the fae live on," he replied. "I am not ignoring the brutality of your actions, but you have long since atoned for that day. From the ashes of that crime, my people were born. You protected us, without payment or worship, or even asking for forgiveness. Even now, you fight for those you care about, even though—I shall add to my eternal vexation—your own life is at risk." Tears shone in his eyes as he leaned in, kissing her softly, reverently. When he pulled back, that warm smile stole her breath as he spoke once more. "So, how could I not fall in love with you? That spark I fell for in Wren. It *burns* like wildfire in you."

Tears sprung to her eyes. Then, as a smile split her cheeks, she closed the distance until their lips were only a whisper apart. "I love you. So damn much."

He drew her into his arms and massaged the small of her back. She leaned in, relishing the comfort he offered, and closed her eyes. They were finding each other again, two souls tentatively navigating the past binding them, and daring to envision a future.

"What was your daughter's name?" he asked.

She turned her head, resting her cheek on his chest.

"Rhea. Her name was Rhea. It means 'red flower' in my native language. The flowers I planted at her grave were a gift from Claudius when he had discovered I was pregnant. They were a gift he'd kept with him since we were taken from the demon realm... I hated him so much back then, but even in my fury, I couldn't deny he was part of her. So, I planted the flowers." She tightened her grip on him, savoring every inch of comfort he offered. "That's why I will always return to the mountains. It's where she rests."

A pounding headache and a restless mind meant sleep was impossible, even curled up at Lorca's side. While he was still dead to the world, she crept out. There was a conversation she'd been dreading since she'd learned of Ellie's fate and felt her own condition deteriorate. That conversation propelled her across the city, right to the door of Claudius's mansion. Only the lord of the mansion wasn't home, nor was he the one she was after.

As she raised her hand to knock, the door swung open.

Titania greeted her, wearing her healer's attire. "What's happened? Is something wrong?"

That was a loaded question, one with a plethora of answers. None of which she wanted to talk about in the doorway of the mansion, not when Claudius might return at any moment. It wasn't a conversation for his ears.

"Can we talk in private?"

Titania glanced back into the foyer, then stepped aside, gesturing for her to enter. Wordlessly, Nimue followed her up the grand staircase and along the hall to Titania's private office. But once the door closed behind her, she could not speak. The whole way over she had practiced what she'd been planning to say, and now she was floundering.

She walked over to the cold fireplace, aware of her old friend watching her in the corner of her eye.

"I need to ask you to promise me something and I know you are going to hate me for even asking," she murmured.

Titania remained where she was. "Go on."

"This situation with Mirena isn't getting any better and we're running out of ways to stop her. Much as I hate to admit it, Ellie might be our best chance, but she's nowhere near ready to face her. Will you still help her when she's awake, even knowing what she is now?" She tried—and failed—to hide the growing desperation in her voice.

A shadow of surprise flashed in Titania's eyes, dimming quickly. "You're talking as if you will not be there."

She didn't answer at first, unsure of how her old friend would react—and painfully aware that if anyone would see through a lie, it was Titania. The woman who had taught her everything she knew.

"I can buy you time. I'm not strong enough to face her now, but that doesn't mean I'm out of tricks. I still have one move left." She let the silence fill the room and the understanding dawned in Titania's eyes. The shock yielded to a darkening look of fury, that mouth twisting into a snarl.

It wasn't any surprise when Titania took a step forward, the look of a friend who knew exactly what Nimue had in mind. "You can't be *serious.* That's a suicide mission."

Nimue had known that was going to be the reaction, but she'd prepared for—at least, mentally she had. That didn't make the fury burning in her friend's eyes any easier to bear. "Don't make me make this a command. I don't want that—look, it might not even come to this."

A shuddering breath racked Titania as she looked away, her eyes shining with unshed tears. "Does Lorca know what you're planning to do?"

"What do you think?" she replied softly, her own heart aching. "Titania, if I do this right, Mirena won't get my power. Ellie will. That means you will have a chance to save us all."

Titania leveled a heartbroken look at her, and Nimue felt her resolve nearly crumble. "You're asking me to...It doesn't need to come to this. Ellie has Lyria's power and when she's awake, she'll be strong enough to stop Mirena. You don't need to do this."

A sad smile pulled at her mouth. As much as she wanted to believe those words, to cling to the hope offered to her, she couldn't. She had to be practical, even if it tore her apart. She closed the distance to Titania, wrapping her arms around her in a warm embrace.

"I can't risk it all on when Ellie might wake up, or if she'll even have control of her powers. All I can do is buy you some time. That way Ellie can be trained and this realm will have a chance. A real, fighting chance." She buried her face in Titania's back. "Look, it might not come to it, but if it does? I need you to fulfill my mission. When Mirena is finished, I need you to bring my people home... and...and I need you to look out for Lorca. Make sure he finds his people. Please. Can you promise me that?"

Titania trembled, and quiet sobs filled the room. Wordlessly, she twisted around, grabbing hold of Nimue. It made her feel like a young demon again, right before the night she challenged the King for his throne. Neither of them had known that that choice would lead them here, that they would face such uncertainty once more.

"I promise you, but that doesn't mean I accept it. We will stop Mirena...and you won't have to do this."

Nimue wished she shared her friend's optimism. Whatever happened, when the time came, she'd do what needed to be done.

CHAPTER 64

"Time and war have divided the six of us. Amara slipped away in the night well over a month ago now, leaving a note that she seeks time to heal. The death of her lover, Kiron, has shattered her. Castille throws himself into pointless battles, alongside Atlas and Claudius. I have not seen them in months. Even Titania prepares to leave, for she seeks a new purpose beyond this broken land. I will be alone, a path I once hungered for, but now fear."

—Excerpt from Nimue's diary

The war room was silent as Sybilla swept in, freshly cleaned, and adorned in a flowing green dress. Until she had her throne, she would wear no crown. That had to be earned...and as she met the gaze of her senior leaders, she felt a trickle of unease. Claudius was absent, sending word that he'd become occupied with damage from the fires.

The heads of the other high noble families sat at the table; Casimir, Tarlin, and Denmor. General Galen was present, along with two other commanders. All rose as her seat was pulled out, scraping softly over the wooden floor. Once she sat, they followed.

Warm sunlight streamed in from the row of windows at the rear of the room and a cool breeze whispered in, dancing among the curtains. The cool sea air had the taint of ash, bringing with it memories of their near failure.

She lifted her chin, refusing to cower beneath their stares. "What is the latest on the army?"

Galen cleared his throat. "They have retreated to their camp and our spies have reported that the dragon culled around seven hundred men. The army is nervous; however, the shield has given them pause."

"And losses?" she ventured reluctantly.

"For the soldiers? Minimal. Currently, it's a little around a hundred, though we predict that number to rise. It is the Merchant Quarter, unfortunately, that suffered the brunt of the losses with the fire. Healers have reported around five hundred deaths so far."

By the spirits...

Her breath caught. It was far more than she'd expected. Guilt bloomed in her chest, thick and hot, and lodged in her throat, barring any words for a moment. It took all she had to remain calm, to shed only the barest hint of grief. There was no time for weakness.

Across the table, the young lord Casimir leaned forward. He was a waiflike man, with ashen skin and long features, and had snake-like eyes. Cutting, predatory. "I speak for those who are not in this room. Why was this shield not established *before* the attack?"

A question she'd expected and prepared for. Closing her eyes, she turned her thoughts inward.

It's time, she said to the spirit within.

Then let us show them.

Her eyes flickered open, and a wreath of light erupted around her. A sharp feeling peeled from her back and Rhea materialized at her side, bathed in ribbons of magic. The men flinched with wide eyes, save for a couple who became statues. No one spoke for a moment, but Sybilla felt a stab of pleasure at their reactions.

She smiled, glancing at Rhea. "Would you like to introduce yourself?"

The spirit inclined her chin. "I am the Spirit of Purgatory and the one who supplies Princess Sybilla with her power. I only recently arrived in the city and circumstances prevented any action before the point at which the shield was erected."

"Do you speak for the other spirits?" a noble asked.

"I speak for those who bless Sybilla in this fight. Beyond my reasoning and motivations, I offer none beyond the support I give now and that is far more than any of my kin might be so inclined to give."

Rhea's form brightened, forcing those closest to lower their gaze, and she retreated into Sybilla. It took a moment for anyone to look up again, and Sybilla took the opportunity to speak before they could ask any questions.

"The spirits wish for us to succeed, requesting that I serve as an anchor for the one you met, so that she may better serve us within this realm. With her grace, I could erect the shield and it is by my magic that it stays. I am deeply sorry that I could not have sorted this out sooner, but beyond my failings, there *are* matters to discuss. Namely, what the fuck happened at the wall?"

The gentle politician melted away, revealing her prickling fury. She leaned back in her chair. Make no mistake. She might be young, but she was not a fool. The response to the attack had been abysmal, and the chaos that had reigned through the city had been a bloody embarrassment. At the first test, they had failed—and it had nearly cost them everything.

One of the commanders cleared his throat. "A flaming boulder collided with the tower, killing the archers' commander and several of the other leaders. It caused chaos, to say the least. We have since restored control."

"Control that shouldn't have been lost in the first place," she said tightly, pausing before she continued. "Empress Alexandria has driven this land into more debt than we can handle and reigns with fear. Make no mistake, we must prove ourselves strong because she *will* send the Gray Army. Does anyone here fancy our chances currently against such a force?"

Silence answered her.

Galen appeared to choose his words carefully. "We are low on men experienced in war. There are going to be errors in the beginning, but this will be rectified. You have my word."

The rest of the meeting passed with a little less tension, and she managed to end it on a mildly promising note. The others went off to their duties, even Helena, without complaint. Only Oren remained, the other two guards standing beyond the door. She felt his gaze track over her as she paced, mulling over the meeting. Her thoughts tangled together, trying to determine the right path forward.

"What did you think of that mess?" she asked, casting a curious glance at him.

His eyes widened fractionally, schooling quickly beneath a mask. "I am a mere guard. Please do not concern yourself with my opinion."

"And if I order it?"

There was a beat in which he did not reply. She almost believed him digging his heels in silence. With a frown, he spoke. "The lords sit at the table for their safety, not for the people who *built* this city. I doubt any of them have even ventured into the Merchant Quarter."

A heaviness pressed down on her shoulders as she sank into her chair. "Do you see me that way?"

When he didn't answer, she lifted her chin and saw he was walking to the door. He paused and turned to her. "Might I show you something?" A trickle of suspicion twisted in her gut. Perhaps sensing this, he offered a small smile and held out a hand. "A little trust, Princess. I swore to keep you safe, didn't I?"

As they rode, they passed beyond the wealthy districts of the city. Once they entered the outskirts of the Merchant Quarter, the stench of ash thick in the air, Oren pulled to a stop. He was at her side in an instant, to help her dismount. Reaching for her hood, he pulled it over her head.

"While we're here, it is best we move unseen for the moment. They may not recognize you, but people are desperate right now. A beautiful woman in a fine dress would be an attractive prize."

Her cheeks warmed, but she managed a small nod, and stepped aside, lest her racing heart betrayed her. A few nice words did that much to her? Fool, stupid little fool.

The sky churned with a growing storm. It left a gray tinge over the narrow street, fringed on either side by tall wooden buildings. This section was a little deeper into the city, so it had been spared much of the damage. From the smell, however, she knew she would not have to walk far. Dampness clung to the air, heavy in every breath she took.

"Now will you tell me why we've come out here?" she asked.

Oren was talking in a low voice to his men, who bowed in response and took the reins of her horse, along with Oren's stallion. Once they had walked away, she strode to Oren's side, but he beat her to the question on her lips.

"Food isn't plentiful here and horses of that quality attract attention," he said softly.

She arched one brow and gestured for him to lead. "If you try *anything* I do not like, I will rip you apart."

He bowed deeply. "Then consider my life in your hands."

As he rose, their eyes connected, and she wondered once more what he had to show her. Had he brought her there to show her the burned ruins of the quarter? To remind her of her failure that she felt so keenly in her chest?

No, it didn't feel at all like that, and as he led her down the street, she considered the alternatives. Her mind ran amok until they veered down a narrow street, twisting like a snake through the gloom. It didn't take long for the first of the charred remnants of shops, warehouses, and homes.

A few times she glimpsed the mangled remains of bodies entangled in the wreckage. Her heart fell. All the lives she had failed. She filled every breath with the scent of death. Let it be a lesson she took to heart, burned to her soul.

When Oren stopped and knocked on the double doors of a warehouse, she frowned beneath her hood. Peering up from beneath her lashes, she studied the innocuous structure, her guard thrown up in an instant.

Rhea stirred at the fringes of her mind, pushing out a warm wave through her blood, and that soothing voice filled her mind. *There is no danger here.*

The warehouse doors opened. A healer greeted them, her gown splattered with blood. Her deep brown skin was flecked with ash, her eyes heavy, weary. When her gaze settled on Oren, her expression brightened.

"Oren, it's been too long. We'd heard you had taken up some fancy position for a noble. Didn't think we'd see you here anymore," she said in a raspy voice.

"As though I could ever stay away from you," he replied, stepping forward as he pressed his forehead to hers. "It's good to see you, Soraya."

"Hmm, well, I suppose you're welcome," Soraya said, her interest moving to Sybilla. "And who might this be?"

"A friend." His tone warned off further inquiry.

Soraya glanced at her again, then shrugged and stepped aside. "I hope you know what you're doing."

Oren ushered her through and down a short hallway and then through an open door. As she went to ask where they were, the sound of children's laughter silenced her. It rose and fell in giggling waves, and Oren stepped aside, giving her a view over the sprawling space.

The warehouse's main area was converted to a makeshift shelter, crammed with tents and areas partitioned off with strung-up fabric. Dozens of beds filled nearly every nook and cranny, and small tables were dotted around covered with folded clothes. A long table was set up by an open window heaped with large pots containing an aromatic stew of some kind. A line of people shuffled along, bowls in hand, which were filled by smiling but weary healers.

The familiar uniforms worn by most of the people made Sybilla pause. She wondered if they were simply merchants who had been displaced in the fires.

A little girl dashed past her, scarcely taller than her hip, squealing with delight as two others chased her. She staggered aside, jostling into Oren's side. An apology caught in her mouth as her gaze snagged on the brands marring the girl's arm. Ice pooled in her gut, chilling her to the bone.

As the children ran back toward them, Oren bent down, growling teasingly. They shrieked, scattering off among the tents. He rose, the soft smile lingering on his mouth. It arrested her for a moment.

"These are the ones the nobility forget. This is only one of so many spread out across the Merchant Quarter. There might be rationing, but the people here seldom see what is allotted to them. All they know is that one day, they were suddenly freed of their chains—but that also meant the loss of whatever awful excuse of a shelter they had." Oren gently ushered her aside, and they sat down on a stack of boxes in the corner. "You asked my thoughts on those meetings, but I ask you this instead; what is the point of your war? This city is full of people from all walks of life—of all colors and creeds. We may be freed of chains, yet little else has changed, and now there is an army outside. People are afraid and confused. We need a leader who *cares*, who truly gives a shit. Otherwise, how are you any better than the Empress?"

CHAPTER 65

"I am alone, wandering this vast land, watching as the mortals rebuild once more. New kingdoms rise from the ashes, built on the ruins of those they destroyed. Young men go off to war and become hardened soldiers. Most never return. I should write more in this diary but I find it harder every day. Darkness haunts my soul, and even in this realm, I feel the distant presence of my throne. Why can it not let me be?"

—Excerpt from Nimue's diary

Nimue sat by her sister's bed, holding her hand, and wondering where the hell it had all gone so wrong. The uncertainty of Ellie's life was a vicious winter storm. Who knew what would become of her once smiling sister? What would happen to the trauma that scarred her? She knew how such agony might manifest, especially in someone with that much power.

She, in her rage and grief, had leveled an entire kingdom.

More than anything, she was helpless to protect her sister, or to even help her on the journey ahead. She knew how to be a demon, how to lie, to survive...but had no idea how to be a goddess.

"I wish you would wake sister," she whispered.

They had so much to talk about. Really, Nimue just wanted to apologize for how poorly she'd handled telling Ellie the truth. Her sister deserved better. To tell Ellie how much she loved her and no matter what future awaited them, that would never change.

With a heavy sigh, she released Ellie's hand and retreated from the room.

Rather than return to her room to sleep, for night had fallen over the city once more, her footsteps led her in another direction. Right to Sybilla's office where the candlelight glowed beneath the door. There was a soft scrape of movement and a gently hissed curse.

She knocked but had already started to push open the door when a protest came—too late. The door was open.

And there was Sybilla.

In Claudius's arms, his lips lifting from her neck. His gaze snapped up, found Nimue's. The world caught its breath as they stared at each other. Her heart pounded and the blood rushed to her ears. For one dizzying moment, she stood frozen to the spot.

Sybilla turned to face Nimue. Her eyes narrowed, defensive and wary.

"One normally waits to be admitted to a room," she said, stepping away from Claudius's embrace.

A pin might've been heard hitting the ground in the seconds that followed.

As Nimue took in the scene, old anger surfaced once more. Bubbling up from the festered wounds within her soul, squeezing her throat painfully.

Claudius pulled away, his gaze on hers, with a look of an apology on his lips. She didn't want to hear it. At that moment, she hated him, hated how he made her feel, hated that she still hurt *because* of him.

"Stay," she snapped in demonic, her voice brimming with power. He lowered his gaze and stepped back. Her gaze returned to Sybilla, and she managed the cool, steady words from her lips. "My apologies for intruding. I'd simply come to discuss if you'd heard anything about my people. I see I timed my visit poorly. I'll go."

She closed the door and hurried off. Behind her, she heard some hushed arguments in her wake. No one followed, and she made it back to her room, slamming the door shut with a rattling thump. Her knees buckled and she slid to the floor. Drawing her legs up, she pressed her face into her hands.

A muffled scream tore from her throat, scraping all the grief long-buried, and the rage that had been her shadow for so many years. Tears burned her eyes as she lifted her head and raked her fingers through her hair. Her hands trembled as she lowered her side.

Why did their daughter have to be born with his eyes? For every time she saw him, it reminded her of their daughter, and part of her broke all over again.

She woke to the sound of the bedroom door flying open, slamming against the wall. Sitting up sharply, she threw up a hand, fire bursting to her fingertips. In that split second, she realized Lorca had returned at some point, and must've slept beside her. For as he jerked awake, and reached for his weapon.

Nora threw her hands up, a shimmering green shield bursting around her. "It's just me!"

Nimue sighed. "Gods, Nora. You could get yourself killed like that."

"Sorry, but this is urgent."

"What's happened?" asked Lorca.

"Sybilla has summoned us. There's been an attack on the food stores!"

CHAPTER 66

"Today, Claudius returned to me, and, like a fool, I welcomed him back to my bed."
—Excerpt from Nimue's diary

By some miracle, Nimue landed without crashing in the street, tucking her wings at her side. Lorca dropped in front, and Nora slid from his back. She lowered to her belly, allowing her passengers to slip off, and once they were clear, she shifted as Lorca did.

Tension hung thick in the air. The loss of food was never good, even less so during a siege. She'd heard Helena speak of their healthy stock that would've seen the city through the harsh winter that was to come.

As she surveyed the grim expressions of the soldiers and the low whispers that swirled and tangled together, she had her doubts. As a demon queen, she'd often aimed at starving out her enemies, breaking their spirits. It was one way to win a siege without the high price of a frontal assault.

The City of Slaves possessed towering walls, thicker than many cities she'd visited, and a secure water source. It had deep tunnels and large areas to store a vast amount of grain, perfect for withstanding an assault.

As they approached the heavy doors of the warehouse, her mind went over all that she had ever taught Mirena, for this was potentially an enemy using her own tactics against her.

There was no resistance from the guards at the door, just lowered eyes and a quiet look of anger. Not at her, or the team, but the at the blow struck against the city.

Inside, Sybilla was in discussion with an older man. The Princess hadn't noticed them enter, and Nimue noted the set of the young woman's shoulders. The bearing of a ruler. Not one forged of an act, but an instinctive set. There was too much graveness in her eyes, and shadows that lined them for it to be anything but honest.

As they neared closer, Nimue glimpsed the first splattering of blood along the wall and the coppery stench soon invaded every breath. Death beckoned her closer.

"A demon attack," Nimue breathed.

Sybilla turned. "I thought the demons were dealt with," she said, moving away from the older man. Her brow furrowed. "There's been no attack in some time. Why now?"

"We'll look into it."

Those golden eyes examined her for a moment, leaving her to wonder what the Princess saw.

"See that you do. I've received reports that four more depositaries were attacked, which means our stocks are now halved," said Sybilla tightly and strode past them. "Report back with your findings."

Nimue watched the Princess leave, the other man close behind. Had the curt tone been because Nimue caught her with Claudius? Sybilla would believe Claudius little more than a merchant, which was no suitable match for her.

An illicit affair then...and with Claudius of all men.

She shook her head. Dorian strode into the space first, Sylvie close behind, with Nimue and the others following. A rotten stench hit them, and her nose wrinkled in response. In the long rectangular room, lit by several flickering torches, were shelves upon shelves heaped with boxes. The bodies of the guards littered the floor; or, rather, what was left of them. The demons had torn them apart as if they were less than paper.

She picked her way around the mess and peered into the boxes, recoiling back with a retching sound. The grain inside was rotten and flies shot up, buzzing around her face. She recoiled, swiping them away.

Decay. Nimue felt a chill steal through her. That had been the power of Tynan, the demon King of Parthenon. He'd had the ability to pass through fields and turn fertile grounds into rotten, blackening crops. His shadow wolves would run ahead, laying siege first before Tynan and his army came in, destroying what was left and cutting down anyone they found.

Since Mirena had butchered him, claiming the Pathenon throne, she'd inherited his powers. It boded ill for the city.

"Nimue! I found something," Dorian called from the other end of the room.

She discovered him at the last shelf, pointing to the floor. Stopping beside him, she froze. Marked in blood was a message, written in demonic, just for her.

You have won nothing. I will take this city...and your sister.

When she stepped back, Dorian was staring at her with a troubled expression, his mouth a thin line before he spoke. "It's her, isn't it?"

"It would seem."

Dorian shook his head and stood, dusting his pants. "I'd hoped we were we done with this demon business. Foolishly, it seems."

By this time, Sylvie had drawn closer and peered at the message, then at Nimue. "What does it say?"

Nimue repeated the message. "I don't think Mirena was happy my sister beat her so easily. Demons don't like to be defeated, especially the rulers."

"You don't sound surprised she's back?" There was that note of suspicion in Sylvie's voice again.

"My sister didn't kill her, just scared her back to the demon realm," said Nimue.

"You remember the fight?" Sylvie's eyes narrowed.

"Titania spoke with me after. Long ago, the three of us used to hunt demons." It was a lie, but Sylvie wouldn't know that.

Dorian straightened up. "If the others are experienced in hunting demons, why won't they help us?"

"Because they are trying to put that life behind them. It...it left scars," Nimue said, trying to put an end to the inquiry. "And I would be too, were it not for my current circumstances."

She regretted her tone, aimed at shutting them out, but she had to keep the secret of what they were. Sylvie didn't seem satisfied, her jaw tight, tension pulling her shoulders back, but she turned away, seeming to drop it. For the moment, anyway. Eventually, Dorian gave a nod, accepting the story.

They had more pressing matters. Namely figuring out Mirena's next move. She'd struck hard and fast. The shield had done little to keep the threat at bay and Nimue was a fool to hope it would.

They spent the rest of the day inspecting the other warehouses and storerooms hit. In each one was the same bloody message. Mirena wanted to ensure Nimue got it. The carnage was the same, and twenty men were dead in total. All the grain was rotten and moldy. By the end, Nimue felt ill, and the food a runner had delivered when they were at the last place didn't entice her.

The city's food stores had been halved in a single attack.

Word would soon spread if it hadn't already.

As they sat out the front, the others dug into a simple meal. Lorca tried to get her to eat, but she refused. Her stomach was in knots and she had no appetite. Silence wrapped around the five of them, broken only by the others eating. Nimue tried to focus on the sounds to stop her mind from wandering, but it didn't work.

The message kept replaying over in her mind. Mirena's mocking voice became crueler and more venomous each time.

She hadn't realized the others had finished their meal until Lorca gently nudged her side, luring her back to the world. Worry clouded his face. She returned a smile of assurance, but it did little to ease the frown, so she kissed his cheek and stood.

Dorian picked up the satchel and slung it over his back. "The attack on the food was to drive desperation up in the city. People are going to become hungry soon, and that won't bode well."

"If I were this demon, I would then focus on whipping up trouble. Do you think she'll go after the water source?"

The city's water came from an underground aquifer. Sybilla had told them it was hard to access, with only two points, which were under heavy guard. Probably more so given the attack.

Nimue made a silent note to speak to Titania and see if Claudius could have his men close by. A few dead bodies in the water might cause disease, which would cause even further issues. Hunger *and* disease? The people would tear the city apart.

"It's a weak point that must be considered as a possible target," Lorca said, appearing at Nimue's side, a hand resting on the small of her back.

Dorian nodded in agreement. "I will speak to Princess Sybilla. What about the wells? Won't they need to be guarded?"

Lorca nodded. "It would stretch men thin over the city, but there might not be much choice. The two main threats to any city during a siege are hunger and disease. The first will make tempers flare, so we should expect riots and aggression from the people. Then I'd say that will be when disease strikes."

Hit us when we're down. It was akin to Nimue's tactics. When she'd taken cities, she never focused initially on breaking the walls. She'd make an initial strike, to get the enemy nervous and aware, then pick away from the inside. Sometimes she'd use spies, other times she'd slip small groups inside. Enough to conduct operations to attack...

"You sneaky bitch," Nimue blurted out. All eyes fell on her, and she went on, saying, "I know what she's going to do next."

She spun on her heel, rushing outside. By the demons, she hoped she was wrong, but everything had been by the book. She cursed her foolishness.

"Mirena is following a method I've seen before." She recounted all the key moments that had happened until that point, then explained the next move.

"It won't be disease. There is a step before that. She's going to sow the seed of doubt among the lower classes and slaves. Right now, they see Sybilla as their savior. Put a crack in that and when the hunger and disease set in, they won't turn on each other—they'll turn on the one source of their pain."

Because Nimue knew that the best tool wasn't your army or starving your enemy. It was using your enemy's people against them, watching as they were ripped apart from within. That way your losses were minimal and, if Mirena did this right, then Sybilla's people would open the gate and welcome back Alexandria's forces.

One by one, the understanding dawned, and the group fell quiet. It was then Nimue saw the fear in Sylvie and Dorian's eyes. There was a genuine concern for Sybilla.

"We must protect the Princess," Sylvie whispered.

Dorian looped his arm around her. "We will." Then he looked at Nimue, searching. "Won't we?"

"That is our mission, isn't it?" answered Nimue.

Much as she didn't like the Princess, she was the way to saving the people of Fenware. A necessary evil.

"The fact they've attacked the food stores means the next blow will be soon. We need to get to the Merchant Quarter now."

CHAPTER 67

"It has been fifty years, and at last Atlas has returned. I missed my friend and am glad he has come back to us, though I wonder where Castille is. The pair of them left together. There is a heaviness about him. He brings wealth, but the shadows following him make me worry. He tells me he has founded a temple on the Mithra Archipelago, which he has made a haven for us."

—Excerpt from Titania's diary

When Flynn returned to the temple, everyone was going about their business. The moment they saw him, a hush fell in his wake, and he felt their burning eyes tracking his every step as if wondering what he might do next.

Inside the main hall, Mathias was waiting for him, his face etched into a deep frown, his golden eyes unreadable. It made Flynn feel small and uncertain, even as he swore he heard Tobin whisper in his ear.

Lift your chin.

Flynn stepped up onto the dais, swallowing the lump in his throat. More fae had gathered in the hall, whispering among themselves. He tried to ignore them, and though he wished that he'd seen Mira before he started the next trial, he remembered her anger.

There was no time to think about anything further as he knelt before Mathias. He'd chosen to take the last two trials back-to-back, so he'd have to deal with the consequences. The time to turn back had passed.

"Flynn, you have passed your second trial and have returned for the third. The Trial of the Mind. Are you ready?" Mathias asked, his gravelly voice boomed through the temple.

It quivered through his soul, his mind responding with a single word. *No.*

But a different word came from his lips. "Yes."

A shadow came down on Mathias's face as he turned and collected a chalice from the table, then held it out for Flynn.

Flynn's hands shook as he reached out and took it. The contents were the same as before, clear and odorless. He still had no idea what it was. The first one had knocked him out, but the second had seemingly done nothing. Would this inflict pain?

"It's time to drink," Mathias murmured.

He hurriedly downed it before he could let himself doubt anymore. The tasteless liquid slid down his throat, settling in his gut. He waited. A second passed, then a faint heat kindled in his gut. It grew hotter, almost as if he'd drunk hot tea. Then, without warning, pain erupted. He threw his head back, an agonized scream tearing out.

Agony lanced through his limbs. He fell backward, his head striking the stone hard. Stars flashed in front of him. He didn't stop screaming, writhing as liquid fire flowed through him, ripping him apart from within.

His chest expanded, trying to breathe, but another wave of crippling pain tore through his body. The temple crumbled away, consumed by darkness, but the pain didn't lessen. Wave after wave rolled through until without warning, the ground disappeared and he fell.

The wind screamed in his ears, whipping at his bruised skin. A soundless cry scraped up his raw throat. He threw his hands up, as if he might catch himself somehow but all he saw was darkness, the end nowhere in sight.

After an eternity, he slowed and his feet touched something solid. The darkness melted away, like snow yielding to spring. A cavernous stone room stretched out around him, nearly twice the size of the one in the temple. Towering pillars of polished stone flanked him, leading to a dais with three thrones, each one occupied. Two of the occupants he knew by sight.

Ronan and Aislynn.

A moon-pale woman sat next to them, her eyes coal-black, bottomless pits that bore into him. There was no warmth on her haunting face.

Lyria.

His heart raced as he walked toward them, his body protesting every step. Pain still throbbed through his whole body, making him feel old, broken. It felt as if he had been stripped down, his skin flayed and broken for this final trial. Dust dried his mouth and no matter how much he tried to summon spit, it never came. He bit back a cough and stopped before the three gods.

Ancient power rolled off them.

Three types of magic. The three true sources.

Ronan watched him closely, none of the original fury that he'd seen before. Instead, there was an eerie calmness about him, matching the other two.

The old spirit God of Balance leaned forward. "You have been summoned for the third trial. The task we set is simple. A lie has been told, one that conceals an ancient truth. Uncover this and you will have passed but, be warned, should you fail, the essence within you will destroy you."

A shiver whispered through him as he managed a shaky nod.

Lyria lifted her hand and snapped her fingers.

The ground fell out from beneath Flynn, sending him tumbling back into darkness.

He awoke in a room that trembled and groaned, dust swirling in the air, choking his lungs. He doubled over, coughs racking his body. The shuddering nearly sent him headfirst into the table. Cursing, he straightened up, squinting as the door was flung open. Aislynn rushed in, wearing a warrior's armor splattered with blood. She darted to the table, frantically searching for something. After a beat, she found whatever she was looking for, snatching up a single sheet of paper. Her gaze flew over the words when the door behind her slammed open again.

Lyria stood at the door, clad in a tattered black dress with a satchel over her shoulder. A shadow flitting over her unreadable face. She hesitated, but as Aislynn turned, the demon goddess shot forward, driving her palm onto her sister's chest. The Primal Goddess froze, eyes wide. Ribbons of darkness erupted from Lyria's hand and plunged into Aislynn. Pain pinched Lyria's face, determination hardening her gaze as she stepped back, pulling a glowing green thread. It pulled taut from Aislynn's chest, then snapped and recoiled back, wrapping itself around Lyria's hand, dancing with the shadows. With her spare hand, she dug out a jar and slipped the thread into it, then screwed a lid on. The thread swirled within its glassy prison, the forest glow playing over Lyria's face.

Aislynn's essence?

She stuffed the jar away in her bag as Aislynn jolted, blinking several times before she focused on Lyria. "Is it time already?"

Lyria nodded coolly. "The army closes in. I've already spoken to Ronan. It's time."

"Does he suspect?" Aislynn asked.

"No. He believes I collected his essence for his rebirth," Lyria mused, a ghost of a smile tugging at that haunting mouth.

Aislynn smiled ruefully, the warmth in her eyes a strange distance from the sad ones he'd seen with Ronan during his second trial. As the pair moved to the door, he realized she carried herself differently. The godly air he'd seen her with earlier had gone.

The door closed behind them and the world funneled away into darkness.

A half-ruined stone courtyard greeted him. One section of the wall was destroyed, reduced to a pile of rocks that spilled across the ground to the middle. There, Ronan, Lyria, and Aislynn stood, their hands linked. The sky raged viciously above them, fire raining down, turning the sky red and murderous. The ground shuddered, but the three deities remained standing, unmoved by the looming disaster.

Their soft chanting rose above the distant cacophony of war cries and drums and ringing metal. It wasn't in a language he knew, the words strange and lyrical. At their feet were three opened jars, a thread of magic swirling within each, all a different color. White, green, and black.

A sphere of light erupted from within their circle, growing rapidly until it nearly consumed its surroundings. The threads lifted from the jars, rising to touch the sphere. Flynn felt a shiver of awe pass through him. This was the origin of the three realms. He had to pinch himself to focus again. This was a trial. Somewhere, in something he'd seen or was about to, was a lie and a truth.

The two goddesses fell silent. Aislynn stepped back, and the spell snapped. Ronan opened his mouth, confusion sparking in his eyes as the sphere shrank. Lyria threw her hand up, a bolt of energy shooting from her fingers and into Ronan's chest. He stilled, his mouth frozen wide. Lyria pivoted sharply on her heel as Aislynn snapped her fingers, a sword materializing in her hand. She burst forward.

"You think you could win?" Aislynn taunted.

Lyria vanished in a plume of smoke, then reappeared right behind Aislynn, slamming her palm into the goddess's back. A bolt of magic shot through Aislynn's heart. Shock paled her face as she slumped, the light sputtering out from her eyes.

"And I am death. I always win." Lyria leaned in close and whispered something else into Aislynn's ear.

She calmly stood once more, letting the body of her sister fall, and she returned to the circle, her dress stained with blood. With a wave of her hand, Ronan moved.

The vision ended, and Flynn tumbled into the abyss.

He was back in the throne room, the three deities watching him. Aislynn was alive and Lyria sat beside her as if Flynn hadn't witnessed the latter murder her sister. None of what they'd shown him matched what he saw here. Besides, he'd seen Aislynn during his second trial, and she'd seemed real enough then.

"So, tell us, what did you see?" Ronan asked.

"I saw the end of the Chaos Realm and the spell that formed my own." He paused, drawing in a deep breath as he mustered his reply. "I saw Lyria murder Aislynn."

But that couldn't be the truth...It was too obvious. He'd seen only two scenes, but the truth was in them. Aislynn had drawn her sword, but had that been in some belief Lyria would betray them? Had the Goddess of Death become corrupted?

"What is the truth within the lie?" Ronan pressed.

He raked his brain over every moment he'd had with Tobin. The lessons. The languages he'd been taught, the history he'd learned in the library. He recalled one of their first conversations, back when Tobin had first educated him on the gods...and his own family's history with them. What had he said dammit?

Perhaps in death, we will know.

Flynn's gaze snapped up. "The lie is that Lyria betrayed Aislynn. I saw Lyria strike her, yes, but the spell wouldn't have worked with her dead." His gaze slid to Lyria. "You didn't betray anyone. That is the truth in what I saw."

None of the deities moved or spoke. Flynn's heart hammered in his chest. Had he been wrong? No, his gut told him that Lyria *was* innocent. Or at least so far as the crime of her betraying Aislynn.

Lyria stood and walked toward him, her bare feet silent across the stone, until she stood before him, in all her terrifying glory. Her dark eyes bore through him, down into the pit of his soul. She reached out, brushing her hand across his cheek, and moving to his chin, lifting it to meet her gaze properly.

"In prior times, the stories would have been strong, painting me as the villain. Now, with what we've shown you, and that which you have learned during your time at the temple, you saw the lie...and the truth within. We are but shadows now," Lyria said mournfully.

"Why me? Why now?" There was still so much he didn't understand.

Her hand fell away. "There was another deity. A fourth. *Our* creator. One forged of pure chaos. She briefly possessed my sister, which was why I struck her down. I needed the goddess close so that I could seal her spirit away in a place beyond the three realms. Unfortunately, the veil between realms is weakening and this evil has broken through. It now controls three of the four demon thrones, and will come to your realm to claim your essence, as well as that of the other two once they claim their power." She snapped her fingers and darkness swirled around her hand. "Our time has passed, but the age of the new gods must begin. Seek the two who bear the essence of my kin, and that of the five ancient demons with their demon queen, for they have hidden in your realm long enough. Only together will you stand any chance of defeating the coming darkness."

CHAPTER 68

"It has felt like a lifetime in this realm, though it pales to our long lives within the demon realm. Yet as I see Amara return to us after two hundred years, there is a quietness about her. She is still as achingly beautiful as I remember...and her power has grown."

—Excerpt from Castille's diary

Aziah sprinted down the long hall, legs burning, heart thundering. She flew like the wind, her feet scarcely touching the floor, as she flung herself around the corners. Every sense was strained, hunting for any trace of the guards that walked the halls. Only silence answered her, broken by the soft pad of her boots over the stone and the rapid draw of her breath.

Where was everyone?

By her guess, there was one way out, which was probably blocked by now. Why bother to chase a rat when there's nowhere to escape?

She arrived at the chamber where she'd slain the priestess. The metallic stench tainted the air, the body now in the middle of the room. That bloody wound grinned at Aziah as she jogged past and down the way she'd come. Near the exit, she passed a narrow hall, a whisper of magic brushing her nape. It was so faint that anyone less trained might've missed it.

Aziah paused, turning toward it. Her gut clenched, and her magic stirred beneath her fingertips, pushing for release. She stared at it for a moment, half-torn to run. She had what she needed about the people after, which was the point of her mission. But her gut told her that to leave at that moment was a mistake.

By the spirits, she hissed internally as she twisted on her heel and jogged toward the source.

It wound deeper into the temple, a pulse of magic rising in her soul. It beat a second heartbeat, waves of magic flowing out through her limbs, pressing against her skin, calling to be free. As she came to a towering black door, magic sparked from her palms. She bit back a curse, pressing her hands to her thighs, trying to quash it. After a straining effort, she forced it back in and set her palm to the door, closing her eyes.

Why, hello there. Who do we have here? A new voice crooned in her mind.

She flinched, slamming the walls up in her mind, trying to drive them out—not that it worked. It felt as though they were everywhere within her at once. A chill stole right down her soul, freezing her to the core. She jerked back. This was a mistake. Something had lured her, she suspected. That explained her sudden urge. It had to be. But as she turned, the door swung open, and her body froze.

She howled at her body to move, but her feet carried her forward as if something else had taken over. Inside was a long rectangular room, bare and simple in every respect but one. At its heart was an enormous stone arch, the symbols carved into its obsidian stone glowing a deep red.

A figure peeled out from the shadows behind the gate. *Hmm, curious. The little traitor. What shall I do with you?*

CHAPTER 69

"Time has changed my kin. Titania has become a healer; Atlas hungers for a mortal life; Claudius has taken to a life of war; Castille carries many shadows with him.... and Nimue. There is a weariness that has only deepened. Even I cannot say I am the same. My power continues to grow, like that of my kin, and with it, my connection to Lyria. She waits for her heir and whispers to me in the night, broken fragments of a soul crying out. The spirits have the essence of the gods but have not chosen new vessels. What do they wait for?"

—Excerpt from Amara's diary

Nimue landed in the market square as demons flooded the space. Their nightmarish howls ricocheted through the buildings, mingling with the screams of those who scattered before them like frightened deer. The beasts leaped over boxes and from behind corners, crashing into people and ripping them apart before they could fight back. Blood-curdling cries choked off with sickening crunches.

Dorian and Sylvie dismounted off her back, and as Lorca landed, Nora jumped off. Free of their passengers, they shifted back in a burst of light. Nimue drew her short swords and commanded flames to her hands, infusing them into the metal.

"Keep close, we move forward as one," Nimue said.

The return to leading felt easier than before. Slowly, Wren was retreating further away, and her demonic nature was pushing through.

Dorian and Sylvie nodded, taking up a flanking position, with Lorca at the rear and Nora at Nimue's side. They moved swiftly, cutting down demons as they passed. By fire and steel, they left carnage in their wake. They reached a row of warehouses where a small group of people stood pressed up against the wall, facing demons closing in for the kill.

She felt their hunger and their madness. The leash on them was so tight, the control so absolute, that there was no room for thought in their minds anymore. They had been rendered little more than beasts without souls. Mirena, it appeared, was leaving nothing to chance.

Nimue released a thundering roar and flung herself forward. Fire exploded from deep within, surging upward through her chest and out from her hands. Bolts ripped from her palms, cleaving the air in streaks of red, slamming into the beasts. They scattered from their prey with yelping cries, turning to her, their glowing eyes burning a molten red.

"Lorca, Nora, get those people into houses and shut the doors. Dorian, Sylvie, you're with me! Let us cut those bastards down to size!"

She sprinted at the demons, shadowed by the fae couple. The wolves snarled viciously. Shadows swirled around them. Nimue leaped at the first, a flurry of fire and steel, as she cut her way through them, moving in sync with the others. Black blood splashed the ground and her skin, but she pushed on, a creature of death and destruction.

A shadow of movement dashed to her left. She pivoted to meet a demon as it launched at her. A dagger slammed into the side of its head and it dropped to her feet, blood pooling from the wound. Dorian shot out, leaping over the body to attack another.

Light burst past her head, crashing into another demon, as Sylvie appeared, swathed in ribbons of light. One curt nod was all Nimue got before the fae woman moved on to her next target.

More demons poured from the shadows, spilling out from the alleyways and streets. Dozens of them and no matter how many they cut down, it didn't same to make any difference.

"Nimue!" Lorca's voice cut across the chaos like a knife. He sprinted to her, splattered in blood but uninjured. "We can't hold them all off here. See—"

He grabbed her and spun her behind him, throwing up his hand to blast out a wave of fire. She pivoted just in time to see a demon turn to ash. Her gaze slid back to Lorca. A thin band of sweat gathered on his brow. Familiar exhaustion tightened his face. Pain flickered down their bond, faint as if he were trying to mask it.

"You need to shift," she said.

"I'm fine," he gritted out.

"*Lorca*." Warning dripped from her voice.

She cut him a sharp look, and his jaw tightened. White light flashed as he shifted, dimming to reveal his gleaming scales and outstretched wings.

But even in that split second, she felt his pain ease, and that was enough for her.

"Take to the sky, see if you can see any pattern," she ordered, then gave him a lingering look, saying in his mind, *if you see anyone who might be that demon, let me know?*

His head dipped before he launched into the sky. A thread of tension in her eased. He was out of the demon's rage. Safe.

She cast her gaze across the fray. Nora was ushering a small group of people into a building, beckoning them with an urgent hand. A dart of movement several feet from the girl grabbed Nimue's attention. *Demon.* Nimue tore off, calling the flames to her hands. She sprinted across the road and hurled herself over an upturned wagon. A beam exploded from her palms. The demon tried to dodge but the flames crashed into it, incinerating it instantly. Only ash remained as she dropped her hands. A wave of nausea welled up in her throat, blackness threatening to consume her.

Her strength was ebbing. Whatever the spirit had done to her was fading.

"Nimue, over here!" Dorian shouted, grabbing her attention.

She blinked the darkness away and jogged toward his voice. Her muscles burned and sweat dripped down her face.

As she rounded the corner, Dorian nearly ran into her. His hands shot out, grabbing her briefly as he steadied himself, then he let go and pointed. She followed his finger to the middle of a square.

A demon crack.

But this one was emerging before their eyes, as though a knife was cleaving the veil between realms, and shadows spilled from the opening. They hit the stone, then took shape, growing rapidly until a beast exploded from the shadows. It leaped at them. Nimue threw herself in front of Dorian, throwing up a wall of fire.

The beast struck the wall, exploding to ash.

She dropped the wall and hurled herself. "Dorian, with me!"

"You're mad!" he replied, but dashed to her side. "Can you close it?"

"I don't think so. Whatever the spirit did to me seems to have stopped my ability to seal the cracks," she replied.

He grimaced. "Then we blast everything that comes through."

Nimue threw up her hands and fire surged out. She twisted her fingers, weaving the fire around the crack. In the corner of her vision, Dorian was firing at anything that got close to her or came from the crack. An idea sparked in her mind. She threw her hands wide, calling out another wave of fire, and threw it around the crack to cocoon it in a blanket of flames.

Pain throbbed through her arms, leaving them shaky, her knees nearly buckling, but stubbornness flared in her gut. She wouldn't let them out. If she couldn't force the portal to close the normal way, then she would smother them. Mirena would realize soon enough her forces weren't getting through.

Nimue, four more cracks have appeared, sent Lorca circling above.

I'm a little busy with one. Try to use your fire to create a bubble around them.

His shadow flashed overhead. *I will, but Nimue you're fading. I can feel it.*

A wave of dizziness swept through her, making her teeter for a moment. Sucking in a sharp breath, she shifted her stance and pulled her hands in closer, making the cocoon smaller until the edges of the crack pressed against it. Resistance burned down her arms. The darkness wanted to be free. It called out, sensing her demonic soul.

The familiar presence of her throne slipped into her mind. *Come back to me. Return to where you belong.*

She shoved the presence away, then squared her shoulders and offered only the most defiant of smiles. *This is where I belong.*

The throne hissed in response, pushing to get back in, to reclaim its dominance over her. A savage roar tore from her lips as she forced a step forward, something wet dripping from her nose, touching her lips, slipping into her mouth. A metallic taste pooled down the back of her nose, down her throat. She pushed forward, defiance tearing through her, and she forced another surge of fire out.

The bubble shrank down, compressing against the crack.

A band of light burst past her. It flared wide, then wrapped around her flames and constricted, pressing the cocoon of fire tight around the crack. Dorian stood beside her, magic pouring from his hands. A trickle of blood seeped from his nose, too.

"Dorian, your nose," she wheezed out.

"Yours, too," he replied. "We're almost there. Just keep going!"

Their shields fused, two sources of spirit magic tangling together. Another wave of darkness pushed out. She could feel its hunger to get out, to destroy. Its icy fury brushed her mind. This wasn't any normal demonic magic. It was twisted and potent, stronger than anything she'd faced before.

The power of three demon thrones combined.

Her legs wobbled, threatening to give out. She was close. She could feel it. One more step forward, she thrust her palms. A new surge of fire erupted from her palms, fueling their shield.

The crack snapped shut.

The resistance gone Nimue dropped to her knees, ragged breaths shaking her body. She was going to be sick. Seconds later, she retched all over the stones. Among the remnants of her last meal were spots of blood.

Dorian staggered to her, looping an arm around her waist.

"Come on. We're not done yet," he urged.

By the demons, she was *exhausted.* Her body was fading. She had only a little longer, but he was right. There were more cracks. More than—

Nimue, seven more have just opened, right in the center of the square. They're...Gods! They're connecting! The energy pouring out of them is forming a sphere.

Dread sunk in her gut. Mirena wasn't playing by Nimue's playbook anymore. This was something new...

Nimue, you're too close—get out of there!

She shifted, destroying tents as her wings snapped out. As Dorian rolled out of the way, she grabbed his cloak with her teeth and launched into the sky. Once they were high enough, she twisted her neck and dropped him onto her back.

Lorca, can you see Nora and Sylvie?

There was an agonizing silence that roared down the bond before he spoke. *I see Sylvie. Getting her now!*

His wings snapped close as he dove sharply, flaring them open at the last second to pluck Sylvie from the ground and surge back up. A trickle of fear ran down Nimue's body as she frantically scanned the chaos. The last few stragglers were trying to escape the demons that filled the square. She couldn't see Nora anywhere.

Nora, where are you? She bellowed it out across the square, trying to find Nora's mind.

But the girl was silent. Where was she?

"Where is she?" shouted Dorian, desperately. "I can't sense her!"

The humming in the air grew louder. Below, more magic spilled from the cracks, pooling together. The sphere was enormous, as large as two wagons, and kept growing. Waves of demonic energy rolled off it, filling the air.

I see her! Lorca shouted as he shifted his wings and angled toward the sphere.

No, don't go! She blurted out, shooting toward him.

The sphere went silent for a split second. The world froze. Nimue powered her wings to Lorca, even as Dorian shouted at her. He saw Nora, but Nimue couldn't stop. She was so close. Just a bit further! Her heart pounded in her chest as she flew harder than she ever had before. The darkness beneath her continued to grow.

Her demonic side stirred sluggishly, awakened once more. She felt it slip into her veins, her dragon form faltering. Two sides at war…and the demon side wanted the control back.

Just get to Lorca, she screamed to herself, trying to force the magic back down.

But she never made it as the sphere erupted. Silence seized the air, then a shockwave slammed into her, shattering every bone in her body. Pain exploded everywhere at once. She fell. The last glimpse she had of Lorca was him tumbling to the ground, and Sylvie clinging for dear life.

The ground rushed to meet her, but she could do nothing to fight it. A new voice slid into her mind.

Did you like my little trick, old friend?

Nimue hit the ground and the abyss devoured her whole. She felt no more.

CHAPTER 70

"I depart this land. I cannot stay here anymore. My power has grown and shows me things...things that I dare not even write upon these pages. Time is running out but I must prepare. By Lyria's command, I leave my kin and begin my journey."

—Excerpt from Amara's diary

Nimue felt like death.

She couldn't even cry. The effort was too taxing, leaving her at the whim of her traitorous body. She drifted in and out of darkness, listless like a leaf drifting down a river. Rising from the murky gloom once more, she willed her body to move, but it yielded to another wave of daggers tearing through her veins. The cold oblivion hauled her back under, and she felt no more.

Nimue jerked awake with a cry. The world was a blinding light, burning her eyes, forcing her to squint. Her body shuddered, only stilling after what felt like an eternity. Little by little, her vision cleared, and she sat back on her haunches, shaking.

It took her a moment to absorb the ruins of the surrounding buildings, and the gaping hole she'd created when she crashed through the roof.

Dorian!

He'd been on her back but was now nowhere in sight. There was no blood or crushed remains to suggest she might've crushed him in her dragon form.

She lumbered weakly to her feet and staggered through the piles of broken bricks and smashed wooden pillars. With every step, her body screamed in protest, as though she were walking across a field of broken glass. A pounding headache thundered behind her eyes, forcing her to squint.

Lorca! Can you hear me?

No reply came, but the bond hummed steadily. He was alive.

She stumbled through an opening in a wall and slid down a tumble of rubble into the market square. It was utterly destroyed. The market stalls were shredded, reduced to tattered cloth and splinters of wood. Many of the buildings had been blown inwards, their windows shattered and roofs missing. Torn chunks of what might once have been people lay scattered on the ground, and the smell of blood hung heavy in the icy air.

"Dorian! Sylvie! Lorca! Nora!" Nimue called their names until her voice was scraped raw.

She wandered the mess slowly, her body fighting every step. Even with her improved healing, it would be a few hours until she could fight again. Determined, she pushed on, picking her way through the debris until she edged toward the center of the square. A crater stretched out before her. She lay on her belly and inched to the edge to peer down.

She froze.

At the bottom, Nora lay curled up in a ball, wrapped in a bubble of green light. Nimue swung over the edge, then slid down along the loose dirt to the bottom. She staggered forward until she found her footing, then kneeled beside Nora. Reaching out, she brushed her fingers along the bubble. Sparks shocked up her arm. She yanked it back with a cry.

Nora stirred with a groan and sat up, the magic retreating into her. "What happened?"

"I'm not precisely sure," Nimue confessed as she eyed the crater.

"I was fighting this demon when suddenly the cracks started to connect. After that, I don't remember anything. I guess I must have blacked out," said Nora, rubbing her temples. "Spirits, my head is pounding."

Nimue! Lorca's voice shot through her mind like a clap of thunder.

She jumped up, glancing around wildly. *Lorca? I'm at the crater. Where are you?*

There was a pause of silence, then a scramble of footfalls before Lorca's head popped over the top of the crater. He leaped down and raced to her. She threw her arms around him and buried her face in his chest. His earthy smell, crisp and rich like the forests of her home, filled her every breath. It was home.

Reluctantly, she pulled away. "Have you seen Dorian and Sylvie?"

"I found them. A little bruised, but otherwise okay."

More footsteps rushed to the crater, and Dorian and Sylvie peered over the edge. The fae leaped down into the crater, rushing straight for Nora, who stumbled into their arms. Nimue felt a stab of envy and looked away. Lorca leaned in, gently squeezing her hand. Looking up, he pressed a kiss to her brow.

After a minute, the trio broke apart.

Dorian spoke first, his face grave. "We never dealt with this demon threat...and now all those people. *Spirits!*"

Sylvie touched his arm, but he turned away. Her mouth tightened and she looked at Nimue angrily. "This is on you."

Lorca stiffened, moving to defend her, but she placed a hand on his arm. This was her fight, even if Sylvie was right.

"You're right," said Nimue slowly. "I'd hoped that after the attacks ceased and we found no more cracks that the threat was neutralized. I kept my senses open for demons but sensed none. Obviously, this was intentional."

Sylvie's eyes narrowed. "Your secrets are going to get us all killed."

No one said a word. A lump lodged in Nimue's throat. Sylvie didn't know how right she was in a way. Her secrets would kill her in the end, whatever happened.

Lorca cleared his throat. "Let us return to the mansion. Sybilla should have our report."

The Princess was pissed, to say the least.

They sat in her office as she paced back and forth, her cheeks red and hands clenched into tight fists. The fight had been a disaster. Over two hundred dead, including thirty healers, which were already in short supply. A good portion of medical supplies had been destroyed as well, which was another loss they couldn't afford.

Nimue didn't miss the shadows beneath Sybilla's eyes. The long silence continued until, finally, Sybilla stopped at her desk and leaned against it, arms folded across her chest. Those golden eyes darkened.

"How the fuck did it all go so wrong?"

The question was angled solely at Nimue. "I believed cracks could not be forcefully created. No demon ruler has ever possessed that ability. The game has changed more than I realized."

"Game?" Sybilla's brow shot up. "This rebellion isn't a *game*."

Nimue stood. Tired and wrung out, her temper slipped. A harsh laugh broke free, like glass shattering on stone. "Of course it is. You simply believed *you* and your aunt were the ones controlling it. This is Mirena's game, and she's been planning it for centuries. The first few attacks were to test you, to see how you'd respond. Now the army is in place, the fourteen-day formality finished, and the real attacks have begun."

Mirena had been her shadow in the Azradan court, eager to learn the inner workings and eventually claim a political position like the one Claudius had held. She had not realized just how perceptive Mirena had been, discovering secrets that Nimue had gone to great lengths to bury.

Sybilla pushed off the desk with a withering look and moved to her window, interlocking her fingers behind her back. The sunlight framed her figure. "How do you know so much about this?"

"My father hunted demons and taught me everything he knew about their kind, including the history of their wars," Nimue answered. Another lie was far easier than telling the truth and might get Sylvie off her back. "I hadn't realized that Mirena was using the tactics of another, with her own touches of course. I won't be so foolish the next time."

She turned to the others. "This demon represents a serious threat to both this rebellion and the greater realms. It is using this fight of yours to achieve its aims. Mirena will seek to open the Hell Gate and I'm unsure whether our efforts are part of her plan or have actually delayed her goal."

It had to be a bit of both. Mirena couldn't have known what Ellie was. Otherwise, she would've slit Ellie's throat when she was her prisoner.

Nimue needed to keep her sister safe, but could she entrust the knowledge of what Ellie really was to Sybilla?

Lorca rose and moved to her side. "Sybilla, the focus must be on ridding this demon threat from the city. Might I advise you to take swift action with the people? They have seen us divert our efforts to other missions rather than the demons, so they may blame you for this attack. For poorly dealing with it."

Anger fired in those amber depths. "You think I have handled this poorly?"

Lorca, to his credit, merely lifted a brow. "Public perception can run away from you if it isn't handled. I have watched my mother nearly lose her throne a few times when she did not deal with the threats our people faced."

Nimue's gaze jerked up, locking on him. He seldom spoke of his past and his family, even with her. It was a wound that ran as deep as her own. She never pried, waiting for him to speak when he felt comfortable enough to do so.

"And your mother knew the difficulties of ruling?" Sylvie inquired archly, coming to the defense of her Princess.

Lorca leveled his gaze at her, unflinching. "My mother was Queen Evanya, the last Dragonir queen, and I am her son, Prince Adrian. So, yes, I know of the troubles she faced and the price we paid for not heeding the signs before our doom."

CHAPTER 71

"Only a week passed before Castille departed after Amara. He did not say this in words, but I have seen how he looks at her. We have lost so much and this I will not deny him. I pray he finds her and that, together, they find the peace they both hunger for."

—Excerpt from Nimue's diary

It was one disaster after another for Sybilla.

First the food, then the markets.

A few calm days passed, which had given her time to do damage control on the market square. Much to her dismay, there was a high level of frustration from the people. The siege had entered another week, and the hard rationing had begun much earlier than anyone had predicted.

Hunger had already set in, and she'd even heard more reports of people hoarding food. It would only get worse as the days grew colder, and the first wisps of snow had fallen. In a few weeks, white would blanket the city.

Already a thin layer of snow dusted the streets. They'd equipped the soldiers with thicker uniforms, but that was all they could do. Increasing their food was not an option. Even her belly grumbled. She pushed back her chair and stood, pressing a palm to her stomach.

When had she eaten last?

It had to have been yesterday evening. Helena had offered her a mug of spiced wine and a small bowl of stew. It would be the last of their meat for some time. The rest was already being cured and stored. If it became necessary, the horses were next, but she was reluctant to cull them yet. The city was large and sprawling. The horse and wagons provided transport for supplies and the injured.

But how long could they hold out?

She'd attempted to summon a vision last night, but that had proven to be a futile adventure. Instead, she'd tossed and turned restlessly until she'd crawled from her bed and headed to her office. There she'd remained, much to Helena's dismay, who tried several times to bring her downstairs, until morning. Oren offered some company, but he'd been quiet since their visit to the Merchant Quarter. Even after she'd sent soldiers in to ensure food was distributed to them, along with some additional supplies. Because she knew he wanted her to go back, to walk among them.

How could she, though? She was barely holding the city and had to keep them safe.

She didn't even notice him until he was standing over her desk, pushing over a plate with some steaming hot stew.

"You need to eat," he grumbled.

"And what about you?"

"They are bringing something up shortly. I was to ensure you ate. Helena's orders," he said, returning to his position by the door.

Her brow lifted. "Aren't you meant to answer to me?"

"I am to keep you alive, which I expect means ensuring you don't starve yourself," he said, his mouth twitching.

She didn't realize how much it meant to see his smile until something in her softened.

For a moment, their eyes met. Her stomach gave a traitorous flip. She quickly looked away, clearing her throat in an effort to divert the conversation, when a knock rattled the door. It seemed she was not to be left alone. Oren shot her a searching look, and when she returned a short nod, he opened the door.

Claudius slipped in, shutting it quietly behind him. "I have good news."

Oren's smile shuttered as he stepped back. She stood up from her desk, gesturing for him to leave the room. The courteous, perfectly respectful air swept across his face as he bowed and shut the door behind him. Though she knew he would remain just outside, she was uneasy having him in the room with Claudius. It left her in knots, none of which she had time to unravel.

Pasting on her practiced smile, she resumed her seat. "Not a disaster? A shame. I've been having quite a few of those lately."

Claudius appeared oblivious to her inner turmoil as he approached her. "I have received word that the ships will arrive within the next few days. It won't cover all the supplies lost, but it will help."

He's only being kind because he wants this city. Her inner voice sneered.

But as he walked around her desk and drew her into his arms, she relaxed. She buried that cruel voice and relaxed into his embrace, pressing her cheek to his chest. The steady thump of his heart calmed her. She shouldn't let him hold her, let alone enjoy it so damn much, but she did. The stupid fool she was.

"I should not be in your arms," she mumbled after a pause.

"Has Helena voiced her concern again?" The teasing note did little to stop her mood from darkening once more. When she didn't reply, he pulled back and cupped her cheek. "This is simply what you wish it to be. I make no demands than those I have already said."

Why? She wanted to ask, but couldn't muster it. The answers her mind conjured gave her sufficient pause. She suspected the truth would bring her pain.

"I can offer you this city, though, in current circumstances, I don't know if I can keep to that bargain," she said tiredly. "I just received word that Alexandria has sent an advance force to the northwestern city of Tarth. They're under siege right now, which means we're unlikely to receive any aid after winter breaks—if we even last that long."

Claudius cursed. "What about the other Northern lords?"

"They are now hunkering down for winter. If we lose Tarth, then this rebellion becomes a losing battle."

Just one more disaster after another...

She was drowning. General Galen had kept control of their men, so there was little resistance there, but the nobles were growing agitated. Their peaceful lives had been uprooted in the promise of a short siege. Now, that promise looked to be broken, which left tension in her court. Helena was scrambling to keep control and ensure alliances, but there were only so many miracles they could expect.

"I have some allies in the North and men that owe me favors. Let me see what I can muster up," said Claudius. "I make no promises, though. It has been some time since I have worked closely with them."

She nodded and wandered to the cold fireplace. Kneeling, she waved her hands over and flames sparked on the fresh wood. The fire grew until a steady heat filled the room. She stood and rubbed her hands together, then faced her palms to the heat. "I knew this fight would be hard, but this feels as though I am losing on every front. My whole life I had believed that my powers would ease some of the troubles other leaders faced. That I could rise above such things."

"Take heart. The ships I promised will be here soon."

Hopefully.

"May the spirits grant them fair winds and calm seas," she said softly.

She didn't even hear him approach until he appeared beside her, those fathomless depths fixed on the fire. "Alexandria wins when you give up. Until then, there is always hope."

Without speaking, she grabbed his hand and threaded his fingers through her own. The crackling fire filled the silence between them, saying all that couldn't be said, and offered the warmth they needed.

Once the last of her attendants left her chambers that night, Sybilla moved to the window overlooking the garden below. Moonlight spilled over the manicured grass and bare trees. Wisps of snow fell softly, dusting the ground. A little gathered on the windowpane, frosting the glass at the edges. She stepped back. She didn't like the cold. During winter, the caravan normally ventured further south toward Midlan where the snows didn't take, and the air remained just a little warmer.

I like the cold, Rhea murmured, rising sleepily up from the dark in Sybilla's mind. Her magic stretched out like a yawn, then retreated. A warm glow lingered in Sybilla's blood.

"That makes one of us," Sybilla said, turning to her bed. Would she get any sleep tonight, or would it elude her once more? She sighed. "I am curious. Now the shield is up; what's next for you?"

Resting.

A spark of irritation flared in Sybilla's chest. "Am I merely a bed to you?"

To your credit, you are one of the more comfortable hosts I've inhabited.

"You managed just fine by yourself before," she mumbled as she pulled back the blankets.

Rhea chuckled. *We can only exist in this realm for a period before we must return to our own. To exist for longer here, we must rest within hosts. Unlike the demons, we do not seek to fully exist within your realm. There would be...consequences for such a desire.*

"Have the spirits spoken to you about your involvement here?"

There have been terse words, but it seems they are leaving me to act as I please. For now.

"And your next move?"

Laughter rumbled softly through her mind. *I gave your city a shield. Do you wish for more?*

"The demon threat." Sybilla slid into her bed and added, "any insight about that?"

Rhea hummed softly in her mind before she spoke. *This demon's reach with the cracks is limited. Though it appears that demons are attacking you from within, I sense there are also mortals at work. I cannot see them, but I feel an echo of their presence. They are hidden from me.*

Sybilla sat up sharply. "Spies in the city?"

She knew there was a good chance there were some in the city. Her birds were hunting for them, but she'd been fairly content in that she'd gotten the worst of them.

Saboteurs, I'd say. Monitor the shield. Mirena will seek to dismantle this as quickly as she can.

It wasn't the answer she wanted, but with the little time she'd spent with Rhea, she knew wouldn't give any further information unless the capricious spirit deigned to do so. It was maddening, but there wasn't anything she could do.

Tomorrow, they'd have to turn their focus to the offensive. She'd have to make the Empress's forces bleed before her own men became too hungry to fight back.

She dreamed she stood in a long stone throne room, lit by enormous flames cradled in iron baskets. Towering pillars flanked the room, stretching up to a glass-capped window that let moonlight spill into the room. The silver and red hues danced together across the polished floor, catching on the flecks of crystal embedded in the stone, like stars reflected at her feet.

Her gaze lifted to the dais at the end of the room. Three thrones, simple by design, with tall backs and arched arms, sat side by side. The left was empty. The middle held a man whose shimmering form concealed any distinguishable features...and on the third sat a woman.

No...

It was Ellie, Nimue's sister. The mortal.

But she was different. Her eyes were glossy black, void of any white, and black tendrils writhed beneath her skin. One slender arm stretched out, holding a tall scythe.

This all felt too vivid to be any kind of dream. This felt like something else. She inched forward cautiously, itching to pinch her arm to wake up, resisting only as those cold black eyes bore into her. It compelled her to keep moving until she came to a halt before the dais, dropping to her knees before she could stop herself.

"Rise," Ellie commanded.

Sybilla did so with wobbly legs, wondering what the hell was happening to her. Something about Ellie made her want to *obey.*

"I require your aid," Ellie said

"What?" *So, not a dream...and not her prophetic vision.*

Had Nimue lied about her sister?

"My sister is none of your concern." Ellie rose slowly and stepped forward, her footfalls silent as she descended from the dais. "I need you to deliver a message to the spirit within you. The time has come for the Primal Goddess to awaken. The Druid girl, Nora, has been chosen. When the time comes, she will be claimed. No one is to interfere."

CHAPTER 72

"Atlas returns to war across the sea. It is not a battle he expects to win, but winning is seldom the point anymore. Perhaps he wishes, like most of us, to feel as close to what he once was. A creature of war and death. Alas, now there are just us three left in this kingdom. How have only seven hundred years passed since our arrival? Why does time move so slowly here?"

—Excerpt from Claudius's diary

Flynn awoke from the third trial with a scream as his soul cracked open. Magic erupted outwards, flooding his limbs, and bursting from his fingers in streams of light. His eyes flew open, blinded for a moment, a soundless cry tearing from his lips. His mind stretch out across the fae, feeling their collective magic, as it pushed beyond the temple grounds. Then he was lifted over the trees, above the town below, then out across the water. A glittering sea ran to the horizon, calling his name.

His mind was pulled toward the thousands of islands that formed the Mithra Archipelago. The air felt still and void of magic. A land sucked dry. Though the trees were lush and green, they felt *dead*, as though what was seen was merely an illusion.

Look deeper, a voice urged.

He reached out his power to the islands and peered closer. A shadowy film lifted, a curtain pulled back, and a flicker of magic brushed his mind.

There you are, he thought.

The magic of the fae, buried deep within the earth, bound by a spell. He could see it now, an invisible chain locked on the archipelago. One grand prison, binding it all away, keeping the fae weak. Only the strongest could still tap the source, but it was mere droplets.

He was pulled back, drawn to his body, to the temple itself, and back into his mortal prison. A part of his soul raged against it, seething to be free. A cold chill dumped over him, shattering the connection to his magic, and his eyes snapped open.

There was no blinding light, just the pale stone ceiling and a face hovering above him. He blinked several times until their features sharpened. A worried smile tugged at a small, heart-shaped mouth. It was moving, but their voice was muffled, as though spoken from far away. A hand touched his shoulder, squeezing softly. Time dragged on, his senses dull, unfocused until his hearing at last returned.

"Flynn, can you hear me?" Mira asked, shaking him again.

That's my name, he thought dimly, memories trickling in, returning his mind to his soul.

The two merged in a burst of light in his chest.

Flynn sat up, wincing. "By the spirits..."

"How do you feel?" she asked gently.

His gaze dropped to his hands. Tendrils of light wove through his fingers. "I'm a demon...but ... this is spirit magic. I thought..."

Mathias's shadow fell over them. Mira stepped back, bowing her head. A strange expression was on her face, one Flynn didn't recognize. Even her stance was new. Back straight, hands at her sides.

Like a warrior.

His gaze drifted beyond her. The hall was empty...but that wasn't right. He'd felt the assembled fae's power, had seen them in his mind's eye, watching him. His brow furrowed. How long had he been under? Questions crowded his mind as he pushed up to his feet, a lightness lingering in his limbs.

The old fae looked at him with a guarded expression.

"Both of you, come with me," he said and strode off without waiting for a response.

Flynn and Mira shared a look, which eased his nerves. At least he wasn't the only one in the dark. Lyria said he was now—or would become in time—the new Spirit God. Whatever *that* entailed, he didn't know, but his mind still struggled to make the connection to his blood. Atlas was his father...unless that was a lie, too?

He wasn't sure what he was anymore.

Confused, he followed Mathias, shadowed by Mira, who kept glancing at him with an unreadable look. It was as though she didn't recognize him, either.

The room was too small. His magic stirred restlessly in his blood, his soul chafing against the four walls. He felt as though he could bring down the Empress by himself, bring his people home, and save Tobin.

Beside him, Mira seemed unaffected, and he suspected his new power was to blame. It was changing him already, erasing the human he'd been.

Mathias cleared his throat, pulling Flynn from his wandering thoughts. "Flynn, you have questions about your power and your blood. The truth that I am about to give you cannot leave these halls. Beyond these grounds, that will be up to you, but I must caution you. At this time, it isn't wise to declare what you are. For though you have your magic now, you must train and learn how to harness it. You have more power in your veins now than most, but to wield it to its full potential will take time."

He wanted to argue. His people didn't have time. Tobin didn't have it either. Mira's gaze darted to him. A silent plea glimmered in those golden depths. He nodded, replying begrudgingly, "I understand."

Mira bowed slightly. "As do I."

Mathias seemed satisfied and sat back in his chair. "I will tell you everything I know. Please sit." He waited until Flynn and Mira were seated then with a heavy sigh, he spoke.

"Your father, Atlas, was an immortal, a demon. He could not sire any children, and he searched desperately for a way to grant his wife a child. The spirits saw this as an opportunity. They granted his wish, but for a price they would only reveal after his child was born. You and your sister were born nine months later. That is when the price was revealed. The spirits possessed the essences of the three gods, taken before they split the realm and died. They decreed that both of you would each be granted the essence of a god. Lyria was granted to your sister and you with Ronan."

Flynn frowned. The story left him with even more questions. "But I'm still a demon...aren't I?"

Mathias nodded. "Yes, at least you were by birth, and only enough was left to ensure any kin of your father might recognize you as one of them. Your father tried to hide you both by separating you and binding your magic. That way, any trace of this deal was concealed from any who might wish you ill."

"And who would want us dead?" he asked.

"Your father only told us that the spirits warned him that someone with immense power might come for you. Beyond that, he said nothing."

Flynn pressed his face into his hands. The story still rang loud in his mind. He thought that freeing his powers would give him the tools he needed to save his people. Learning that he was nothing more than a pawn of the spirits and gods, forged to become a weapon, left his stomach in knots.

Closing his eyes, he tried to think about what he should do. Lyria wanted him to gather a team of gods and demons, all to defeat the coming darkness. This goddess of chaos was rising once more. Lyria and her siblings had barely defeated her before. Back then, they were trained in their powers...but him? He had no idea how he was meant to save anyone...

And he was now further from rescuing his people than he'd ever been.

A steady hand fell on his shoulder, squeezing softly. "Flynn passed your trials, as I have passed mine. You know where we intend to go."

Mathias laughed softly, but it was a weary sound, an old man in defeat. "I confess I hoped you would fail, but such were the desires of an old man. After all, your father was confident in your success. He said that should you pass the trials, the bind on your powers would be removed. This would grant you less of an assault by your powers and afford time to learn control."

Flynn sat up sharply. "You wanted me to fail, but why?"

"Because he doesn't have faith you will fulfill this destiny, that you will bring ruin on the fae," finished Mira grimly. "But Mathias, you forget something. Flynn has the power of a god now."

Mathias levelled a weary look back. "And you forget, Mira, that it took all three gods to defeat the darkness the first time. Their plan cost them their lives and that of the millions caught in the crossfire." Mathias stood, irritation sparking, his patience thinning. "You have passed the trials, but do you have what it takes to truly embrace your destiny? Can you pay the same price as those before you did?"

To that, Flynn fell silent. The price of victory had cost Ronan his life. Aislynn had died anyway because she had been possessed in the final moments by the chaos goddess, and Lyria died alone in her new realm. Was he truly ready for that fate?

He didn't know.

Mira's hand squeezed his shoulder. "He can and will, I know it. Right now, your people are being taken. Flynn and I have power now, which means we can help. Let us get your people back. A first test, as you will, of our abilities. You can send Ashara and Kiya with me. They're my teachers, so they can train me as they go and can help Flynn master his magic." She leaned forward, a hard gleam sharpening her eye. "But let us be frank, you owe Flynn."

Flynn's gaze flew to her. *Power? Since when?* His mouth parted, the question poised to his lips. That had been what they'd sequestered her away for? He wondered why all the secrecy. It was something he'd ask her later when they were alone.

Mathias appeared to mull this over as he leaned back in his chair, one brow lifted. "I owe him, do I?"

"Tobin is his mate, something you knew about for some time and did nothing." There was a note of fury in Mira's voice. "I know you swore an oath to Tobin that you would ensure Flynn was given all that he needed. I mean, that *was* the agreement if anything happened to Tobin...and I heard from the others that it was Tobin who stepped in to be taken to spare some of the others here."

A heavy silence filled the room.

Flynn couldn't breathe. All that time and Mathias had known Tobin was his mate? His mind twisted to the promise his mate had made, trying not to linger too much on it.

Mathias's face was a mask unto itself, for which Flynn couldn't read. Those golden pools yielded no response while leveled steadily on Mira. Finally, he cleared his throat. "Ashara said you were an observant one."

"And I learn languages quickly as it turns out," Mira replied.

Flynn had grown still as a statue as Mathias had spoken. The words of the old fae were roaring in his mind. All those training sessions, the lingering looks, the *kiss.* He sat forward, a hand over his mouth, as a scream threatened to tear out. Tobin had never said a damn word. The damned fool. Why hadn't he told Flynn? He wanted to shake Tobin, scream at him, demand why he'd kept the truth hidden.

I'm his mate.

From what he'd understood in the past few weeks of fae was what that word meant. Soul bound. His heart thudded hard in his chest, followed by a wave of growing anger.

He stood up sharply. "I think we're done here."

Mira and Mathias looked at him, both surprised at his hard tone. Mira's gaze softened as she spoke. "Flynn?"

His focus was on Mathias, his blood heating. "You knew we were mates and you still tried to stop me. Did you make him keep it from me as well?"

Please say no, please say that it was Tobin's foolish decision.

Mathias didn't even blink as he said, "I did."

"*Why?*"

Mathias hissed in exasperation. "You're to be a *god*. What room is there for a god to love?"

Flynn had heard enough. "I'm leaving now to get him back, along with any others I can, with or without your support. If your people mean anything to you, then send the two Mira said, and we will go. We will get your people back and I will prove you wrong."

At dusk, he met Mira, along with the two fae women, at the temple gate. The pair stood a head taller than Mira, all muscle, dark skin, and tight curly obsidian hair. Their luminous gold eyes watched him approach. He realized they must be siblings. They bore the same sloped nose and strong mouth. One stood a fraction taller and had a scar beneath her left eye. The other had shorter hair she wore braided close to her head in neat rows. Interest glimmered on her face as she took him in, while her taller sister was harder to read.

Mira moved to greet him and set a hand on his shoulder, offering a friendly squeeze. She stepped back, then gestured to the taller of the two. "This is Ashara," she said, then gestured to the other, "and her sister, Kiya. They've been my mentors these past few weeks, and I know you have many questions about that. I will answer all that I can, but time is of the essence."

Kiya held out her hand. "Congratulations on your trials. I had my doubts about you, but I am glad you proved me wrong. Know this, however, we join this mission not for you but for our kin. We will teach you control but fail us and I will remove your head. I have no interest in dealing with weakness."

He bowed to them. He wasn't so arrogant to believe he controlled the magic that now roared in his veins. They wanted to get their people back as much as he did, too. He would do his best to earn their respect, and prove to them he was worthy of their training.

Ashara spoke. "We need to leave now. I have spoken to our sisters on the island of Desirelle. Our kin have been taken to the barracks there. They'll be trained there for perhaps a week or more. Word has it, a contingent of men and ships will be sent to Danomir. Rebellion has sparked and the Empress wishes it crushed."

Dread pooled in Flynn's gut. He nodded grimly, eager to get going and to learn as much as he could. Ashara set off first, leading the way. The rest of them fell in behind, with Mira and Flynn at the rear.

He cast a final look at the temple grounds. Mathias stood at the entrance, the looming pillars on either side. Flynn said a silent goodbye, then hurried off after the others.

They walked in relative silence back down the winding path toward town. Night crept over the forest. A cool breeze whispered lazily through the woods, rustling the leaves, offering a slight reprieve to the damp air. Sweat dripped from his brow by the time they emerged from the path at the edge of town.

Lanterns hung from homes and stores, lighting the streets, and dispelling much of the shadows. The place was quieter than their arrival, with eyes peering through shuttered windows and only a handful of fae about on the street. They watched the group walk past with guarded expressions and tight mouths, as if they knew what they were going to do. Even with the power in his veins awakened, he felt stripped bare, unsteady.

Kiya dropped back to his side. "First lesson, lift your head, be proud of what you are. Embrace the power."

He took strength from her words and forced his head up and his shoulders back. A little of his discomfort eased. He *had* passed the trials, which ought to have killed him, and had attained the magic he was after. The first part was over. Now he just had to control it, get Tobin back, and then return to Danomir.

"Better," she remarked with the ghost of a smile, and she nudged his shoulder as she spoke once more. "Perhaps there is some hope for you after all."

CHAPTER 73

"After a hundred years in the arms of other people, we find ourselves entangled once more...but it feels different now. I no longer feel adrift. A new desire has been lit within me. I am afraid to broach it with Claudius, for this is a path no demon has attempted before. Not with success, anyway. I cannot deny this anymore. I wish for a child."

—Excerpt from Nimue's diary

A new day of the siege dawned.

The sun inched slowly upward from the sea, golden fingers stretching out over the water until it brushed the city's edge. Shadows retreated to nooks and crevices. The cold air warmed, and the bite of the breeze dulled.

The city entered a lull, a quiet before the storm. Even as diseases prowled the streets, striking at unsuspecting homes, evading measures put in place, a sense of normalcy took hold.

From high upon the tower, Nimue watched it all in dragon form. She wasn't sure what brought her back to the place where she'd rescued Lorca. It was one of the few places up high she could stretch out her long body and unfurl her wings in the morning light without knocking anything over. Somehow, she found her mind quieter there.

It was the closest she had to her time as a climber.

She rose slowly, flexing her wings against the morning chill, and lumbered over to the edge. The sun had lifted higher now, and the blue sky emerged through streaks of white clouds. Her gaze settled on the distant army.

It was camped at the tree line, a sprawling force that grew larger each day. The Empress had sent reinforcements. Perhaps more from Midlan, or the cities further down the coast. Whatever Nimue had burned in her last attack had been replaced.

Nimue? Lorca's voice brushed her mind.

I'm at the tower I saved you at. Is everything okay?

Beyond being in a city under siege? Amusement crackled down the bond. *I'm in the library. There's something I want to show you.*

Her head jerked up. *What is it?*

It's hard to explain. Can you come here?

Is everything okay?

There was a long silence before he answered. *You should see this.*

Though she considered pushing the matter, she launched off the edge, snapping her wings wide at the last second. A gust of wind caught her and she lifted upward, gliding comfortably over the rooftops.

Thick bands of daylight pierced through the smattering of clouds inching lazily across the sky. There would be no snow today. She realized it was something she missed from her old life in Fenware. The vicious snowstorms that lashed the mountains, the nights huddled by fires, sharing stories, drinking spiced mead.

Before she knew it, she had reached the wide street that was within walking distance of the mansion. Less chance of people seeing her land terribly.

She picked her spot, eyeing the middle of the street, and angled down. The air hissed in her ears as raced toward the ground. Her heart leaped. She kept her wings steady as she swooped low, then snapped them up, sharply cutting her speed. Thrusting her feet down, she gave another flap and she hit the ground with a hard stumble.

Nearly roaring in delight, she shifted back and jogged toward the mansion. The quiet morning streets would soon fill with people trying to make the best of the siege, endure it the only way they knew how—by pretending it wasn't happening.

The mansion's gates were flung open and a wagon trundled out carrying a group of healers. Another was in the courtyard as she strode in, with supplies being loaded up by weary-eyed men and women. Slowing to a walk, she moved around them, offering a nod of respect, and headed inside.

The foyer was its usual hive of activity. Healers finishing their shifts were stumbling out from the direction of the ballroom where the injured lay, while new ones stepped in to replace them. Helena appeared at the top of the stairs, crisply dressed, with that unflappable calm about her as she spoke to a group of nobles. She met Nimue's stare, gave a curt nod, then turned her attention back to the men.

Nimue hurried off in the direction of the library and walked inside. Lorca was fussing over something on the table and started as she walked over.

"Nimue!"

There was something on the table behind him, but she couldn't make out what it was. His body blocked her view.

"What is behind you?" A teasing note lit her voice.

He shifted nervously for a moment. "This is a terrible idea."

"What is?" She didn't like the uncertainty in his eyes as she moved forward, reaching for him.

He turned and unwrapped the bundle. Inside were two short swords, far more ornate than the pair she'd been using. The blades glinted sharply, connected to a hilt of leather and metal with a red jewel glittering on either side.

Gingerly, she lifted them. They were perfectly balanced and weighted better than her current ones. She stepped back, tightening her grip on the hilts, and moved into a set, swinging and thrusting. As she stilled, she found his gaze on her.

"I melted down that sword you hated," he confessed. "And I had a weapons master use it in making those. I also found some red jewels, which I thought you might like, for...for your daughter."

She stilled, her gaze falling to the swords. The sword that had killed her was gone. Lorca had reforged into something new and combined it with a token for her daughter. Tears welled before she could stop them. Lorca moved close and his hand caressed her face.

"Why?" she asked gently.

"At first, I wished to destroy the sword that Litania had used to kill you. It brought you such pain and I wanted it gone...but as it melted down, I thought I might reforge it into something new. I just didn't know what, but then I saw how you were with twin short swords."

"You destroyed it for me?" No one had ever done something like that for her.

It had always been her role to play that part for others. That Lorca had done this to shield her from pain blindsided her. A part of her had wanted to destroy the sword herself, but this result was better. She could hold it and reclaim the weapon that had nearly killed her...and the red jewels in honor of Rhea.

"D-do you like it?" he asked quietly.

She gently set the blades aside and closed the distance, then took his hands in her own, squeezing them softly. "I love them. Thank you."

"Good, good."

The nervousness in his air melted away, making her realize just much he must have fretted over the swords. She released his hands, then reached up and leaned in, pressing her forehead to his. Both of their fates were unknown, but one small gesture left her wishing more than ever before to have more time.

Something that was rapidly running out.

They spent the next few hours going over maps, family histories, and everything they could learn about the Gray Army. Lorca read the manuscripts aloud as Nimue transcribed them into notebooks in a demonic script. Her hand cramped, so she sat back and rested for a few minutes. This mortal body had been a novel thing at the start and something she'd longed for in her immortal years but the everyday aches and pains had quickly worn thin. The power boost the spirit had given her was also fading again, faster than she was comfortable to admit. She could shift, which was a mercy, but her body felt full of holes, the magic bleeding out steadily.

"You slept little last night," Lorca said as he sat up from his spot on the table. "You were tossing and turning, calling out Rhea's name."

She flinched at the mention of her daughter. "It's nothing new. What about you? Do...do you dream of the fall?"

They had spoken little about his past. She hadn't wanted to push, but his quietness about it worried her. During their research, they'd run out of materials about Litania. She'd died young, her husband killed in battle weeks later, leaving her sixteen-year-old daughter to ascend the throne. Sybilla's bloodline. Very few personal diaries existed and what texts detailed about her described a quiet empress, clever but prone to bouts of sadness. She often sequestered herself away.

That was it.

Mirena and Litania had become entangled at some point, though it was impossible to say if that was by choice or coercion. Had Litania submitted for power? Or was she coerced? She'd been a young girl in love, tempted by life beyond the mountains.

He sighed. "Sometimes, but it's all the same. Fire and death."

She stood and reached for his hand. "Lorca—"

He pulled away and got off the table. "It doesn't matter now, does it? It's three hundred years ago. She's dead. They're all dead."

A chill seeped into her heart. The Dragonirs had been hers to protect from demons and wyverns alike. She'd shielded the worst storms from their homes and kept enemies at bay. But when the real challenge arose, she had failed them...and now Lorca suffered. There was nothing to destroy, nothing within reach. Mirena was the cause behind it all, but Nimue was too weak to end her.

And now they risked losing another city to Mirena.

"Hey, *stop that,*" he said.

She looked up sharply. "Stop what?"

"That demon murdered you. The destruction of my people is not your fault." He raked his fingers through his hair.

"We have to stop Mirena. Here, in this city," she said vehemently.

She had to destroy Mirena's connection to his realm. Long ago, they had thought that if she and her kin returned to the demon realm, they might restore balance to all three realms. Perhaps that would've worked once, but their selfish desire to be free had shattered any chance of returning.

If things became dire, she had one last trick up her sleeve—but that was a path from which there was no going back.

Lorca's hand cupped her chin and lifted her gaze. "What is going on in that mind of yours?"

"Destruction and war," she replied with a smile.

But the teasing lilt only deepened his frown and worry crept into his eyes. He knew her well enough to know that there were few lines she would not cross for her people. She wanted to tell him she wasn't planning anything crazy. Which *was* true...but not for long. To shatter Mirena's connection would bear a heavy price.

"Nimue, whatever you're planning, don't shut me out," he begged.

But she was already sinking further into her mind, churning through ideas. She wouldn't fail him again or the rest of the people she cared for. Mirena would pay. She would make sure of it.

Whatever it took.

Nimue and Lorca walked in silence from the library. His arm was snaked around her waist, but he felt an ocean from her, silent in his thoughts. Twice she opened her mouth to talk, but then closed it. What could she say? Promises that she wouldn't do whatever was required to defeat Mirena? It would only be lies.

A distant clatter and a cacophony of voices floated up from the floor below. That steady sound she loathed in the morning now filled the void between them. She glanced at him, hoping that a look might entice him into conversation. Instead, those green eyes stared ahead.

A sense of unease welled within her, hollowing out her chest. She itched to take his hand, but even that felt too much. A right she didn't deserve. More than ever, she wished she was back at full strength and that Mirena was in front of her, that she could rip her limb from limb. Make her scream and beg for mercy.

Lorca staggered. A curse shot from his lips, his hand shooting out to catch himself on the wall. Nimue burst to his side, sliding one arm around him. Pain pinched his face and his eyes were scrunched shut.

"Lorca?"

"It's...it's fine," he gritted out.

"You're *not* fine—how long have you been fighting this? Why didn't you go back to rest?" she snapped.

"I was fine," he replied. "I *am* fine. Let's just get to the room."

She hauled him the last bit and kicked open the door. His skin glowed as she hurled him into the room and stepped back. Lorca sank to his knees and threw his head back, an inhuman cry of agony bursting from his chest.

White light erupted as he threw his arms wide. When it dimmed, he slumped forward in his dragon form, sprawling out. His head sunk to the ground and a low groan rumbled through his chest.

For a moment, she couldn't speak. Anger burned through her like a raging inferno. Why hadn't he said anything? He didn't need to suffer! But as he turned his head groggily to her, their bond ebbed and flowed with a weak trickle of energy cooling her temper. A gut-wrenching fear washed over her.

"Why didn't you say anything?" The anger had yielded to an aching panic that shredded her to ribbons. "You said you were fine, as though you weren't getting worse. Why didn't you tell me?"

I didn't realize I was that close. It just...It came quickly. A note of unease brushed her mind.

She kneeled, gingerly reaching for his snout. "Is it getting worse?"

As he leaned into her hand, shutting his eyes, she felt a shiver of fear lance through her heart. One eye cracked open and she felt his fear. For her, for his future, their mission...and the fear he might never see another Dragonir.

I don't know...

CHAPTER 74

"This morning, I felt my daughter kick for the first time. I do not know how I know it is a girl, but I do. I can feel her. Claudius was out exploring. The fae seldom leave us be and he is curious to wander undisturbed. When he returns, I hope she kicks again. He sometimes tries to hide his excitement, but I see his smiles. Nervous but hopeful."

—Excerpt from Nimue's diary

Flynn leaned over the railing of the ship and watched as the last remnants of his breakfast tumbled into the frothy waves. At last, his stomach ceased spasming. He stepped back, wiping his mouth.

Kiya was beside him, faring no better. After she had finished, she straightened up with a grimace. He took out his waterskin and offered it to her. With a shaky smile, she took a quick swig before heaving again.

Flynn slipped the skin back into his satchel and leaned against the railing. The hot sun beat down mercilessly, bright and glaring off the jewel-blue water. How it was still so warm when he knew it was winter in Danomir surprised him. Tobin had mentioned something about ancient magic running through the islands, ensuring a consistent climate.

Suddenly, he wished he paid more attention to those lessons, instead of just staring at Tobin longingly. He forced his gaze across the deck. The sailors moved about with ropes, buckets, tools in hand, as they went about their tasks. A few scrambled up the masts with nimble hands. A pang of longing for the cliffs cut through him. He sighed and headed over to sit in the shade. Kira, appearing more settled, joined him.

"Mira mentioned you used to scale the mountains, that it was her job and yours, too," she said.

"Our livelihood was tied to was a flower that only grew up high. We climbers were the ones who harvested it," he explained. "I miss the cliffs. There was just something freeing about being that high up. The views from the outcrops were beyond anything you could imagine."

Kiya snorted. "Wouldn't catch me up there. I like my feet on solid ground."

Flynn smiled. "So, no heights or seas?"

"I enjoy swimming, but sailing does not entice me. My sister likes jumping on ships for runs between the islands. I, for one, prefer keeping my feet planted on dry land," she said before her face twisted again and she rushed over to the rail.

Nothing came out, but tremors racked her body. When she finished again, he offered her some more water. "Small sips otherwise you'll get worse."

She scowled but took the skin and sipped it tentatively. "How are you okay now?"

His stomach was still uneasy, but he felt a little better, for the moment anyway. "Don't worry, you'll feel better soon enough."

She didn't appear convinced, but as she went to say something, Ashara strode over. The woman walked with the air of a warrior; straight-backed, square shoulders, steady confidence emanating from her. Her iron gaze slid to Kiya and softened.

"I'll have the healer bring you something," she said. Turning to him, her air resumed its reserved tone. "Come with me. We need to get some training in before we arrive."

He cast a friendly smile at Kiya, then followed her sister to the stern of the ship. The quartermaster stood there, one hand on the wheel, moving it gently. He glanced at Flynn, and lingered for a moment before returning to his task at hand.

Ashara waited for him at the railing. "Now we are going to see what we're working with. Stand beside me and point one palm at the water."

He did as she said, though he felt a little absurd doing so. Ashara's gaze burned on him as if it saw right down into his soul and could read his every thought. "Like this?"

"Now, close your eyes. Calm your thoughts. Look within yourself, *feel* your magic. Call it to your fingers and hold it there."

At her order, he closed his eyes and turned his gaze inward. A vast abyss of pure light swirled around him, warm and soothing. He pictured himself stretching a hand out to the magic and summoning it. Power sparked in his chest, and out across his arms. His eyes flew open as light erupted on his fingers. For a split second, it glowed like a sun, tendrils peeling off and gliding over his hand, then it flashed and exploded outwards with a deafening bang.

Flynn flew back, crashing into the railing, smacking his head. Stars flashed across his vision as he attempted to stand.

He wobbled to his feet. "I don't know what happened..."

"I do." Ashara pressed her lips together for a moment, silent.

"You do?"

"I want you to do it again but, this time, do not summon it to your fingertips. I want you to keep it just beneath the skin and hold it there for five seconds, then push it back in."

"Just that?"

Her brow rose. "If you use too much power at once and lose control you may just end up killing us all. That *is* something I'd like to avoid."

So would he. A determined air filled his lungs as he closed his eyes again. The light blazed around him, a vast expanse of raw magic, with no end in sight. He felt his mind want to drift again, as it had before, but he fought back the urge. Releasing the air from his lungs, he called on the magic and pushed it down into his arms. Just as it went to squeeze out his fingertips, he pulled it back and counted.

One.

Heat built, and pressure started throbbing in his head.

Two.

A sharp pain lanced down his neck and into his chest, straight to his heart.

Three.

The magic surged, straining against his skin. It fought for release. He felt it howl angrily at him, furious at being taunted with freedom.

Four.

It lashed against his control, then shrank back, eddying within his chest like a caged beast.

Five.

He hauled it back in, but a tendril of magic slipped from his control. It shot down his arm and burst out. His eyes flew open as a tiny bolt erupted from his palm. Although he didn't fly back that time, irritation flared at his inability to control his power.

"Again," ordered Ashara.

He pictured his people in his mind and Tobin, too, standing among them. Then he tried again.

The days stretched on, and a familiar routine settled in for all of them. Flynn rose early to spar with Kiya, who only permitted him a wooden sword. They trained until midday when they broke for a short meal. Once this was done, Kiya went down to work with Mira, conducting private lessons below. He wasn't permitted to ask questions or intrude.

Not that he had time. Ashara kept him busy with magic lessons until his head pounded and sweat dripped from his brow. It was more exhausting than the sword work, but he pushed on.

He tried not to think about Tobin or his people. Thoughts like that left him with a gaping sense of dread, his stomach twisting into knots until he was ready to throw up again. The focus for the moment was finding where the fae were imprisoned. Ashara said she had contacts in the city, but she was incredibly cagey whenever he asked. Sometimes he caught her glancing warily at the sailors and, in particular, the captain.

It made him watch the crew.

By the time the sun touched the horizon, stretching out shards of amber and red across the sky, he was bone-tired and aching. He stumbled down to his quarters, which he shared with the others. Mira was already curled up asleep in her cot, but unlike on previous nights, Kiya was absent. He moved toward his bed when a shadow filled the doorway behind him. Startled, he twisted on his heel, heart pounding.

Kiya's mouth twitched. "Come with me."

She set off, leaving him wide-eyed as he hurried after her. "Where are we going?"

"Below."

Kiya moved swiftly, silent as a wraith, with one hand held up, threaded with ribbons of magic. It lit the gloomy interior, chasing back the shadows.

Their quarters were two decks below the main deck, with two more beneath. A sailor had informed him they were storage holds. He'd gotten curious late one night, but it was as the sailor said. Nothing but barrels of fresh water, crates of dried food, and some preserved fruit cushioned in beds of hay. He hadn't been back down since.

Kiya climbed down the steep steps first, then snapped her fingers to call on tendrils of light. A makeshift bed had been constructed. Around it was a circle carved into the wooden floor. He wondered if the captain knew about it. Probably not. He imagined such men didn't like their belongings being messed with.

"Mira spoke to me of your connection to Tobin," Kiya said quietly. "The link between mates, even those who haven't formalized it in a ceremony, is strong. We're going to try to connect with him."

Flynn froze. "You know we're mates?"

"A lot of us could tell Tobin had an interest in you." Kiya's mouth twitched again. "Ashara wondered, but it's considered rude to pry into such things. Mates are a sacred thing, not something we gossip about."

"But how can I connect with him?"

This time Kiya smiled. "Fates are two souls tethered together the moment both are in the world. It is said that the thread grows tighter, inevitably drawing the pair together. It is that connection I'm going to use. Well, try at least."

He felt a renewed spike of anger for Mathias.

"Why didn't Mathias tell me back on the island? Is this another way to control me and keep me from saving Tobin and the others?"

"Don't be angry at Mathias. He doesn't know of my ability. It's a long story, but one I will share later. Now, lie down. We have but a short time before one of the crew comes down for his rounds," said Kiya.

He stretched out on the wooden bed. Kiya moved silently to his head, then knelt and gently pressed her hands to his temple. He opened his mouth to speak, but darkness sucked him under, sending him tumbling into oblivion.

The next moment he jolted upright, gasping. He wasn't in the ship's hold anymore. Rather, he was in the clearing he used to spar with Tobin. The sun was bright, but he could not feel its warmth, nor taste the salt air on his lips.

A gasp came from behind him.

He pivoted and his heart froze in his chest. He didn't dare to move, nor breathe. A few feet away, staring at him with a disbelieving expression, was Tobin.

"W-what is this?" Tobin asked hoarsely. "What kind of damn dream is this?"

Flynn was already moving forward before he realized it. "This isn't a dream. I'm here. Well, perhaps not fully. Kiya made this happen."

At the mention of her name, Tobin jolted, and all the color drained from his cheeks. "No, no, no, don't tell me you're coming for me!"

He flinched back. "What? Of course, I'm coming for you! Why wouldn't I?"

"It isn't safe," insisted Tobin. "Please, turn around wherever you are, finish the trials. Then go save your people."

"And lose my mate?" It was the first time he'd said it aloud. It felt...easier than he expected. He wanted to say it again. "Because that is what I am to you, isn't it?"

Tobin paled. "But your trials—"

"I finished them. The last two back-to-back."

A presence brushed his mind. Kiya. *You need to tell him to pass a message to Cazamere. The nest is empty.*

"What are you talking about?" he blurted out, but Tobin's brow furrowed questioningly. "Kiya. She has a message for you, well, for someone called Cazamere."

Tobin stilled. "What's the message?"

"The nest is empty." Flynn frowned. "What does it mean?"

"Madness. Tell her I'll pass it on, but I don't like it."

I don't care, chuckled Kiya. *I'm going now. You have a few minutes. Make the most of it.*

Flynn relayed it, then felt her presence ebb away. "She's gone now, says we've—"

Tobin was in front of him in a flash, crushing his mouth to his. For a moment, he was stunned, but heat sparked, and he returned the kiss. Maybe it was Kiya's magic, but he could feel Tobin, hard and male, and smelling as maddeningly good as he had during those sessions. He yanked him closer as he clutched at his tunic.

But then Tobin pulled away. Flynn leaned in, trying to kiss him again, but Tobin only gave a chaste peck before pressing their foreheads together. "Tell me about your trials and all that I missed."

Flynn's hand rested on Tobin's hip. "Can't that wait? There are other ways I'd much prefer to catch up."

Laughter tumbled from Tobin. Honest, raw. It shook Flynn to his core. He didn't think he'd ever become indifferent to that sound. Later, once the dust was settled, he'd make it his mission to make Tobin laugh like that every day.

"I want to feel you, to breathe you in, taste you properly, and know it's real, not a fantasy," Tobin growled.

Flynn's cheeks heated. His mind was already conjuring all sorts of images, which were going to make mornings very awkward.

"Fine." He kissed Tobin again. "I'll tell you all about it."

He explained about the trials, but couldn't bring himself to tell Tobin what he was. Mainly because he wasn't precisely sure. He'd explain it in person once he'd figured out how to tell Tobin properly.

When he finished, Tobin kissed him again, a proud smile splitting his cheeks. "I knew you would succeed."

Flynn grinned back when he felt a tug in his gut. The world faded at the edges of his vision, then quickly closed in. "No, no, it's too soon! I want more time!"

Kiya didn't respond.

The world tumbled from beneath him. His hand snapped out to grab Tobin passed through Tobin's vanishing form—

He sat up, the world momentarily dark around him. His eyes adjusted and focused. Standing up, he started walking when his foot hit something. Looking down, he froze. Kiya was sprawled out cold.

"What—?"

Something hard hit him from behind, and he felt no more.

CHAPTER 75

"Nimue and I seek the fae in the mountains. Their magic is famous and their deep connection to the spirits might just be what we need. I worry though what price they might expect..."

—Excerpt from Claudius's diary

The shock of the shield must've worn off because a week after it had gone up, the army was back. The trebuchets had been rebuilt and fireballs blitzed for hours every day, followed by other assorted projectiles. All collided harmlessly against the shield and were destroyed on impact. It should've calmed the men, reassuring them that the magic was strong.

But as Sybilla walked along the wall, she felt the men's unease. She wished Rhea was with her, but the spirit had slipped from her body in the early hours of the morning.

Their leaders stood back, staring at the army just outside. A couple bowed slightly as she walked past, but most appeared to not even realize she was there at all. She wanted to talk to them, but words of encouragement fell flat.

Once she reached the end of her route, she headed back down to the horses. She swung up and nudged her horse forward. Normally, she cantered, but she wasn't in a hurry. Not to return to her office where another mountain of letters waited, or to listen to the complaints of nobles. There had been evidence to suggest they were barely rationing and had stockpiled supplies, even as some of the city was already feeling the first pangs of hunger.

Wagons of weary healers trundled past, heading toward the docks where many of the tents had been moved.

She glanced at Oren, but his focus was on their surroundings, hunting for any threat to her life. Since Claudius's last visit, he'd withdrawn from her. She hated it, and her mood darkened on the ride back to the mansion.

Helena met her at the entrance.

"The high nobles are requesting a meeting with you," she informed her.

Sybilla followed her inside, the headache returning. They'd had a meeting this morning. What did they want now? She nodded absently and rubbed the back of her neck. "I don't suppose there is anything more pressing that might remove me?"

"You would abandon me to those vultures?" Helena drawled.

"A noble sacrifice I would deeply appreciate."

Helena snorted. "Alas, I must decline. Does this evening suit?"

"I have little choice in the matter, do I?" Sybilla already knew the answer.

"This evening, then. Given our rations, I would suggest the meeting be before dinner. That way their hunger won't encourage them to stay for long and if they complain, I get the delight of informing them of the limited food supplies." The corner of Helena's mouth twitched. At that moment, a healer called for her, diverting her attention from Sybilla. Helena nodded at the woman with a frown.

Sybilla glanced at Helena. "Is everything okay?"

"It's just the afternoon report. I'll draft up the final list of injured and dead for you after I meet with her. Are you heading to your office now or private chambers?"

A rest was tempting, but Sybilla knew the pile of reports that awaited her. "I'll be in my office if you require me."

When she arrived at her office, Sybilla sank into her chair. The exhaustion hauled her under, pulling her into darkness.

No dreams assailed her, nor nightmares to leave her screaming. The dreamless abyss wrapped around her, quiet as death, offering a piece she momentarily clung to.

Alas, it was not to last. A hand grabbed her shoulder, jerking her awake. Her eyes flew open, heart pounding in her throat.

"What has happened?"

Helena stood over her, pale as death. "A message from the wall. The shield is failing."

CHAPTER 76

"The fae say that they will aid us. They provide us with magical tonics, which we are to drink before tonight's ceremony."

—Excerpt from Nimue's diary

Titania was heading out when Claudius rode into the courtyard. Wondering what had brought him back early, she glimpsed a bruise on his neck. And there was no mistaking what had caused it. The question was who? There was no way in hell had Nimue forgiven him so easily.

"Claudius?"

He blinked, then looked at her, as if he'd just realized she was there. "Titania, I thought you would've left by now."

"I'm about to. So, who—" She caught a whiff of the scent, then stepped back as understanding dawned. "*Are you fucking mad?*"

His cheeks turned scarlet. "It's not what you think—"

"You're in bed with the Princess of this rebellion?" she said accusingly. Dropping her hand, she attempted to steady herself before speaking again. "What the hell are you thinking? Or perhaps you weren't thinking because I honestly cannot think of any rational reason you might have to be sleeping with her. Given there is no chance for anything to end well."

He looked away. At that moment, Titania felt she scarcely knew him at all.

"We haven't—"

"Do you *really* wish to split hairs now?" Titania retorted.

He glanced away, leaving her with the satisfaction that he appeared sufficiently scolded. Demons below, she'd never been one to judge any of their kin for bed partners—living long lives and such—but they'd always tried to show a degree of sense. Never anyone with power or position, certainly no one capable of exposing them.

Everything that damn Princess was.

He sighed deeply. "I never thought this would happen, but... I cannot explain it. Have you ever met someone who caught you unawares?" After a pause, he continued on. "Was it not like that for you with your wife?"

She looked away, trying not to think of the wife she'd loved and lost. "Of course, it was, but what of Nimue?"

Eight hundred years of questions and mysteries filled the long silence that followed. Only when those jeweled depths slid back to her, revealing the same aching grief she'd seen in Nimue, did a little of her anger die away. It wasn't the matter of who he chose that upset her; but rather, his timing, and that old voice that warned how bad it was for a demon to fall for a mortal. After all, it had never worked out well for any of them. Atlas was enslaved and mortal; she had lost her wife in a horrific attack, and Castille's wife had been burned alive.

"I can never hope—nor ask—for her forgiveness...and even if I had it, our time for what we had is gone," he eventually replied.

"You owe her the truth."

"I know, and I will tell her when I can. What I have with Sybilla, I understand cannot be anything beyond what it is."

She threw up her hands. "You're a fool to think this will end any other way but destruction and pain."

And with that, she strode into the shadows and vanished from sight.

A low sea fog drifted lazily in from the sea, whispering among the docks and warehouses, threading through shuttered windows and beneath locked doors.

The late hours of the night rendered the city quiet, except for the soft music warbling from one of the few brothels still open a few streets away. Such things always survived, even during a siege.

Titania took a short break outside the warehouse she was working, her clothes stained with blood and vomit. Though she reeked, the fetid odor never bothered her. Despite insisting she didn't need a rest, Rell bullied her outside and gave her a waterskin, telling her not to return to work until it was empty.

When Rell finally let her back inside, Titania threw herself back into work.

There had been no new attacks of late, so their role was tending to the injured who couldn't move. Those fit enough were returned to their homes. Leaving those who had lost limbs or required regular wound monitoring kept her on her feet. Every so often Titania would have to call a soldier in to remove someone who had passed.

Morning yielded to a bitter day. Gray clouds blanketed the sky, casting a dreary light over the city. Snow passed through the shield, dusting a thin layer of white across the rooftops. The tents kept most of the water off, but several had developed leaks, requiring buckets to catch the water. She helped empty them when they grew full, pouring them into the restless seas that lashed the docks.

When she broke for a short meal, at the order of the healer running the tents she was working, she found Rell in the rest area. The girl was sitting on a stack of crates, absently chewing on some dried fruit, which she held out to Titania. With a murmured thanks, Titania sat beside her.

"How many?" Rell asked.

"Six and you?"

"Fifteen."

Demons below... "That many?"

"They had bad burns. We kept them as clean as best we could, but infection took to them. They were gone within hours." Rell's gaze dropped to a piece of fruit in her palm. "I tried to heal one, but they were too far gone."

"The hazard of war, I'm afraid," Titania said, and added in a low voice, "It'll only get worse."

Rell leaned back, casting a long look over the tents. "I'm not against this fight. I know why we're doing it. The slaves in this city are now free, well, as free as the rest of us. But it doesn't make this any easier."

Titania wanted to tell Rell how right she was. In all the bloody conflicts, sieges, battles, that she'd been in and witnessed, it never got easier. It was different in the demon realm. Their kind was returned to the pit, then reborn. They might not have the same memories, though on occasion they did, but it meant they weren't gone. In this realm, her kin became accustomed to loss...but even after two thousand years, it didn't feel any easier.

She absently nibbled at the fruit in her hand, finishing it slowly. Still hungry, she dug a sweet roll out of her bag. It broke easily in her hand, and she offered the larger piece to Rell. The young girl murmured a thank you before taking it and wasted no time sinking into the roll.

"Your mother must worry about you," Titania remarked.

Something shuttered in Rell's eyes. "All mothers worry. Mercifully, mine has a fondness for healers. She's a scholar herself but encouraged me to learn more about medicine. I liked it well enough, and my magic lends itself well when I can use it at least."

"She has not tried to keep you locked away?"

A ghost of a smile pulled at Rell's mouth. "My mother knows how poorly that would—"

Their conversation was cut off as the shield flashed overhead. Titania's gaze snapped up as another fireball slammed into the shield, exploding on impact.

"It won't break, will it?" Rell asked.

"No, of course not." Titania tried to sound sure, but inside, she was not so convinced.

The spirits were powerful, but their power wasn't absolute. After all, their love had supposedly blessed Toranelle...and the city burned regardless.

The peace was not to last.

Shouts erupted. Jumping up from her patient, she ducked to the entrance and peeled back the cloth. A crack split the air. Soldiers and healers scrambled back as the crack began to grow.

Titania sprinted to the closest soldier, grabbing his sword. She had it out and was running off before he realized. His shouts fell away as she ran toward the crack.

Demonic magic spilled out. A wolf demon exploded from the shadows. She was right in its path as it launched at her. At the last second, she rolled out of the way and leaped to her feet, pivoting as it came at her again. She side-stepped and slashed her sword down, cleaving its head from its neck.

It hit the ground with a muted thump.

No smoke. Her gaze flew to the portal. More demon wolves. She tightened her grip. This would be easy. Child's play. The corner of her mouth tipped. She stepped forward—

A thunderous explosion ripped from the crack, the shockwave crashing into her, sending her staggering back. She threw her hands out to steady herself. The crack had widened. A clawed paw thrust through, followed by another, and a shadowy creature pried its way out. It dropped to the ground.

Titania stilled.

The creature loomed over her with thick muscular limbs and a barrel body coated in a layer of black scales. A row of horns ran from the tip of its long tail, along its body, and down its head. Four glowing red eyes locked on Titania.

"You know what I am, don't you?" she whispered.

The creature hissed, thrashing its tail back and forth. It dug its claws into the ground, then exploded forward. Titania stayed motionless for a second, then dropped low, sliding under the creature as it jumped. She leaped to her feet and jumped onto its back, driving her sword through the scales. The beast thrashed wildly in an attempt to throw her off.

Her hand slipped.

It bucked again, this time successfully dislodging Titania, and she hit the ground hard. She scrambled up to her feet as the beast stalked toward her. The sword was still embedded in its back, but not deep enough. She just had to get on its back again.

The soldiers had cleared out of the way and healers were retreating into the shadows. The tents hid her from most of their view. Perhaps she could...

A figure flashed behind the beast.

Rell threw a hand out, white light bursting from her palm, crashing into the back of the beast. It threw its head back with a savage roar, splitting the air like a crack of thunder, and thrashed its tail straight into Rell. She went flying across the square into a tent.

"No!"

Titania race forward throwing one hand wide. Darkness erupted from her palm, shooting skywards before it arced back down, dropping around her and the beast. Rell's panicked cry filled the void. Titania ignored it as she sprinted forward and jumped, throwing herself onto the beast's back. Her hand found the hilt of the sword and she drove it down. A pained cry cut off suddenly as the beast crumpled to the ground.

Titania sat up shakily, looking at Rell, who sat up, wide-eyed.

"What *are* you, Titania?"

CHAPTER 77

"The fae, it seems, held up their bargain. Claudius sends word that Nimue is pregnant. I cannot believe it. A demon carrying a child? It fills me with hope...and worry. Some natural laws ought not to be broken and I fear this is a line that should not be crossed."

—Excerpt from Atlas's diary

Much to Nimue's dismay, Lorca's condition hadn't improved. He shifted uncontrollably from human to dragon form, with the former leaving him in writhing agony. Every moan and cry lanced daggers through her heart.

Healers came and went, but few knew what to do with a dragon. The two healers who had tended to him after his injuries beyond the wall couldn't be found.

Sybilla was painfully absent, off dealing with the assailing army and the troubles within the walls. Which meant no spirit help until she returned. He wasn't critical for the moment and didn't appear to be getting worse, so Nimue hoped some rest would settle his body.

She sat by his side, stroking his scales softly, then holding him when he changed back. His screams filled her ears, and his skin glistened with sweat. She wanted to heal him, but her dragon magic had dried up, along with the power gifted by the spirit.

The door cracked open. Nora's head appeared, then she slipped in, casting a worried look over Lorca. "I heard he's not well. What's wrong?"

Nimue briefly explained how Lorca had spent too long in his dragon form, which was why his body was in agony in his human form. "I just don't know why he's gotten worse. I tried to ask him but even awake, there's no talking to him."

Nora squeezed down beside Nimue and brushed the side of Lorca's neck. "I can feel his magic. It's all twisted up. There's no balance."

"Can you do anything?"

Nora sat back, a thoughtful look furrowing her brow. "Perhaps? The problem is, my magic is primal, which means I can't control all the spirit magic inside him. I can ease his pain, but that's about it."

"Please," said Nimue. "Do what you can to help him."

She watched as Nora set her hands on Lorca's neck. A faint green glow appeared beneath her palm. Lorca's twitching body stilled, his raging thoughts calming. Nimue felt his pain easing through their bond. After a few moments, Nora sat back, casting her a questioning glance.

"You have spirit magic..."

Nimue smiled wryly. "Alas, my magic is being difficult once more and Sybilla is absent." She rose shakily and stepped over Nora and one of Lorca's sprawled legs. "Can you stay with him? I want to check on my sister."

"Of course. Take all the time you need."

Unfortunately, Ellie's condition wasn't much better. Ancient demonic magic still choked the air, unseen, but leaving an uneasy feeling whispering through Nimue. She sat down on the bed, taking her sister's cold hand.

"What are you waiting for, Ellie? Why won't you wake up?"

Nimue tried to peer into her sister's mind, but it was a fortress. Even demon to demon goddess, she was still refused entry. She withdrew with a sigh and stood up. A cold breeze nipped through an open window, likely done by a maid to keep some fresh air moving through. She wandered over to close it as the door behind her opened with a gentle creak.

"Oh, you're here!" a woman exclaimed behind her.

Nimue's eyes narrowed. It was a maid. "Have you been tending to my sister?"

"One of three. We are the only ones allowed to tend to her," the woman said. "I'm Alice. The others are Lilian and Mera. We've been working here since we were small, so the Princess trusts us."

Alice was simply dressed. Her face was lit by a warm smile and kind eyes. There was no magic about her, not even a whiff of fae, which suited Nimue.

"Has she shown any movements?" asked Nimue. "I come when I can but..."

"Some mumblings every few days but I can't make much sense of it. I've dealt with bedridden folk before, but she's never soiled herself, nor is showing any signs of wasting away. I change the bedding, clean the room and wash her as best I can." Alice cast a long look at Ellie before it returned to Nimue. "Is she a dragon, too?"

Nimue shook her head. "No, but magic protects her."

That and her body is changing. She's becoming something new. Nimue hoped her sister would recognize her when she woke, but there weren't any guarantees. And the fates were seldom kind to her.

"Well, I should imagine she'll wake soon enough. We'll need all the magical folk we have to protect this city," Alice ventured.

Nimue didn't bother saying that there was no guarantee Ellie would protect the city. She might simply leave. Lyria, by what little recorded history there was of her in the demon realm, cared little about connecting with the world she forged. She might even burn the city to the ground, if she so desired.

There was just no telling what her sister would be if—no, *when*—she woke.

As she walked back to the room, an agonized scream, half tangled in a dragon's roar, tore through the air.

Lorca.

She was off racing before the scream cut off, sprinting straight for the bedroom. The door flew open, and Nora stumbled out. Relief flashed on the girl's face.

"Something is wrong. He changed back to his human form," Nora said in a rush.

Nimue rushed past her into the room. In the middle of the floor, Lorca lay twisting and clawing at the air, a haggard scream filling the room. Sweat glistened on his skin, his gaze unfocused on the ceiling, grimacing in pain. She rushed over, dropping beside him, but as soon as her hand brushed his skin, a new scream ripped out. He wrenched from her as if her touch burned.

She spun on her knees, looking for Nora. "Come here!"

Nodding, the girl rushed in and dropped to her side. She reached out, brushing her hand over Lorca's. His screams tapered off, but he still twisted about and groaned as waves of pain racked his body. Every sound tore at Nimue's soul. She stood up.

"I'm going to find Sybilla." Before she left, she cast a lingering look over Lorca, worry squeezing her heart. "Hold on, Lorca, just *hold on*."

"Go!" urged Nora. "I'll keep him as stable as I can, but he needs that spirit. It's his only hope now."

Nimue dashed from the room.

CHAPTER 78

"A terrible pain roared through my mind today—grief so deep it dropped me to my knees and left tears streaming down my face. I think I scared my lover, Elara, who came rushing from our room. Hours later, that grief became a raging storm of fury. It was a vengeance I knew well. This was the rage of a demon queen, the kind who leveled empires."

—Excerpt from Titania's diary

Aziah choked back a scream as the hammer slammed down onto her legs, shattering bone and splitting flesh. A roaring agony pumped through her veins like molten metal, waves of it continuously crashing over her. The man raised the hammer again, moving up to her thigh.

"This ends when you talk!" he snarled.

As far as torturers went, this one was below average. Hell, even she had inflicted far worse. However, she'd never got herself captured before, and she was not relishing the experience.

She spat into his eye. "I'm going to murder you, *slowly.*"

Cursing, he drove the hammer onto her other leg. His inhuman fae strength meant every blow would break her bones. Nausea surged up her throat and she twisted her head sharply, hurling up the putrid gruel she'd forced down hours before. Some of it splashed his shoes. He jumped back with a hiss, then stepped forward and drove his fist into the side of her head.

Darkness dragged her under.

When she woke hours later, she was dangling by her wrists. Her legs were healed like they always were after each session. In her cell a few times, she'd tried to stand, but the pain had sent her tumbling back down.

Her shoulders ached, which told her she'd been up for a while, and there wasn't much feeling left in her wrists. But at least she could rest her legs.

The room she'd been moved to was small, lit by a tiny, barred window to her right. Powdery gray light spilled through, barely pushing back the shadows that crowded the room. A table had been set up with an array of torture tools, each one gleaming and sharpened. Many she recognized when she'd been required to do the same upon the Empress's enemies.

She went over her faculties; none of her senses seemed affected. Her physical body was healing, and she wasn't drugged, so far as she could tell. The attempts before had felt childish. Aziah trusted her training, focusing on the lessons she learned as a trainee assassin. Her teacher had been brutal but effective.

Turning her mind inwards, she kept her mind on her goals, breaking them into steps. Doing this kept her from thinking about what kind of pain was going to come. That was inevitable and something she had no control over.

You have mastery over your body and mind. They can only take what you permit them, her teacher had told her.

It kept her busy for what felt like an eternity until the door swung open. A new torturer entered. A woman, this time. Torturers were rarely women but, in her experience, they often had much more creative ways to give pain to their victims. She kept her gaze on the woman, meeting fathomless pits set in a stone-like face.

"Oh, did your friend give up?" crooned Aziah.

The woman turned to the table and ran her hand over the selection of tools. "The man has *no* delicacy in such matters. He thought he could break a fae assassin. I told him your training meant his efforts would be futile."

"And you have a much finer touch?" Aziah's mind was whirling. This was someone who knew exactly what they were doing.

Selecting a knife, the woman turned to Aziah. "You are trained to deal with immense amounts of physical and psychological pain. You have one weakness, though."

"Oh?" *That* sparked Aziah's interest.

The woman grinned mirthlessly. "Your mate bond."

Ice flooded her veins. All pretense of humor vanished. "If you hurt him—"

"I don't need him. All I need is you." The woman stepped up and plunged the knife into Aziah's chest.

She braced for the agony of the cut, but it never came. Her gaze dropped to the knife. The skin shimmered around the blade. Confusion erupted in her mind. What the—? Slowly, the woman withdrew the knife, and then Aziah felt it. The sharp tug in her soul as the bond was pulled from her chest.

Panic exploded. Without the bond, she'd have no way to feel if Gabriel was alive or not, and it would make finding him brutal. He'd think she was dead...and she knew the madness he would be subjected to. That loss *broke* the fae.

"No, no, no!"

The woman grinned and pulled another inch. Pain splintered through Aziah's soul, shredding through her. Her thoughts scattered, reduced to ash. The room shrank to just the two of them, the world beyond forgotten. Gabriel flashed in her mind, on his knees, crying out as he clutched his chest. She screamed down their bond that she was okay, but he didn't hear her.

"Tell me how to break the shield around the City of Slaves or I'll break your bond," the woman taunted.

Aziah shook her head. She'd sworn an oath to the royal family. If she broke, all that she'd sacrificed would be for nothing. All that had died for her mission would be wasted deaths. But she couldn't condemn Gabriel to madness... Frustration roared through her soul.

The blade withdrew a little further.

"I—"

The woman twisted the blade suddenly, the pressure on the bond releasing abruptly. She yanked it out and pivoted.

The door flew open.

Gabriel.

What? Aziah couldn't stop the rush of relief that flooded through her.

He filled the doorway, clad in his old warrior's garb, one hand holding a flaming sword. He raised it, pointing it at the woman. "I'm going to *end* you."

The woman shot forward, just as Gabriel did. Aziah watched with bated breath as he swung and came at her, narrowly missing her as she dodged his blows. She was faster than Aziah expected and got in close more than once, slashing with the knife.

"Watch that blade! It'll cut our bond!"

And if she was in the room when it happened, the magical whiplash would be devastating to them both.

Gabriel ducked one of the torturer's blows and dropped low, sweeping his foot and knocking the woman down. As she fell back, he spun and slashed his weapon right through her neck. Shock flashed her face, frozen in death, as the head and body tumbled separately to the floor. Blood splashed his clothes and his face, but he still looked achingly beautiful to her.

Just as he always would.

Gabriel rushed to her side and ripped her binds from the ceiling. She dropped into his arms, too weak and numb to move for a moment. His hand brushed her side, pushing some magic into her. The warmth chased back the aches and pains, and moments later, he helped her stand. Her legs wobbled, but she managed a few steps forward.

Midway across the room, he stopped. "Can you stand guard for a second?"

It was an odd request, but she slipped shakily from him and staggered to the door. Turning back, she watched Gabriel kneel and search the woman, looking for something. A warm wave of relief crashed over her head, and she turned back to the door, opening it—

The same woman stood before her. A cold feeling dumped over her, and pain exploded in her head. Aziah screamed as she fell back, her head striking the floor.

The woman was over her in a flash, a hand around Aziah's throat, squeezing hard. She twisted desperately, but as she tried to look behind her, she froze.

The torturer's body was gone.

And so was Gabriel.

Aziah's eyes flew to her attacker, and another burst of agony hit her. The woman leaned in close, with cold eyes, and the stink of death. A cruel smile tugged at her thin mouth. "Thank you for opening your mind to me. Now, let's find out about that pesky shield, shall we?"

Aziah tried to shove her head back, but as the woman plunged into her mind all she could do was scream.

CHAPTER 79

"Word comes from the mountains only a few days after I felt the pain from Nimue. The fae had been driven out and are now on an exodus across the land. According to one of my spies, they have been banished."
—Excerpt from Titania's diary

Nimue flew first to the wall. She glided high above it, keeping just shy of the shield as she scanned the faces below. Soldiers and archers were in position along the top. Barrels had been set up at regular intervals on raised pedestals with funnels positioned in front of them. Sand, perhaps? To be heated and poured down upon attackers? As she passed over a few, she realized a few contained oils. An expensive commodity to be sure...but a flammable resource nonetheless...

She flew on, spying tents set up closer to the wall, cluttering the streets. Makeshift barracks to keep men close by, ready to respond if the shield fell at any moment.

All those men, but none of the higher-ups she knew, and no glimpse of Sybilla. The next stop was the barracks. She roared as she glided in, the men scattering just as she shifted her wings and swooped down to land. This time, she hit the ground with a hard trot and tucked her wings in, and shrank to her human form.

She turned to the closest man. "Have you seen Princess Sybilla?"

The man stared at her, confused. Irritation cut through like a knife. She didn't have time for this. Lorca didn't have it. Another man approached in a finer uniform, with a sword strapped to his back.

"I'm the one in charge here. As for Princess Sybilla, she left to visit the docks. There was another attack. She should still be—"

Nimue twisted from him and shifted back, snapping out her wings, and launched into the sky, leaving behind the confused faces of the men. Driving her wings, she rose higher and shot over the rooftops. Catching a gust of warm air, she banked toward the docks. The wharves and roads were cluttered with tents and people, so she landed a street back and shifted back.

Without pausing, she broke into a run. The mention of an attack drove her on until she reached the docks. The chaos slammed into her; soldiers and healers rushing about half-destroyed tents, upturned wagons, and debris. It was a mess. A cacophony of shouts from everywhere at once rose to a dizzying pitch.

Nimue slowed to a jog, darting through the fray as she scanned for anyone that looked mildly important. After a few minutes, she came across a healer in more ornate robes. She tapped the woman on the shoulder, who spun sharply, a reprimand poised on her scowling face.

"Who are you? I have work to do!"

"I am looking for Princess Sybilla—"

The old woman scowled. "Do I look like a damn princess?"

Nimue's temper snapped. Her hand shot out, grabbing the woman by the collar, and lifting her off her feet. Surprise and fear paled her face. "*Where is the Princess?*"

One trembling hand pointed across the docks. "Last I saw she was at the end wharf talking with the healers there."

Nimue tossed the woman aside and sprinted off in the direction given. No one cast her any curious looks. They were all focused on cleaning up after the attack, which must've happened quickly because Nimue hadn't been called. None of her team had.

She ran along the dock, weaving through the fray as desperation clawed at her. Pain throbbed dully through the bond, which meant Nora was keeping the worst of Lorca's discomfort down for the moment. The bitter wind slammed at her when she dashed from the last line of tents to where a group of healers was gathered. Huddled together, their backs to the wind, they didn't sense her until she stopped, and her haggard breaths filled the air.

Sybilla emerged among the parting crowd. "What's wrong?"

"Lorca, he's not in a good way. He keeps shifting between forms and he's in so much pain. I thought it might ease when Nora came. She said his magic was in knots. I need your friend." Nimue straightened up. "*Please,* I need help."

Something flickered in Sybilla's eyes. The Princess murmured something to the healers, then slipped away from them, gesturing for Nimue to follow. Dread coiled tightly within her chest, a beast poised to strike. She shoved it back down and walked after Sybilla until they were out of earshot of the healers. A few glanced curiously their way, but didn't come any closer.

Sybilla's eyes bled to a frosty blue, the contrast startling. "Hello, Nimue."

There was a softness to that voice that threw Nimue off. Had she misread what she'd seen in Sybilla's eyes? "Hello, spirit."

"What's wrong with Lorca?"

Nimue detailed what Nora had picked up before asking, "Is it because of me?"

"Yes, your other nature is at odds with his. Right now, that turmoil is making his body sensitive. The proximity to you is hurting him," said the spirit. "I don't know if I can stabilize him. Dragonir magic is tricky and not my specialty."

"But you'll try?"

The spirit nodded. "Of course, mo—"

In a blink, Nimue was shoved aside. She staggered and twisted around. A figure rushed past her and plunged a blade into Sybilla's gut. An inhuman cry, two voices entangled, choked out as the Princess sank to her knees, clutching her stomach. Healers hurried forward, but Sybilla's arms flew wide. A burst of light ripped from her chest, shaping quickly into a woman surrounded by swirling wreaths of magic.

The attacker was swiftly rendered headless by a guard.

Nimue stepped forward, but a deafening bang ripped through the sky. The shield shimmered brightly for a second, then exploded. Shimmering specks of magic fell like snow as she stared, still as death, at the naked sky.

The shield had fallen.

PART 4

FALL

CHAPTER 80

"The fae marched across the land in a great procession. They made no claim on this land and kept to themselves. Eventually, they arrived in the port city of Castor. They say they seek the Mithra Archipelago, and that the islands call to them. I hear them whisper of a demon that drove from their homes...and their vows of revenge."

—Excerpt from Atlas's diary

Sybilla staggered to her feet, one hand clutching her side, blood trickling through her fingers. Around her, screams pitched into the air. People rushed past, but she was still as a statue, blood pounding in her ears.

Someone was in front of her, reaching out, talking to her but the words slid over her skin like water. The world sang one singularly loud note, devouring all else, and it took a moment to realize it was a healer standing in front of her. She blinked, trying to dispel the mist that threatened to smother her senses.

The healer's face sharpened into focus. "Can you hear me?"

She swayed, and two hands caught her as she fell back. "Sybilla!"

It was Oren.

As she sank to her knees, he was at her side, hands at her back. His guarded eyes were gentle as they regarded her, and as he spoke to her, raw grief tore his voice, the words lost to the ringing in her ears.

"Oren, I—"

A bright light ripped from her chest, as though she were being split in two. Her head jerked back in a scream that sliced through the air like a knife. Tears burned her vision blurry as the pressure suddenly snapped off, and she fell forward. Once more, she was caught before she hit the ground. As she forced her head up, she froze.

Rhea's form shimmered before her.

Before Sybilla could utter a word, Nimue appeared. Her dark eyes, like the vast shadows that crowded the city, flickered between her and Rhea. Something flashed across Nimue's face but vanished before Sybilla had a chance to make sense of it.

Another wave of molten pain rolled through her, and she gave a low groan. When she managed to pry her eyes open, it was the look of utter devastation that darkened Nimue's face that chased away any biting response.

"What happened?" she asked.

"It's Lorca. He's hurt. Dying." The words tumbled from Nimue so fast that Sybilla almost missed it. "I need—"

Nimue's gaze slid to Rhea, and Sybilla knew what she was after. The help she so desperately needed.

"I'll go," Rhea declared.

Sybilla pushed herself up, ignoring Oren's protests. His hand never left her side though, not even as she fought to remain standing. She looked at Rhea, whose gaze never wavered from Nimue.

"Can you save him?" Sybilla asked.

Rhea leveled a look that reminded her she wasn't dealing with any mere mortal.

"I make no promises, but I shall do all that is within my power. Consequences be damned."

"Why?" Nimue asked, one brow lifted.

"Because we need someone to deal with the threat outside the city. Two dragons are better than one," Rhea replied, as if it were the most sensible explanation in the world. "I will do this while you go out there."

Nimue looked in the direction the mansion lay, and defiance ebbed from her shoulders.

"I accept the deal."

Rhea's form shimmered for a moment as she brushed a hand against Nimue's arm. "We need a dragon at full strength to remind the army out there that this city is not for the Empress anymore."

A long silence played out between the two, leaving Sybilla shifting uneasily on her feet. Just what was it between those two? It felt more than both being spirits.

Nimue cleared her throat and turned to leave. Sybilla stepped forward. "Wait! Take me with you to the wall."

All at once, Oren and the healer rushed in with comments. She pushed away from him and pressed her hand hard on the still bleeding wound. Heat flared low from her belly, surging up through her hands and into the wound in a flash of light. She hissed as the fiery heat seared the injury. It wasn't ideal, and she knew she ought to rest, but there wasn't time for that.

Nimue stared at her, that shuttered expression unreadable but inclined her head after a pause. "Very well. Looks like you're coming for a ride, Princess."

People were not meant to fly, Sybilla decided as she jumped from Nimue's back and onto the wall. The world lurched as her feet hit the stone, and what little she'd eaten that day surged up her throat. She pressed a hand to her mouth, swallowing it back down with a shuddering groan.

Sybilla glanced over at the distant army. "Don't get yourself killed. Lorca will destroy me if anything happens to you."

Nimue bowed her head, then launched into the sky. Sybilla watched her vanish among the low cloud that settled over the battlefield. She turned away from the wall and hurried straight for Galen.

The men parted as she approached, bowing their heads. She lifted her chin and straightened her back. This was her fight, as much as it was theirs. She would prove to them she was the ruler they needed.

Galen pulled his focus from the army, took one look at her bloodied side, and stilled. "What the hell happened to you? You need a healer."

She waved a hand. "I'll be fine, trust me. I heal fast. Now, report how we're looking."

His mouth tightened to a thin line, a heavy silence reigning between them as fire roared across the sky. Perhaps it was the sound of buildings burning, of men screaming, or even the crumbling stonework striking the ground below, but he relented with a sigh.

"The men are in position, but it seems the Empress's army has grown. The forest has made an exact count difficult, but we're so badly outnumbered I would advise against any attack out there. It'll be a slaughter." He paused as Nimue's deafening roar thundered across the battlefield. "Where's the other dragon?"

"He'll be here shortly," she said.

Hopefully.

He turned to her again. A look of awkwardness overcame him. "A...delivery came for you. Lady Adara had some armor made for you." He paused for a moment. "Are you sure about this?"

"Yes."

"This is foolish," he muttered.

Without turning to him, she lifted a hand to his shoulder and squeezed. "Then it shall be a glorious end in fire and blood. What more could one ask?"

"This is madness," he grumbled.

"We're all a little mad here." She turned and faced him, meeting those weary eyes with a gentle touch of his arm. "Galen, Trust me. I can do this."

He nodded and jerked a thumb to the closest tower, his face unreadable. "The men will direct you to a room so you can change. Helena sent an attendant to help you dress as well."

Stifling the magic in her hand, she strode off to the tower. A soldier at the door led her the rest of the way inside. It was a tiny room, packed with a few crates and her sword. A young woman, one of Helena's rescued slaves, offered a steady bow.

Sybilla changed with the woman's help and donned the armor. It was lighter than she expected and shone like gold. When she finished, she stepped back and tested out a few movements. As much as she could do in such a small room.

The woman braided her hair down her back. Then the work was done. Practical, fit for battle. Sybilla rose, offered a quiet thank you, and strode out. This time, the men cast her surprised looks. This wasn't the attire of someone planning to stand back and watch from the battlements as men died for her glory.

She returned to Galen's side, and he eyed the sword at her hip. "Is that what I think it is?"

Her father's sword, the one she'd been found with. It was her last link to her family and on the day she ventured into battle; she wanted it with her. A token of luck, and a reminder of the future she was forging. She thought of the freed slaves within her city, and of those in other cities, still in chains. Oren was right. So many didn't *care,* but she also knew she wasn't alone in her determination to fight and break those chains.

Her parents had dreamed of that. It had cost them their lives. Now she would finish their mission. Not alone, but with every soldier who stood at her side.

And that fight, that first step into battle, would be with that fated sword.

"Dragon's breath? Yes, it is," she said, one hand resting on its hilt.

From the distant clouds above the advancing army, a golden dragon descended in an eruption of fire.

She tightened her grip on her sword. "And so it begins."

CHAPTER 81

"Titania has journeyed to the mountains. I wished to join her, but unrest in Midlan has meant our modest home is threatened. There is too much of our past to leave unattended. To my surprise, Claudius appeared this morning. I asked him about Nimue and their child. He simply said their child is gone and nothing of why he left or of Nimue's brutal vengeance against the fae."

—Excerpt of Atlas's diary

Rell still wouldn't talk to her. Even as they bundled the injured onto wagons and rolled out of the docks. The girl had grown quiet, and stared straight ahead, even as Titania kept looking at her, hoping to explain. They trundled in uneasy silence down the streets.

The wagon stopped in front of a modest two-story home. Orders were barked from the soldiers out the front, and the injured were ferried inside. Titania tried to get close to Rell a couple of times, but the girl quickly moved away.

It stung every time. She rose once more and started toward Rell, who had finished reapplying the last of the bandages, and asked, "Can we talk?"

"You're a demon," Rell muttered as her head lifted, her golden gaze piercing. "A real damned demon."

Titania stilled. No one around appeared to have caught what Rell said, and the man stretched out at her feet was out cold.

"I am."

Rell's lip curled. "There have been attacks for weeks, and you were with us the whole time. Why fight back now?"

Titania bit her lip. How to explain all the mess that was raging within her?

"I've *been* fighting."

"Could...could you stop that army?"

Titania stiffened. The idea of being that close to an army again sent flashes of the past rushing through her mind. Her mouth dried up. "No, but even if I had that power, it's not that simple."

"Isn't it?"

A few healers drifted close, so they lapsed into silence again. Rell's gaze burned through her. It was just the same as her wife, Aliya's infamous looks, cutting like a blade.

Demons below. How long had it been since she'd even thought of her wife's name?

The candlelight flickered precariously overhead. A chill brushed the nape of her neck, prickling the magic within her. She stood up sharply, eyes on the door. "Rell, whatever you hear, *stay inside.*"

Rell jumped up. "Demons?"

"I'll deal with it."

Titania didn't wait for a response. The cold feeling sharpened as she opened the front door. An icy wind slammed into her, biting her cheeks. There were demons close by. She could feel them. A low growl rumbled from the darkness as two wolves, their eyes burning like glowing coals, moved toward her.

They didn't attack, but their snarls filled the air, echoing softly down the street.

She snapped her fingers, summoning the darkness. Wreaths of smoke flared across her hands, wrapping up her arms. The beasts shrank back with a hiss.

"Leave."

The demons lowered their heads, but did not retreat.

The door behind Titania opened, and someone gasped. Titania wanted to drive the healer back inside but didn't dare remove her gaze from the demons. They were just as likely to attack at any moment, and she still wasn't sure why they'd come.

"*Demons,*" Rell hissed.

"I told you to stay inside," Titania growled.

"You sound like my mother," Rell muttered in Toranellan, likely thinking Titania wouldn't understand.

"She sounds like a smart woman!"

"Wait, what?"

There was no time to explain that Titania knew more languages than most. She edged forward, raising one hand as dark ribbons stretched out from her fingertips.

A blast of energy ripped from her, tearing across the cobblestone street. The beasts turned, but were too slow. The shadows crashed into them, destroying them on impact. Plumes of smoke were all that remained. Titania breathed a sigh of relief and turned to reassure Rell.

An explosion ripped through the air. The sky turned black, extinguishing the stars and moon. Even the torches along the streets went out.

"Oh, spirits, no!" Rell was off before Titania could stop her.

She ran after the girl, grabbing her wrist. "Where are you going?"

"That's close to my home! Let go. I have to see if she's okay." Rell's desperation tore at Titania as she tried to pull free.

"Fine. I'll come with you. Take this."

She thrust one of the smaller daggers that she kept hidden in the folds of her dress at Rell. The girl stared at it for a second, then grabbed it. It wasn't much, but if she got herself pinned by a wolf, then it might just save her life.

They set off. Rell sprinted ahead, leading the way. Screams soon erupted. First panicked and then choked off. Titania pushed her magic to her hands, summoning the shadows. Her senses sharpened. The stench of blood filled the air, thickening as they rounded the corner. A shadow flashed, leaping right for Rell. Titania threw her hands up, and a wall of darkness shot up in front of them.

A force slammed into it, jolting her arms. Throwing her hands down to dispel the shield, she leaped over the body of a demon wolf, its neck broken.

All around, demons filled the streets, dozens of them launching at the houses. Doors were ripped off and windows destroyed. Screams of terror filled the air. This wasn't a hunt, Titania realized. Mirena had called her demons to slaughter these people. To run the streets red with blood.

"Where's your home?" she shouted.

Rell raced ahead. "This way!"

"Stay with me!" Titania cursed, sprinting after the girl as she ran to a broken doorway.

Titania grabbed Rell at the last second. The girl cried out, clawing to push past, but she held firm. "I'll go in first or so help me I'll knock you out myself."

She didn't wait to see if the girl agreed as she made her way silently into the narrow hall. A small living area with shredded, upturned furniture was at her right, and another dining area ran off it. She lifted her hands, stretching out her mind through the house, hunting for the demon when a resounding crash came from upstairs. Titania raced up the stairs, two at a time, and dashed through an open doorway.

A beast lunged. She stepped back, narrowly missing it. Pivoting, she raised her hands, ready to attack it, when the beast collided with a sword. The bloodied point glinted through the demon's back as it fell to the ground. A woman, tall and slender, with dark skin and braided ebony hair, yanked the sword from the beast's chest. She rose gracefully and with a spare hand, wiped the blood from her cheek.

Titania froze, her heart seizing her chest.

No, no, no...It's not possible.

The woman turned, and Titania dropped to her knees.

"Aliya?"

And Amara's long distant proclamation to Titania rang clear in her mind like a clap of thunder.

In the City of Slaves, you will meet your destiny.

CHAPTER 82

"I am going to kill that son of a bitch for what he did."
—Excerpt from Titania's diary

Nimue dived through the clouds, roaring so loudly the ground trembled and the thundering sky answered in bolts of lightning. Fire poured from her, just as it had when she'd rained her wrath down upon the fae eight hundred years ago, driving them from the mountains. And as the inferno crashed over the trebuchets and the men who tried to flee, she once more embraced the monster at her core.

As all before her burned, men dashed into the forest, as if it might shield them. She turned her gaze upon them, unleashing another wave of fire. It roared down to claim its next victims. At the last second, it crashed into something invisible and dispersed.

A shield.

Her wings snapped in and she sliced through the smoky air, the wind whistling in her ears. The ground rushed to meet her, and she unleashed another blast. It crashed into the shield, doing nothing to break it, she threw her wings out and surged up over the forest.

Something silver flashed in the corner of her gaze. She banked sharply as a hiss passed by her head. Another followed, and as she rolled out of the way, a metal bolt narrowly missed her wing.

A volley of bolts shot up from the trees. No matter how hard she dodged, they came closer until she flew up into the cloud.

Heart slamming like a war drum against her chest, she circled, watching the forest below through wisps of white and gray. From her vantage point, the missiles could not reach her and plummeted harmlessly to the field below.

The drums thundered across the battlefield, matching the rumbling boots that stepped upon the charred earth. And marching as if she had not just rained fire down upon them all, the army reappeared.

A thousand men had become charred corpses, and still, the army plowed onwards. Even as she cut them down from above, tearing through the advancing force with her fire, there was no end. More men appeared from the treeline, an unending sea of death.

Archers fired volleys of arrows at the city, turning the sky black, and forcing Nimue higher above the chaos. No matter how much destruction she brought, it didn't appear to make a dent in their numbers as they continued toward the city gates.

Defending the city from the sky wasn't enough.

She circled back around, gliding low along the front of the wall. Landing hard, she positioned herself in front of the main gate, flaring her wings wide.

All she had to do was hold the gate. Keep the army out and the streets free of blood. She was not afraid, and she called on the fire, spurred by the spirit's gift of strength to her.

There were men to burn and an army to defeat.

The drums of war beat loud across the battlefield, swelling in the air, then fading and exposing the distant moans and pleas of dying men. Hundreds of bloodied corpses littered the earth, many trampled by the army that marched over them.

Nimue wrought her fire upon the swaths of men, reducing them to piles of blackened corpses, their deaths too swift for her hunger.

The army pushed on, even as another volley of arrows rained down, forcing Nimue to rise into the clouds.

A gap in the arrows opened. She shot down, burning a trail of men who had almost reached the gate. The wind howled viciously as the ground rushed to meet her. Throwing her wings out, and dropping her feet down, she landed with a hard drop back at the gate.

As she turned to face the army, a thunderous roar ripped through the air. Familiarity sparked a distant memory. A gap emerged in the men and from it, galloped an enormous beast.

It matched her in size and had a leathery hide, with a row of spikes down its spine and along each leg. It opened its mouth to reveal vicious rows of jagged teeth. Nimue knew the beast well. She'd employed dozens of them at the front of her army in another life. They were designed to break the lines of enemy forces and scale walls. Those taloned paws could cut stone like it was butter. And fire was useless against it.

A shadow shrieker, a beast that once marched ahead of her demonic army. One forged of her creation. Just another of her tactics Mirena was throwing back in her face.

It was then she realized the tie between the Empress and Mirena ran deeper than she ever considered before.

She stalked forward, snarling viciously, posturing her wings wide to make herself seem larger. Wreaths of fire eddied around her teeth.

The shrieker rushed forward, roaring. Nimue launched into the sky as the beast jumped to catch her. One talon slashed high, narrowly scraping her back thigh. Powering higher, she rolled sharply and plunged back down. The beast leaped up to meet her, swiping its enormous claws.

They collided hard and crashed to the ground, wrestling with claws and gnashing teeth. She fought to pin it down, desperately trying to sink her teeth into its neck. Jumping back, she slammed her tail into its side, sending it staggering.

Scrambling to stay out of the way of its claws, she slashed at every inch of skin she could. Hot blood sprayed, the stench of it swirling thickly around her.

More than once it cut through her scales, splattering her blood on the ground. Pain lashed through her, but she fought on. She surged up onto her hind legs and slashed her front claws as it rose to meet her. This time, her longer limbs came into play as she cut across the monster's chest and slammed down onto its back.

It tried to buck her off, but she sank her teeth into its neck and tore with her remaining strength. A gurgled cry choked off and the beast died beneath her. Nimue scrambled off, tail flicking back and forth. She eyed the row of advancing men...and watched as two more shriekers exploded from the ranks.

Well, fuck.

CHAPTER 83

"I went to see her but Nimue sleeps deep beneath the earth, recovering from the destruction she rained down on the fae. I stayed for a few days, hoping she might wake, but every day there felt like hell. Everywhere I looked, I saw my daughter, lifeless and blue, staring at me with empty eyes. I can't stay here...I can't."
—Excerpt from Claudius's diary

Flynn stirred groggily from the darkness that enveloped him. His head pounded as he tried to open his eyes. A stabbing pain lanced through his head as he finally managed to take stock of his surroundings. The room still rocked, telling him they were still underway. Sunlight streamed in through a crack in the wood, but there was no telling if it was the same day, or if more time had passed.

A wave of panic washed over him. He peered around the room and spotted three shackled figures hunched over, their soft breaths whispering through the air signaling they were still alive.

"Mira! Ashara! Kiya!" No one stirred.

He struggled to stand, but chains pinned his wrists to the wall behind his back. Looking down, he found his ankles were chained together as well. The bands around his hands rattled as he lifted them, testing the metal's strength. His wrists protested, but Flynn refused to stop. He turned his mind inwards, feeling the light stir once more to his call.

It rushed through his body, flooding down to his fingertips.

Breathe, Flynn. You can do this. Just try not to blow a hole in the side of the ship...

He pushed it slowly to his fingers and pressed his palms against the chain securing him to the wall. Heat welled along his skin, flashing brightly for a second, filling the room with luminous light. When it dimmed, his body jerked forward, and the chain shattered. Pulling his hands around to his front, he tried again with his ankles. It took two more attempts until he broke free.

His bones ached as he staggered to his feet, teetering awkwardly like a newborn deer. The ship rocked, sending him staggering forward into the wall. It lurched back and he grabbed hold of the beam above his head, clinging on until the ship steadied again. His heart thudded as he hurried to the others, kneeling first by Ashara. He gently leaned her forward so he could get to her shackles when she stirred with a groan.

Ashara blinked. "W-what the hell happened?"

He relayed what little he remembered, and she looked at her sister, the worry easing in her eyes. "Can you sit forward? I'm going to try to free you."

She stared at him for a second, then leaned forward and lifted her wrists as much as the chains permitted. The faces of everyone relying on him flashed through his mind. His thoughts calmed, and he gently grasped the chains. He forced his energy slowly down to his palms and held it just beneath the skin. The heat welled in his hands, but he stayed steady, focused solely on the task at hand.

Then he pushed.

The chains shattered, and shards of metal clattered to the ground. Ashara moved her hands to her ankles. Sparks flashed in her hand, then sputtered out. A frown deepened her brow as she looked up at him. "Can you...?"

Nodding silently, he shattered her chains. As she stood, he went to work on the others, slowly and with measured breaths. When he finished, he stood shakily and his whole body trembled. His legs wobbled, threatening to buckle at any moment. Nausea rolled around like a monster in his gut, clenching sharply. He doubled over, wincing.

"Perhaps there is hope for you yet," Ashara remarked with a ghost of a smile.

Kiya awoke next, followed by Mira. His old friend was at his side in a flash, one hand cupping his chin as she examined him. Her blue eyes peered at him, lingered for a moment, then withdraw as she moved back. He wondered what she saw.

"Do you feel it, Kiya?" Ashara asked as she bent down and pressed her palm to the floor. After a beat, she rose, frowning.

"We've slowed."

If the heavy looks were anything to go by, it wasn't good news.

Ashara strode to the door. "We need to get topside now."

Flynn followed Ashara, the other two close behind. They hurried along the hall, where they came into the crews' quarters...and stopped as carnage greeted them. The sailor's bodies were strewn about the room, ripped to pieces. Not one body was left whole. It looked like what was left were the remnants of some creature's meal.

He twisted away and threw up.

"We have to keep moving," Ashara said, but he didn't miss the thread of unease in her voice. It was like she knew what likely killed the men.

Mira nudged him, but he let himself be led from the room. He waded as gently as he could through the mess, his boots squelching through the pools of sticky blood. They arrived at the ladder, which Ashara climbed first. Halfway up, she gestured for him to stop before she pushed the hatch above open. Moonlight spilled down, framing her as she vanished onto the deck.

The world held its breath in a moment of silence.

The ship lurched slowly. The others waited in silence until a shadow fell over the hatch. Ashara's face took shape. She gestured for them to come up with a finger to her lips, then she was gone again. Flynn scrambled up.

More body parts littered the deck. He counted at least four heads. The rest of the crew, perhaps? The blood was sticky, not fully dried, which meant it wasn't old. Ice slipped down his spine.

"What happened?" he asked softly.

To this surprise, it was Mira who spoke as she inspected the shredded remains of an arm and held it up. "Sirens. Like the ones that attacked us when we first arrived in the archipelago."

Ashara strode to the railing and peered out. "That looks like Rivenelle, so I'd say so. The idiot captain probably thought he could save time by cutting through this path."

"None of these look like the captain. Do you think he might still be alive?" He studied the corpses.

A look of fury darkened her gaze as she stalked off. "If he is, I'm going to make him *wish* he was dead. Alas, I doubt anyone else is alive. The fact we were left alone is miracle enough."

Flynn didn't know about that, making him wonder had someone intervened or that some other force kept them safe. He shifted on his feet, glancing about anxiously.

He tracked Ashara across the deck until she went down another hatch. As he followed, Kiya called out, "Leave her be. There aren't any of those creatures left onboard."

"How can you be sure?" he asked.

"I would sense them if there were." Kiya offered nothing beyond that as she and Mira fanned out across the deck.

He discovered another set of body parts up near the wheel. There he paused, looking out across the glittering water. In the distance, he could make out the shape of an island with several sharp peaks. Behind it was another series of smaller islands, far enough away that he wasn't worried about sailing into them...

But just how they were going to sail now? The crew was dead. They'd need more than four people to sail a ship. Perhaps Ashara had the knowledge, but Kiya hated water, so she likely didn't know how. He certainly never learned, and Mira was the same.

He pushed off from the wheel and started toward Kiya, who was kneeling by a body. A hatch clicked from behind, making him turn. Ashara emerged. Her eyes widened as she spotted something behind him. "Watch out!"

Four sirens prowled across the deck, three holding spears, one without.

Kiya swept past him, light sparking in her hands too. "As we trained, Mira."

The girl nodded, and sparks appeared at her fingertips. Spirit magic.

Flynn stepped forward when a hand grasped his arm, stopping him. Ashara thrust a sword into his hand.

"Now you can show us how well Tobin trained you," she said.

He lifted the blade. "Let's cut them down to size, shall we?"

One of the sirens let out a shriek, and all hell broke loose.

CHAPTER 84

"After I drove the fae from the mountains, I slept for months, sometimes a year or more, waking only for short periods. Even now, I seek sleep because in my dreams I can hold my daughter again...and I feel no pain. And every time I wake, I feel this stupid hope he will return to me."

—Excerpt from Nimue's diary

Sybilla held her breath as the creatures shot toward Nimue. The archers leveled dozens of arrows onto them, but they merely bounced off their thick hides. One had nearly beaten Nimue. Could she beat two? Sybilla's heart raced in her chest, blood roaring in her ear. She clung to the stone wall, digging her nails in, wondering why the hell the dragon wasn't breathing fire anymore.

Nimue burst forward, roaring viciously, and crashed into the first one in a flurry of claws and gnashing teeth. The other raced over, closing in on her, and Sybilla's heart froze. There was no way she could win, but sending men outside would be suicide as well. She had to do *something.*

One of the beasts grabbed Nimue by the tail, tearing her off the other. A sickening cry tore out as she frantically fought to get free.

Sybilla's guards stepped back in alarm, but she didn't care. The magic swelled up from the pit of her soul, pushing up through her limbs. It surged out from her fingers, wrapping around her body. She threw her palms forward, forcing all that power to a singular point between her hands. A blazing sphere erupted. The rest of the world tumbled away.

She pushed more magic toward her hands. Sweat beaded along her brow. An ache surged down her limbs, but she held on, gritting her teeth. She picked her spot, held for a second, and released.

The magic erupted free in a deafening bang, a single beam of pure energy that split the air like a knife and slammed into the ground. One beast went flying, crashing into the wall; the other was thrown off. Nimue latched onto its throat and ripped it out before tearing over to the other.

A shadow flashed overhead, plunging toward the fight below.

Lorca.

He collided into the beast, snapping viciously at its neck, ripping chunks out until it dropped dead beneath him.

Sybilla staggered back, breathing a sigh of relief. Her legs wobbled. A warm hand slid to her back, tendrils of magic pouring through. The dizziness ebbed away, and she straightened up. A dull ache still lingered in her head, but it was slowly fading. She didn't have to turn to see who had helped her. A smile lifted her mouth.

"Thank you."

Rhea's hand slid away, and her form shimmered. A troubled expression was on her face. "I can't stay much longer."

A thread of panic tightened sharply in her. "What?"

"Healing Lorca and you...I have used too much power." Her form shimmered again, growing fainter by the second.

"Is there anything I can do?"

Rhea shook her head. "I must return to my home but—"

The spirit vanished. Sybilla stared at the spot Rhea had just been standing.

But what?

"Your Highness, a runner for you!" Oren's voice yanked her from her stupor.

The young man, red-faced and sweaty, held out a missive. She tore the letter open and ran her gaze down the page. The air rushed from her lungs.

If this message reaches you, it means our runner made it through. Demons have begun an attack on the city barracks. Requesting aid, urgent.

—Lady Adara

She dropped the letter and headed toward the tower. “Captain Oren, gather the horses and any men that can be spared. We ride to the city barracks!”

Sybilla and her guards raced down the cobbled street. She leaned over her horse’s neck, clutching the reins. The wind whipped past her, plunging icy needles deep into her bones.

Her heart raced faster the closer they got to the barracks. Sweat glistened on her brow, rivulets running down the side of her face. Her thoughts eddied around, losing the barracks.

“There, up ahead!” Oren shouted.

She yanked on her reins, and the horse reared up onto its back legs. Clinging on as it dropped back down, it strained against her control.

The barrack’s walls loomed at the end of the street, the barred gate was slammed shut but repeatedly pounding into it was a creature unlike any she’d seen before. This was smaller than the one Nimue had fought. Perhaps the size of a draft horse, with muscled limbs and a spiked tail. As it charged against the gate, a metallic groan echoed down the street. The gate wouldn’t hold for much longer.

Dozens of wolf-like creatures paced the surrounding wall as if they were its protective shield.

“We must kill that thing before it breaks the gate,” she ordered, turning to Oren. “Your best men with me. The rest take down those wolves and clear us a path.”

“As you command.”

As he rattled off orders, she jumped down from her horse and pulled her sword out. The metal hissed out of the sheath. She strode forward, shadowed by her men.

The first of the wolves turned, followed by the rest. A collective snarl met them. Sybilla steeled herself. Fighting was in her blood.

Magic flared from her fingers, flashing down the sword, wrapping it in ribbons of light. The demons hissed. She thrust the blade into the sky, shooting a bolt of light. The monster at the gate stopped its assault and turned, fixing a pair of glowing red eyes on her. Its lip pulled back in a low snarl.

"Now I have your attention." She lowered her sword and shifted her feet.

Light eddied around her form. Oren's men took up formation around her, with the good captain at her side. If he was afraid, he didn't show it. She offered him a flash of a smile.

Chaos was unleashed in a flash. Demons and men collided, a clash of metal and claw. The beast shot toward her. She dug her heels in, fighting the urge to run. Heart pounding, she held on, and so did her men.

The men swarmed in, slashing at its legs. It reared back, swiping viciously, trying to get them off. She sprinted around it. Dropping low, she felt the hiss of the air as its powerful tail swept overhead, missing her by inches.

The tail lashed straight at her again. She swung her blade and sliced clean through it. The beast threw its head back with a roar. Sybilla moved back out of reach of its claws and raised her hand. A bolt of light erupted from her palm and plowed into the creature's side. A deafening shriek rattled the street.

As it landed back down on all fours, the men rushed in. The beast slapped two of its attackers away. Sybilla heard the sickening crunch of bone on impact as they went flying and hit the ground. Rising onto its hind legs, the creature latched its burning gaze on her.

She tightened her grip on her sword. *For my people.*

The beast launched forward. An arrow hissed past her, a glint of metal and feather landing hard in a glowing red eye. She turned, and another arrow flew past and struck the other eye. A wounded cry split the air as the creature staggered to a stop, pawing at its face. She watched as it ripped the arrows out and black blood poured freely down its face. Then, to her horror, the eyes regrew.

"*What?*"

A figure materialized beside her, whistling low. "Well, *that* is rather rude."

An arrow was lifted, the line pulled taut—

She turned to see the archer and froze. Claudius. Time slowed for a moment, the feather nicking his cheek as he released the arrow. He reached back, plucking another, and fired it off a second later. He glanced at her and smiled.

"You're *here?*"

"I will explain later. Let's kill this creature first."

Nodding resolutely, she turned back to the beast. It raised a paw to pull out the arrows, but Claudius shot forward, firing off more into the socket. The demon staggered back with a howling cry. Sybilla saw her chance, shouting for the men to close in, and give her an opening. She knew the spot. It kept protecting it in every attack.

"Keep its focus on you, Claudius!" She circled its back.

The bloodied stump of its tail was already healing. Claudius fired arrows into its front, keeping it lumbering toward him. Sybilla sheathed her sword.

She dashed forward and jumped, digging one foot into the small of its tail. It flicked instinctively, propelling her onto its back. She scrambled up its matted fur. The beast roared, bucking hard, but she clung on. There was no way she was being thrown off. Gripping its matted fur, she clawed her way forward until she sat closer to its neck.

Arrow after arrow sunk into its side. The beast took off, racing toward Claudius.

She fired a bolt of energy into its side. It lashed its head, trying to reach her.

Gritting her teeth, she yanked her sword out with one hand. The creature reared, trying to throw her off. A fetid stench burned her eyes and twisted her stomach. Biting back a cough, she gripped hard until it dropped back down.

The beast stilled, and Sybilla plunged her sword into the nape of its neck. Hot blood sprayed back over her, splashing her lips with its acrid taste. Rising, she threw her body onto the hilt, driving it down through muscle and bone until it broke through to the other side and the beast slumped down.

It whimpered but didn't move. She'd cut its spine.

"Hurry," she shouted. "Remove its head!"

Oren sprinted from the ranks of his men. She sat back, still holding on, as he hacked at the creature with his sword. Several heavy cuts and the head rolled away, the black blood pooling across the stones. With a gasp of relief, she yanked her sword out and scrambled off. Her legs wobbled for a second, but a hand slid to the small of her back. A warm, heady smell fell over her.

"You're no coward, Princess." Heat laced Claudius's words.

She offered him a shaky smile. "What are you doing here?"

"I came with my personal guards to have them assigned to the fight. You?"

"Reports of an attack. These were all the men that could be spared," she said. Claudius had around thirty men with him, less than she expected. She'd thought a man of his power would have more. "Is that all your men?"

"All that are available." He doubled over with a gasp, clutching at his head. A strange string of words rushed from his lips, a language she'd heard once before.

In the visions, she had of Nimue.

Her body stiffened. *Was he...?*

The thought cut off as he stood up and turned to speak to a nearby man. "Cain, take the men. I have to go."

Sybilla stepped forward. "Where do you have to go?"

"The wall," he said.

"What?"

He stared at her, then suddenly reached out, cupping her jaw. A flicker of regret touched those jeweled depths. He kissed her, then stepped back. "Whatever happens next, know that whatever is between us *isn't* a lie."

Then he strode away and jumped up into his saddle. She moved to follow, but he already raced off into the city.

CHAPTER 85

"A golden dragon sought sanctuary in my mountains. They took human form and kneeled at my feet, saying the fae were hunting them for their magic. I took her hand, lifting her up. 'This shall be your home now,' I told her."

—Excerpt from Nimue's diary

No one in the room moved a muscle.

Titania's heart, though, drummed hard. Talons raked her lungs, the need to breathe building. She didn't dare, though. As if any sound might dispel the illusion, or that it might somehow take Aliya away. A loss she couldn't endure again.

Aliya inched forward, her dark eyes guarded, wary. There was none of the warmth and love that Titania remembered, nothing she had clung to in the years that followed the fall of Toranelle.

"Mother? What's going on?" Rell whispered.

Titania flinched at every word. She kept staring at Aliya, watching as her wife came closer and reached out, uncertain fingers brushing her cheek. The lightest of touches. A hand snatched back.

"You're *here?*" Aliya stepped back. "What game are you playing?"

At that, Titania rose to her feet. "Game? What are you talking about? I thought—"

"Thought what?" A shadow of anger flashed in Aliya's face, and a scarlet stain deepened those cheeks. "When the city fell, I was injured, but when I finally woke,

I looked for you but found no trace. Finally, I found my friend, Keelan, and he told me you left the city for Danomir."

Her friend, not *their* friend.

"I thought you were dead," Titania whispered hoarsely. "I fought for days but Toranelle fell...and I..."

Aliya froze. "You thought I was dead?"

"I was in Toranelle's Healing Guild that morning when the attack came. When the walls fell, I knew they'd go to the citadel." Flashes of that day came thick and fast, crowding her mind, choking her voice for the moment. Screams of the dying, a city falling, roared in her ears. She tasted the ash in her mouth. "I ran as fast as the shadows would carry me, slaughtering any soldier who got in my way. When I got there, the citadel was destroyed and our bond was silent. I couldn't sense you Aliya. I couldn't feel you anymore. Why would you think I would ever willingly leave you?"

It felt like only the two of them were in the room; two wary souls circling each other. Uncertainty and hope entangled.

"Titania, I..."

"Yes?"

Titania... A familiar voice thundered in her mind. She doubled over with a gasp, clutching at her head. Nimue was calling her. The thread connecting them all pulled taut in her chest.

Forgive me, but this city will fall without your help. Come to me. I need you both. Please, just come to me.

The pressure ebbed from her mind. Nimue was gone. She opened her eyes and saw Aliya and Rell watching her, worry in their eyes. For the first time, Titania realized how similar the two were, and cursed herself that she hadn't seen it sooner.

"I have to go," she said. "I've been summoned."

A shadow appeared on Aliya's face. "By who?"

"It's a long story, but one long overdue. It's time I stepped from the shadows." Titania straightened up. She was still afraid the memories would freeze her again on the battlefield, and that she would falter. But this was what she was born to do. She was a warrior.

Rell moved back, but Aliya's hand lingered, clutching Titania's upper hand. "Stay—*please.*"

It killed her to pull away, and she had no idea how she managed it. "I will return to you but, please, head to Lord Delmont's mansion. Tell the guards I sent you. You'll be safe there and when this is over, I will come for you."

Aliya opened her mouth. The look Titania knew brooked an argument, but she moved forward, silencing her with a kiss. Her hand lingered, cradling Aliya's cheek, wishing the moment would never end, even as the city raged with madness. She'd found her destiny, and yet once more, she was being parted from Aliya.

Her wife touched Titania's hand. "Come back to me."

Titania didn't want to make another promise, so she kissed Aliya again, before pulling away. She squeezed Rell's arm before hurrying out.

CHAPTER 86

"The world of man has come to my mountains. Desperate mortals fleeing the war in the lowlands. They plead for sanctuary. I warn them that dragons call this place home and that they must earn the trust of the dragons. If they can achieve that, they will be permitted to stay."

—Excerpt from Nimue's diary

Nimue roared into the darkness of her soul, calling on the threads connecting her to the others. Pain hissed back, sharp and lancing, behind her eyes. Warmth flooded her mind, chasing back the pain.

A savage cry ripped through the air as Lorca unleashed a blast of fire on the forces attacking them from below.

He glanced back at her. *Are you okay?*

As the rain fell over his midnight scales, a breath caught in her throat. All worries about the army fell away. He was alive and with her.

But no sooner had a reply formed in her mind had a volley of arrows launched into the sky. She leaped into action, soaring high above him and unleashing a burst of fire. Her blue flame collided with the arrows, rendering them ash. Wreaths of smoke whirled about her teeth.

Get to the sky! She threw her wings out and powered upward with everything she had.

The cacophony of war drums and men's shouts carried across the battlefield. It howled through her body, stirring the darkness that was once more pushing up from its slumber, splintering through her body. She just had to hold it together a little longer.

They rose higher, out of range of the archers. Despite their efforts, the army was nearly at the wall. The soldiers at the top were doing their best to cull the numbers.

Lorca, go to the wall. Once they pour the oil light it. Then see if they have any barrels you can carry.

Lorca soared beside her, pinning a heavy look her way. *Watch yourself. And Nimue... give them hell.*

As he shot off to the wall, she circled above the forces. Burned corpses littered the field, paving the way for the advancing army as more men rushed to fill the gaps. She snarled and snapped her wings in, diving for the rear of the forces near the tree line. The wind screamed in her ears, whistling over her body. A row of archers at the trees lifted their bows, arrows knocked.

She released a burst of fire, striking first, then snapped her wings out and banked sharply along the tree line. Powering forward, she descended her fiery vengeance on every man who marched from the trees.

A prickle of magic brushed her mind, cold as ice. The shield, she suspected.

Where the forest curved, she drove her wings hard and lifted. Exhaustion burned through her, but she fought it back, refusing to stop. A surge of adrenaline sparked, flooding through her like liquid fire. She angled in for another approach when the bodies of the burned archers started to move.

The charred flesh crumbled away, and the men pulled their bows from the piles of ash, then lifted them to her once more.

An old memory stirred and a chill seeped into her heart.

No, it's not possible! She'd burned all the records all those years ago...hadn't she? Doubt crept in, refusing to let go. If Mirena had managed in thousands what Nimue had only practiced in small numbers, then things were far worse than anyone could imagine.

She recalled her conversation with Titania. All other avenues of defense were tumbling away, leaving her with few options left to stop Mirena's advance.

Slamming her wings in tight, she plunged toward the archers, picking out the closest one. He pulled back his string. She threw her wings out and her claws down, snatching the man as she surged back up into the air. He made no sound, going limp in her clutches as she rose high above the raging battle, passing through a thin layer of cloud.

She shifted him to her front claw and looked down. His skin turned ashen, cracking, as his glassy black eyes met hers...and then he *smiled.* A cold breeze surged against her, and the man's body crumbled to dust, floating away in a cloud of ash. Her heart pounded viciously in her chest as her mind spiraled into the past, back to her life as a demon queen.

To forge additional forces without having to wait for more demons to crawl from the pit, she'd created undead soldiers with full fighting capability. She'd succeeded, for a time, but the price had been great, so she'd abandoned the project and burned all records.

She watched the ash vanish, blood howling in her ears, devouring the cries of battle below. A single word rose to her mind, one she'd prayed to Lyria that would never be uttered, or even thought of, again.

Unease bubbled through her mind. This fight would be a slaughter. The city would fall. This was Mirena's plan all along. She'd let Sybilla grow confident thinking she was facing an army of a few thousand men, not one forged of shades, immortal creatures that would simply respawn unless the source of their magic was destroyed.

Nimue snapped her wings and plunged through the clouds, aiming straight for the city. She flew over the raging army as it advanced toward the walls. Drums of oil spilled down over the wall, staining the stone black, dripping like blood, and gathered in a line along the base. She was halfway to the city when Lorca appeared, unleashing a burst of fire, igniting the oil. It exploded along the ground, catching the soldiers in a raging inferno, and rose up the walls in columns of fire.

She powered onwards to the wall when a voice slid into her mind, rising from the darkness, one of the threads pulling taut.

Nimue, I've come.

Claudius.

Her gaze snapped to the top of the wall, his golden hair gleaming in the firelight. And beside him, Titania. Relief poured through her. They'd answered her call.

She opened her mind to respond when something crashed into her back. Pain erupted through her limbs. A heaviness washed over her, tearing the air from her lungs, and the world exploded into light as her dragon side was silenced, forcing a shift. Someone screamed, tearing through her mind, and her stomach flipped as she felt herself fall.

Darkness rushed to devour her, consuming the battlefield from her view. From the corner of her eye, she saw Lorca, falling from the sky, his limp mortal body dropping like a stone to the ground.

CHAPTER 87

"I hear whispers of a kingdom being born in the mountains, of an alliance between dragons and humans. I sit in my office and wonder just what the hell kind of game Nimue is playing?"

—Excerpt from Atlas's diary

Titania sprinted up the tower two steps at a time, and flew out the door, swathed in ribbons of shadow. Racing along the wall, the battle raging in her ears; she darted between the men. The thread tightened in her chest, pulling her forward through the fray; a familiar presence brushing her mind as she emerged through the throng to a clear section.

The Princess stood in her armor, straight-backed and hands clasped. And at her side, every bit the warrior, was Claudius, staring out across the fray, his expression grave. Titania slowed and stopped at his side, the shadows melting away. Men shouted in alarm, scrambling to her. Claudius spun, his hand snapping up.

"She's with me!"

The soldiers crept forward until Sybilla stepped in their way. "Stand down. If he says she's with him, then she is. Return to your posts!"

A thread of power hummed in the girl's voice, and magic burned in those golden pools. For a moment, she reminded her of a younger Nimue, before her friend had claimed the Azradan throne.

Sensing her gaze, the Princess looked at her, then at Claudius. "We will talk about this later."

Sybilla swept away, vanishing among the fray.

At the distant tree line, Nimue swooped down, laying waste to the ranks of men with a storm of fire. As a line of burned corpses stretched out in her friend's wake more men marched from the tree line. She felt her dark powers stir, pushing up and through her limbs, eddying in her chest.

"You feel it?" She stretched out a hand, closing her eyes.

"This is Mirena's magic."

Her eyes flickered open. An old memory brushed her mind, dancing just out of reach. Irritation flared in her chest. Her hand dropped, curling into a fist. She *knew* that magic, but from where? Was it from one of Nimue's experiments back when she had been Queen in the demon realm?

Nimue swooped down for another attack, but this time she grabbed one of the men from the tree line, then flew above the clouds. Titania frowned, her magic surging again, snapping to be released. It paced in her chest, snarling. She gazed skyward again and saw Nimue, her claws absent, flying back to the wall.

"*Release the oil!*" shouted the Princess.

Along the wall, men tipped over wooden barrels mounted on frames and a thick black oil spilled out. The foul stench struck her nose. Desperation flooded her mind, tugging at the thread binding her to her queen. She could feel it spilling from Nimue, thick and fast, and her chest suddenly went painfully tight.

A flash of darkness erupted just behind Nimue right before something crashed into her. White light exploded, dimming quickly, and she began to fall.

"Claudius, grab—"

But he had already thrown himself off the wall, the wind flinging him toward Nimue. Titania grabbed the ledge, the vast army spread out before her, hesitated for a split second, then threw herself over. Darkness surrounded her, the wind roaring in her ears as she dropped to the field below. As she landed, a figure tumbling toward the ground caught her gaze.

A man.

Lorca.

She threw out her hand, throwing up a protective bubble around his body, catching him just before he hit the ground. There was no time to think as the advancing forces rushed at her. Titania turned her attention to the soldiers. Ribbons of darkness spilled from her. Throwing her hands wide, the ribbons sharpened to spears, and she thrust her palms forward, hurling them at the advancing horde.

The spears collided with sickening crunches, spearing them to the ground. She moved forward, summoning more of them to the air when, before her eyes, the dead soldiers turned to ash. A memory pushed up of her marching into the library to find Nimue burning a pile of books, frantic and splattered with blood from their latest battle. Horror blazed in her queen's eyes as she threw another book into the flames.

Titania now realized what stood before her.

She pivoted sharply on her heel, throwing up a shield of darkness, and dashed in Lorca's direction. The men came closer, their war cries roaring around her. Fires blazed on her left, the burning wall throwing off dizzying waves of heat. Sweat dripped down her skin as she found Lorca rising shakily to his feet.

A soldier came at them, his sword drawn. Titania seized a blade from the ground and drove it up as the soldier attacked. The blade sank clean through his chest. He staggered back and then shattered into dust. She called on another spear, this one firm in her hands, and then gathered her shield around Lorca when she reached his side.

"Titania?" he cried, looking around in confusion. "Where's Nimue!"

"Can you shift?"

Concentration tightened his face, then faded into a frown. A shadow of unease flickered in his eyes. "No, I can't."

"And your fire?"

He held up a hand, fire sparking in his fingers. "It feels weaker."

It was better than nothing.

A force slammed into her shield. She staggered, wincing as the pressure grew. There was a sword at his hip. "Take your sword. We're going to have to fight our way through this mess to them!"

Nodding grimly, he pulled out his sword. The fire in his hand leaped down, wrapping around the blade. A steely look hardened his face, one to rival any demon. "Ready when you are."

She tightened her grip on her spear. "Try not to die. Nimue will kill me if you do."

He snorted. "I imagine she won't be thrilled if I let you die, either."

The corner of her mouth twitched. She had no intention of dying. Her wife awaited her in the city. Gritting her teeth, she dropped the shield, and the pair of them plunged into the fray.

Soldiers came at her thick and fast. The old panic still writhed beneath the surface, but she dug deep, gritting her teeth. Aliya's face burned brightly, and she clung to it, chanting the oath she'd sworn as she surged forward.

She was not broken, not anymore. And as she ducked and weaved, swinging her spear effortlessly and driving it into her enemies, the warrior within her awakened.

Among the chaos, she spied Claudius and Nimue fighting close by, the latter slower in her movements. Exhaustion shadowed her vicious attacks. Whatever had been done to her, it had left Nimue faltering. Titania had to get to her.

Lorca saw her, his movements faltering for a second. Nimue stiffened, looking across the fray at each other. Time slowed. Titania watched the pair share a silent exchange between them. Then Nimue's gaze darted behind him, eyes widening. Her mouth opened, as if in a warning. Titania pivoted sharply, hurling her spear into a man as he launched at Lorca. The spear slammed mid-air into his chest, disintegrating him before he hit the ground.

Another came at him from behind.

"Oh, no you don't!" She summoned another spear and threw it, striking his throat and turning him to dust. The last few men fell, and Titania rushed to Claudius.

"Drop!" she yelled.

He dropped and she jumped, one hand on his back, vaulting clean over as she threw a hand out, firing a bolt of darkness that slammed into a soldier. Straightening up, she raised her palms, wrapping a wall of shadows around the four of them. At once, the soldiers slammed against it; the force shuddering through her body. Clenching her teeth, she held her hands wide, holding them steady. Lorca rushed to Nimue's side, dropping as she sank to her knees.

"Why'd you shift mid-air like that?" he teased, kissing her hair as he held her in his arms.

Nimue laughed weakly, wincing. A look Titania knew well. The damage was worse than she was letting anyone see.

"I can assure you, it was not my plan."

The shield shuddered. Titania cursed. "Hate to break up this touching reunion but we need to get back to—" Something hard crashed against her shield, dropping her to her knees. Pain lanced through her arms as if they were being ripped from their sockets. Curses tumbled from her lips as she forced herself up, gritting her teeth and widening her stance.

"Can you extend this darkness over the battlefield?" asked Claudius.

One brow lifted. "If I could do that, I would have already. I haven't wielded that power in—"

Nimue threw her back with an agonized scream, clutching at her chest. Pain erupted inside Titania, and as she trembled, fighting to stay standing, Claudius doubled over. Her demonic magic flared suddenly, growing tenfold before retreating once more.

Oh no.

"Nimue, what is it?" Lorca asked.

But Titania knew. She could *feel* it. Words died on her lips. The cracks had given her snatches of her old realm...but the power now humming through her body felt different. Sharper. Her gaze dropped to Nimue, who gripped the earth with her nails dug deep as she drew in shaky breaths.

"It's open, isn't it?"

Nimue let out a long groan, swaying on all fours before she sat up, pale as death.

"Not fully, but...I can feel it—" Her breath caught, but Titania knew exactly what she was going to say. The flash of fear in those ancient depths was enough.

Nimue could feel her throne. It was calling to her.

Titania turned her focus to Claudius. Time was running out. He knew it too, but neither of them had wielded the level of magic they once did. For that, they needed blood—

And a lot. Even draining Lorca dry wouldn't be enough, as if Nimue would ever permit that.

They had run out of options, their identity was exposed, and Mirena was opening the Hell Gate.

CHAPTER 88

"The lowland kingdoms have become restless at the rumors of a growing kingdom in the mountains and now I have received a message from Amara. She has summoned me back to her side. For the first time since coming to this land, I saw fear in her eyes."

—Excerpt from Castille's diary

Flynn dropped to the deck as another spear flew at him, landing with a heavy thud in the mast above his head. He jumped up to his feet, swinging the sword hard as a siren charged at him. They collided in a flurry of blows and snarls, and it took all he had to match her speed.

It was hard. The siren ducked and weaved, pivoting sharply out of his arcs before rushing in. He dodged a slash of her claws when his back hit the railing. In a flash, her hand shot out, grabbing at his wrist. Sharp nails sank deep, forcing him to drop his sword. It clattered heavily to the deck, and then the claws were at his throat.

Desperately, he thrust his palms against her chest and sank his mind into the well of raging magic within. It exploded out, a flash of light blinding him. The pressure on his throat vanished. Sucking in a gulp of air, a wave of dizziness swept through him as he fell to his knees.

His vision cleared. The siren was dead on the deck, a hole blown right through her chest. Black blood pooled around her body.

He had no time to think as another two sirens vaulted over the railing, landing on the other side of the body. They hissed, looks of rage on their faces, their fury at their dead sister welling in the air. He raised his palms, calling on the magic once more, when a hand grabbed his neck from behind.

A bolt of pain shot down his spine. Flynn hit the ground with a gasp. Someone shouted his name, but a deafening roar filled his ears. A drum beat like thunder. His heart. Claws dug into his neck once more, and a cold, fetid breath brushed his cheek.

"Time to die, godling," the siren crooned. *"Chaos sends her regards."*

Who? The question died on his lips.

A talon raked across his neck, slicing flesh. He tried to move, but his body refused to obey. Waves of crippling pain, each more savage than the last ran down his spine.

He felt himself slipping. Desperately, he tried to summon his magic, but he couldn't control it, nor demand its obedience, even as he felt it, just out of reach, a torrent of ancient magic.

The world slowed to a crawl. It would be so easy to let everything go, he thought, but then a shape came into focus. A glowing figure kneeled before him, on their face a look of bitter disappointment.

Ronan.

"Get *up,* you fool. You're to be a god. Are you going to let these pathetic creatures kill you?"

I can't move, he tried to say.

The god rose sneering at him, arms folded across his chest. *"Get up!"*

The order cracked through his mind like a clap of thunder. A sense of calm came over him. He stilled, the pain a distant thought. Focusing on Ronan's command, he forced his hands up, even as his arms trembled. The god's mocking question fueled him, a burst of defiance flooding his limbs.

He was to become a god. How could he let sirens defeat him?

The fetid breath brushed his cheek again. "What was that, godling? A final plea before I slit your throat?"

He realized he'd spoken, and the words bubbled up once more, rising to his lips. Power raged in his chest, infusing every inch of his body. His hands rose, facing the pair that now stood in front of him. They laughed, leaning in as they licked their lips. Their foul stench reached his nostrils, fueling his rage.

Latching onto the words, he pushed them out. "You're wrong."

"About what?" The siren's claw dug deeper into his neck, the blood running freely down his skin, but he felt no pain.

"I'm not a *godling.*" He closed his eyes. The magic surged up, answering his call, a wave of pure energy. His eyes opened, and he threw his hands wide. Energy erupted from his chest. "I. Am. A. *God*!"

The siren's screams filled his ears. Almost instantly, they ceased and silence reigned. The howl of his blood grew quiet, his heartbeat slowing as the light dimmed. At his feet, their black blood splattered across the deck. A metallic taste burned his lips, but he was beyond caring. Waves of power vibrated through his whole being. He felt his soul fight to be free, to stretch out once more beyond his body.

Slowly, he calmed himself until his heart beat normally once more. The other sirens were torn apart, their bloodied remains scattered across the deck. Where were the others? Had he harmed them with the reckless use of his power?

His gaze snagged on a glowing sphere at the far end of the ship.

"*Mira? Ashara? Kiya?*" Their names scraped his throat raw as he stumbled forward.

His legs nearly buckled, the magic retreating within, as he raced across the deck, not caring if he stepped on blood or flesh.

The sphere faded. Kiya was out cold on the ground, a nasty cut on her forehead. Standing over her were Ashara and Mira, one hand linked, with the other facing out. Tendrils of light danced over their fingers, then slid back under their skin. Sweat glistened on their brows. They looked exhausted, barely standing, but also like a true pair of warriors. Ashara spoke first.

"Now *that* was the power of a god," she mused, the corner of her mouth tipped up. "A little warning next time would be nice."

Laughter spilled from his lips, the brittle sound like shattered glass. Wincing, he pressed a hand to his throat. Had he really seen Ronan, or was it simply an illusion from the lack of air?

"I'll try, but I make no promises." Every word hurt and his whole body felt frayed at the edges.

Mira let go of Ashara and stepped around Kiya, walking over to him. She studied him closely before hauling him into her arms. "Don't scare me like that again."

He leaned into her hug, letting it anchor him for a moment. His soul settled, the urge to leave his body gone for the moment. "Only if you tell me how the hell you suddenly have magic."

She pulled back when a slow clap came behind him. He pivoted sharply. Big mistake. The world lurched, his head spinning for a second. Four figures stood in the middle of the ship, two men and two women. He blinked slowly, his vision sharpening. No, not four.

Two.

Castille and a hooded woman. Slender brown hands slipped out from the folds of a gray cloak and pushed back the hood, revealing a striking young woman with luminous golden eyes. A pin glimmered at her collar, that of a red flower.

Ashara moved to his side, her arm looped around Kiya's waist, who looked like she could barely stand. Ashara bowed as deeply as she could while supporting her sister, as did Mira. Flynn remembered where he'd seen her.

Her portrait adorned one of the pillars at the temple, right beside his father and Castille.

The latter stepped forward, clasping his hands together. "Apologies for our delay! Might I introduce my wife, Amara?"

CHAPTER 89

"The humans have earned the respect of the dragons. For the actions of a few who battled demons that attacked the dragon's nest, they have been blessed with a gift. The form of a dragon."
—Excerpt from Nimue's diary

Nimue threw her head back, an inhuman scream clawing its way out of her throat. A shockwave jolted through her body as dark talons clawed deep within her mind, tearing back her walls, and crawling inside her.

The world crumbled away, abandoning her on an empty battlefield. The city loomed in the distance, an empty husk, stretching out its shadowy presence over the field. A full moon glimmered brightly in the sky, casting the world in a silvery hue.

Nimue pressed her palms onto the cold earth and tried to stand. A wave of nausea pushed up her throat. She doubled over, heaving bile and blood onto the ground. Her stomach clenched, and tremors racked her body until her gut felt empty. Exhausted, she closed her eyes.

A warm hand settled on her shoulder. Nimue's eyes opened in panic. Ellie was there, smiling softly, one hand outstretched.

Nimue slid her fingers into her sister's grip, and was hauled up.

"Is this a dream? Are you really...?"

Ellie's mouth twitched. "Here? In a manner of speaking, yes."

She ought to have found joy that her sister was awake...but staring into those eyes, once so bright and youthful, were darkened with something ancient and unreadable. It was as though she were staring at a stranger, a thought that cleaved her soul in two.

"Why are you here? I have to go back. The gate is activating."

Ellie inclined her head. "Mirena's demons slaughtering people as we speak. She has you right where she wanted you; outside the city and focused on the army. But don't you see? That was never the real threat. "

"But how can you know all of this?"

Ellie's gaze dropped. "I wish I could explain that there was more time. My mind is a mess and I don't know when I'm going to lose myself again. While I have this moment of clarity, I had to come to you. To help."

Exhausted to the bone, Nimue stared at her blood-stained hands. "I don't have the power I used to."

"You can't defeat Mirena, not as you are." Ellie's jaw tightened. For a second, she was silent, and her gaze darkened. "But I can help you buy time so you can do what you've been planning."

Their eyes met, and Nimue felt icy hands wrap around her heart.

"You won't try to stop me?"

Ellie closed the distance, cupping her cheek. "There is no guarantee what will happen after. Now, time is running out. Sybilla will need to find the one acting as a conduit for the undead army. It's the only way to stop their assault. As for you and the others, find the portal that will lead you to the Hell Gate."

Nimue glanced across the empty battlefield. "I don't know if you've noticed, but there is an army between Sybilla and that forest."

"Which is why you and I are going to give her an opening. I can briefly lend you my strength, and this will suppress your dragon side. But it will only last for a few hours, so move fast."

Questions flooded her mind. Nimue tore her gaze from the battlefield and thrust out her hand. "I guess we better get started."

Ellie grabbed her hand. "Sisters, no matter the form, till the very end."

"Sisters."

Ellie squeezed her hand and closed her eyes. Ribbons of magic spilled from her ashen skin, wrapping around the both of them, growing rapidly, until a wall of pure energy raged around them. The roar filled Nimue's ears, like that of a storm growing stronger with every second. Ellie's eyes opened and two black pools stared back at her. All traces of her mortal sister were gone.

She was staring into the eyes of a goddess as Ellie struck her in the chest—

Her eyes flew open, the misty field gone, and she was back with her friends, Lorca, and the dark shield Titania held around them. At once, she felt her dragon side buried; the fire snuffed out. Demonic magic roared in her veins, crackling just beneath the surface. It snarled to be unleashed and at that moment; she felt like her old self. A demon queen once more, the full force of her dark powers at her control.

Hurry, sister. Ellie's voice whispered.

Nimue nodded and stood. This time, her legs stood firm.

"Nimue?" Lorca spoke her name with an air of concern.

She turned to him, offering a shaky smile. "Ellie says hi."

A shadow of dark magic clung to his skin. It had to be the spell blocking his dragon form. Could she...?

His mouth opened, but it was Titania who spoke next. "Do I even want to know?"

"Probably not." She smiled faintly at her before she stepped to Lorca, brushing his cheek. "This is going to hurt."

"What?"

She thrust her palm into his chest, the shadows bursting from his skin. He sank to his knees with a gasp. After a second, her heart thudding hard in her chest, he looked up, his green eyes glowing. The spell had been broken.

"What did you do?"

"I broke the demonic binding that made you shift in mid-air. You should be able to take dragon form now, so I need you to take Titania and Claudius back to the wall."

He pushed himself unsteadily to his feet. "And what do you plan on doing?"

"My sister and I are going to disrupt a spell. Don't worry, I just need to buy Sybilla a bit of time before we can deal with that annoying Hell Gate. Trust me. I have no intention of dying on this battlefield. There's a much bigger threat we need to face afterward." She closed the distance, kissing him firmly. Stepping back, she moved out of reach. "Go. Ellie can't lend me her strength for long."

Sensing the urgency in her voice, he nodded. "Come back to me."

The urge to promise she would, died on her lips. "I have to go now."

His lips parted, then shut before he appeared to find his voice. "I want you to know I am glad you revealed your true self to me. It let me fall in love with you all over again."

Tears burned her eyes, but she quickly blinked them away. "Go. I'll see you soon." She turned to Titania. "It's time."

Titania expanded the shield, giving him room to shift. Sweat dripped from her brow, but her stance remained strong, her gaze steady.

Light flashed as Lorca shifted. Claudius strode past, climbing on first. Once the shield dropped, everything would happen fast. The others offered her one last look, each a mix of assurance, worry, and hope.

"Ready, Nimue?" Titania asked.

"Ready."

Titania's hands dropped. The shield vanished as she leaped onto Lorca's back, who instantly launched into the sky. The soldiers rushed in, but Nimue threw her hands up, sending a shockwave crashing against them, their bodies reduced to dust on impact. Another wave of magic howled through her, surging out from her hands, spreading even further. She gritted her teeth, sending wave after wave across the battlefield.

Clouds of dust whipped up, the army destroyed as she wrought her fury on them. A savage scream welled up from the pit of her soul. Thousands of years of fury and darkness were summoned once more, the wrath of a queen unleashed.

She had become death once more, pushing out her wicked powers, laying waste to thousands.

And by Lyria's grace, it was *glorious.*

She dug her heels in and thrust out more power, without mercy or hesitation. This was what she was born to do. A monster unchained, smiling wickedly. From the moment she had crawled from the demon pit thousands of years ago, to her ascension to Queen, death and chaos burned through her soul.

A primal scream tore from her lips as she hurled her power from her hands and slammed them down into the earth. The ground exploded outwards, tearing gaping wounds in the earth and splintering outwards. A wave of darkness roared outwards, decimating the army as they tried to escape her wrath.

The shockwave crashed against the forest, slamming up against a shield. The resistance sparked a rush of anger; the darkness raging at being defied. She channeled all her power into one point, then drove it forward. Palms out in front, she stalked toward the forest, a wall of pure darkness touching the sky at her command.

One word welled up in her throat, poised like a blade on her lips.

"Break."

The shield shattered. Her magic exploded forward, flooding through the trees. Screams erupted, and human cries of horror as the wave covered all in its wake.

Then, the tide turned and the energy rushed back. In a flash, she dropped to her knees, a wave of exhaustion crashing into her. Deep breaths shuddered through her body. Something wet touched her lips, tasting sharp and metallic. Blood.

Nimue staggered to her feet, alone and battered on the battlefield. All traces of the undead shades were gone, the illusion broken for the moment. She opened her mind, latching onto her bond with Lorca, and at once, his relief burst through.

Nimue! You're alive.

Of course. I told you to not to worry. Can you come for me?

It was chaos back at the wall. Lorca landed and Nimue slid down from his back, running one hand along his side to rest at his head. Titania and Claudius stood with them as soldiers rushed over, swords drawn. Shouts erupted, thick with fear and tension. Instinctively, ribbons of magic burst from Nimue's hands, encircling her arms. Titania snapped her fingers, power spilling from them, as she offered Nimue a reassuring wink. The wind whipped around them, tousling Claudius' hair, as his eyes turned black. Even Lorca snarled protectively beside her, unfurling his wings, flames eddying around his mouth.

The men stopped, keeping their distance, whispering among themselves. No one moved an inch closer, but they kept their swords lifted. She almost laughed. The act gave them the illusion of safety, even if the four of them could slaughter everyone within minutes if the need arose.

"*Step aside!*" Sybilla's voice cut the air like a crack of lightning.

The men parted. Sybilla swept through them, shadowed by her guards and General Galen. Blood splattered one side of her face. The Princess's gaze was wary as she looked over at the four.

Nimue squared her shoulders and stepped forward. Two thousand years of hiding what they were had ended. She knew what she had to do.

The guards moved closer to their Princess, hands dropping to their swords. She returned Sybilla's stare, unflinching. One monarch eyeing the other.

"It's obvious you're not Wren of Fenware. So, who are you?" asked Sybilla.

Nimue snapped her fingers, black ribbons dancing across her skin. "I'm a demon." *Nimue...*Lorca's voice slid into her mind. She pushed on. "I am Queen Nimue of the Azradan throne, one of the monarchs of the demon realm."

Sybilla's gaze narrowed. "Hell of a title. And what of everyone else with you?"

Nimue didn't miss the way Claudius stiffened. "Titania, my general, and Claudius, my adviser and right hand. Lorca is, as he said, a Dragonir prince." She paused, hearing the whispers of surprise and alarm ripple over the surrounding soldiers. Steeling her spine, she continued on. "Now, as fun as these introductions are, there are bigger problems. You must find a sorcerer in those woods and kill him. He's acting as a conduit to the demon realm and will soon resurrect the army I destroyed. They are immortal soldiers, and unless you stop him, they will breach the walls and slaughter everyone inside."

Silence fell. Nimue's heart thudded hard, leaving her twitchy. Every second that ticked by left her increasingly restless. The darkness inside her snarled louder, clawing at her soul. Sybilla glanced toward the treeline.

"Why didn't *you* kill him?"

"A goddess granted me her powers for a moment. It was enough to buy you some time. What I must do now is to—" A bolt of pain tore up her spine, driving hard into her head. The connection to her throne roared in her soul, tearing through her. Her knees buckled and she sagged for a moment against Lorca. Steadying herself, she continued. "Listen, Princess, I don't have *time* for this. Demons are slaughtering your people as we speak. The Hell Gate is activating and Alexandria's real army will march on this city soon if her undead one cannot be summoned. And if I fail at my mission, you're *also* going to be fighting a demon army. Maybe not at this moment in this city but it will come for you. It will come for us all. Do you fancy your chances, then?"

Lorca nudged her with his head, but she slid a hand to his neck, staying him for the moment as they awaited Sybilla's response.

"How do I know you won't turn on us?" Sybilla asked, her gaze narrowing.

Nimue stepped back, took hold of one of the horns on Lorca's spin, and swung onto his back. As she settled there, she levelled a grim look at the Princess.

"You don't, but I would suggest dealing with the army at your gate. There is a sorcerer who has created an army of shadow men, creatures that will lay waste to everything you love. Kill him and you may stand a chance of winning this fight."

Sybilla stared back, silent, and hands curled into fists at her side. She made no move to stop them, so Nimue glanced to the others. "Are you coming, Claudius?"

There was no guarantee any of them were coming back, and she would not deny him a chance for goodbye.

He shook his head. "I'll follow our bond and meet you. I need to do something first." He glanced over at Sybilla who avoided his gaze, staring solely at Nimue with an unfathomable expression.

Titania cautiously got on behind Nimue, never looking away from the men. Nimue glanced over at her shoulder. "Ready?"

Titania grinned. "Let's break that gate."

Sybilla stepped forward, raising her hand to stop the advance of her men and guards. "Wait! How do I know you are not lying?"

Nimue's brow lifted. "Do you wish to gamble your city on me being wrong? Go, or don't, my fight isn't on that battlefield. Yours is."

A beat passed before Sybilla released a string of curses, then spoke again. "And where will I find this sorcerer?"

"They'll have a hell of a lot of demonic magic radiating from them." Nimue saw the flicker of doubt in Sybilla's eyes. "Trust your instincts and your men. You are royalty and a warrior. I've seen it. Now is the time to show it."

CHAPTER 90

"The Dragonirs and Dragons have now declared to the lowlands that the mountains are their home. Their kingdom is born."
—Excerpt from Nimue's diary

When the others departed, Claudius turned to Sybilla, hesitating as he reached out. She flinched. A shadow flashed across his face, and he snatched his hand back, his jaw tightening. Sybilla's confusion warred with her anger, the sting of his lies bitter in her mouth, and tears burned her eyes. She rapidly blinked them away.

"Sybilla..."

"*Your Highness,*" she corrected, her voice like shattered glass.

His jaw tightened and he bowed. His cool practiced mask rivaled even the proudest noble's, taking hold. "Fight well, your Highness."

With that, he sprinted off the wall, vaulting into the air with a roaring gust of wind. She held her breath until he vanished into the city.

"Your Highness? Your orders?" Galen's voice broke her train of thought.

She blinked the tears away and took a steadying breath. All eyes were on her, awaiting her command. The empty battlefield taunted her. Mere moments before, they'd had thousands of 'men' at their gate, their doom imminent, and now it was empty because of Nimue's terrifying power. She studied the treeline. It was quiet, but the thick shadows concealed the army she knew lay within.

She turned to Galen, knowing what she had to do. "Come with me."

As she walked with her general, she sensed Oren's eyes on her. He was at her side, closer than perhaps was protocol but she didn't care. Everything within her had been strung taut, and she was about to snap.

When they arrived at the nearest tower, he opened the door for her. Their eyes met. She expected smug satisfaction that he was right. Though he had never said the words, she knew of his disapproval. But it was kindness in his eyes, not pity, just a look of loyalty. This was a man who had not faltered at her side, remaining as steadfast as her shadows.

She broke her gaze away first, leading Galen into one of the meeting rooms. Gray light streamed in from a single narrow window, lighting the small and gloomy space.

"You have a plan and I am not going to like it, am I?" Galen strode to the window, hands clasped behind his back.

"We can't risk a full assault on the forest. There aren't the numbers to do that and defend the city as well, especially while we have half of our men already trying to deal with the demons running through our streets." She could still hear screams ring out across the city, even in the confines of that small room. Doing her best to block it out, she focused her mind on the task at hand. A plan began to formulate.

A bold, stupid, and utterly reckless plan.

Galen groaned, and she imagined him as her father for the moment; worried, but aware of her nature all the same. "I know that look."

"Consider this a test of loyalty and how well you can keep a secret."

"Spirits above, you're serious about going out there, aren't you?"

"Not alone."

"*Sybilla.*" Her brow shot up at her name and he cursed. "You are the future leader of our people. If you die, this whole fight is for nothing."

"We have very few people with any kind of magic and even fewer who can fight. Would you send one of them, entrust our whole future to them?" She snapped her fingers and magic flared at her feet, lighting the room in an ethereal glow. "I won't go alone, but we can't send our army."

"And if you die?"

She strode toward him, still bathed in light and magic. "My life will never be safe or my own until my aunt is dead. Let me show you I can give us a fighting chance and strike a blow at her. Let us make her bleed. If I can cut this sorcerer down, then we can fight a force of real men. Ones we can kill."

Hesitation and doubt warred in his eyes. She saw it, the desire to hide her away. It warmed her heart. She offered him a small smile. In that room, she let him see her fear and her fire, and that she would not be argued against.

He sighed, nodding reluctantly. "Very well but you have a plan, right?"

"I do. Have my guards ready and send your fastest runners to the mansion. I need you to retrieve some people for me. We'll leave as soon as they arrive."

Galen didn't argue further and bowed deeply. He gave a sad smile and said, "I always knew you were stubborn like your father."

Sybilla swept to the door. "Bring Dorian, Sylvie, and Nora to the gate. I'll meet them there."

Were it not for the gravity of the situation and how much was pinned on Galen bringing the others to her, she might've laughed at the look on Oren's face when she told him they wouldn't need horses.

She waited for what felt like an eternity, alternating between pacing and leaning against a wall. The momentary pause in the battle had rendered the city unnervingly quiet, as if it were all a terrible dream.

"Your Highness. Riders approach!" called Oren.

She stopped and breathed a sigh of relief. Galen had come through.

Dorian, Sylvie, and Nora dismounted, striding over with grim expressions. As much as she hated involving the young Druid, there was no one else with her power.

Sybilla strode forward. "Thank you for coming."

"What do you need us to do?" asked Dorian.

She filled them in with as much detail as she could, then faced Nora. "I've heard stories of the Druids' abilities to control the earth, and Sylvie has spoken of how truly exceptional you are. We have to get to that forest without crossing the battlefield. Can you create a pathway for us to travel underground?"

Nora's eyes widened, flashing to the gate as if she was seeing the vast field that lay between the city and the forest. "I've only ever used my power to play tricks on people. How can I possibly do anything like that?"

"You are stronger than you believe." Sybilla stepped forward, setting a hand on the girl's shoulders. "We don't have a lot of time. Their archers would pick us off before we even got close. All that I ask is that you try."

Nora's brow furrowed. "You really think I can do this?"

"Yes."

A fire lit in Nora's eyes. "Okay, I'll try."

CHAPTER 91

"I depart this land hoping to find a new adventure. I cannot stand to be in the company of Claudius; Amara and Castille have long since departed themselves for unknown lands; Atlas is off on another campaign and Nimue... I wish to step beyond this false title of spirit many of us have and cast aside my role as a warrior. I wonder what else I might find beyond these shores."

—Excerpt from Titania's diary

The throne called to Nimue.

The crooning voice taunted her. A shadowy hand stretched out, beckoning her. Leaning down on Lorca's back, she touched his neck and opened their bond to the demonic pull.

I can sense it. Do you feel that every day?

There was no point in lying about it. *It was dull until recently. I could ignore it before. We need to follow it.*

Lorca did as she asked, though she felt his reluctance through their bond.

They flew deep into the heart of the city, leaving Nimue unsurprised when Lorca landed outside a familiar graveyard. It was the very one that led to where they'd last fought Mirena.

As she climbed down, the whispers rose to near shouts in her head. Wincing, she rubbed her temples when a hand slid to the base of her neck. She didn't have to see who it was. Magic hummed through their bond, dulling the pain.

"Better?" He studied her closely.

"A little."

The sound of horse hooves signaled the arrival of Claudius. He dismounted and approached them, raising his brow. "Of course, we're back here. I was hoping our connection was misleading me."

"Someone sounds terrified," said Titania and threw him an arch look. "Perhaps you should leave this to warriors?"

Claudius's lip curled defiantly, and he flicked a hand in Lorca's direction. "He's no warrior."

Titania laughed. "He's handled himself well enough."

Nimue stepped forward, pulling away from Lorca's touch, and turned to face everyone.

"We move in fast. The focus will be to find the portal and try to sever the link from this end. There's no way of telling if the portal feeds to the same location as the Hell Gate or if it's a conduit, meaning if we go through—"

"We're back in paradise?" Titania finished with a wry smile.

"Something like that. Is everyone ready? There is no turning back from this point."

The others nodded. It was time.

A thin band of silver light peeked out from beneath the door. The air hummed with ancient demonic magic, which prickled along her skin, raising the hairs on her arms. Ice slid down her spine. The throne tightened its grip again; the voices returning with a vengeance.

Just as it had been two thousand years ago when I was ready to—

Her thoughts cut off as the door swung open before anyone touched it.

"I am under the distinct impression we are expected," said Claudius, but there was no amusement in his voice.

"Then we best not keep Mirena waiting." Nimue strode through first.

The second she crossed the threshold a wave of demonic energy washed over her. The power within her swelled, flooding through her limbs, spilling out of her fingers. Black ribbons wreathed themselves around her arms. She drew her swords from her sheathes and moved further inside.

In the middle of the room, an enormous portal pulsated with energy, larger than any she had seen before. Tendrils of shadows swirled across the floor, stretching toward her as if sensing who—and what—she was.

The others followed, falling in at her side, though none said a word.

Nimue drew a deep breath, letting the magic soak into her bones and fill her. She exhaled and stepped forward. "Make sure nothing disturbs me."

Majesty infused her words. Glancing back, she saw that Titania and Claudius had bowed. She hadn't meant to command them...Shaking her head; she returned her focus to the portal. Even though much of Ellie's power had left her, enough still coursed through her veins that the pain of her failing body was silent.

She lifted her twin blades, infusing them with dark magic. An orb sparked in between, growing larger as she forced more energy through the blades. Sweat gathered on her brow. Heat built in her limbs, but she kept the blades steady.

"Nimue! Watch out!" Lorca's voice boomed through the room.

A shadow flashed in the corner of her gaze. Her heart leaped as Lorca rushed past her, colliding with something with a muted thud. Chaos erupted behind her. Savage snarls ricocheted off the walls, swelling with growing numbers. From the shadows emerged the wolves.

And the door slammed shut.

They were locked in, and she couldn't move a muscle. If she let her concentration slip, she'd have to start over and there was no time for that. Gritting her teeth, she clawed up every scrap of power she had and thrust it through the blades. The orb doubled in size.

Her legs wobbled, nearly sending her to the floor, but she breathed in and steadied. The battle raged around her with the others fighting desperately to keep the demons away. All she needed was a few more seconds. She was so close. She could feel it. Gripping both hilts, she forced out a final burst of magic, and the orb was at last ready.

She moved closer to the portal, her body screaming in protest, daggers of pain cutting through her. Every inch forward hurt more than the last, but she pushed on.

Her strength was already failing, and her control slipping. Curses spilled from her lips. She was so close.

A scene materialized within the portal. She recognized her throne room, even after two thousand years. But it appeared Mirena had made some changes. Bones and discarded weapons littered the floor, draped in webs and dust. Three skulls lay under the throne, perhaps those of the murdered rulers. The walls had fallen and a gaping hole in the roof showed the familiar red sky, bathing the room in a bloody hue. All around were signs of death and destruction.

Mirena had reduced the Azradan court to ruins.

Grief howled through Nimue like a storm without end. She hadn't wanted to be queen when she was ripped from the realm...and it had been her decision not to return. But by Lyria's grace, she hadn't wanted her people to die. Tears burned her eyes, the bitter taste of shame and failure filling her mouth. Their deaths were on her head.

Anger erupted in a blinding rush of heat, tearing from her throat in a primal scream. She lifted the swords and the orb higher. The city would not fall, and the Hell Gate would not open. Not if she had a damn word to say about it.

"No!" Lorca's howling cry cut her thoughts like a knife.

Time slowed to a crawl.

She turned her head. Her heart stopped dead. Lorca was thrown past her, blood splattered across his face. Their eyes met in a split second. A thousand emotions screamed between them.

She watched, frozen, as he flew through the portal.

"LORCA!"

CHAPTER 92

"It has been nearly five hundred years since I last spoke to Nimue. I had visited several times, but she slumbered during every visit...and when I felt her awaken, I had to leave. Each time this deep terror seized me...and I found myself unable to face the look I knew would burn in her eyes."

—Excerpt from Claudius's diary

Sybilla stood with bated breath as Nora stepped back and spread out her hands. A quiet chant spilled from her lips as green magic sparked at her fingertips. Oren stiffened, but remained faithfully at her side. Her hand shot out, dropping over his, and their eyes met. The tension slowly bled from his shoulders, and she returned her focus to Nora.

The girl flung both hands at the ground, palms facing down, and energy blasted out with a deafening bang, crashing into the earth...

And nothing happened.

Silence reigned dominion over them as Sybilla scarcely dared to breathe. As the seconds crept by, Nora remained as still as a statue. Something snapped within Sybilla. Her feet ferried her forward and she crouched down beside the girl.

"You are not defined by your pain. This power is your connection to your people. It is who you are. The shadows of your past are part of you, threads in a tapestry that you weave." Sybilla reached out, tucking a strand of Nora's hair behind her ear, then met those glimmering green eyes with a smile. "You are *power.* This land is connected to you. Now, make it yield."

Nora nodded shakily.

Sybilla dipped her head, and returned to Oren's side.

When Nora stood once more, there was no hesitation or meekness in her bearing. The girl had faded away, leaving someone truly powerful in her place. Her hands snapped wide, making Sybilla's breath catch in her throat. Sparks of green light flared in Nora's hands, burning brighter before she dropped, slamming her hands into the earth.

Dirt flew up, churned apart by a steady beam of magic. The ground shuddered and groaned, the road tearing open like the mouth of a yawning beast. It grew wider and took shape, becoming large enough for them to walk through.

"I did it!" cried Nora.

Sybilla moved to her side. "I knew you could. Now, shall you do the honors?"

With a nod, Nora strode ahead, her two parents hurrying after her. Sybilla trailed at the rear with Oren beside her as they descended deeper underground.

Nora's magic lit their way as they continued their journey.

Sybilla tried to focus, but nerves rattled through her, making it hard to focus. When a hand brushed hers, she flinched, shooting Oren a startled look.

His hand fell away, leaving her missing his touch as he spoke. "So, what is the plan once we get there?"

"Sneak into the camp, find the source, kill him, then escape."

Oren's breath hitched in his throat. "That's your plan?"

"It's a simple plan," she amended with a dry smile. "There wasn't much time to get it all pretty, I'm afraid."

Nora quickened her pace. The tunnel echoed with their heavy footfalls and labored breaths.

When they slowed once more, Sybilla sensed they were approaching the camp. Her magic stirred restlessly beneath her skin, chafing against the dark magic above. They were close. Doubts crept in, taunting her with visions of a burned city and a field of dead.

"Lift your chin, your Highness," Oren whispered, reaching out in the dimly lit tunnel to touch her hand.

She threaded her fingers through his, squeezing them for comfort. "I will not fail. I can't."

Oren offered a small smile, assuring and proud, but said nothing. Perhaps because there was nothing to say that would completely erase her fears and doubts. They would always be her companion. She just had to manage them, just as she had when she was small. This rebellion was her destiny, the throne her future. Defeating this new threat was just one step in that direction, a future she had been born for.

The green light dimmed, and the earth stilled. Sybilla drew closer and saw the magic retreat into Nora's hands. The path ahead sloped up and a pale gray light spilled in. Dust floated in the air, shimmering for a moment with the remnants of Nora's magic.

"We're here," Nora whispered.

Sybilla stopped at her side. "You can head back to the city."

"The tunnel is already collapsing. You'll need me to get back." Nora forced a smile, but it was brittle at the edges, as she'd break at the slightest touch.

Sybilla slipped past the others and crept up the tunnel. At the mouth, she popped her head up, scanning for any sign of life. The shadowy forest permitted only thin bands of gray light through, dancing across the leaf litter and fallen twigs and rotting trees. Leaves rustled gently in the bitter breeze that pinched her cheeks red and whipped at the loose strands of hair from her braid. White clouds swirled around her lips as she emerged, poised to fight as the others followed.

Magic crackled just beneath her skin, itching for release. Scanning the shadowy woods, she reached with her mind through the trees. Nothing but the ancient woods greeted her for several moments until something cold brushed against her. A breathless gasp broke from her lips as tendrils of ice threaded their way down her body.

"This way." She set off, footfalls crunching quietly across the leaf litter.

When the trees thinned, the camp emerged through the gloom, and she ducked behind a tree. Pressing into the shadows, she studied the neat arrangement of tents and patrols of soldiers. Most bore an array of symbols on their chests, marks of the lords they served. A chill stole down her spine.

"Where to?" Oren asked.

Sybilla focused on the chill her probe had picked up. "They're in the middle of the camp, I think."

Which was going to be difficult to get to without being seen. They didn't have the luxury of nightfall and there wouldn't be a moonless night for several more days. She studied the men, who appeared well-rested, primed for battle. The few she spied sitting around the fire pits or moving about the camp had no marks of hunger or exhaustion.

"Wait—Where did Nora go?" Dorian's voice snapped her back from the camp.

Unease clawed her gut. Sybilla scanned the shadows but couldn't sense the girl. It was as if she'd never been there at all. From Dorian and Sylvie's worried exchange, they couldn't sense her either. How had she slipped away with no one noticing? Nora had mentioned practicing some new tricks of hers, but Sybilla had thought she'd meant offensive abilities.

A group of soldiers marched past. Oren's hand shot up, hauling her into the shadows. Pressed hard against his lean form, he shielded her from view. The warmth of his breath brushed her neck. Cursing under her breath, she waited until the soldiers were gone before prying herself out of his embrace.

She closed her eyes and pushed out another wave of magic, hunting for any sign of Nora. When she reached the edge of her reach, she pulled back and cursed, opening her eyes slowly. "I can't find her."

Dorian reached for Sylvie, but she pulled away, studying the camp with renewed interest. "What the hell is she—?"

A thunderous explosion ripped through the air. Screams followed by shouts for help sounded off farther into the camp. A wave of magic blasted into Sybilla, a faint green glow briefly sparking in the distance.

"Nora. She's created a distraction. Let's go!"

A pair of soldiers sprinted past when Oren shot out from the trees, grabbing the first one by the nape. As he spun, Oren slammed his hand into the back of the man's neck, and he crumpled like a broken doll.

The other soldier turned, but Sybilla was already racing from the trees, magic bursting from her fingers. He turned to her. She threw her weight forward and hurled a bolt of light, slamming right into his chest, sending him flying into a nearby tent.

Sylvie and Dorian rushed over. Ribbons of light flared around their arms and hands.

"You two continue. We shall find Nora and keep this distraction going."

There wasn't any time to argue before they were gone, leaving her alone with Oren, who had already put on the soldier's cloak and was striding over to the other man. Taking the soldier's cloak off, he handed it to her.

"This should provide us with a little cover."

She fastened the cloak into place and started following the cold magic. Oren fell into stride beside her, one hand resting on the hilt of his sword.

Soldiers dashed by, oblivious to their presence.

Another series of screams ricocheted across the camp, thick with fear and agony. Whatever Nora was doing, it sounded as though she was ripping the men apart.

Or worse.

Sybilla pushed on, plunging deeper into the array of tents. The chill in her chest expanded, stretching out icy fingers along her limbs, and the thread she'd been following snapped tight. She stopped, catching her breath, as she stared at a large tent with guards at its entrance, who stood unmoved by the chaos.

Her heart racing, she stepped out from the shadows magic sparking at her fingers and wrapping up her arms. The guards turned. Understanding dawned on their faces as she walked forward. One slipped inside and the other advanced, drawing his sword.

She glanced behind him as a man swept out. Coal-black eyes found hers, brimming with demonic magic. His lips tightened into a thin line as he registered her magic.

"You're not the one who broke my spell." Disappointment dripped from every word.

"I'm afraid not. You'll have to deal with me instead."

He glanced at Oren, then back at her. "Just the pair of you? Is your Princess truly that stupid?"

A burst of screams sounded off in the distance. Sybilla snorted. "You truly think I came alone?"

"You surprise me, Princess." He stepped forward as his guards moved to shadow him. Raising a hand, he gestured for them to stand aside. "I'm going to enjoy killing you. The Empress will pay me handsomely for your head."

She drew her sword and shifted her feet into position. "Then come and take it."

CHAPTER 93

"I return to the mainland after years abroad and journey to the mountains. There, the people who call themselves Dragonirs have built a flourishing kingdom; cities scattered across the sprawling mountains, villages interspersed among the cliffs and valleys. I see dragons among them, the ancient creatures at peace with their allies. It seems Claudius was wrong all those years ago. Nimue is capable of something other than destruction."

—Excerpt from Titania's diary

Nimue's scream tore from her throat, agony howling in every note. The sphere exploded, the shockwave crashing into her. Sliding back, she drove one hand down, catching herself. Blood pounded hard in her ears, devouring all other sounds, as she pushed herself back up.

He couldn't be gone. Not to that place. Anywhere but there. He was a creature of spirit magic. The demon realm would devour him. Only their bond told her it hadn't—yet.

She started striding toward the portal when a hand latched onto her wrist. Spinning back with a snarl, she slammed her fist into Claudius's jaw. He staggered back, cursing.

Claudius held his jaw, staring back with burning eyes. "You go into that realm and Mirena will kill you—"

"And if I leave him there then he will die!" she roared.

"You're the only one who can close the portal," he argued.

Titania was at his side in a flash, grabbing his upper arm. "Then we will go with her to make sure Mirena doesn't get close. We just have to grab him and then return." Titania shot Nimue a look. "We will *all* return."

"Let's go then."

She burst into a sprint and jumped through. Heat washed over her, sparking across her skin. For a moment, she was weightless, lost in an abyss of darkness. Only the thread that bound her to Lorca propelled her forward, a rush of wind howling in her ears. The dark fell away in a flash, and she dropped, landing on a cold stone floor.

Before she even stood, she realized this *wasn't* her throne room.

It wasn't the demon realm.

A towering stone arch loomed before her, the edges marked with symbols that turned her blood cold. One by one, those symbols began to glow, leaving the air thickening with demonic magic. No, this was far more dangerous.

The Hell Gate.

Wrenching her gaze away, she scanned the room frantically when she spotted Lorca sprawled out, face down on the stone. Nimue hurried over to his side. With her heart racing, she rolled him over. His eyes blinked groggily open.

"W-what happened?" He sat up, wincing.

Before she could speak, Titania released a string of curses. "*By Lyria's grace,* is that who I think it is?"

Looking up, Nimue saw Titania and Claudius striding across the room. Dozens of figures were chained to the wall, their wrists bound above their heads. Wearing little more than tattered scraps of cloth that hung off their skeletal frames, they were barely human, unrecognizable.

The last one, she realized after a shocking moment, wasn't human.

"That's Aziah!" said Claudius, jogging over.

"Who?" Nimue replied.

"Sybilla's assassin."

The one the Princess had sent to look into her people at the temple construction. If she was there, then it meant...

Her feet were moving her forward before she realized it. She stopped. A man hung up on the wall next to Aziah caught her attention. "Vaughn?"

The man she had once loved, and nearly married during her time as Wren, was barely recognizable. He was skin and bone and festering wounds.

She reached up with trembling hands, brushing his tattered hair from his brow. A weak groan tumbled from his lips as his eyes slowly opened. For a second, he stared and as he worked his lips to speak, tears welled in her eyes. While she'd been in the city, the Empress had been brutalizing her people.

"Wren?"

"I'm here, Vaughn. I am right here." She reached up and ripped the chains away.

Vaughn dropped into her arms, and she carefully lowered him to the ground. Guilt howled through her soul, tearing at the edges, leaving her rage to fester and twist in her gut like a knife. The fury she'd released on the battlefield erupted once more, spilling through her limbs.

"Rest now. We'll get you out of here," she vowed, standing up.

The others were already pulling the others down, twelve in total including Aziah. The assassin remained unconscious and only a few others stirred before falling unconscious once more

"What the hell were these people doing here? Why were they—"

Titania was cut off by the door flinging open, and soldiers spilling into the room. Nimue looked at them, then back at the portal. The Hell Gate was awakening, and there was no way the three of them had the power to shut it down.

Only one path remained.

Time slowed to a crawl. Her throne was calling her, an invisible hand outstretched, beckoning her closer.

"Nimue, what are you doing?" Titania shouted from across the fray.

Nimue kept moving to the dais where the Hell Gate stood.

"Nimue!" Lorca's voice howled across the room, making her turn.

Their eyes met across the fighting. The world held its breath. Understanding dawned in his eyes, a plea already rising to his lips. He exploded forward, cutting down the soldiers with vicious savagery. As if he didn't care about the death he brought. It tore at her soul, but she couldn't let him stop her.

If she went through, she'd have more than enough power to stop the gate.

Her gaze snapped to Titania. "Promise me you will do what I asked!"

"Nimue!"

"*Promise me!*"

Titania's gaze hardened, but the fight was gone in her eyes. "I promise!"

She looked at Lorca as he cut down the last man who stood in his way. Claudius fought at his back, protecting him. She had so much she wanted to say to him, that she forgave him for what he did all those years ago. But there was no time for that, and she wanted her last words to be for Lorca.

She met his gaze, raising her hand to the gate, and smiled through her tears. "I will find my way back to you, in this life or the next."

His eyes widened as he took a step forward, reaching out with a hand, as if that might close the distance between them. A guttural roar ripped down the bond, plunging a knife of his grief right through her soul.

"Don't do this! Please!" Tears burned in his gaze as he rushed forward. *"There is—"*

"I love you."

And she stepped through the Hell Gate, crying out as she was ripped from the mortal realm. The last thing she saw was Lorca falling to his knees, screaming her name.

"NIMUE!"

Forgive me, she whispered as their bond sputtered, weakening as she tumbled down through the abyss.

The darkness fell away, yielding to the familiar ruins of her court. The bodies of her people scattered the surrounding floor, an affront to Lyria's teaching, who commanded all dead demons to be returned to the pit. Nimue's gaze lifted from the carnage to the empty throne and the woman standing beside it.

Mirena.

"All hail Queen Nimue. How do you like what I've done with your court?"

CHAPTER 94

"There has been an increase in demon cracks appearing across Danomir. More demons have entered this realm. I reached out to Amara, but my old friend is silent."
—Excerpt from Titania's diary

Sybilla collided with the sorcerer in a clash of magic and metal. Her power swelled up from her soul, surging out to her palms. Surprise flashed in his eyes, shadows flaring along his arms, but she was faster. A band of light thundered from her, striking the man in his chest and ripping the sword from his grasp.

He staggered back, clutching at his chest. Grinning, she lifted her sword.

"Is that *all* you offer?" taunted Sybilla.

He dusted himself off, scowling. "I see you're not as weak as the last fool I dealt with."

The more he talked, the better she could read his magic. She just needed a little longer, then she'd have her opening. Patience, as Omi once told her. When fighting someone more experienced, you just had to show a bit of patience and *watch.* Find your opening.

Or make one if necessary.

Magic sparked down her blade. He burst forward. She side-stepped, swung the blade and—

It sailed through a plume of smoke.

Cursing, she twisted on her heel and swung again. Again, it sailed through the smoke. Laughter echoed around her, the man unseen. If he lived and raised the undead army all would be lost

Sybilla steadied her nerves and tossed her sword aside. Light spilled from her fingers and wrapped around her body, chasing back the shadows. Ancient blood ran in her veins, the power of empresses. She reached down into the core of her soul, where the silver thread of her vision magic twisted away. It was too risky to force a full vision.

Luckily, she didn't need that.

Turn now! Her instinct howled. Sybilla twisted and threw up a wall of light. A black blade cleaved right through the middle, descending right to her chest. Cursing, she shattered the shield and dived to the side, rolling up to her feet. Spinning around, she hurled a bolt. He vanished again. The hairs on her neck lifted.

Sybilla dropped to her knees and slammed her palms onto the ground. The earth ruptured, fissures tearing the ground open. Driving up to her feet, she slammed her palms together, summoning an orb of pure light. His form shimmered, vanishing from view.

She closed her eyes. The light blazed loudly above her, but she held strong. A cold chill slipped over her skin, stealing into her bones.

Dropping her palms, she pivoted as a hand shot out, clamping around her throat. Nails dug in, biting into the skin, and she was lifted. Those cold pits stared her down, but she wasn't afraid.

The fool was right where she wanted him.

Laughter bubbled up her throat, tumbling from her lips. His brow furrowed.

"What the hell is so funny?"

"I win."

Her hand dipped to his side as he spoke, yanking out one of the blades fastened to his chest, hidden beneath the fold of his cloak. His gaze dropped, but it was too late. Sybilla plunged the knife up through his chin, driving it deep into his skull. With a scream, blood streaming from the wound, he fell to the ground.

The soldiers rushed over, but she spun to face them, throwing her palms forward. Bolts of magic exploded from her, slamming into their bodies, cutting right through armor and flesh. They crumpled to the ground, blood pooling around their bodies. She dropped her hands, breathing hard, as she felt her power withdraw back in.

"Sy—" Oren's voice choked off abruptly.

Sybilla turned sharply, a scream tearing from her throat. *"No!"*

Oren stood at the edge of the clearing, a bloody sword jutting from his chest. It was yanked out and his body crumpled to the dirt, blank eyes staring at her. A soldier loomed over his corpse, his dark gaze flitting from the men dead on the ground, then back to her. Fury twisted his face.

"I'm going to—"

She thrust her palm up, firing off a single shot. He was dead before he hit the ground. The cold fury over what he'd done flooded her body as she rushed forward to Oren's side. As she hauled him into her arms, she saw the surrounding carnage. Half a dozen soldiers had been cut down by his sword.

A scream snapped loose from her gut, tearing up her throat, and she threw her head back with a savage cry.

Magic erupted skywards, crashing into the clouds and parting them like a blade. Sunlight fell over her, but she howled, a rush of energy tearing outwards. This guard, her quiet shadow, was dead. The man who had laughed and teased and smiled, coaxing her from the darkest of her reveries. His silent faith, even as she dabbled in a reckless affair. Even then, he kept her safe.

Right to the very end, just as he'd sworn.

A hand suddenly fell onto her shoulder. "Sybilla, we have to go."

Nora.

Power flooded back into her, the light dimming. She stared into Oren's eyes. His death wouldn't be in vain. None of those who fought and died for her would be for nothing. Cursing that he would have no proper burial, she staggered to her feet.

The world lurched, sending her careening forward, right into the arms of another. Looking up, Dorian offered her a sympathetic nod, then helped her stand. They had to escape. She knew that, but the idea of leaving Oren behind tore at her heart.

"We have to go. Now their sorcerer is dead, they will rally their forces. We have to return to the city." Dorian still had his arm around her, but she pulled away, looking at Nora.

"Can you make a tunnel?"

Nora shook her head, raising a hand. A tiny tendril of magic slid down her hand before vanishing. "All burned out. We will have to return the old-fashioned way. I saw some horses back the way we came."

"And the archers?"

"I kept them pretty distracted and destroyed much of their stores." When she stared at Nora, the girl grinned. "What? I wasn't about to gamble everything on having enough magic to do another tunnel."

She would've laughed, but a series of nearing shouts signaled the soldiers' approach. "Let's go."

Striding across the clearing, she grabbed her sword and sheathed it at her hip. She cast one last look at Oren, stifling the grief that rose, and returned to the others.

"This way. Follow me," Nora said, breaking into a jog.

She hurried after her, weaving through the camp. Dorian and Sylvie moved swiftly to her side. Alarm bells cried out, echoing through the forest. Boots drummed heavy footfalls in their wake, closing in rapidly.

Up ahead, a group of soldiers appeared, cutting off their path. Sylvie threw her palms up, roaring as magic shot from her palms. It slammed into the men, sending them flying out of the way.

"Nora, which way?" she shouted.

Nora rushed past her. "This way. We're close!"

More soldiers appeared in front of them. Sybilla yanked out her sword, sprinting straight at the closest man. He held up his sword to attack, but she dropped low, sliding past him and slashing her blade along his legs. His screams followed her as she continued to slash at the other soldiers with Dorian's help, all the while keeping Nora close. No one would get close to the girl.

A blade cleaved the air in front of Sybilla, diving for her throat.

She snapped her hand upward, a burst of light shooting out. A man screamed and the light dimmed, revealing him staggering back, clutching the bloodied stump of his hand. A sword lying at his feet. She dug her heels in and spun sharply. A second attacker, recovering quickly, straightened up to come at her again.

One step forward and she slammed her palms together, then yanked them apart, stretching out a wall of light. Sybilla grinned wickedly and thrust the wall at him, turning his body to ash.

Shaking her head, she sprinted back to the others, and they took off again. Near the tree line, she spotted several horses saddled up, adorned in the finery of battle horses primed for war. Hesitation flared in her mind. She'd heard stories of such beasts and how they seldom permitted unknown riders.

Nora showed none of this concern as she dashed to one of them, grabbed the reins, and leaped up into the saddle. The beast reared, neighing as it tried to thrust her off. Nora dropped low and pressed her palm to its side, whispering into its ear. Tension bled from it as it dropped back down. Shouts came from behind them.

"They're taking the horses!"

"Quick, get them! Do not let them get away!"

Sybilla sprinted to one of the horses, swinging up into the saddle. The war horse shifted restlessly beneath her but didn't fight as she dug her heels in. It raced forward, nearly ripping the reins from her hands. Hunkering down low, she urged the beast onwards as it thundered from the camp. The last of the trees fell away and they broke the treeline, galloping hard across the battlefield.

The remnants of the trebuchets and army scattered the field, leaving the charred stench of death thick in the air. Even the biting chill and salty tang of the sea did little to chase it away. She focused on the looming shape of the city, a dark beast hunkered beside the stormy ocean...and the outstretched fingers of the docks. Her heart seized in her chest.

A spark of hope lit in her chest before she could stop it.

The distant shouts of the army fell away as they reached the middle of the battlefield. Navigating the paths divided by traps and trenches was hard, slowing their sprint to the city. She pushed her horse on, refusing to slow. They were close. The shadow of the wall was stretching out to them.

"Arrows!" Sylvie screamed.

She twisted in her saddle, the blood freezing in her veins. From the tree line marched archers. It was less than she expected...but more than she liked. Turning back around, she bent low in the saddle and flicked the reins.

"Keep going! We're almost out of range!"

The path suddenly narrowed, forcing them into a line.

Or would've but Nora was cut off. A ditch stood between them and the city. Sybilla's breath hitched in her throat as the girl's horse jumped. The front hooves touched down. Relief flooded through her.

But as she landed, an arrow slammed into Nora's back. The girl jolted forward awkwardly as the beast landed fully and threw her off. Sybilla screamed as she yanked on the reins, twisting sharply to Nora. She jumped down before her horse stopped and dashed to the girl. Blood was already staining the back of her tunic. Sybilla sat Nora up, eyeing where the arrow had sunk deep...right near her heart.

No, no, no!

Sylvie was at her side in a flash, lifting the girl from her arms and hauling her up onto Dorian's horse. Sybilla pushed up to her feet, refusing to let her mind spiral as Nora's skin paled, her eyes growing unfocused. Life was bleeding from her. She had to get her back to the city and find a healer.

She strode to the horse and froze. The sky was dark and filled with arrows, hundreds of them descending like a rain of death.

CHAPTER 95

"A spike in demon attacks has left a trail of bodies across the kingdom."
—Excerpt from Titania's diary

Nimue surveyed the ruins of her old home. The silence was unnerving and somehow it felt as if the dead were watching her, whispering their judgments with malice and scorn. She squared her shoulders, pulling on a mask of indifference.

"It could do with some color." She stood and dusted herself off, though her clothes were thoroughly bloodied and torn from the fighting.

Mirena laughed coldly. "That's *all* you have to say? I saw your fury, Nimue, when you peered into the portal and witnessed what I'd done. Why bother to lie?"

Her brow lifted. "We're demons."

She let the silence settle between them. All Nimue needed was time and was more than content to drag it out. Mirena might hold the power of three thrones, which put the advantage solely on her side, but Nimue had played this game before. It wasn't the first time she'd been up against a stronger opponent.

"And pray tell, why did you come through? You must know I'm going to kill you." Mirena pushed away from the ruined throne and stepped down from the dais. The silence of her footfalls was unsettling. It was as though she were little more than a specter, a dangerous thing to even consider because Nimue could sense all the magic of four thrones was within her.

She casually inspected her surroundings, keeping just enough distance from Mirena, who appeared increasingly amused by this.

"I was always going to die in this place." Nimue chuckled softly, casting a lingering look at the throne. "That's the price to be paid by any ruler."

"By you, perhaps," Mirena retorted.

Nimue surveyed what was left of her home, trying her best to appear indifferent. "So, what is your grand plan? If I'm to die, I'd like to think it was for something actually impressive and not something as petty as revenge."

When no answer came immediately, Nimue glanced back and watched as the smile on Mirena's face deepened. "You believe this whole mess is about you? Oh, my dear, you are but a means to an end. Your power will add to my own and I will complete my mission."

"And that *is?*"

Mirena took a step forward, the smile melting away to a cold, dead expression. Her hair turned scarlet, spilling down her back like liquid fire, and framed a face that changed before her very eyes. A new figure stood before them, no longer wearing the face that Nimue recognized as Mirena.

"Restore the three realms to what they once were—whole and mine."

All the air rushed from Nimue, rendering her mute as her mind processed those words. Fear she had known before, but this coldness that stole through her blood, flooding her heart, was a terror she'd never felt before.

"You're the one the gods were fighting when they split the Chaos realm," whispered Nimue.

"Good, you're finally understanding." Mirena took a step forward, tipping her hand to the sky. An orb of shadows materialized and lifted upwards, growing larger until it floated near the arched roof. Threads of blue light sparked through, splashing the jeweled tones across the floor. "Now, I know you studied your history with your precious Keeper. Tell me what I am."

Nimue found her voice, even as her heart slammed against her ribs, making every breath feel as though she were inhaling shards of glass.

"The Goddess of Chaos."

Her last-ditch mission, at that moment, became imperative and all hopes she had of ever returning, even by the slimmest of margins, vanished. At least this way, she would give everyone back in the primal realm a fighting chance.

"Now are you going to surrender? You are no match for me."

"*No.*"

One thin brow lifted, the corner of the goddess's mouth curling upwards. "If you wish for my power, then by ancient law, you must challenge me. Even you cannot defy the rules set in place by Lyria. This was her domain after all."

Something dark flashed in Mirena's eyes as she slowly nodded. "Very well. Queen Nimue of the Azradan Court, I hereby challenge you for your throne."

Ancient laughter whispered through her mind. Ice flooded her veins, rushing to her heart. She'd forgotten how the challenge felt, the rush of power, the thrill of a fight. It wasn't her body responding; no, it was the throne. The promise of a new ruler, a fresh mind to devour…and it had been bound to Nimue for so long, a challenging host by any standard.

She strode across the floor to a glowing red ring, nearly filling the entire throne room. Two symbols marked the stone: challenger and ruler. Nimue stepped into hers, the throne at her back. Her heart gave a skittering leap as she reached back, drawing both her swords out, and steadied as she shifted her feet into position.

Mirena, a chilling picture of calm, snapped her fingers. A short sword appeared in each hand, glimmering black blades.

Nimue's old swords.

She pointed with one of hers. "I'm going to enjoy ripping them from your corpse."

"Plucky, aren't you? Not that it matters. You will be dead soon enough, just like the other demon rulers," taunted Mirena.

The Goddess exploded forward, shadows tearing the air in her wake. Nimue yanked up her blades as Mirena collided with her, metal ringing out. They broke apart, but Nimue pushed on, throwing everything she had into the fight. Every blow was met, and the ferocity returned in equal fervor.

Sweat dripped from her body, every inch burning, even as Mirena fought back, with no trace of exhaustion. Within minutes, the battle shifted. A mocking grin lit Mirena's face, stirring Nimue's rising fury. Curses tumbled from her mouth as she fought, parrying, and slashing in a blur of metal. Instinct had her dancing across the floor, narrowly deflecting every thrust and slash.

As they circled, she shot a glance at the portal, which hummed with growing energy. Mirena rushed at her. She drew her sword up to block the blow, but it was too late. At the last second, Mirena dropped low, spun, and slashed the blade across Nimue's side. Blood splashed the stone.

Her arms shook, almost buckling under the weight of Mirena's attack. Darkness nudged the edge of her vision, rising to claim her. She called a vision of Lorca to her mind and pushed back, defending herself from Mirena's dizzying blows.

"Why do you bother to keep fighting?" Mirena taunted, as she rushed in for another attack.

Nimue smiled, even as a wave of pain roared down her side, almost sending her buckling to the floor. "You really want to know?"

Mirena stepped back to come in with another attack. Nimue took her chance, and dropped her weight into her front foot to pivot, slamming her leg into Mirena's side. The Demon Queen went flying across the floor. Nimue strode over, blood dripping in her wake, as Mirena snarled, scrambling swiftly to her feet.

"Nice trick—You didn't answer my question, however."

"And *you* have had every reason to kill me. You're holding back—why?"

Nimue knew why. Her enemy had revealed a fatal flaw...and she hadn't even realized it. For all the studying Mirena had supposedly done on Nimue, she hadn't learned the biggest lesson of all. The reason she'd stayed queen longer than any other ruler.

"Because I am savoring this moment. Watching you bleed and breaking you slowly." Mirena laughed, a hollow sound that ricocheted around the throne room. Mirena circled her slowly as if she was magnanimously granting Nimue a reprieve.

"It seems you didn't think this whole thing through. Surely someone as ancient as yourself should have realized that Lyria put measures in place to protect her realm."

Mirena stopped. "Oh?"

"You killed the Keepers of your courts, didn't you?" Nimue didn't wait for Mirena to answer, though the flash of unease in those dark pits said enough. "You did, which means you never took the time to study ancient history. You see there was so much the Keepers never wrote down. The failsafe, for instance, for situations such as these."

"What fail—"

Nimue plunged both swords into the stone, right where the pool of blood gathered beneath her and thrust all her magic down. Her blood would've done most of the job, but with that of all the dead whose blood stained the floor? Mirena had no idea what she'd done.

Ancient magic sparked across the floor.

"Azradan has but one translation in the language of the gods. *The Gate*. Let's see what happens when I open another one, shall we?"

With a shudder, the floor cracked, and a shockwave of magic erupted upward. Nimue tried to scream, but the rush of magic devoured her whole. The ground fell away, sending her tumbling into the abyss. Above she could see the retreating shape of her court, stone tumbling down, destroying what was left of her throne.

You will never have my throne, thought Nimue as the cold talons of death latched onto her. *I take Azradan to my death, where not even you can follow me, and from that place, my power will flow through to Ellie. Out of your cold, monstrous hands.*

She smiled, surrendering to the song that rose from the abyss. Death had come for her—

I win.

CHAPTER 96

"I return from the mountains at a loss. Nimue will not leave her home there. She said there is some threat facing her people...one she is determined to face alone."
—Excerpt from Titania's diary

SNAP!

The thread in her chest broke, and Titania dropped to her knees with a gasp. Confusion tore through her, a thousand thoughts roaring at once. She looked at Claudius and the horror and grief blazing in his eyes showed he felt it, too.

Lorca threw his head back and roared; a savage, wild sound, broken in every note. The walls shook as his body exploded into light, and his dragon form took over. Fire tore outwards as he threw his head back and howled.

The inferno shot toward them. Titania threw up a shield around the injured and Claudius, the heat slamming into her.

"He's going to kill us all!" Claudius shouted.

She didn't know what to say. Her soul was crying, the grief shredding her at the seams. The bond was shattered, the absence of it gutting. Tears burned her eyes, but she forced back the sobs.

The heat snuffed out suddenly, and the pressure eased off her shield. She dropped it to see that Lorca had reverted to his human form. On his knees, he stared at the remnants of the Hell Gate.

The pile of stone rubble still thrummed with power, but Nimue had done it. She'd bought them time.

She walked over, ignoring the layer of ash that dusted the floor and the stench of death that filled her every breath. At the touch of her fingers brushing his shoulder, he buckled over with a hoarse scream. The room shuddered violently, and the open portal flickered.

"Lorca, we have to go—"

The ground trembled again. She grabbed him, dragging him up. To her surprise, he didn't fight her. He had no fight left in him, just a hollow look that gutted her. It was like staring into a mirror showing how she felt after the fall of Toranelle.

Claudius was already hauling the survivors through the portal as she guided Lorca over. Wordlessly, she watched him pull away and scoop Aziah into his arms. When he vanished, she grabbed the last of the survivors—the man that Nimue had spoken to—and joined Lorca who was staring at where the Hell Gate had stood.

"She can't be gone," he whispered. "I—"

An ocean of regret and grief raged between them. She offered him a somber nod and strode through the portal, hoping he would follow.

CHAPTER 97

"Nimue is no more. I...I can't sense her. Reports arrive by the day of a storm assailing the mountains, of fire raining from the sky...and of dragons fleeing their home. I fear the worst."

—Excerpt from Titania's diary

Arrows slammed into the ground, bringing a hail of death. Light flared from Sybilla's hands as she threw up a wall of magic, incinerating dozens on impact. Another volley followed seconds later, crashing against her shield with a hard jolt. Her arms quivered as the heat built rapidly in her arms. She flexed her fingers, pushing the wall wider.

Her horse reared and bolted off, making it barely a few feet before arrows slammed into its side. The beast crashed to the ground, as more sunk into its side and neck. Sylvie dashed for her horse, but it, too, bolted across the field and was felled in an instant.

"Can you feel that?" Dorian shouted.

She didn't know what he was talking about at first. All her focus was on holding the wall of light. A biting response died as the ground underfoot rumbled. Seconds later, the war drums bellowed across the battlefield. The sound thundered through her chest, a death march drawing closer. A glance at Dorian confirmed her fears.

"You need to get back to the city," said Sybilla.

"I will not abandon you! You are my Princess."

"Sylvie can stay by my side, but you have to get Nora back. She'll be dead if you stay." Arrows crashed against the barrier. Her legs wobbled, threatening to give out. Gritting her teeth, she stepped one foot back and thrust her palms forward, pushing the wall forward. "Now, *go.* That is an order."

There was a hushed conversation between the pair, but she tuned it out. She had to figure out her next move. Once the army arrived, she'd be overwhelmed. Rationally, she ought to have claimed the horse for herself. Galen would've insisted. But she couldn't, in any conscience betray Nora like that. Consequences be damned, she would fight and level the whole gods' damned army if she had to.

She wasn't dying until she'd cleaved her aunt's head from her body and sat on that damn throne. It was *hers* and by the grace of the spirits, she'd claim it.

The retreating gallop brushed her ears. Sylvie stepped to her side, drawing her sword. "We are not dying here today."

"I like the sound of that."

The assault of arrows had stopped, and the air was broken only by the heavy drums and approaching chants. The cacophony of their cries and footfalls churned through her body. A trickle of ice slid into her mind, lifting the hairs on her nape. Sybilla thinned the wall, just enough to see beyond it.

The marching army was closing in fast. A mounted force barreled across the battlefield heading straight for them. Sybilla dropped the shield, drawing all her power to her hands. Ribbons of light flared up her arms. She dug in her heels, choosing her targets. Blood roared in her ears, drowning out the chaos, and a chilling calm washed over her. A spark flared in her soul, erupting outwards, spilling down her body, lighting her skin with an ethereal glow.

The first four horsemen bore down on her with dizzying speed, swords drawn. She snapped up her hands and a band of light exploded out; the force pushing her feet hard into the dirt. A deafening bang split the air. The light collided with the first of the riders, destroying him instantly. Sparks flashed upward into the sky. Three others quickly followed suit.

Another group of riders darted through the fray, galloping toward them. Sybilla roared, another bolt ripping from her palms, crashing hard into the next wave of attackers. One evaded the blast and raised his weapon, a look of fury on his face.

Sylvie leaped past her, grabbing the side of the man's saddle to jump up behind him and plunge her sword into his chest.

Soon Sylvie was surrounded by soldiers and lost from Sybilla's view. She could only pray for her survival while she fought for her own.

One of the soldiers broke away and rode toward her, swinging his sword as he tried to mow her down. Barely dodging the horse's hooves, her attacker's blade sliced across her cheek. A sticky trickle of blood dribbled down the side of her face and stained her lips.

She dropped low, pushing a burst of magic down her blade, and swung it wide in a circle. Light tore outwards, driving the men back from her. Within minutes, a score of dead bodies scattered the ground at her feet.

Time slowed to a crawl, the world holding its breath for a single moment. Spirit magic still pulsed through her, ribbons of light glowing around her whole body as she raised her sword. Muscles in her arms quivered. She was tired, the rush of the fight the only reason she hadn't collapsed.

More men appeared surrounding her. One stepped forward, breaking the circle. Her gaze narrowed on him. He grinned cockily, moving closer with both hands on his weapon.

"Time to die, little girl," he sneered.

But in the distance, she heard shouts and the sound of others approaching. The man turned, his focus gone for a second. Sybilla took her chance and hurled a bolt of magic into his throat. He was dead before his body struck the earth. The other soldiers had no chance to react as a swath of men rushed into the fray, descending on her attackers.

"Who *are* you?" she shouted across the chaos.

One of them turned. "Lord Delmont sent us. We have come from Mithra Archipelago."

True to his word, pointed ears jutted from the long black hair tied at his neck. *Fae.* The bastard hadn't just brought any army. He'd brought the fae to their cause. She didn't know whether she wanted to strangle or kiss him. Perhaps both.

"Well, shall we cut these men down to size?"

He shot a startled look over at her. "We need to get you back to the safety of the wall."

"Not until this fight is won!"

His mouth opened to argue, but the look on her face stopped him. He reluctantly dipped his chin.

"Let us break this army! Drive the bastards back!"

If anyone was surprised at the profanities that spilled from her lips, no one cared. She rushed forward, shadowed by her new guards and Sylvie who, although injured could still wield her sword. The screams of the dying filled the air, rising to a deafening cacophony she thought even the spirits would hear.

The blood-soaked ground turned soft underfoot, saturated and strewn with entrails and limbs. A fetid stench filled every breath as she fought on and still more came at her with weapons held ready to cut her down.

But none came close enough to land a killing blow.

The fae at her side ensured that. The rush of battle propelled her deeper into the mess. There was a battle to win. She surged forward, her guards moving in harmony with her. Their blades attacked in rhythm, leaving no opening for any soldier to get in close.

Overhead, the darkening sky began to rain. Within seconds, it became an assaulting force. Lightning splintered across the sky, splashing white across the bloody carnage. The ground softened and soon her boots were sinking into mud, making each step harder than the last.

The heat burning through her legs tore like a hundred open wounds. She tried to lift her feet, but her pace was slowing. Every breath felt like her chest was full of broken glass. The rush of the battle was fleeing her. The light sputtered on her hands, leaving only thin tendrils.

The attacking soldiers were getting close. Their stench eddied around her, filling every gulp of air, and leaving the taste thick on her lips. Bloodied water washed from her face, running red streaks down her armor.

She swung her blade to meet the blow of another, her arm jolting hard on impact. Coal-black eyes met hers.

"You're looking tired there, little girl," the soldier sneered.

"Fuck you." She slammed her head into his.

He staggered back with a curse, and she spun, slashing her sword across his neck, slicing a gaping smile. Blood gushed down his body as he sank to his knees.

Everywhere she looked men died and screamed, but still, so many of Alexandria's forces were scattered among the fray. Was the tide even turning? Or were they losing, and she hadn't sensed it yet?

Thunder boomed across the sky, lightning splashing through the clouds as the rain descended heavier than before. The thickening stench of bodies choked the air, soaking into her skin and down into her bones.

She drew in trembling breaths, her legs wobbling beneath her, threatening to send her careening into the mud and filth. The guards closed in around her, shielding her from the chaos.

"We have to get you out of here," one of them said.

She shot him a fiery look. "Like hell. I'll leave when this battle is done."

"You're nearly dead on your feet."

"And I will *not* abandon my men!"

"And if you die?" he bit back.

Opening her mouth to spit a response, she felt the ground tremble. Shouts rippled across the battlefield and the enemy soldiers turned and headed to the tree line. She froze.

Carving through the battlefield came mounted riders, laying waste to all who tried to run. Soldiers wearing green, their battle horses adorned in Northern armor. Her heart thudded as the riders galloped after the retreating army, fleeing across the battlefield.

And from across the cacophony broke the cheers of her men.

"The army is retreating!"

Sybilla tipped her face to the sky, letting the rain wash away the blood and dirt. The city had survived. They had *won*. Perhaps not the war, but a battle had been won. A blow struck to her aunt. And as she settled her gaze across her army, she let herself breathe.

I'm coming for you, Alexandria.

CHAPTER 98

"I can no longer stomach the horrors of war, nor can I stay with my kin any longer. There must be something more to this world, a chance to have a family. Perhaps I am a fool, a demon cursed, but I strike out, venturing into the unknown."
—Excerpt from Atlas's diary

The seas were glass as the sails swelled with a steady wind, propelling them among the islands. Flynn stood at the prow, hair whipping in the breeze, his eyes fastened on the distant slopes. His heart drummed restlessly in his chest, leaving his fingers dancing restlessly along the wooden railing. No matter what he did to distract himself, he couldn't sway his thoughts.

Tobin's face was bright and clear in his mind, ringing with a single word. He held it close to his chest, letting it warm him, and imagined the day they would meet again.

Mate.

When they met again, he'd have a long discussion with Tobin about it. But would Tobin even want a god as his mate? He leaned forward, staring down into the water as it cut alongside the hull. A low groan rumbled from his chest.

"I could hear your thoughts from the wheel." Mira's soothing voice brushed his ear as she placed a soothing hand on his shoulder. "Are you feeling sick? I'm sure—"

"I'm okay." He pushed back from the railing and rubbed the back of his neck. "What do you think of Amara?"

The stranger in question stood at the wheel, her hands held out in front. Her eyes peered out from beneath her hood, thrumming with power. Even from across the deck, he could feel her propelling the ship along the water. Whether she was manipulating the water or wind, he didn't know, but she was the reason they were on the move at all. And even as the night yielded to the day, she remained there, steadfast with hands outstretched.

Castille remained close to his wife.

As if sensing his attention, Castille looked at him across the deck and grinned. Flynn returned one awkwardly, but it was hard to maintain. Thankfully, Mira looped her arm through his, guiding him back to the railing.

"We're going to get him back."

He nodded absently, his thoughts drifting to Ashara and Kiya. The pair were sleeping downstairs; well, it was probably just Kiya, while Ashara watched over her. The attack had left Kiya weakened and she still needed time to recover. They'd gone down below a few hours ago and had yet to come up.

"Are you going to tell me about your new little tricks?" He eyed her hands, recalling the light that had danced through her fingers.

Spirit magic.

She smiled. "Surprised you, didn't I? When we came to the temple, I felt so lost. How was I meant to fight by your side? Ashara came to me one night and asked if was serious about learning how to wield a sword. When I told her I was, she agreed to train me. I thought it was pretty silly given I had no magic."

"Clearly that state didn't last," he teased.

The corner of her mouth tipped up. "No. As it turned out, I wasn't completely powerless. You recall us taking tea steeped in the red flower powder each year?"

Flynn nodded. It was a part of their post-harvest rituals. Everyone over the age of five had some of the tea. It was supposed to grant good health over the winter, which, mostly it did. Few ever became sick in Fenware. But how did that translate to magic?

"Of course, but, well, how did that change you?"

"Our people have been taking it for hundreds of years. Ashara thinks it slowly built up a small amount of magic in us. Enough for my body to take on what they could give to me. It took a little work, but after some time, I could conjure and can now create my own magic." The smile faded from her lips. "Flynn, I think that is why our people were taken."

"What?"

She grabbed his upper arm. "Think about it. A whole village of people with bodies primed to become vessels. Ashara said I could have been imbued with spirit or demon magic. I was just an empty vessel ready to be filled."

He fell silent, his stomach twisting into knots. Had that been why they were taken? Mulling this over, he glanced at Mira. She wasn't telling him everything. What she said didn't explain all the secrecy...and her theory of the village unnerved him. What if she was right?

As he looked out across the glittering water, he glimpsed the hint of gray among the swaths of green forests. His heart gave a traitorous leap. There were so many unknowns in his life and the power of a god burning in his veins. The trials were over, but the fight had just begun.

Whatever the truth of Fenware's attack, of what his future would hold, and of what Mira's secrecy might mean, he would face it. And soon, he would have Tobin by his side to brave the coming storm.

CHAPTER 99

"I can feel Chaos stretching out her touch, piercing the veil between realms. She is coming. By the gods, may we have the strength needed for what is to come."
—Excerpt from Amara's diary

Rhea wandered the ancient woods of Purgatory, the realm where souls came when they died before moving onto whatever life they were reborn into. The starlit sky glittered overhead, barely visible through the gaps in the canopy. Eddies of dust swirled and floated around her. The warm, humid night brushed against her skin, lifting the hairs along her bare arms.

The bands of moonlight cutting down across the path lit her way. Even without the tug in her chest, an invisible thread pulling her forward, the realm itself was whispering the way. She'd felt the disturbance a few hours ago, and it had taken time to trek through the realm to trace the source. Whatever had upset the realm had left it all out of balance.

She wondered what it was. Only the dead came to purgatory and their arrival was natural, peaceful. This had felt violent and abrupt, an affront to the natural order of the realm. As guardian, it was her duty to investigate, to safeguard the sanctity of the realm. Her first intruder. A flutter of excitement skittered through her chest, catching her breath.

As the trees thinned, yielding to a sprawling meadow—The Field of Souls—she slowed her pace. The wind pushed her, propelling her forward. A low hiss rumbled from the forest. Whatever had the realm so unsettled was close. She peered through the trees...and stilled.

A figure lay sprawled in the middle of the field. The shimmer which always accompanied the dead in this realm was absent.

Intrigued, Rhea emerged from the safety of the trees and inched across the meadow. As she neared closer, her heart stuttered in her chest and her mouth dropped open. Before she knew it, she was running to the newcomer. She reached out, her hand trembling, and brushed the hair from the woman's face.

Nimue.

Rhea moved her hand to Nimue's chest. The heart was silent. Closing her eyes, she hunted for the spark of life, the remnant of Nimue's soul...and there it was, a glowing thread in the dark. She stretched out, latching onto it.

A prayer spilled from her lips as she pressed her palm down firmly, pulling the thread up from the darkness. She bent over, brushing her lips against the shell of Nimue's ear.

"Rise."

SPECIAL THANKS

This has been a behemoth of a project and not a journey ventured alone. A deep thank you must be given to every reader who began this journey in The Girl of Ash and Snow. I hope you're not too mad at me for the ending of this one but have faith. The journey continues!

To my wonderful love, Kyona. No words can express my adoration and gratitude for loving me, supporting me, and just dealing with all my chaos. You are my Lorca, the calm to my storm, and where I am home.

For my family and friends, thank you so freaking much. Your unending support, love (and occasional passive-aggressive threats to keep certain characters alive—yes, I'm looking at you, Vanessa) keep me going every day. Hopefully, some of you aren't too mad over the ending of this one...but have a little faith in me? After all, there are still two more books for me to break your hearts. Continue at your own peril.

To my discord family, you have maintained your support through all the highs and lows. To Wolfie, Heather, Ancient, Marjorie, Sib, Tarragonsoda, and everyone else I have missed, thank you. You are the reason I have gotten this far and I am so deeply honored to know you all. Your comments, tips, and tricks, memes, and music have kept me going when this project nearly got too much.

To my editor, Kerry. Words can never express enough my respect for you and the magic you weave with my stories. I am so grateful to work with you and cannot wait to share future projects. You always know what to do, and how to polish my work but keep my voice, and make my stories shine.

A special mention must be afforded to the team at Miblart, whose amazing talent created the book cover! Once again, you nailed the brief. You are a company that is easy to work with, prompt and kind, and as such, I look forward to other endeavors.

To my Tiktok community, I can't forget you. It's been a wild journey these past few months and I look forward to sharing more of my work with you.

C.M. Quinn

ABOUT AUTHOR

C.M. Quinn is an Australian self-published queer fantasy author based out of Western Australia. She has been writing since she was thirteen and certainly has no plans to slow down any time soon. Between losing herself in the worlds she writes about, tending to her four cats, or exploring, she is never far from her computer.

www.ingramcontent.com/pod-product-compliance
Lightning Source LLC
Chambersburg PA
CBHW070151120726
47909CB00001B/60
* 9 7 8 0 6 4 5 3 1 5 3 2 5 *